HER HOLIDAY
MIRACLE

BY
JOANNA NEIL

MILLS
BOON

Published in Great Britain 2016
By Mills & Boon, an imprint of HarperCollins*Publishers*
1 London Bridge Street, London, SE1 9GF

© 2016 Joanna Neil

ISBN: 978-0-263-25432-7

Printed and bound in Spain
by CPI, Barcelona

Joanna Neil loves writing romance, and has written more than sixty books for Harlequin Mills & Boon. Before her writing career started she had a variety of jobs, which included being a telephonist, a clerk, as well as nursing and work in a hospital pharmacy. She was an infant teacher for a number of years before her love of writing took over. Her hobbies include dressmaking, cooking and gardening.

Cursed with a poor sense of direction and a propensity to read, **Annie Claydon** spent much of her childhood lost in books. A degree in English Literature followed by a career in computing didn't lead directly to her perfect job—writing romance for Mills & Boon—but she has no regrets in taking the scenic route. She lives in London: a city where getting lost can be a joy.

Dear Reader,

What better place is there to while away the hours than on a beautiful Caribbean island? The gentle lap of surf on the sand, palm trees swaying in a soft, warm breeze… In this idyllic setting a girl can surely soak up the sun and forget her troubles.

Or can she? Setbacks in the form of a tropical storm and its aftermath might not present too great a problem—but when it comes to dealing with an incredibly good-looking plantation owner set on keeping her away from his equally handsome young cousin, what's a girl to do? How can she possibly resist his all-out charm offensive?

There's only one option when temptation arises in Paradise…isn't there?

I hope you enjoy reading my latest book…

With love,

Joanna

CHAPTER ONE

AT LAST. REBECCA GAVE a soft sigh of relief as a sixty-foot-long catamaran smoothly eased into position alongside the dock. The sound of calypso music came from on board, floating on the air waves towards her, and her spirits lifted in an instant. She'd been patiently standing in the queue for some time, wilting in the heat despite her light camisole top and loose cotton skirt, but now there was an end in sight. She would soon be on the last part of her journey to the beautiful Caribbean island of St Marie-Rose.

Just up ahead of her a man straightened as the boat approached. She'd noticed him earlier—in fact there was no way she could have missed him. He had midnight-black hair and sculpted, lightly tanned features, and he stood out from the crowd—tall, muscular, supremely fit-looking, wearing pale chinos and a white T-shirt that outlined broad shoulders and well-muscled biceps. He'd been looking around, taking in his surroundings. Presently, though, he seemed preoccupied, deep in thought, not at all like the others who lined the quayside.

Perhaps he felt her glance resting on him just then, because he half turned towards her and looked directly at her, his dark gaze meshing with hers for a heart-stopping instant. His eyes widened and his glance moved over her, taking in her slender yet curvaceous figure, the long copper-coloured hair that tumbled past her shoulders in a mass of unruly curls. All at once he seemed stunned, as though he couldn't take his eyes off her.

Heat swept along her cheekbones and she looked away, embarrassed for her own part to have been caught staring. Somehow she hadn't seemed able to help herself… there was just something about him… He probably wasn't a tourist, she decided. There was nothing of the loose-limbed, laid-back sunseeker about him.

Actually, much the same could be said of her right now. She didn't feel at all touristy. After being cooped up in an aeroplane for almost a dozen hours, followed by a short taxi ride to this port, she was more than ready for the last leg of her journey. At least she hoped this was the last leg. It was already late afternoon, and she really wanted to arrive at the house before nightfall. With any luck her sister, Emma, would be there to greet her. She smiled, a thrill of excitement running through her at the prospect—it would be so good to see Emma again.

Up to now, though, nothing had gone quite to plan—instead of flying directly to the island she'd found herself stranded here, on the verdant, equally lovely tropical island of Martinique, waiting for a ferry to take her across the sparkling blue sea to her final destination.

The people in the queue began to move slowly forward. 'Ah, looks like we're boarding at last,' someone said behind her. 'Finally!'

It was a male voice. She turned to glance at him. He was a young man—in his mid-twenties, she guessed, much the same as herself. She was twenty-six. He had blond hair and blue eyes, and a ready smile. Dressed for the heat, he wore three-quarter-length shorts and a T-shirt. Clearly he was in a good mood—most likely returning with his friends from a day trip to Martinique. The three young men with him were chatting to one another, lively and exuberant.

He returned her gaze and waved a hand towards the boat. 'Shall we? I'm William, by the way. William Tempest.'

He looked at her questioningly and she responded in a soft voice, 'Rebecca…Rebecca Flynn…most people call me Becky.'

'Hi, Becky. We should be able to get some refreshments on board. Perhaps I could buy you a drink? I'm not hitting on you,' he hastened to explain. 'Well, maybe I would in different circumstances. It's just that I noticed earlier you were looking a bit fed up and I thought maybe you could do with something to cool you down and perk you up—perhaps an iced juice of some sort—they do a good orange and mango mix?'

'Do they?' So he'd noticed her wilting. What was it that had given her away? Was it her hot cheeks or the way her curls clung damply to her temples? She should have taken the time to pin her hair back while she was on the plane.

She'd no experience of the facilities on board ferries in the Caribbean, but now she moistened her lips with the tip of her tongue in anticipation.

'A cold drink sounds wonderful. I'd like that.' She added as an afterthought, 'This whole thing is a bit of an adventure for me.'

'Are you here on holiday?'

'Sort of. More of an extended break, shall we say?

Things were getting me down back home and I needed to get away.'

'Really? I'm sorry. I feel a bit that way, too. I've had a break-up with my girlfriend…it was really hard to take. It was a while ago, and I keep trying to put it all behind me, but it's difficult.'

'Yes. I know how that feels.'

Together, chatting amiably, they walked the short distance along the quay to the boarding ramp and stepped on to the deck of the boat.

It was strange… She didn't know him from Adam, but she liked him instantly, in a platonic, unthreatening kind of way. All her usual English reserve seemed to be disappearing fast—melting away in the tropical sunshine.

Perhaps it was the heady atmosphere of the Caribbean beginning to exert its hold on her—or maybe the energetic beat of the music coming from the boat was serving to loosen her up. Whatever the reason, she'd throw all her inhibitions away right now for the chance of downing a long, cold glass of something. Anything.

William looked around. 'Where do you want to sit? Would you like to be under cover, or do you want to look out over the sea?'

'Both, I think.' She smiled. 'I've been stuck on a plane for several hours, so it will be great to move around and feel the fresh air for a bit.'

He nodded, his mouth curving. 'Sounds great. We can get to know one another—it'll take about an hour to get to St Marie-Rose.'

He was friendly and open with her, and as they chatted Rebecca was startled to find herself responding readily, a bit like a flower opening up to the sun. Why did she feel so at odds with herself about that? He'd already told her that he was getting over a broken relationship. Would it hurt to talk some more and maybe confide in him in return? He was easygoing and sociable and that was what she needed right now.

'So what's been getting you down?' he asked.

'Oh, a few things... I was ill, and my boyfriend decided that he couldn't handle it.'

'Ouch! That's a tough one. It must have been difficult for you.'

'Yes...'

It had been a few months since her relationship with Drew had disintegrated, and what had happened over that time had certainly taken its toll of her... Complications after her appendicitis had added to her problems and left her feeling low, and Drew had been less than supportive. After her appendix had burst, peritonitis had almost killed her, with the poisons in her bloodstream keeping her in the hospital's Intensive Care Unit for a couple of weeks.

But her problems hadn't ended there. The doctors told her she might be infertile because of the scar tissue from those complications, and that was when Drew had decided to bow out. She had been devastated, overwhelmed by everything that had happened to her. How could she cope with the possibility of never having children? That question haunted her still.

It had all been a bit of a struggle. She desperately needed a change of scene—a chance to put herself back together again. Wasn't it time she tried to relax and let her hair down? It could hardly matter what happened here, what she decided to tell William—he was only going to be around for a short time, after all.

She found a seat on one of the benches under the awning and put her bags down on the floor by her feet while he went to fetch the drinks. Padded bench seats were arranged along the deck, facing a central four-sided counter where dusky-skinned youths were busy cutting up all manner of fruits—oranges, melons, passion fruit, limes. There were a couple of urns available for hot drinks, along with juice dispensers and water coolers. She glanced around. There were even potted palms placed at discreet intervals on deck, all adding to the holiday atmosphere.

The man she'd seen earlier had gone to stand by the rail, looking out over the sea. He braced himself, leaning back against a stanchion, as the boat's engine started up. He glanced her way, watching as William came towards her with a tall glass of iced juice. She couldn't tell what the man was thinking. His gaze was smoke-dark—brooding, almost. As though he was disturbed to see her with another man. That couldn't be so, though, could it?

For some reason he bothered her. Perhaps it was because in some way—maybe in the way he stood apart from the others—he reminded her of Drew. Though her ex had never possessed those bone-melting good looks, or that way of looking at the world as if it was his to command.

'Don't worry about him.' William must have seen her cautious glance, and now, as she accepted the drink he handed her, she looked at him quizzically.

'I won't. Do you know him?'

He nodded. 'He's my cousin. He's been over to Martinique on business—I think he probably wants some space to mull things over.'

'Oh, I see…I think.' She frowned and tried to put the man out of her mind, turning her attention to William and chatting to him about nothing in particular.

He was good company. He was fun and he made her chuckle, and at one point he even pulled her to her feet and had her dancing with him to the hot, rhythmic music that spilled out from the loudspeakers overhead.

Other passengers were already moving to the beat, and from time to time William's friends came to join them. She laughed with them and exchanged banter, simply enjoying the freedom of letting herself go for a while. Her hair tumbled this way and that over her bare shoulders and her skirt gently swirled around her thighs as she sashayed to the beat of steel drums. She hadn't felt this unrestrained in a long time.

The music stopped for a moment as the latest song came to an end and she stood still, attuning herself to the rhythm of the boat as it crested the waves.

'Shall we go and stand by the deck rail for a while?' William suggested, and she nodded, going with him and turning her face to the cooling breeze as the boat ploughed through the waves.

Standing with her by the rail, he put an arm around her shoulders to point out dolphins in the distance, playing in the clear, crystal water.

She felt a prickling at the back of her neck and looked around, suddenly distracted. The man at the rail flicked a glance in her direction, inclining his head in acknowledgement, his eyes narrowed against the glare of the sun. Was he still intent on watching her? Or was it William he was keeping an eye on?

William spoke to her, cutting into her thoughts. 'Perhaps we might see each other again—hang around together from time to time? Don't get me wrong—I know you're not looking for a relationship and neither am I—but we do have something in common. We've both been hurt and we could be friends, maybe?'

'Yes, I'd like that.' It would be good to have a friend out here.

She looked out over the blue water once more. The island of St Marie-Rose was drawing closer, its green-clad mountains beckoning, while picturesque white-painted houses nestled among the trees on the hillsides—a perfect invitation to visit.

'Whereabouts are you staying?' he asked.

'Tamarind Bay. My sister's renting a house there... well, nothing quite so grand as a *house*—it's more of a cabin, really. She was lucky to get it—it's quite secluded, apparently, near to a small private marina. The owner of the property is a friend.'

He frowned. 'That's the opposite direction from me. We're all staying at a rental place in the north of the island. Still...' He brightened. 'It's not too far away. It's not that big an island. You could go from one end to the other in two or three hours.' He smiled. 'There aren't that many bars and nightclubs in Tamarind Bay. I'm sure I'll manage to find you again. Maybe I could have your phone number? I could help cheer you up.' He made a wry face. 'Heck—we could cheer each other up.'

She nodded and smiled in response, but she wasn't about to commit to anything. She wasn't averse to having fun—in fact it would be great—but above all she'd come out here to spend time with Emma.

The catamaran moved into place alongside the dock at St Marie-Rose just a few minutes later and they readied themselves to disembark. Ahead of them, William's cousin was among the first to leave the boat.

William helped her with her bags as they negotiated the steps to the quay. She paused for a moment to look around, feeling a deep sense of satisfaction as she took in the curve of the bay, with its wide strip of golden sand and palms that tilted towards the sun, their green fronds drifting gently in the light breeze.

'Are you going to be okay getting to your sister's place?' William asked as they stood among the melee of disembarking passengers. 'Tamarind Bay's about an hour's drive south from here.' He seemed concerned, anxious to stay with her, but also aware of his friends waiting for him a short distance away. 'I could find you a taxi. Better still, I could ask my cousin—'

'No, please don't do that,' she said hurriedly. 'Don't worry about me. I'll be absolutely fine. Go and join your mates. Enjoy the rest of your holiday.'

'Okay...' He frowned. 'I suppose so...if you're sure?'

'I am.'

Reluctantly he walked away, and she looked around to see if there were any cabs left for hire. A man thrust a leaflet into her hands—an advertisement for sea trips to the local islands—and she glanced at it briefly. In the meantime passengers were still getting off the ferry, descending upon every waiting vehicle.

'I help you, lady—yes?' A dark-skinned, athletic-looking young man came to stand beside Becky on the dock. 'You need help with your bags?'

'No...no, thank you.' Becky gave him a tentative smile. She'd been warned by the tour company about hustlers, and though he seemed innocent enough she was cautious. Perhaps he had a car somewhere, but from his manner she seriously doubted he was a legitimate cab driver. 'I'll be fine. I'm sure I can manage.'

Unfortunately, her suitcase was still back at the airport, but she had her hand luggage with her—a holdall and a roomy bag.

He shook his head. 'You give me money—I take your bags for you.' He bent down and started to grasp the handles of her overnight bag.

'No, no…please don't do that… I can manage,' she said again, but he wasn't listening.

'I take care of it for you,' he said.

'No—I'd rather you didn't do that.'

She tried to reach for her bag but he was too quick for her, deftly swinging it away from her into the air. She sucked in a sharp breath. How on earth was she going to deal with him? Should she kick up a fuss? Call Security? Where *was* Security around here?

Even as the thoughts darted through her head the man she'd seen earlier stepped forward. He moved so fast she blinked in surprise, watching as he came up to the stranger, gripped the handles of her bag firmly and wrenched them from him. Rebecca was stunned. He was lithe and supple, his body honed to perfection. It was simply amazing to watch him in action.

His steel-grey gaze cut through the young man like a lance. 'She told you that she didn't want your help. Now *I'm* telling you—leave her alone.'

It was clear he meant business. It was there in the clipped tone of his voice and in the firm thrust of his taut, angular jaw. Even Rebecca was in awe of him, and she was an innocent bystander.

'Okay. Okay.' The young man held up his hands in submission, backing off. 'I didn't mean any harm. I'm going.' He looked wary, taken completely aback by the opposition that seemed to have erupted out of nowhere.

Her rescuer watched him leave. 'He won't bother you any more,' he said.

'No. I see that.' She sent him a grateful glance, her green eyes drinking him in. The youth was hurrying away along the quayside, anxious to stay out of trouble. 'Thank you. I wasn't sure whether there were any security people around here. They didn't seem necessary. Everything looked so peaceful.'

His mouth made a wry curve. 'It is—usually. But anywhere you go you might find people who want to supplement their income any way they can.'

'I suppose so.' She used the leaflet to fan her cheeks against the heat. How did he manage to look so cool and in control? He must be used to the conditions out here.

'I'm Cade, by the way,' he said. 'I'm William's cousin. He may have mentioned me.'

He held out a hand to her and she slipped her palm briefly into his. His grasp was firm and reassuringly strong.

'Rebecca,' she answered. 'Yes, he did. Thanks again for your help.'

'You're welcome.' He gave her a thoughtful look. 'I couldn't help overhearing some of your conversation with William on board. You said you were staying at Tamarind Bay—that's roughly where I'm headed. Near there, anyway. I have a place in the hills above the bay. I could give you a lift, if you like?'

'Um…that's okay, thanks. I don't mind waiting for a taxi. I don't want to put you out.' She didn't know him, after all, so why would she trust her safety to him?

'You could be in for a long wait…' His glance shifted

over her. 'To be frank, a woman on her own—a beautiful young woman at that—could invite unwanted attention…as you've already discovered.' He reached into the pocket of his chinos and showed her a business card. 'Perhaps this will help to put your mind at ease.'

Dr Cade Byfield, she read. *Emergency Medicine Physician, Mountview Hospital, St Marie-Rose.*

'People know me around here,' he said. 'I make the trip to and from Martinique on a regular basis. Ask the officials at the end of the dock if you need reassurance.'

That sounded reasonable enough. She'd seen one of them acknowledge him with a nod a short time ago. 'A doctor?' she said quietly. 'So you live out here?'

He nodded. 'I have done for the last few years, anyway. I'm from Florida, originally, but my parents settled on the island some years ago.' He glanced at her questioningly. 'And you?'

'I'm English—from a busy town in Hertfordshire.'

'Ah, I thought I recognised the accent.' He smiled fleetingly and waved a hand in the direction of the harbour wall. 'My car's parked over there. Shall we go? I promise you, you'll be safe with me.'

'Okay.' As she nodded he placed the palm of his hand in the small of her back, sending small whorls of sensation eddying through her spine. She tried not to think about the touch of his warm, strong fingers on her body as she walked with him.

'We could have done with your help as a doctor on the plane coming over here,' she murmured as they set off along the quayside.

'Really? Why is that?'

'We had to divert to Martinique to drop off a man who was taken ill. He was sitting in the seat across the aisle from me when he collapsed. He looked dreadful—pale and waxy. The pilot had to radio for help and they made sure they had an ambulance waiting for him at the airport.'

He frowned. 'It must have been serious if they had to do that. What was wrong with him? Do you know?'

She nodded. 'He complained of chest pain radiating to his ears and gums, and then he lost consciousness. I felt for a pulse but there wasn't one.'

He sent her a quick, concerned look. 'Sounds like a heart attack. What happened?'

She pulled a face. 'There was general panic all around me for a moment or two. Then I started chest compressions while a flight attendant rushed to get a portable defibrillator. We managed to shock his heart and establish a rhythm and restored blood flow to his vital organs.' Her mouth flattened. 'I thought he was going to be all right, but then things went wrong again and his heart went into an irregular rhythm and stopped for a second time.'

Cade sucked in his breath. 'He was obviously in a very bad way—that must have been scary for you.'

'It *was* worrying,' she admitted. 'But I'm a doctor, too, so I suppose the training kicked in. They had adrenaline on board in the aircraft's medical kit, so I gave him intravenous doses until he started to recover.'

His eyes widened with interest. 'Are you an emergency doctor?'

'No. My specialty's paediatrics.'

'So, do you work in a hospital or general practice?'

By now they were approaching his car—a dark metallic red sports utility vehicle. It managed to look both sleek and sturdy at the same time, and she guessed it would be capable of managing most types of terrain.

She said quietly, 'I was working in a neonatal unit, but actually I'm taking a break from medicine right now.' How could she bear to go into work every day and be surrounded by babies, knowing she might never hold one of her own? It was like a pain deep inside her. 'At least I thought I was taking a break until I stepped on the plane. My plans certainly went wrong after that.'

He opened the passenger door for her and ushered her inside. He was frowning again. 'Obviously you weren't heading for Martinique at the outset. Wouldn't it have been easier to fly the rest of the way from there instead of getting the ferry?'

'Probably.' She was thankful he hadn't asked about her reasons for having a break from her career, but maybe he assumed she was just taking a holiday. 'There wasn't another flight until tomorrow morning,' she explained. 'Once we stopped at Martinique the flight crew had worked their allotted hours, apparently. I didn't want to mess about. I wanted to get here on time to be with my sister—and my luggage had already been taken off the plane.' She pulled a face. 'I'm not quite sure where it is at the moment...en route to Barbados, I think. I've filled in all the appropriate forms, so hopefully I'll be reunited with it at some point.'

'You've had an eventful journey.' He slid into the driver's seat and switched on the engine. 'Let's hope things go smoothly for you from now on.'

'Yes, we should look on the bright side, shouldn't we?' She leaned back against the luxurious upholstery and felt the cool waft of a delicate breeze fan her cheeks as the air-conditioning kicked in. 'Oh, that feels good.'

He gave her a sideways glance. 'How long are you planning on staying over here?'

'Three months to begin with—maybe longer, but if so I might need to find work of some sort. I'm not in a hurry to do that yet—I suppose I'm looking for a change of direction. I may even decide to go home when the three months is up. I just want to spend time with Emma—my sister. She's over here on a temporary contract with the nursing directorate.' She frowned. 'She messaged me a short time ago when I was on the boat, to say she'd been called out on a job—some last-minute thing that cropped up. I'm just hoping she'll be back before too long.'

His cool, thoughtful gaze swept over her before he turned his attention back to the road ahead. 'Talking of jobs, it seems a bit strange for you to be taking time out so early in your career. You're very fortunate if you can afford to do that. A lot of people would envy you.'

She winced inwardly. Was that a veiled criticism? After seeing her on the boat, getting on so well with his cousin, he probably thought she was a bored rich girl looking for thrills.

'Perhaps they might. You're right—it's good to have enough money to be able to choose—but I don't see myself as "fortunate", really,' she countered. 'My parents died when I was twelve. They left money in trust for me and my sister, so we're both comfortably off, but I'd much rather they were still around. We were brought up by an aunt and uncle. They've been good to us, but they had their own two little girls to care for. It can't have been easy for them.'

'No, I expect not. I'm sorry.' He studied her briefly. 'Does it bother you, leaving them behind to come here?'

'Oh, yes—I'll miss them all…especially my cousins. But we're all older now, going our separate ways.' She was pensive for a moment or two, lost in thought. 'I suppose we were lucky that there was no rivalry or resentment bubbling away in the background because we were taking up the love and attention that should have been reserved for family. In fact we get on very well with one another. My aunt and uncle did a good job.'

'Four youngsters must have made for quite a lively household?'

'Yes, it was a bit rumbustious at times. We had a lot of fun…holidays and family picnics and generally hanging out together.'

'I never had that experience.' There was a slight thread of regret in his voice. 'I was an only child—that's probably what makes me value my cousin's friendship all the more. We're very close—a bit like brothers.'

She sent him a curious glance. 'Really? I didn't get that impression. You kept to yourself on the ferry and didn't really have any contact with him—he said you'd been to Martinique on business and needed some space.'

'That's right. I had to go over there to talk to some clients—I have a plantation in the hills, a few miles from Tamarind Bay, so I make the journey to Martinique on a fairly regular basis to see people about supplies and exports and so on.'

'Wow!' She smiled. 'I'm impressed…a plantation owner…that's inspiring.'

'Not so much.' His mouth made a wry twist. 'I took it over a couple of years ago, when it was completely run down, and I'm learning a few lessons on the way. It's taking a lot of effort to get it going once more, but we've made a reasonable start, I think.'

'It sounds as though you have a busy life.' She wanted to know more about the plantation, but he hadn't yet commented about leaving his cousin to his own devices. Why had he done that if they were so close? 'You said, "We've made a reasonable start"—is William part of that? Where does he fit in? If you're so close, I don't understand why you didn't want to talk to him on the boat?'

'He works for me, but he's on holiday at the moment. As for when we were on the boat—he was with his friends and I didn't want to intrude...more especially since he seemed to be very taken with *you*. In fact, I'd say he was smitten...so much so that I doubt he'd have thanked me for getting in the way.'

She looked at him in mock surprise. 'Smitten? We'd only just met!' Why would he have reached that conclusion? Was he jealous of the attention William had been giving her? Of course he hadn't heard the bulk of their conversation, or he would have known they were just going to be friends. William liked her, but he was still getting over the break-up with his girlfriend and wasn't making any romantic overtures. 'You're reading too much into the situation.'

'I don't think so.' Again, that wry smile. His glance drifted over her, taking in her slender curves, the way her camisole top nipped in at the waist and her skirt draped itself over the swell of her hips. 'What chance did he have against a flame-haired beauty with emerald-green eyes and a come-hither smile? He was done for the moment he looked at you.' He pulled a face. 'Heaven knows—*I* was done for.'

She stifled an uncertain laugh. Did he really feel that way about her? And that was the second time he'd commented on her looks. 'Well, thanks for the compliment… I think…' He made her sound like some kind of Delilah… 'But if it really was as you say, do you imagine he'd have some sort of a problem getting involved with me? I couldn't help feeling you were keeping a weather eye on him.'

'I was, to be honest.'

She blinked, startled by his frank admission. 'You were?'

He frowned. 'I was…most of the time. At least I was trying to, when I wasn't distracted by thinking about you. There's something about you—a vulnerability that I sensed, maybe. I suppose it must have brought out the protective instinct in me.' He sighed and gave his head a shake, as though he was trying to pull himself together. 'Perhaps William feels it, too. Either way, I don't want to see him land in hot water. My aunt asked me to watch out for him over the next few months. He may not look it, but he's vulnerable, too, right now. He's easily led and he's been hurt in the past.'

'Haven't we all?' She said it under her breath, but he gave her a quick, sharp glance before concentrating on negotiating a twisty bend in the road.

Rebecca gazed out of the window, watching the landscape unfold in all its glory. It was easier than trying to fathom him out. She sensed there was a lot more to Cade Byfield than she'd learned so far. He was attracted to her, but he was fighting it, and at the same time she had a sneaking feeling he didn't trust her around his cousin. She wasn't at all sure why.

Not that it mattered. Did she even trust *herself* right now? She was here to chill out, to get over the breakdown of her relationship with Drew and the turmoil that had caused…and hopefully to recover from the aftermath of the illness that had thrown her life into disarray these last few months.

The road wound its way through forested slopes, and their journey of discovery helped to take her mind off things. Beneath the thick canopy of trees she glimpsed the occasional flight of a colourful parrot or a yellow-chested peewee, and on the ground, which was thickly covered with broad-spanning ferns, she caught sight of small green lizards darting through the undergrowth. There were wild flowers hidden among the foliage along the route—waxy lilac anthuriums and the pretty scarlet rosettes of bromeliads peeking out here and there. It was beautiful, and all new to her.

'You said you often go to Martinique on business?' she murmured, turning her attention back to Cade. 'Wouldn't it be quicker and easier for *you* to fly?'

He nodded. 'That's true. But I like having the chance to unwind on board the ferry. It gives me time to clear my head and maybe get things into perspective. In a place like this you don't always want to be rushing about. I get plenty of that in my job at the hospital.'

He pointed out the pristine waters of a yachting harbour as they rounded a curve in the road. 'We must be getting fairly close to where you'll be staying, I think.'

'Oh…' She gave a small gasp of delight as she looked out over the hillside and down into the rocky cove. 'It's so lovely. It's perfection.' Beyond the shoreline, outlined beneath the deep blue of the sea, she saw the turquoise ridge of a coral reef. 'It's even better than the way Emma described it to me.'

'Yes, it's an exquisite island—a beautiful place to live…and work. I've travelled the world, but I always love to come back here.' He negotiated a winding road down to the scattering of houses that made up the small hamlet. 'Yours is the cabin, you said?'

'Yes… I think I can see it amongst the trees. Emma sent me pictures of it.'

Excitement bubbled up inside her as she caught sight of a timber-clad house with white-framed windows and a white-painted wooden balustrade enclosing a wide veranda. The sun was setting on the horizon, casting a golden glow over the hills as they drew up in front of the house. Everything looked tranquil and untouched by the outside world. She sat for a moment, taking it all in. She could be happy here. She felt it deep inside. Surely this was a place of healing, where she could mend her body and her spirit?

'Presumably your sister would have been expecting you earlier? How will you get into the property if she's not here now?'

She frowned. 'It's been a couple of hours since her text message—I would have thought she'd be home by now. But she said she would leave a key in a safe place where I'd be sure to find it.' She laughed softly. 'Knowing Emma, that probably means it could be under a rock marked *"Key is here".*'

He laughed with her. 'I dare say the locals are all on good terms with your sister. You can rest easy. We don't get a lot of crime out here.'

He parked the car in front of the cabin a few minutes later. It was set against a backcloth of leafy trees and dense shrubbery, its location completely private, and everything smelled fresh and open to nature.

Cade waited while Rebecca knocked on the door.

When there was no answer she stifled her disappointment and went in search of the key.

'It was hidden in a box under the veranda,' she told him. 'Would you like to come in for a drink of some sort? I expect there'll be juice in the fridge—or coffee?'

'Thanks. I'll have a coffee, if you have the makings. I'll see you settled in and then I should be on my way. I have to get over to the plantation to meet up with my estate manager.'

'You work late out here?'

He nodded. 'Occasionally. Sometimes it's necessary if problems crop up. My manager wants to see me about getting a new truck—the one we have at the moment keeps breaking down. He lives in a cottage on the plantation, so it's not as if he'll be put out too much. I need to get it sorted.'

All this on top of his work as a doctor? He obviously believed in keeping busy. She stepped on to the veranda and unlocked the front door. 'Come in.'

'Thanks.'

They both took a moment to look around. The living room was simply furnished, with a polished light oak floor, a couple of settees and a coffee table, and opened out into a light and airy kitchen-diner at one end. The units there were cream-coloured, with pale oak worktops that were easy on the eye. Two sets of French doors led from the kitchen and the living room out on to the veranda that swept around the building, giving a view through the trees of the delightful cove below.

'I'll just see if Emma has any coffee.' Rebecca checked the cupboards, then set out porcelain mugs on the oak table while she waited for the kettle to boil. There was a note from Emma propped up against the sugar bowl. 'She doesn't know when she'll be back,' Rebecca said, quickly scanning it. 'She says the landlord will stop by tomorrow morning to sort out a problem with the window shutters.'

She frowned. It definitely sounded as though she would not be back tonight.

'Ah, I might have known it—Emma's left some food for supper,' she murmured, continuing to read and then going to rummage in the fridge. 'We might as well help ourselves…there's plenty for both of us, from the looks of things. Spiced chicken drumsticks and salad, with savoury rice.' She turned to him. 'How does that sound?'

He pulled in a breath. 'Too tempting to refuse,' he admitted with a grin. 'It seems to be quite a while since I had lunch.'

'Mmm…me, too,' she agreed, taking dishes and platters from the fridge. She frowned. 'I wish I knew how long she was going to be. I was so looking forward to seeing her again.'

'Is she older than you or younger?' he asked as they sat down to eat a minute or so later.

'Older by just a year. But for all that she's always sort of looked after me…kept me on the straight and narrow, so to speak—our cousins, too. They're three or four years younger than us.' She waved a hand over the food she had set out. 'Help yourself.'

She'd always looked to Emma for guidance over the years. Perhaps Emma would know how she could get over her illness and the break-up with Drew and restore her self-confidence once more. When her consultant had said she might have difficulty in having children because of scar tissue blocking her fallopian tubes it had come as a devastating blow. Rebecca had withdrawn into herself for a while and shut out the outside world. She hadn't wanted to face up to anything for some time.

As for now… A recklessness seemed to have taken her over. She'd left her job, left the country, put everything behind her. And she'd met a handsome young man on the ferry coming over here—not to mention the fact that now she was sharing a meal with a perfect stranger in the privacy of a secluded cabin. Had she lost her senses? Perhaps she was hell bent on self-destruction. She didn't want to take anyone down with her, but was she headed that way? Emma would surely put her right.

She shook the thoughts from her mind. Better to think of something completely different. 'What kind of plantation do you have?' she asked now. 'What do you grow there?'

Cade had been watching her, she realised, clearly curious about her introspection, but now he followed her lead and answered readily. 'Cocoa—everything depends on producing a good crop.'

'You said it had been run down—why would that happen?'

'Because of disease in the plants, the weather—hurricane winds, tropical storms—and low prices. A lot of people out here gave up on cocoa and turned to banana-growing instead. It must have seemed like the better option.'

'But you think you can make a go of it where others have failed?'

He nodded. 'I'll certainly have a good try.' He finished off his chicken and wiped his hands on a paper serviette. 'That was delicious.'

She inclined her head briefly. 'Emma's always been a good cook.'

They talked some more about food in general, and his hopes for the plantation, and then her phone rang, cutting in on their conversation.

'Perhaps it's Emma. I should answer it,' she said quickly.

'Of course. Please—go ahead.'

She stood up and walked across the kitchen to take the call. It wasn't Emma, though, and a swift wave of disappointment washed over her.

'Hi, Becky…it's William. I'm just checking that you managed to get to your sister's all right. I was concerned about you. I hated leaving you alone at the harbour.'

'Oh, hi, William. Yes, I did, thanks. You didn't need to worry about me. I'm fine.' Out of the corner of her vision she saw Cade brace himself slightly. His head went back a fraction.

'That's good. Listen, I'm coming over to the bay tomorrow evening. Maybe we could go for a drink together?'

'I'd like that… It depends what my sister's doing, though. She isn't here right now.'

'She could come with us.'

She thought about it. 'Okay, then. Yes, we could do that. It sounds good. I'll let you know if anything changes.'

'Great. I'll meet you in Selwyn's Bar at around eight o'clock?'

'Selwyn's Bar? Yes. Eight o'clock, then. I'll look forward to it.' She was smiling as she said it, and when she cut the call she turned to look at Cade once more. 'That was your cousin,' she said unnecessarily. 'He was just checking to see that I got here all right.'

'So I gathered.' He stood up, his features guarded. 'You'll be seeing him again, from the sound of things?'

'Looks like it.' She sent him a quick, challenging look. He seemed tense. 'Do you have a problem with that?'

'Not really... Maybe...' He shrugged awkwardly. 'Like I said, I don't want to see him get hurt. He's just come out of a bad relationship and he's vulnerable right now. I know it doesn't seem that way...'

'Surely he's old enough to take care of himself?'

'You'd think so, wouldn't you? But some people take a while longer than others.'

'He seemed fine to me.' Her green eyes flashed. 'Anyway, why do you imagine I'm likely to be such a problem for him?'

'Are you *kidding*?' His mouth made a crooked shape as his glance drifted over her. 'The way you look, I suspect you'd be a problem for a saint,' he said, with feeling. 'My cousin stands no chance at all.'

A wave of heat ran through her cheeks. 'Well, I'm flattered you imagine I have such powers...'

He smiled. 'I suppose I want you to go easy on him. I sense you just want to have a good time and enjoy your stay here—and there's absolutely nothing wrong with that.' His dark eyes glinted. 'I'd be only too happy to help you do that. As for William—he's here for the duration, while you'll be moving on in a short time. I can't help thinking that if you and he get together I'll be left to pick up the pieces again.'

'I'm sure you and your aunt are being overly concerned... I've never thought of myself as a heartbreaker.' Still, something in her prompted her to say, 'Anyway, you could always come with us to the bar.'

Even as the words left her lips she wondered what on earth she was thinking. 'He suggested my sister might want to come along,' she added, 'so you could join us and make up a foursome.'

'I'd like that,' he said. 'I'll look forward to it—I'll come and pick you up.' His smoky gaze rested on her once more. 'It's a great pity William saw you first,' he said softly. 'I'd be more than ready for the challenge.'

She looked at him directly, her green glance unwavering. 'I've said before that we're just going to be friends…but even if that wasn't the case I'm not some prize to be won.'

'Like I said, I have his interests at heart. I won't stand by and see him hurt.'

She wasn't sure whether that was a threat or a promise.

He left soon after that, and she watched him drive away. She ought to be feeling relaxed, at peace with herself, but instead she felt a sense of nervous anticipation— a vague worry starting up inside her. What was she doing, getting involved with Cade and his cousin? Hadn't she been through enough turmoil—and could William really get hurt because of *her*?

Her mouth made a crooked twist. She doubted Cade was the kind of man who would let that happen. She frowned. Perhaps that was what bothered her. What did he have in mind? Somehow she suspected a man like him would leave nothing to chance. Wasn't that why he'd been waiting around on the dock after William had left?

CHAPTER TWO

'I WAS SO worried when you didn't come back here last night.' Rebecca watched her sister search through the clothes in her wardrobe. 'Does it happen very often—that you don't manage to get home?'

'Sometimes—it depends on the circumstances.' Emma held up a pale green dress that had an off-the-shoulder neckline and a skater skirt. 'How about this one? It'll go beautifully with your eyes.'

'Oh, that looks great. Thanks. I'll try it on.'

They were getting ready for their night out at Selwyn's Bar, and as most of Rebecca's clothes were still in her suitcase, travelling between airports, she was having to rely on Emma to help her out. Luckily they were of a similar shape and size.

'So what happened last night?'

'We had to go to a rural area up in the hills.' Emma frowned. 'A couple of people have gone down with headaches and fever, and we're not quite sure yet what we're dealing with. We looked after them, made them comfortable, and sent blood samples and so on to the hospital. We shan't know what's wrong with them until we get the results back in a couple of days.'

'So you'll be going back there?'

Emma nodded. 'I have to wait for a call from the chief nursing officer. They'll send a Jeep to take me back to the village.'

The girls finished dressing, and Rebecca added a final touch of blusher to her cheeks just as a rapping noise sounded on the cabin's front door. Her stomach muscles tensed. That would be Cade, of course. He was a few minutes early and she didn't feel at all ready for him. She hadn't had time to compose herself, but she didn't know why that bothered her. Why was she nervous about meeting up with him again?

'I'll get it.'

Her sister left the room and Rebecca took a moment to quickly check her hair in the bedroom mirror. She'd pinned it up for the evening, doing her best to tame the unruly curls, though a few spiralling tendrils had escaped to frame her face. Satisfied that she looked okay, she smoothed down the dress. The silky material skimmed her hips lovingly and fell in soft folds almost to her knees.

Emma was already opening the door, greeting Cade with a cheerful, 'Hi, there. You must be the man Becky's been telling me about. Come in.' There was a pause as he entered the cabin. Then, 'She says you have a plantation up in the hills?' Emma said. 'That is *so* exciting! I've never met an estate owner before—or seen a cocoa plantation.'

'You should come and visit, then,' Cade answered cheerfully. 'I'd love to show you and Rebecca around— you could come tomorrow, if you like?'

'That sounds great.'

'Good. It's a date, then. Late afternoon would be

best for me—I could pick you both up after I leave the hospital.'

'You have to work at the weekend?'

'I do, unfortunately.'

He hadn't wasted any time in issuing the invitation, had he?

His deep voice sent ripples of tingling sensation coursing along Rebecca's spine. She tried to shake it off. How did he manage to have this effect on her? She wasn't looking for any kind of involvement or attachment, yet he'd figured constantly in her thoughts ever since she'd watched him drive away the evening before. It was disturbing. Hanging out with William would be one thing—his cousin was a different matter entirely. With Cade she sensed danger at every turn... Her nervous system had gone into overdrive and was sending out vigorous warning signals that she would ignore at her peril.

'Hello again.' She took a deep breath as she walked into the room, and knew a perverse sense of gratification as she saw Cade's grey eyes widen in appreciation.

He said nothing for a second or two, but then his dark gaze swept over both girls and he commented softly, 'It's clear to see that you're sisters. You have the same high cheekbones and perfect jawline. You both look lovely.'

'Why, thank you!' Emma laughingly touched his arm, her long chestnut hair fleetingly brushing his shoulder as she moved in close to him.

She was wearing a simply styled blue dress with thin shoulder straps, leaving her arms bare. As for Cade, he looked cool and immaculate in a freshly laundered shirt and pale-coloured trousers.

'Just give me a minute to get my bag,' Emma said, 'and we can be on our way. I've been to Selwyn's Bar before,' she confided. 'I love it there.'

Cade led the way to his car a few minutes later and saw them seated comfortably. Rebecca chose to sit in the back seat alongside Emma. It didn't feel as though they'd had much time to talk, since Emma hadn't arrived home until mid-afternoon, and she doubted they'd have much chance to confide in one another this evening. It was good to be together again, though.

'How long have you been working out here, Emma?' Cade asked as he turned the car on to the coast road.

'A couple of months. I'm having a great time out here. The work hasn't been too difficult up to now—mostly we've been running health clinics and visiting the more remote villages. We've been giving vaccinations and checking out the under-fives to make sure they're okay.'

He glanced in the rearview mirror. 'Is that the sort of thing *you* might want to do, Rebecca—work with the under-fives, I mean? Not now, obviously, but maybe later? You talked about wanting a change of direction.'

Rebecca's face paled at the unexpected question. 'Um... I'm not sure. It's something I'd have to think about.'

'I suppose in neonatal your work was much more specialised?'

'Yes. Some of the babies were very ill. They might have been born prematurely, or they had heart defects or lung complaints and so on.'

'Is that why you stopped doing the job—because it was too harrowing?'

She swallowed hard. 'In a way, yes.'

She didn't want to talk about this. Delving into the different aspects of her work was far too painful, and it brought up a host of reminders she would rather ignore. It had been so hard going back to work after her illness. She hadn't been able to bear to hold those tiny babies in her arms when she might never have one of her own. She hadn't realised how badly she had been affected until she'd cradled those sweet, frail infants.

Beside her, Emma shifted closer in a silent gesture of support. 'Sometimes it's good to do something different for a while—to explore other opportunities. But for the moment Becky's taking time out to recharge her batteries. She's worked really hard over the last few years, qualifying as a doctor and taking her specialist exams. She hasn't really had much time for herself and she's well overdue for an extended holiday.'

'Of course. I understand.'

Seeing the reflection of his dark eyes in the rearview mirror, Rebecca knew he didn't understand at all. How could he? As far as he was concerned she was young, energetic, on the cusp of life—why would she need to take time out? But she wasn't going to explain her circumstances to someone she'd only just met. And talking about it was upsetting.

She hadn't been able to discuss things much with Drew, because his negative, unhelpful reaction had made matters worse. Whatever future they might have contemplated had been wiped out when he'd realised there was a possibility she might not be able to have children. She'd been devastated by his response to her predicament.

As for now, she wondered if any man she met might respond in the same way? She couldn't even think about her situation without feeling shaky and unhappy. It was too soon…the emotional wound ran too deep and was still too raw.

'They do marvellous mojitos at Selwyn's,' Emma said brightly, changing the subject. 'You'll like them, Becky. They make them with white rum, fresh limes and a sprig of mint. *Yum*.'

'Sounds good.' Rebecca made an effort to pull herself together. She glanced at Cade once more. 'What do you like to drink, Cade?'

'I like rum, too—it's the national drink out here in the islands—but mostly I drink lager. Maybe I'll have a rum cocktail this evening, but after that I'll stick with non-alcoholic lager because I'm on the early shift tomorrow at the hospital… And, of course, I'm driving.'

'Ah…you drew the short straw.' Emma chuckled sympathetically. 'They serve food at Selwyn's, so you could always try soaking up the rum with a tenderloin steak or some such.'

He smiled. 'I might do that.'

William was waiting for them, greeting all three of them with enthusiasm when they stepped on to the boardwalk leading to Selwyn's Bar a few minutes later. The bar was made of wooden decking and built over a shallow tidal strait where mangroves emerged in a dense tangle of arching roots from the flood plain left by the ebb and flow of salt water. There was lush greenery all around, and the sounds of the forest mingled with the lively music coming from speakers positioned under the solid awning. Tables covered in white cloths were set out alongside the balustrade, so that customers could sit and eat and look out over the water.

William was smiling, wearing a T-shirt and knee-length cut-off shorts. 'Hey, it's great to see you again,' he said, giving Rebecca a quick hug and nodding amiably to his cousin. 'And this must be Emma…' He turned to Emma. 'Hi, there. Becky told me you're a nurse? It must be a whole new experience for you to come out here and work in the Caribbean. How are you finding it?'

'It's great…' Emma said. 'It's very different to what I've known before, back in the UK, but it's really good—most of the time. Some things can be a bit frustrating—like equipment shortages or breakdowns—and of course everything tends to move at a slower pace.'

He nodded. 'I know what you mean. Food stores can run out of staples like bread and milk, if you don't get there early in the day, and the Internet can go down when you're in the middle of something.'

'And if your truck breaks down you might have to wait for a part to be sent over from one of the other islands,' Cade put in, with feeling. 'That's happened to us more than once.' He smiled and led them over to the bar. 'I'll get the drinks in. Mojitos, was it?'

'That would be lovely.' Rebecca glanced at him. 'So, did you talk with your estate manager about getting a new truck?'

'I did. It'll take a while to sort out, but things will start to run a lot more smoothly for us once it arrives.'

They took their drinks to a table by the rail and the four of them chatted while they looked at menus and decided what they wanted to eat.

'We could share a seafood and chicken platter?' Cade suggested after a minute or two, and they all agreed. It sounded appetising…saffron rice with grilled spiced chicken and mixed seafood.

Rebecca looked out over the water and watched graceful white egrets searching for titbits in the shallows. In the distance, where the mangroves gave way to tall dogwood trees, she saw a blue-and-gold macaw spread its wings and take flight.

She smiled. 'I love it here,' she said softly. 'It's so restful.'

'It's good to see you looking relaxed,' William commented. 'You were a bit stressed after your journey yesterday.'

Smiling, she said, 'Well, twelve hours on a plane and then finding they've lost your luggage can do that to you.'

Cade lifted a dark brow. 'Have your cases still not caught up with you yet?'

'Not yet. I rang the airport this morning, to check, but nothing doing so far. They don't seem to have any idea where they might be.' Rebecca's mouth curved a fraction. 'It pays to have a sister who'll share her clothes with you.'

'Yeah, I guess so.' He leaned towards her and added quietly, so that only she could hear, 'If that's Emma's dress it certainly suits you…and it fits like a glove.'

Warm colour flooded her cheeks. 'Thanks.'

William was still thinking about the boat journey. 'Actually, I thought there was more to it than lost luggage…there were a few moments when you were off guard and you went a bit quiet.'

'I was fine,' she said. 'I'm still fine. Who could be stressed in a place like this?'

He grinned. 'You're probably right.'

Rebecca sent him a fleeting, thoughtful glance. Was it possible William was more perceptive than she'd given him credit for? Maybe through his own experiences William understood deep down how it was to be out of sync with everything around him and his general air of good humour was something of an effort for him.

She was conscious all the time, though, of Cade's watchful gaze. He still wasn't happy about her getting to know William to any great extent—she could feel it in her bones—and he'd even managed to arrange the seating at the table so that his cousin was placed next to Emma and sitting diagonally across from Rebecca. Of course that could have come about in the natural course of events—maybe she was reading too much into things.

Cade said now, 'Perhaps you were quiet because you were thinking about that man on the plane—the one who was taken ill?'

'Yes, that was probably it.'

William and Emma listened interestedly as she quickly recounted what had happened.

'That must have been so worrying.' Emma frowned. 'I wonder how he's doing?'

'His condition's stable,' Rebecca said. 'I phoned the hospital this morning. Apparently he's been assessed, and they've made the decision to do heart bypass surgery tomorrow.'

'That must have cheered you up—to know that you enabled that to happen.' Cade smiled. 'It's good that you followed up on him—I was wondering how he was doing, too.'

'From the way the nurse spoke, I'm sure he'll be fine. I think he's in good hands.'

William was momentarily subdued. 'I'm surrounded by medics,' he said, in a voice tinged with awe. 'What *I* do is nothing in comparison.'

'You shouldn't feel that way,' Emma said. 'We all have something to offer.' She studied him briefly. 'You work on Cade's plantation, don't you? What do you do there?'

'I help out in all areas—getting to know the job from the bottom up, so to speak. Cade thinks that's the best way for me to start.'

He told them about his role in ordering new seedlings and supervising the planting.

'When we took over the plantation there were a number of mature trees that were viable—a lot of them are ready for harvesting now,' Cade put in. 'They have to be at least three years old before they produce pods—five years is best for a good crop—but we want to plant seedlings every year to ensure quality and continuity. You'll be able to see what we're doing when you come and take a look around tomorrow.'

'I'll look forward to that,' Rebecca said.

Emma nodded. 'Me, too… Provided I'm not called away to work.' She pulled a face. 'I'd arranged to take a few days off, with Rebecca coming over, but we're not sure if there's some kind of outbreak happening up in the hills.'

A waitress brought their food over to the table and they spent the next hour or so talking about this and that while sampling the delicious dishes on offer. Rebecca ate shrimp sautéed with peppers and onions in a spicy ginger and lime sauce, along with crab cake and rice accompanied by a tasty green salad. Dessert was a delicious concoction of caramelised pineapple with a drizzle of lime, vanilla and rum syrup, and a scoop of ice cream.

'Mmm…that was heavenly,' Rebecca murmured, pushing away her plate when she had eaten her fill. She laid a hand on her stomach. 'I don't think I'll be able to eat another morsel for at least a week!'

William laughed. 'Let's hope it's not as long as that. I was thinking of tempting you with my own recipe for melt-in-the-mouth chocolate tart when you come over to the plantation tomorrow.'

'Oh…chocolate…you've found my weak spot—stay away from me!' She laughed with him. 'So you're planning on being there, too? That's great. But what about your friends on holiday in the north of the island? I thought you would want to be with them?'

'They're going back to Miami,' he said, his mouth turning down a fraction at the corners. 'To go on with their university courses or work commitments. I met them over there, when I was studying food and agricultural sciences, and we stayed in touch after I finished my course. But my vacation ends today, and I'm due back home tomorrow—so, yes, with any luck I'll see you there. I live in one of the cottages on the plantation.'

'That's handy.'

'Yes.' He leaned towards her and spoke confidentially. 'It's rent-free, courtesy of my cousin, so I'm more than happy. I owe him—though he's very dismissive of his generosity.'

Rebecca returned his smile. Cade couldn't hear what they were saying, but all the while she felt his brooding gaze resting on her. He obviously felt great responsibility towards his cousin. She understood his concerns, at least in part, but outwardly William was fun and that was what she needed right now. She responded to his lively, engaging manner, but it wasn't as if she was setting out to capture his heart.

Emma was in a playful mood, too, unwinding after her busy time at work, and was more than ready to let her hair down. She teased William and laughed with Cade.

Both girls drank mojitos, and then at Cade's persuasion Rebecca tried another cocktail, made up of dark rum, lemon juice, grenadine syrup and Angostura bitters. The evening passed quickly and in a bit of a haze after that. She was enjoying herself, but the others had to prepare for work the next day, and so all too soon their night out came to an end.

'I'll drop by the cabin around three-thirty tomorrow, if that's okay?' Cade said as he delivered the girls safely home.

The moon was a silvery orb, glimmering through the branches of the trees, casting shadows all around and highlighting the night-scented jasmine. The heady fragrance of the white flowers lingered on the air.

'Yes, that should be all right. All being well, we'll be ready and waiting.' Emma waved him off as he slid back into the driver's seat of his car and disappeared into the night.

Things didn't turn out quite as they'd expected, though. Rebecca was disappointed when, early the next afternoon, Emma received a text message calling her out to work. Several more people had gone down with the mystery illness in the village high up in the hills, and the nurse in charge wanted extra staff on hand to be available to deal with the ailing patients. They were very ill, apparently, with high temperatures and headaches.

'We think it's some kind of bacterial infection,' Emma told Rebecca. 'We'll probably have to give antibiotics as a precautionary measure.'

'Shall I go with you?' Rebecca asked. 'It sounds as though you could do with some help.'

Emma shook her head. 'No, Becky,' she said firmly. 'You've not long recovered from an illness yourself— you might still be under par and we don't want to risk you going down with anything. Anyway, I doubt the nursing director will allow it.'

'But what about the risk to yourself?' Rebecca was worried, instantly on the alert. 'What if it's typhoid fever? I heard a whisper that there have been sporadic outbreaks on a couple of the other islands.'

Emma shrugged. 'I've had all my vaccinations, so I should be okay. We take precautions, anyway, with gloves and masks where we think it's necessary.'

Rebecca was still anxious, though she stayed quiet, not wanting to upset her sister. The typhoid vaccination wasn't always a hundred per cent reliable—you still had to be careful not to eat or drink contaminated food or water. 'You'll keep in touch, won't you? Phone me and let me know what's happening?'

'Of course I will.' Emma gave Rebecca a hug and then glanced at her watch. 'The Jeep will be here to pick me up in half an hour,' she said. She pulled a face. 'It's such a shame—I was really looking forward to seeing the plantation. You'll have to tell me all about it.'

Rebecca frowned. 'I might ring and cancel…but I'm sure Cade will invite us another time. He and William both seemed keen for us to visit.'

'They did, didn't they?' Emma smiled. 'William's so sweet. He has such an innocent, boyish look about him. He was telling me how much his mother loves chocolate—but she's as thin as a rake, apparently. She's really pleased about him working on the plantation. He's had a bad time lately, from the sound of things…and now his father has been taken ill.'

She hurried away to her bedroom to start packing a few things into a holdall.

Rebecca followed her. She wondered aloud what was wrong with William's father, but Emma wasn't sure.

'Some sort of virus, I think,' she said. 'They're still trying to figure it out, but it seems to be affecting his heart. It's very worrying, by all accounts.'

No wonder Cade was being protective towards his cousin. It sounded as though he had a lot on his plate right now.

Rebecca searched through one of the cupboards. 'I'll give you a hand. Do you need fresh towels—moisturiser and so on?'

'Yes, thanks.'

Emma left for the village a short time later, and Rebecca tried in vain to phone Cade. Each time she tried she received the unavailable tone. Then, some half an hour later, he knocked on the cabin door.

'Oh, hi,' Rebecca said, trying not to let herself be distracted by his flawlessly turned out appearance. He was wearing a crisply laundered shirt, a pale blue silk tie, and dark trousers that emphasised the tautness of his flat stomach and his powerful, long legs. 'I'm afraid Emma isn't here—she was called away to work. I tried to ring you to cancel, but your phone seemed to be switched off.'

He nodded, frowning. 'I was driving. I tend to switch the car phone off if I'm not on call. Some of the roads in the hills can be tricky—very winding and steep—so I like to give them my full attention, especially if there's been heavy rain or a storm.' He sent her a questioning look. 'I'm sorry she isn't here, but there's no reason for you not to come along, is there?'

'Uh…no…if that's all right with you?' Her brows drew together. 'I know Emma's disappointed to be missing out.'

'It's okay—she can come another time. We'll arrange something. It's no problem.'

She brightened. 'All right, then, if you're sure.' It felt strange to be going without Emma, but since he'd taken the trouble to come out of his way to fetch her, she didn't want to argue the point. 'I'll just get a light jacket.'

A moment later she slipped the jacket on over her T-shirt, then checked her jeans pocket for her key and cash card, transferring them to a small bag. 'I'm ready,' she said at last.

'Good. I told my manager to expect us just after four. His wife's arranging afternoon tea on the terrace for us.'

'Afternoon tea?' She smiled, giving him a quick glance as she slid into the passenger seat beside him. 'It sounds lovely—but isn't that a very English tradition?'

He smiled. 'It is, but I hoped you might like it. I could certainly do with something—I've been on duty since seven this morning and I'm starving. It isn't always easy to stop and grab something to eat and drink when you're coping with emergencies.'

'No, it isn't.' She recalled her time as a junior doctor, working long hours and fitting in breaks wherever possible. 'Have you been very busy today, then?'

She frowned. He looked clean and fresh after his exertions, but maybe he'd managed to shower and change at the hospital. Come to think of it, his black hair *was* faintly glistening with moisture.

'We have… The usual variety of patients, with chest pains, viruses, bleeding…' He glanced at her, his mouth twisting faintly as he started on the road up into the hills. 'Even though this is the Caribbean, and we have lots of tourists around, enjoying the beaches and water sports quite safely, people still get ill—people who live and work here.'

'I never thought otherwise.' Perhaps he'd mistaken her frown for a look of disbelief that there could ever be trouble in Paradise.

'No?' He didn't say any more, concentrating his attention on the winding road that led ever upwards.

As she gazed out of the window Rebecca saw the cloud-covered peaks of the mountains rising majestically in the distance. The landscape was awe-inspiring, vibrant and rugged.

They arrived at the plantation a few minutes later, and Rebecca looked around in wonder at this dark green jewel set in the midst of the rainforest. All around her were cacao trees, standing about twenty feet high, with glossy green leaves as big as her hand. The tree bark was covered with mosses and lichens, and small, delicate orchids peeped out from crevices here and there. Large pink fruit pods hung from the branches, ready to be harvested.

Set amongst these trees were other, taller ones. She recognised banana and coconut palms. She looked at them, a little puzzled, wondering what they were doing here in the middle of a cocoa plantation.

Interpreting her glance, Cade said, 'They provide shade for the cacao—otherwise the hot sun would shrivel them. The cocoa trees are quite fragile, especially when they're young, so they need protection. I planted these trees when I first took over the plantation so that I could shield the young plants. They grew very quickly.'

'Ah, I see.' The banana leaves were huge, spreading shade, and the nearby coconut palms added extra security.

'Up ahead they're harvesting the pods—we can go and watch for a while, if you want?'

'I'd like that—thanks.'

She went with him to an area where workers moved among the more mature trees, hooking the pods from the branches with long-handled implements. The pods fell to the ground, where young men and women with machetes cut them open and removed the white beans from inside. They dropped the large seeds into clean metal buckets.

'They'll empty the beans into wooden boxes and cover them with banana leaves to keep in the heat,' Cade told her. 'We let them ferment for a few days before drying them, so that the colour and flavour can develop.'

'It's fascinating,' she said simply. 'I'd no idea the beans were white to begin with.'

His mobile phone pinged and he took it from his pocket and glanced at a text message on the screen. 'If you're interested I can show you more of the process,' he said, 'but maybe we should go and have tea first. It's all ready and waiting for us at the house, apparently.'

'Okay.' She smiled and started to walk with him towards the white-painted building in the distance. 'Is William there? I was expecting to see him this afternoon.'

A muscle flicked briefly in his jaw. 'Actually, no...

Perhaps I should have mentioned it earlier… I'm afraid William won't be back until much later today—he's gone to a neighbouring island to organise the transportation of our new truck. Things will go a lot quicker for us if he takes charge of it, I think.'

She shot him a quick, penetrating glance. 'You sent him to do that today?'

He nodded. 'The dealer called this morning. It seemed to me like a good opportunity to follow up on things right away.'

He sounded nonchalant, though she suspected he was covering his actions. The truth was he hadn't wanted her spending more time around his cousin.

'Really?' She eyed him doubtfully.

Had it been so necessary for William to go this afternoon? Wouldn't a phone call have been enough to set things in motion? She frowned. It wasn't up to her to interfere, or tell him his business, but she was suddenly on edge, wary of Cade's motives. Did he think she was such a bad influence?

'It's a shame he isn't here,' she said. 'I know he was looking forward to seeing Emma and me today.'

His dark eyes glinted in a way that only confirmed her suspicions. He'd deliberately sent his cousin on this errand.

'I'm sure he was, but I dare say there'll be other opportunities for you to get together.'

He laid a hand lightly in the small of her back, and with that gentle possessive touch it dawned on her that maybe he wanted to keep her all to himself. His dark gaze moved over her and a small ripple of panic ran through her—a feeling of nervousness mingled with a strange sadness. She couldn't get involved with anyone, could she? Any relationships she had from now on would have to be light-hearted, fleeting—nothing of any great significance. She didn't want to risk getting the same reaction she'd had from Drew. Once had been quite enough.

They'd arrived at the plantation house by now, and were standing in front of wide veranda steps. It was a beautiful house, built of stone to withstand the ravages of Caribbean storms, and meant to last a lifetime. There were lots of glass doors opening out on to the decking, giving her a glimpse of a light and airy interior.

Just then a woman came hurrying from the house. She was in her mid-forties, Rebecca guessed, with neat brown hair cut into a silky layered bob, and hazel eyes that were filled with anxiety.

'Cade—there's been an accident in the east section. One of the lads has hurt his hand—a machete cut. Don says it's bleeding quite badly.'

'Thanks, Harriet,' he said, looking worried. 'I'll go and get my medical bag.' He glanced at Rebecca as he moved towards the house. 'I'm afraid I'll have to go and deal with this right away. Will you stay here and let Harriet look after you? I'll be back as soon as I can.'

'It's all right. I understand—you have to go, of course.'

All her instincts as a doctor kicked in as soon as she realised that this was an emergency. If the cut had gone deep the boy would need stitches at the very least. If there had been major damage to the muscles and tendons of his hand he might require an operation in order to save the function. There was also the possibility that Cade might need help with administering an anaesthetic...

Deep down, she knew she didn't have a choice. 'Perhaps I should go with you to see him?'

He didn't argue the point. 'Are you sure you want to do that?' He raised questioning dark brows, and when she nodded said, 'Thanks. We'll take the runabout.' He pointed to an open-sided vehicle parked on the drive. 'It'll get us there in a few minutes.'

He went into the house and came out a minute later with a large immediate care response pack.

She was impressed. 'It looks as though you're very well prepared for any eventuality,' she commented, as they climbed aboard the four-seater golf buggy and set off.

He nodded. 'I always keep a medical kit in the car, too. I'm on call outside the hospital sometimes, so I need to be ready for anything.'

'I can understand that.' A worrying thought occurred to her. 'Does this sort of thing happen often here on the plantation?'

'No, not at all. We're really careful to show our workers the correct way of going on, but I suppose it's inevitable that accidents happen from time to time. The aim is to keep them to a minimum.' He frowned. 'One way I've changed things is by paying everyone a proper wage, instead of giving payment for how much they produce. It seems to be working out for the better so far.'

They arrived at the east section a short time later, and he jumped down from the runabout and hurried over to where a small crowd of native workers had gathered. There were murmurs of concern, people talking all at once, but as soon as Cade appeared the group quietened and opened up to give him access to his patient.

He knelt down beside the injured boy, a lad of about seventeen years old. He was holding his hand to stem the blood flow, his face etched with pain. He was pale and in shock.

'Let me see, Thomas.' Cade examined the wound—a deep cut across the back of the hand between the thumb and first finger. 'Can you move your fingers? Open and close your hand for me?'

After examining him carefully, Cade gave an almost imperceptible nod.

'I think you're fortunate—there's been no major damage. You've lost quite a bit of blood, and obviously you're in shock. I think we'll need to clean up the wound and put in a few stitches.' He studied the boy thoughtfully. 'I could take you to the hospital, or we could do it back at the house. What would you prefer?'

'Will you do it here…please?'

'Okay.' Cade rummaged in his medical bag and brought out a pack of sterile dressings. 'I'm going to put a pad over the wound to stem the bleeding and then cover it with a dressing. Once we get you to the house we'll clean it up properly and put some sutures in place.'

All the while he was speaking, he was working efficiently to protect the injured hand.

'Okay, let's get you into the runabout.' He signalled to two of the workers to help get the boy settled in the back of the buggy. 'How did you come to hurt yourself, Thomas, do you know?'

Thomas shook his head. 'It happened so suddenly… I was cutting open a pod with my machete and I saw something out of the corner of my eye—it might have been a small lizard, running through the undergrowth.'

'Hmm…that's a difficult one. These things happen

sometimes, but you need to try to keep your attention on the blade at all times.' Cade frowned. 'Maybe we should issue everyone with leather gloves?'

'Too hot, boss,' one of the workers said. 'No one would want to wear them.'

'Well, we'll have to think of something—maybe we can find gloves that have air holes… I don't want any more accidents if I can help it.' He glanced at the other worker once more. 'Benjamin, will you make sure Thomas's parents know what's happened? Tell them he'll be okay.'

'I will, boss.'

Cade nodded, and saw the boy settled into the buggy while Rebecca slid into the seat beside the patient, making sure that he was securely strapped in and that his arm was supported in a comfortable position.

Back at the house, Cade helped Thomas through the front door and into a room that seemed to serve as a clinic. Rebecca looked around, taking in the clean lines, the treatment couch laid with fresh tissue roll, the glass-fronted cupboards stocked with all kinds of medical supplies. In one corner there was a sink unit with stainless-steel taps and dispensers for soap and paper towels.

'Sit down here, Thomas. Let me adjust the backrest for you.' Cade settled the boy on the couch and then went over to the sink to wash his hands.

Rebecca joined him there. 'Do you want me to help anaesthetise the hand?' she asked, and he nodded.

'Thanks. We'll use lidocaine, and then clean the wound with sterile water. He'll need several stitches to hold it in place.'

She worked with him to tend the boy's injured hand,

and when Cade had finished applying the sutures she covered the wound with a sterile dressing, fixing it in place with tape.

'I'll give you some antibiotics, Thomas,' Cade said, 'so that you don't get an infection. It's important to keep the wound clean, okay? I'll need to see you back here in a week's time, to check that everything's healing as it should.' He looked at the boy carefully. 'Are you okay with that?'

Thomas nodded. 'Yes, thanks.' He was still pale, but at least he appeared to be recovering from the initial shock of the accident.

'Mrs Chalmers will give you tea and something to eat in the kitchen,' Cade said, helping him to get down from the couch. 'Take your time—your father will be along in a while to take you home, but there's no rush.'

Thomas smiled. 'Thanks, Dr Byfield. I'm sorry to be so much trouble.'

'You're no trouble, Thomas. I don't like to see anyone injured—especially on my property. I want you to take extra-special care from now on.'

'I will. Thanks again.'

Cade took him along to the kitchen—a large, superbly equipped room with doors that opened out on to a wide area of the veranda. A table and chairs were set out there, and Harriet Chalmers was waiting with reviving tea, home-baked scones and fruit preserves.

Thomas's father arrived just as the boy began to tuck in, using his good hand, and Cade spoke to the man for a few minutes, inviting him to sit down and eat with his son before turning his attention back to Rebecca.

'We'll leave them to it,' he said. 'Harriet's set out some sandwiches for us in the breakfast room—through here.'

He led the way from the kitchen to a small room, surrounded on two sides by floor-to-ceiling glass doors. It was simply furnished, with a white table and chairs, and a white-painted dresser displaying plates and dishes that added a pleasing splash of colour. Here and there were green ferns, extending their delicate fronds to bring a touch of the outside into the room.

An arrangement of pale yellow orchids on the breakfast table caught Rebecca's attention and she gave a small gasp of delight. 'Aren't they beautiful?' she said, smiling. 'This room is lovely. It's so cool and fresh and restful.'

'I'm glad you like it.' Cade returned the smile and pulled out a chair for her. 'Harriet fetches the flowers from the garden. She looks after the house for me and prepares food—she thinks I'll starve if I'm left to my own devices.' He thought about that for a moment or two, a small line furrowing his brow. 'Actually, she's probably right about that. I've never been any good at cooking—apart from eggs or pancakes.'

'You're lucky to have her, then.'

She looked at the array of food that had been set out. There were perfectly cut triangular-shaped sandwiches arranged on a platter, decorated with a crisp-looking side salad. Alongside that were skillets filled with chicken kebabs made with peppers and mushroom, bowls with savoury rice, and a mango salsa dip.

'Oh, what I would give for someone to cook for *me*! Beyond price!'

They ate the food, drank hot tea and talked about Cade's hopes for the plantation.

'Did you start all this with William in mind?' she asked after a while. 'It must have seemed relevant that he was studying food and agricultural science at university.'

He nodded. 'That did come into it,' he admitted. 'But my father was always interested in growing food, so I suppose I developed an interest along the way.'

'What does he do? Does he have some sort of farm or plantation? Or work on one?' She wondered why he didn't work with his father if they shared the same passions.

'He lives back in Florida now, and works on one of the teams doing restoration work in the Everglades. His interests have changed over the years.'

His tone was faintly cynical and she immediately picked up on that. Was there some kind of problem between him and his father?

'Do you see much of him? It must be difficult for you…working at the hospital *and* running the plantation.'

'We keep in touch. I see him at least once a month—but when he and my mother split up my priority was to make sure *she* was all right.'

'Oh, I'm sorry. I didn't realise—does your mother live on the island?'

'She does.' He smiled. 'She was part of the inspiration behind the cocoa plantation—she and her sister… William's mother. They're both hugely interested in how it will turn out. She lives fairly close—just a mile or so away—so I see her often.'

'That's good. Family's important.'

'Yes. You tend to find that out when you don't have it—as you know. I guess we've both lost out, though in different ways.' He sent her a penetrating glance. 'It must be disruptive for you, with Emma being called away? All your plans for doing stuff together must have been put on hold for the time being?'

'Yes.' Her mouth flattened. 'It's a bit of a blow, but it can't be helped. I'll probably take the time to go and look around the island. From what William told me there are lots of places to see, beaches to lie on, markets to visit. I'd like to see the other islands at some point, but I suppose I've plenty of time to do that with Emma.'

'Well, yes, from the sound of things you'll be here for a few months, so there should be plenty of opportunity for you to explore.' He looked at her oddly. 'I guess it's great to get the chance to take time out from your career.' He frowned. 'Though from what I saw this afternoon when you helped with Thomas, the way you talked to him, and from what happened on your plane over here, you're a highly skilled, competent physician. It seems strange that you've put it all on hold to come halfway around the world.'

'Does it?' She picked up her cup and drank slowly. 'You're quite right—people don't often get the chance to do that, do they? Maybe I'm just taking advantage of my special circumstances and making the most of things.' She spoke nonchalantly, as though it didn't matter one way or the other, but as she viewed him over the rim of her cup she knew he didn't accept her answer.

'Did something happen, back in Hertfordshire?' he asked. 'Something that sent you on the run?'

She hesitated for a second or two. Then, 'Nothing that I want to talk about,' she said flatly.

He pulled in a quick breath. 'I'm sorry. I shouldn't have pried.'

'It's okay.' She glanced at her watch. 'It's getting late. Perhaps I should call for a taxi to take me home. I've taken up enough of your time.'

'Not at all… I have to stay here to supervise the workers, but I'll arrange for Benjamin to take you home. I'm glad you came along this afternoon. Maybe we could meet up for a drink this evening?'

She shook her head. 'I'm sorry, but I'm afraid I've already made plans.'

He frowned. 'With William?'

'With a friend of Emma's.'

'Oh, I see.' He relaxed a little. 'Is she one of Emma's nursing colleagues?'

'No—actually, he's Emma's landlord. He dropped by earlier today, to check that everything was okay with the property, and after we'd talked for a bit he asked me out. I thought, why not? Since Emma isn't going to be around.' She paused momentarily, sensing Cade's sudden tension in the bracing of his shoulders and the narrowing of his eyes. She sent him a quick glance from under her lashes. 'I suppose that only confirms your opinion of me as some kind of good-time girl?'

He returned her gaze with penetrating scrutiny. 'Oh, I don't know about that, Rebecca. You seem to be intent on enjoying your stay out here in the Caribbean—good luck to you in that. I'd be only too glad to help you make the most of your stay on the island in any way I can.' He frowned. 'I can't help thinking, though, that there's a whole lot more to you than meets the eye... I guess I'll just have to bide my time and look forward to getting to know you better.'

CHAPTER THREE

REBECCA LISTENED TO the wind howling about the cabin and shivered unconsciously. Already it had whipped up trouble and blown down a fencepost. It could be that a freak tropical storm was threatening but, whatever the situation, she had to go outside and fix the post before the whole fence collapsed.

The weather had changed overnight, and she wasn't sure what to make of it. It was definitely a bit scary... though she doubted she'd be worried about it if Cade were there with her. Somehow with him around she was fairly certain she would feel safe and secure. But he wasn't here. Nor was he likely to be.

She hadn't known what to make of his comments the other night. She'd tried to keep her feelings hidden deep inside herself, but it looked as though he'd guessed she was holding something back.

Now, as she went outside, she wondered what made him tick. He was obviously a perceptive, ambitious, intelligent man, who cared deeply for the people around him. He even knew the names of all his workers—that had surprised her, because she'd seen for herself that there were a good many of them employed on the plantation, but in a moment alone with the housekeeper

Harriet had confirmed he knew every one. From other things he'd said, he knew their families, too, and about their hopes and their worries.

She straightened the wooden post in the ground and hit it squarely with a mallet she'd found in the outhouse, but her efforts didn't appear to be having much impact. It still remained stubbornly loose and tipped over to one side.

'Try holding the mallet further back along the handle. It'll give you more leverage.'

Startled, she looked up to see Cade standing by the wide-spreading fig tree. Its glossy leaves lifted fitfully in the breeze and sent dappled shade over the garden. 'Cade,' she said in surprise. 'Hello.'

He looked incredibly good, dressed in a dark, beautifully tailored suit, his jacket open to reveal a pale blue shirt and deeper blue tie.

'I didn't hear you arrive. Is everything okay? I wasn't expecting to see you.' Her copper curls flicked about her face and she pushed them away with the back of her hand.

'I was coming home from the hospital and I thought I'd drop by to see how you were doing. I've been on call or I'd have come sooner. It's been a couple of days since you were up at the plantation, hasn't it?'

'Yes… Though I saw William yesterday. He's been keeping me up to date with things. He said he'd brought the truck over and everything is going well with the harvesting—and that Thomas wants to be back at work but you think he should wait until the stitches are removed.'

She wielded the mallet once more and this time the post sank a few centimetres into the ground. It was still not enough, though, and she stared at it in frustration. She wasn't making much headway. The wind had done a good job in dislodging the post and tipping over the fence—even now it was buffeting around her, promising mayhem.

He reached for the mallet. 'May I?' he said, and she nodded, handing it over. He hammered the post effortlessly into place with a couple of hefty swings. 'Shouldn't your landlord be doing these repairs for you?' he asked, attempting to straighten the rest of the fence slats and fixing them to the main post with the nails she handed to him.

She shrugged, causing her loose-fitting top to slide downwards, leaving a shoulder bare. 'It was hardly worth fetching him out for such a minor thing—though I'm sure he would have obliged if necessary.'

His glance moved over the smooth expanse of creamy flesh exposed inadvertently and her cheeks flushed with heat.

'I've no doubt you're right,' he said, 'but I hope he fixed the window shutters for you—there's a storm brewing and you'll need to be able to batten things down.'

'Yes, he did. It was something simple—a couple of rivets missing. It wasn't worth bringing a workman in to do it, he said. He did the repair himself.'

'I'm glad that's sorted. That's partly why I came over here—to make sure you were all right and prepared for the weather.' He hammered a nail home and then studied her thoughtfully. 'So how did your date with him go?'

'It went well, actually,' she said brightly.

It was somehow good to know that Cade cared about

her enough to check that she was okay…but perhaps she ought to remain cautious in her dealings with him. It might be just as well if he realised she wasn't confining her attention to William, considering he seemed to have such a problem with that—even though 'that' was just friendship! She wasn't sure what she wanted in the love department any more…

'He's surprisingly young for a landlord—in his early thirties,' she said. 'But I guess it's a family-run enterprise. His parents are in business over here, dealing in property. He showed me round some of the houses they own and then took me to a nightclub in a resort along the coast. We had a great time.'

His eyes narrowed. He didn't seem too happy with her answer. 'Are you going to be seeing him again?'

'Possibly.' She'd enjoyed her evening with him, and they'd met up for coffee the next day, but when he would have taken things further she'd held back, doubts creeping in. He was keen, but she wasn't ready for that level of involvement. 'We exchanged phone numbers, but I'm a bit cautious about making too many arrangements until I know when Emma's going to be coming back. I don't want her returning to an empty house.'

'I suppose that's understandable.' His shoulders relaxed a bit. 'Have you heard anything from her? William told me you were getting anxious. She's been gone for a couple of days now, hasn't she? Though that's probably to be expected if there's an outbreak of some sort?'

Finishing up, and checking the fence was secure, he returned the mallet to her.

'Thanks.' She nodded agreement. 'I think there must be something wrong with the phones—a problem with the signal up there in the hills, or some such.

She promised she would call me, but perhaps there was a local storm. Otherwise I'm sure she would have been in touch. It's a bit of a worry.' She put the mallet into the storage shed and padlocked the door. 'Shall we go into the house?'

'Good idea—we definitely need to get out of this wind. I just need to fetch something from my car—I have your luggage in the boot, courtesy of the airline authorities.'

She stared at him, her eyes widening in astonishment. 'You *do*?'

He nodded. 'I gave them a call and chased things up, since you weren't having much success… William mentioned it still hadn't turned up. I hope that's all right with you? My handling things? I've had more dealings with people out here…'

'All right? *Definitely* it's all right. You tracked it down? Oh, that's wonderful! I was beginning to think it was gone for ever! How on earth did you manage it?'

He made a crooked smile. 'It was a process of elimination—tracing the route it was most likely to have followed, starting with the trip to Barbados, then back to Martinique. It did a bit of a detour along the way, but I got them to forward it here.'

'Bless you for that. Oh, *wow*!' She wanted to hug him, but contented herself with touching his arm in a brief show of gratitude. They walked around to the front of the house and she watched as he lifted her cases from his SUV. 'Bring them inside, will you? Thanks. Oh, it's *so* good to have them back!'

'I thought you'd be pleased.' He looked around as he stepped into the cabin. 'Where do you want them? In your bedroom?'

'Yes, please—it's through here.' She showed him the way to the second bedroom.

He glanced at the neatly made bed with its mosquito net drapes and then at the desk with her laptop computer set up in a corner of the room. There were doors leading on to the veranda.

'Your sister did well to find this place,' he said, placing the cases at the end of the bed. 'It seems to have everything going for it.' He straightened and looked around properly.

He was very tall, very muscular—an overwhelming male presence in the confines of the small room.

'It does.' She moved to the door, suddenly very much aware of him and a little uncomfortable to be standing in a bedroom with him. 'Come through to the kitchen. I'll make us some coffee.'

'That would be great, thanks.' He went with her and helped set out mugs, cream and sugar on the table, while she added freshly ground coffee to the filter machine and searched for cookies in the cupboard.

'These are made with cinnamon,' she said, opening a packet and sliding them on to a plate, pushing it towards him. 'I found them in the bakery in the village. Help yourself. They're delicious.'

'Thanks.' He took off his jacket, draping it over the back of a chair, and waited while she poured coffee. Then he sat down with her at the table.

'Do you really think there's a storm coming?' she asked. She sipped the hot liquid.

'I'd say it's practically on top of us,' he said. 'It's already affected the south part of the island and it's moving towards us all the time. The wind's building up and it won't be too long before the rain starts.'

She bit her lip. 'Perhaps I shouldn't be keeping you here—you still have to drive up into the hills. I'm not sure what to expect, but from what I've been hearing on the radio these things are a lot more powerful than the storms we get back in England.'

'Are you worried about that?'

'I'm not sure. I suppose so… It's the not knowing that's the worry.'

'I could stay with you—we can see it out together?'

He glanced at her and she gave an almost imperceptible nod, relief flooding through her.

'Would you? I think that would make me feel much better.'

'Of course.' He drank his coffee and then headed purposefully towards the door. 'First thing to do is to close the shutters,' he said. 'It'll make things dark in here, so you might want to put on the lights and check if you have any candles.'

'Do you think the power might fail?'

'It could do. It often happens—lines come down… services get disrupted. You get used to it after a while. The water sometimes goes off as well, so it might be useful to fill some containers as a precaution.'

He went outside and started closing the shutters. As he'd said, it became dark in the house once the doors and windows were blacked out, and he finished the task only just in time as the first drops of rain started to fall. It very soon became pounding, torrential rain.

She looked outside as he came back in through the kitchen door and the sky was ominously dark, with storm clouds gathered overhead. He shut the door behind him and she busied herself pouring more coffee and listening to the reports on the radio.

'They say it's heading north towards the other islands,' she said. 'I hope Emma and her colleagues are okay.'

He frowned. 'I expect they'll be fine away from the coast. Situated here, by the sea, we're probably bearing the brunt of it.'

Thunder boomed overhead, shaking the cabin, and her eyes widened in dismay. She tried to ignore the tumult outside, talking to him about anything and everything— about the beautiful Caribbean islands and beach barbecues, the colourful wildlife that lived in the trees around the cabin—and he told her about his work at the hospital, how he'd come to medicine through his interest in the work of the doctors back in Florida, where he'd grown up.

As the day wore on flashes like strobe lightning sparked through the gaps in the shutters and the wind screamed around the cabin. This was nothing like the mild storms she'd experienced back home. This was violent, booming, nature at its most destructive.

'It'll be okay. It sounds worse than it really is.'

'If you say so. It's been going on for hours.' She went over to the stove. She needed to keep busy. 'It's getting late,' she said. 'I could make us some soup, and there are some crusty rolls and butter we can have with it.'

'That sounds great.'

Another thunderclap shook the cabin and there was an almighty rumble overhead, followed by a shrill clattering on the roof. She jumped slightly and felt the colour drain from her face. It seemed as though the very fabric of the house was being torn apart.

Cade came over to her and put his arms around her, holding her close. 'We'll be all right,' he reassured her.

'It was probably just a few loose shingles on the roof. This place is solidly built.'

She nodded, knowing he was doing his best to comfort her. It was soothing, having him draw her to him this way. He wasn't at all bothered by the hurricane force that hurled itself in a fury around the building. That knowledge in itself was calming, and she leaned into him, gaining strength from him, glad of the steady thud of his heartbeat beneath her breast. His powerful body shielded her, offered protection while the storm raged around them. She was ashamed of herself for needing that comforting gesture, but all the time she was thankful that he steadfastly held her.

Even so, there was another inherent danger in being in close proximity to him in this way. She was becoming far too aware of him—of his strength, his lithe, supple body, the way the lightest touch of his hands evoked a tingling response.

'I think I'll be okay now,' she said after a while. She couldn't let him go on supporting her this way. It was too intimate, too tempting to stay here, locked in his embrace. If this carried on she might want to make a habit of it—and that wouldn't do at all, would it?

'Are you sure?' He looked at her, his gaze smoke-dark as he tried to read what was in her mind. 'I promise you I'm quite happy to go on holding you for as long as you like.'

Heat flickered in his grey eyes and a half-smile pulled at the corners of his mouth. She was feverishly conscious of the warmth of his body, the taut muscles of his thighs pressuring hers, of the way his long body offered refuge.

'I'm sure. I'll be fine.' She couldn't allow herself

to respond to his mischievous invitation. Instead she carefully began to ease herself away from him, and in the end he reluctantly let her go. 'I'll…I'll see to the soup,' she said.

He watched her as she worked. 'Did you have a boyfriend back in Hertfordshire?' he asked. 'I can't imagine a girl like you not being scooped up by some determined man. Have you left someone behind—someone who's nursing a broken heart, maybe?'

She gave a small choked laugh at that. Even now it brought a lump to her throat to think about Drew. She didn't have feelings for him any more, but the hurt and associated fall-out from their relationship still lingered.

'There was someone, but it didn't work out,' she said. 'You could say I've decided to move on.'

'Ah.' He was silent for a moment, his glance drifting over her. 'I thought there had to be something like that.'

She stirred the soup and set out bowls on the table. 'What about you?' she asked. 'You have everything going for you, but I don't see a woman around.'

His mouth flattened a little. 'Perhaps I've learned to be cautious over the years. Women tend to come with their own agendas, I've found… They want marriage, wealth, status—all perfectly reasonable ambitions, but no good if they come at the expense of true, basic human feelings.'

'So you've been hurt? Someone let you down?' She said it in a matter-of-fact way, glancing at him as she served up the hot vegetable broth. 'Just because you've had one or two bad experiences it doesn't necessarily mean that *all* women think along those lines.'

He shrugged. 'Maybe not.'

He wasn't convinced of that, obviously. 'Is that why

you're so concerned about William—you think he might be hurt in a similar way?'

'In part. He fell for someone, but she led him a bit of a dance and cheated on him. He was heartbroken. Then his father was taken ill, and he became the main breadwinner in his household, and things became too much for him for a while.'

She frowned. 'And now?'

'Now he seems to be coping well enough. My uncle's in hospital, being treated for a virus that has affected his heart muscle. They had to sell the house to fund the medical bills, and now they live in a property on the plantation. It's made me all the more anxious to make a success of things, so that I can give them a livelihood. William will become a partner one day, and maybe my uncle, too.'

So there was more than his own land-owning expectations resting on the venture. 'I'm sorry for what you're all going through.' She sucked in a breath. 'Is your uncle going to be all right?'

He pulled a face. 'We hope so. The doctors are giving him supportive treatment, along with a low-salt diet, and they're making sure he gets plenty of rest. It all depends on how serious the damage is and whether his heart can recover from it.'

'I'd no idea it was so bad. William manages to hide his feelings well, doesn't he?'

'He does.'

They sat at the kitchen table, savouring the food, and by mutual unspoken agreement changed the subject, talking about how the storm might affect the plantation.

'It's possible we could lose a few trees,' he said. 'But the main harvest is in, and in general the crop and the houses are protected, so things may not be too bad. The biggest worry is the road network. Rivers tend to swell and flood, and you often find that debris is swept along in their path.' His phone bleeped but he ignored it, going on with his soup.

'I imagine the authorities are used to dealing with—' She broke off as another thunderclap exploded in the distance and all the lights went out. 'Oh, no…there goes the power.'

He stood up and went over to the worktop, where she'd set out hurricane lamps and candles. 'Good— these are battery-operated,' he said, bringing one of the lamps over to the table. It gave out a decent light, so they were able to finish their meal in relative comfort.

When she started to clear the table a little while later she was suddenly aware of the gentle splash of water droplets dampening her hair and her clothes. 'Oh, dear…' She glanced upwards, searching for the source, and discovered a dark patch of moisture spreading across the ceiling.

'I guess I was right about the shingles on the roof,' Cade said, making a wry face. 'There must be a tear in the roofing felt. I'd better do a quick check on the rest of the house.'

He took one of the hurricane lamps with him and went from room to room, searching for more seepage. Rebecca went with him, dismayed to see similar patches of water forming on her bedroom ceiling.

'I'll do what I can to stop the leaks temporarily,' Cade said, 'but your landlord will have to get things fixed as soon as he gets the chance.'

'I'll let him know. Is there anything I can do to help?'

'You could see if there are any sheets of polythene

or something similar that I can use to mask the tears,' he suggested.

'Will bin liners do?'

'They'll be fine. I could do with some tape, as well.'

She searched in one of the kitchen drawers and pulled out a roll of plastic liners, handing them to him. 'I think we have some PVC tape in a toolbox in the loft. I'll get it for you—the loft access is in the hallway. There's a pull-down ladder.'

'Okay, leave it with me.'

She didn't leave him. Instead she stood at the foot of the ladder and held a second lamp to give him more light as he accessed the roof space. It took several minutes for him to locate the leaks and fix the waterproof sheeting in place, but finally he came back down the ladder to her.

'That should hold things until you can get a permanent repair done,' he said, walking back with her into the kitchen. 'At least the storm's beginning to move on…it's heading further up the coast, I imagine. We've had the worst of it here, I think.'

His mobile phone was on the table, flashing to show that another message had been received.

'Do you need to answer that text message?' she asked. 'It might be important.'

'Yes, you're right. Perhaps I should. I'm not on call right now, but given the circumstances…' He glanced at his phone and read the message on screen, then winced. 'It's the hospital—they texted earlier—there's been an influx of patients injured in the storm and they're putting out a general call for any medics available to go and help.'

'So you'll be going back there? Will it be safe for you

to drive?' She was worried for him, but knew instinctively that he wouldn't be comfortable staying here with her when there were patients who needed him.

'I expect so—I don't really have a choice. I have to go and help out.' He frowned. 'I don't want to leave you here,' he said. 'If the storm doubles back for any reason that roof could be totally destroyed. I'd feel much happier if you were to come and stay up at the plantation house until things are sorted here.'

She shook her head. 'Thanks for the offer, but I can't go anywhere—what would I do about Emma?' She wasn't thinking clearly, was concerned for her sister, worried about leaving the cabin, and anxious because she knew she ought to go and help out in the emergency. 'I haven't been able to get in touch with her. She won't know what's happening. Anyway, I'm sure I'll be all right staying here now that the roof leaks have been sorted.'

'No, you won't,' he said firmly. 'That's only a temporary fix.' He reached for her, grasping her arms in a gentle but firm hold. 'You can leave a note for Emma to tell her where you are. Apart from the risk of the roof giving out, the power is still down. At least up at the plantation house we have a generator for when the electricity cuts out. Emma will be fine, I'm sure. The phones are probably temporarily out where she is—I expect you'll be able to talk to her soon enough.'

'I don't know...' Her brow furrowed. 'I need to see her...make sure she's all right. It isn't like her not to keep in touch. I need to go up to the village and try to find her.'

'But not right now—in the middle of a storm.' He tugged her close to him. 'Think about it, Rebecca... You can't stay here, and you won't be able to get in touch with your sister until things calm down a bit. You have to come with me—let me take care of you.'

She shook her head. 'I don't need you to tell me what to do, Cade. I'll be perfectly all right here now that the storm's moving on. I can look after myself.'

'Sure, you can… But there's no way I'm going to leave you here alone. These storms are fickle. You don't know what might happen.' He looked down at her, his eyes sparking with determination. 'You can't stay here. I won't let you.'

'Oh, really?' She raised her brows. 'I don't see that you have a choice. It's *my* decision to make, not yours.'

'Is it? Maybe I can persuade you otherwise…'

Before she had time to realise his intention he swooped, claiming her mouth in a fierce, possessive kiss that caused the blood to course through her body in an overwhelming tide of heat. Her lips parted beneath the sensual onslaught and she clung to him as her limbs responded by trembling under the passionate intensity of his embrace.

It was like nothing she'd ever experienced before. His kisses made her feverish with desire, the touch of his hands turned her flesh to fire as they shaped her curves, leaving her desperate for more. It was so unexpected— such a coaxing, tantalising raid on her defences. Her resistance crumbled. She wanted to stay here, locked in his arms, having him hold her, with his long, hard body pressuring hers and promising heaven on earth.

But these moments of bliss came to an abrupt halt as an almighty crash rocked the wall of the cabin. She froze, shocked into stillness by the noise and the sheer terror of wondering what might have happened.

'The storm—' she said. 'The wall—surely it's strong enough to stand up to the storm? Something must have happened outside—some damage—'

'It's probably a tree that's come down.' Reluctantly, he released her, then went to the kitchen door and looked out. 'I was right,' he said, closing the door abruptly. 'The wind must have weakened it and finally it collapsed. We need to get out of here, Rebecca. You know what I'm saying makes sense, don't you?'

She nodded. 'Yes, okay. I suppose so.' Even *she* couldn't argue if trees were crashing down around them. Who could tell if the cabin wall would give way at some point? There were trees surrounding the house.

'I'll get your cases and load them into the car.' He started towards the bedroom. 'Is there anything else you need to take with you?'

'No, I don't think so.'

'You'll need a jacket—the wind's dying down, but it's still raining out there.' He pulled his own jacket from the back of the chair and shrugged it on.

She nodded. She could hear the rain, still frantic, hitting the roof shingles and spattering against the door and the shutters. 'Okay. I'll get it. But maybe we should head for the hospital—I'm a medic…I could help.'

'I'd rather you didn't—for whatever reason, you've turned your back on medicine for a while. Besides, you're not familiar with the terrain out here…the way things operate…and anyway I'd feel better if I knew you were safe up at the plantation house. It will be one less worry for me.'

She frowned. 'I'm sure I could make myself useful in some way.'

Perhaps the people up at the plantation would need

help of some sort. If he didn't want her working along-side him, at least she could offer support where it was needed.

They hurried out to the car a minute or so later and he stacked her luggage in the boot, alongside his medical bag and equipment. She took a moment to take a quick glance around. Most of the garden had withstood the brunt of the storm, but a couple of trees had succumbed to the elements, which had left several branches twisted and torn. One of them had split along the length of its trunk and fallen against the cabin wall.

Cade set out along the road to the plantation. It was disturbing to see the destruction in some places along the way. Crops were ruined, plantains and banana trees had been brought down. Fields were flooded where rivers had overflowed, and landslides had caused devastation. In one part the road was blocked by an accumulation of detritus that Cade had to toss to one side so that they could continue their journey.

She slid out of the car and went to stand at his side. 'There's no need for both of us to get wet,' he said, but she helped him move the debris despite his protests.

They set off once again, driving ever higher into the hills, and soon came to a small settlement. A dozen or so houses were clustered in what in any other circumstances would have been a breathtakingly lovely part of the island, where several waterfalls cascaded into a blue lake.

'Look—over there…' Rebecca pointed to what looked like an abandoned car, slewed at an angle where a slip road veered off to the west and formed a narrow bridge over a stream. 'Something's wrong. We should stop and take a look.'

He nodded, edging his SUV on to the slip road and following it as far as he could do so safely. Further on the road's surface disappeared under a tangle of broken concrete and stone. The bridge had collapsed and water flowed all around, swamping the saloon car that had apparently been heading towards the village in the distance. As the bridge had collapsed the car must have been hurled into the water, and now it was tilted precariously on one side, lifted up at its front end by a grassy mound.

As they moved closer Rebecca pulled a swift intake of air into her lungs. 'There are people still in the car,' she said urgently. 'We have to help them.'

Cade brought the car to a standstill on a dry stretch of the road above the level of the water. He was already getting out of the SUV as she spoke, and grabbing his medical bag from the boot before heading towards the car. Rebecca followed, gasping as the cold water swirled around her denim-clad legs and slowed her progress.

She waded forward, peering into the stranded vehicle. There were signs of movement inside. A youngish man—the driver—was slumped to one side, leaning towards the passenger seat, a trickle of blood running down his temple. Beside him a woman was apparently unconscious. The back of the car was under water.

Rebecca pulled at the doors but they were jammed solid. 'They must have locked automatically, somehow.'

'I'll get a wrench,' Cade said. 'We'll have to smash the side windows.'

He ran back to his vehicle and returned a moment later to swing the wrench at the glass. It gave way, shattering into a thousand pieces, and quickly Cade cleared a gap so that he could reach in and release the door catch.

The man began to come round. 'What's happening?' he said. Then, as his thoughts became more focussed, he added, 'The bridge—'

'You've been in an accident,' Cade told him. 'You've banged your head. Are you hurt anywhere else?'

'Just a headache,' the man answered. Then suddenly, 'My wife—Jane—' He looked around. 'I think she's bleeding.' He was dazed and shocked, not thinking clearly.

Cade helped the man out of the car and, seeing that he was going to take care of him, Rebecca slid into the driver's seat so that she could tend to the passenger. The woman's airway was clear, she was breathing fitfully and there was a faint, erratic pulse. After a while, she stirred, and Rebecca gave a swift sigh of relief.

'Jane,' she said urgently, 'are you in pain at all?'

'It…hurts…to breathe,' the woman said. 'My chest… hurts.'

Rebecca quickly checked her over. 'I think you've broken some of your ribs, Jane,' she said. 'Don't worry. We'll get you to hospital.'

'My baby…?' The woman frowned. 'Is my baby all right?'

'Your baby?' Rebecca echoed. 'Are you pregnant?'

'No…no…my *baby*…' She tried to twist around, gasping in pain at the effort, and with dawning horror Rebecca realised that she was looking at the back seat. It was completely submerged in water.

'Oh, no…'

She started to slide out of the driver's seat, but Cade was already on his way. The man must have told him about the infant because he looked shocked to the core, determination written in the clenched set of his jaw as he wrenched open the back door of the car.

'There's a child seat,' he said. 'I just need to feel for the release catch.'

It seemed like an age to Rebecca that he struggled to locate and press the buttons that would free the seat, but it must have been only seconds. He lifted the baby seat out of the water and she gasped as she saw the limp, lifeless form of the child fastened in there, her head lolling backwards, golden curls plastered wetly to her deathly white forehead.

'No, no…no… This can't be happening.' Rebecca was out of the car now, trying desperately to get to the baby, her legs hampered by the strong current of the water that eddied all around her.

'I have her,' Cade said briskly. 'I'll take care of her. See to the woman.'

It was like a cold slap across the face, bringing her to her senses.

'See to the woman. Get her out of the car. Get her and the man out of danger.'

She did as he said, moving like an automaton, but all the while her mind was on the child. She wanted to be with her, looking after her. The child was about a year old, with pale, chubby cheeks, and there was a bluish tinge to her rosebud mouth. Rebecca's heart squeezed in anguish. It wasn't fair. It wasn't right. Things like this should never happen.

She led the man and his wife to safety and sat them down on a grassy hillock set back from the water. The man was showing signs of concussion, the woman coping with the effects of the broken ribs that hampered her breathing. They were supposedly the lucky ones… if you could call losing a child anything remotely to do with luck.

She felt sick, her lungs heaving with the effort of holding back her emotions. 'I'll get something to cover you,' she said, aware that both the survivors might go into deep shock at any time. 'Stay there.'

'But my little girl—' The woman called out in desperation.

'We'll take care of her. I'll be back in a minute.'

Cade was working on the child. He'd taken her out of the car seat and laid her flat on her back on the ground near to his SUV. He was giving chest compressions. She heard the whispered rhythm of his voice as he accompanied his actions by counting the number of times he pressed down on the infant's chest with two fingers.

'Twenty-eight, twenty-nine, thirty…' Two breaths into the baby's mouth. Then he started the chest compressions again. 'One, two, three, four…'

Rebecca searched in the boot of his car and opened up his medical bag. Her hands were shaking, but she managed to find two carefully folded foil blankets. She didn't dare think any more about what was going on with the child. It was heartbreaking to witness Cade's efforts.

'Twelve…thirteen…fourteen…'

He was doing everything he could for the baby. Was it too late? How long had she been underwater? She couldn't bear to dwell on it.

'I'll phone the hospital to tell them to expect us,' she told him, and he nodded, not stopping for a second, keeping up the compressions in perfect rhythmic timing.

'Twenty-nine…thirty.' Two breaths.

Hurrying back to the parents, she wrapped the heat-retaining blankets around them and gave them what comfort she could. They were desperate to be with their child, but both were dazed and injured and in no fit state to go anywhere without help just then.

Moving away so that they couldn't hear, she phoned the hospital and told the emergency team that they were bringing in an infant, suspected drowning, an adult with broken ribs, query internal injuries, and a man with concussion from a head injury.

She looked over to where Cade was working on the infant and heard a choking sound. Hurrying back to him, she saw that he was lying her down in the recovery position on her left side. She had vomited.

'Is she breathing?' she asked in a strained voice, hardly daring to believe it was possible.

'Yes,' he said simply. 'She suddenly choked and coughed up water from her lungs. Will you get the oxygen and an infant mask for me from the medical pack?'

'Of course.'

Going quickly to the back of his car, she searched the emergency response kit once more. A tear trickled down her cheek and she dashed it away.

'We don't know how long she was without oxygen, do we?' she asked, handing him the equipment he needed. There was the awful possibility that the little girl could have suffered brain damage… 'But the water was cold…'

'Yes, that will have helped.'

The cold water would have the effect of stimulating the diving reflex in a young child, slowing the heartrate and constricting the peripheral arteries, so that oxygenated blood was diverted to the heart and brain where it was most needed. There was a chance she would be all right.

She watched for a moment as he gave the baby oxygen through the small face mask. Then she said, 'I should go and talk to the parents. I'll start to get them into your car.'

He nodded. 'I'll feel happier if you sit in the back with the mother and the baby—the father can go in front with me.'

'Okay.'

He looked at her, studying her thoughtfully, a frown creasing his brow. 'Are you all right?'

The question startled her for a second or two. Of course she was distraught—seeing the baby in that condition had totally unnerved her. But she realised that she had subconsciously laid a hand over her abdomen. Perhaps it was meant to be a protective hand, laid over her womb—over that place which might never hold a child.

Sometimes she thought she felt pain where the adhesions left by her former illness had marred her fallopian tubes, but it might be a purely psychological reaction. It would be so much worse to give birth to a child, to nurture it and then to lose it in such a dreadful manner as these parents had almost experienced—might yet still experience.

'Yes, I'm okay. I'm just anxious to get this family to safety.' She looked at him, full of respect and awe for what he had achieved. The baby wasn't out of danger yet by a long way, but her lips had begun to pink up a little and her cheeks were less pale than before. 'You did a wonderful thing just now. I'm so overwhelmed by how you responded. You were so calm, so determined.'

'You would have done the same thing. As I recall

you were ready to leave the adults to come and help the child… It was instinctive once you knew the parents weren't in immediate danger.'

She reached for another, smaller foil blanket from his pack. 'We should try to warm her—take off her wet clothes and wrap her in the blanket,' she said. 'She needs to be in the hospital.'

'Yes, we'll do that. And we'll be on our way in a minute or two. I just want to make sure she's stable before we set off. Her heartrate is a bit erratic at the moment, but it will probably settle once she's less chilled.'

They worked together to get everyone settled in his SUV. Reunited with her baby, the mother laid a gentle hand on the child, needing a connection of some sort despite the discomfort of her own injuries.

'Her name's Annie,' she said. 'She's my angel.'

Rebecca sat on the other side of the child, holding the oxygen mask in place and making sure that she was still breathing. The infant's pulse was slow—a protective reflex, no doubt—but once she was in the hospital the emergency team would do everything they could to resuscitate her. There was always the danger of pneumonia after a near drowning. The lungs had been flooded with water and there would be constant worry about the after-effects.

The journey seemed interminable, but in fact it only took around three quarters of an hour. Cade drove as swiftly as he dared, negotiating bends in the road and checking all the time for trees that might have come down along the way. Twice they had to get out and move fallen branches from the road.

Eventually, though, they arrived at the hospital and handed over their charges to the waiting team of doctors and nurses. Annie was whisked away to the resuscitation room and her parents were taken to Radiology for X-rays.

'I could take you home,' Cade said, 'but I expect you'll want to wait for news of how Annie's doing?'

'Yes, please… I'd rather wait. I don't think I could settle, otherwise.'

He nodded. 'Me, too. We'll go to my office. They'll come and find us when they have some information.'

'Okay.' She went with him along the corridor, not fully aware of how she'd arrived there, just putting one foot in front of another. The last hour had been traumatic. The child's parents must be feeling as though they were caught up in a nightmare.

He showed her into his office—a light, comfortably furnished room with a polished wooden desk to one side and a couple of upholstered chairs for visitors. There was also a two-seater couch against one wall. He shut the door and she stared blankly around her, not really taking anything in.

'You probably want to go and help your colleagues with all their other patients,' she said quietly, trying to gather her thoughts. 'I'll just stay here for a while and get myself together, if that's all right?'

'I'll stay until I know you're okay,' Cade said. 'I wondered if it all might be too much for you.' He came over to her and wrapped his arms around her. 'You're too emotionally involved with your patients, aren't you? Is that why you gave up on your job?'

'I don't… I can't talk about it,' she said huskily. 'Please don't ask me. I can't even think straight right now. I just—I just need to know that little girl is going to be all right.'

'I know.' He held her tight, as though he would give her his strength and the will to go on. 'I feel the same way. I'm worried about her, but I'm concerned about *you*, too, Rebecca. I want to help you any way I can. You can trust me… I need you to know that.'

She didn't answer him. She closed her eyes and pressed her cheek against his shirt-front, wishing that things could be different… It would be such a relief to know that she could put her faith in someone—know that it would all come out all right in the end. But deep down she knew that wasn't going to happen.

Cade was a good man, but he couldn't turn her life around, and he had his own problems and aspirations to deal with.

CHAPTER FOUR

REBECCA WENT WITH Cade over to the couch, where he sat down beside her. He'd managed to find some fresh clothes for them to change into—clean scrubs, the outfits made up of the loose-fitting trousers and shirts that were used by the medical staff in the Emergency Unit—and now that she was at least dry she was beginning to feel a little better.

He laid an arm around her shoulders in a gesture that seemed entirely natural and right, and she was content for the moment to sit and talk to him and try to regain her emotional strength.

Her reaction to the events of the day had unnerved her. She had always thought of herself as decisive and independent, but over the course of the last few months she felt as though the stuffing had been knocked out of her. Somehow Cade must have picked up on that.

'How are you feeling now?' he asked. 'That was traumatic, wasn't it?'

She nodded. 'I'm okay. It was difficult for both of us. Are *you* all right? It must have been so much worse for you…trying to save the little girl…not knowing if she would breathe again.'

'I just did what had to be done. You don't really think

about it, do you, when you're faced with something like that? Like you said about that man on the plane—you follow your instincts, go with the training.'

'Yes, I suppose so… But it was awesome, what you did. You kept going. You didn't give up for a second. I'm so proud of you.'

'I'm a doctor,' he said simply. 'That's the reason I took up medicine…to save lives and help where I can.' He looked at her, lifting a hand to gently ease back the fiery curls that fell across her temple. 'I was worried about you, Rebecca. You were upset and anxious for the baby, but there was more to it than that, wasn't there? Something was troubling you deep down inside, at your very core—I wish you would talk to me about it, tell me what's wrong. Is it something to do with the reason you gave up your job back home? Did you lose a patient…a child in your care?'

She didn't answer him directly. It hurt too much to tell him the truth about her situation, and perhaps she was afraid it would change the way he felt about her.

'It happens sometimes…occasionally,' she said. 'You lose a patient despite everyone's best efforts. You do everything you can but there's nothing you can do if your best is not enough. There are times when medical science doesn't provide the answer.'

A knock at the door interrupted her and she tensed, brought back with a jolt to the reality of where they were. Cade eased himself away from her and instantly she felt the loss of his warm body and his gentle support. It was a wrench, losing the comfort of his embrace. She'd wanted to stay like that, wrapped up in his arms.

'Hi, Cade.' The consultant in charge of baby Annie's care came into the room. 'I only have a minute or two—things are hectic out there.'

'Hi, James.' Cade introduced Rebecca to his friend and colleague, who acknowledged her with a smile.

'I'm very pleased to meet you. Cade said you were the one who pointed out the car and saw that the family was in trouble.' James became serious. 'I came to let you know that we're doing everything we can to warm the baby. I've just been to talk to the parents, to try to reassure them, but it will be some time before we see any definite change in her condition.' He winced. 'She's lucky to be alive.'

Cade nodded, getting to his feet and going over to a worktop at the side of the room to switch on a coffee machine. 'We thought she'd already gone when we found her. It was a shock for both of us.' He set out mugs on the counter. 'Do you have time to grab a coffee?'

'Just a quick one, thanks. I can imagine how you must have felt. But, as I said, we're doing all we can. We're giving her warmed oxygen and an infusion of warmed intravenous fluids, so her core temperature should begin to rise gradually. We'll just have to hope there are no complications—and at the same time be prepared for them. There are often setbacks in these cases, unfortunately.'

Rebecca shuddered inwardly. She didn't want to dwell on that. All her hopes rested on the baby making a complete recovery.

They drank coffee and he updated them on the condition of the infant's parents. 'Mrs Tennyson has three fractured ribs, and her husband is suffering from concussion—as you suspected. They've both been given painkillers, and we'll keep them under observation for a while to make sure there are no other problems. Of course they're not going anywhere for some time—they're at Annie's bedside.'

'It sounds as though they're in good hands,' Rebecca commented, 'even though you must have a lot more patients than usual to look after. I noticed all the people milling about in the waiting room and in the corridors.' She'd seen men and women nursing injuries to arms and legs, and children with a number of bad cuts and grazes. 'It must be a difficult time for you.'

'You're right—it is. We've put out a call for more doctors—it's been difficult for some to get in, though, given the condition of the roads.'

'Well, *I'm* here,' Cade said. 'I can help.'

'Me, too.' Rebecca said, and saw the surprise on his colleague's face. 'I'm a doctor,' she explained, 'though my specialty's not emergency. If you can get me clearance, I'm happy to help out wherever I'm needed.'

She would rather do that than wait around, wondering what was happening with the baby.

'That's great news.' James's face lit up with enthusiasm. 'I can sort that out for you right away if you're sure you want to do that? We need as many medics as we can get.' Then he frowned. 'Do you have any training in obstetrics? We have a woman being brought in by ambulance—she went into labour several hours ago but only called for the ambulance when the contractions started to get more frequent. It's her first child. We're trying to get hold of an obstetrician to attend her as soon as she gets here, but they're swamped in Maternity.'

He looked at her hopefully.

'We really need someone to attend her as soon as possible. The paramedics are looking after her just now, but from what they've said when they radioed in it looks as though it might be a difficult birth.'

She felt the blood drain from her face, and her stomach lurched at the mention of obstetrics, but she nodded. 'I did a specialist course before going on to do my neonatal training. I'll go and see her, if you want.'

Cade sent her a narrow-eyed look and she braced herself. He must be wondering why she'd paled, but she hoped he wouldn't ask. When she'd volunteered she'd had in mind that she would be working with trauma patients—not mothers and babies—but she would do this despite her reservations. She didn't see that she had any choice. She couldn't stand by and do nothing when there was chaos and suffering all around her, could she?

'Bless you for that. She should be here any minute— I'll take you to the admissions ward now…and I'll get my secretary to sort out the necessary paperwork for you to sign.'

'Okay.' She pulled in a deep breath. 'Lead the way.'

They all walked along the corridor to the main area of the Emergency Unit, and James was pointing out the list of patients waiting to be seen when a nurse came up to them.

'We've had a call from the paramedics bringing Mrs Nelson in. Their vehicle has been hit by a tree—no one's hurt, but they're stuck out there. They're about a ten-minute drive away from the hospital. The birth's imminent, and it looks like a breech presentation.'

'Thanks, Greta.' James remained calm. 'Tell them I'll get someone out there to them.' He glanced at Rebecca. 'Are you up for it?'

'Yes—I guess so. But I'll need transport to get out

to them.' She frowned. 'I don't know how easy it will be to get a taxi with conditions as they are.'

'I'll take you,' Cade said briskly, stepping forward. 'If it's a breech birth it may be better to have two of us present. I'll get directions—from the sound of things we should leave right away.'

'Okay.'

She went with him to the car park, keeping her head down against the wind that buffeted around them. The rain here was a steady downpour that quickly soaked through her jacket, but she ignored it, thinking ahead to the woman in the ambulance. A breech birth meant that the baby was not in the usual head-down position. Usually it would be best to deliver the infant by caesarean section—an operation that was the safest option for mother and baby. That was not going to be possible in these circumstances, when the woman's labour was far advanced.

'We'll be there in a few minutes.' Cade drove carefully to where the ambulance was stranded. 'Are you sure you're up for this?' he asked. 'I didn't want to say anything in front of James, but I saw your reaction when he said it was a case for an obstetrician. I can take over if it's going to be a problem for you.'

'I wouldn't have offered if I wasn't up to it,' she said briskly. 'I'll be fine.'

'Okay. This is it, I think,' Cade said in a while.

They saw the ambulance on a straight stretch of a road that was lined with trees, and even in the darkness of late evening it was clear to see the devastation that had been caused to the side of the vehicle when a papaya tree had crashed down on to it. It was a miracle no one inside had been hurt, but no doubt a good deal of the equipment had been damaged.

The emergency services had been called out to deal with the accident, but so many similar incidents were taking up their resources that it would be some time before help arrived.

Rebecca slid out of the car and hurried to find her patient. The woman was being tended by the paramedics—a man and a woman—who stood to one side as Rebecca entered the ambulance.

'Hi, I'm Jimena,' the woman paramedic said. She was tall, with curly black hair, and she looked strong and capable. 'We're *really* glad you could make it out here to us—aren't we, Kenzie?' She looked at her patient for confirmation.

Kenzie Nelson nodded. Beads of sweat had broken out on the young woman's brow and Rebecca guessed she was in pain from her contractions and under stress after the accident.

Jimena continued, 'We've been giving her gas and air, but it isn't really helping with the pain. Contractions are regular—every five minutes—she's six centimetres dilated, and her waters have broken.'

'It sounds as if things are well under way,' Rebecca said with an encouraging smile. She introduced herself and Cade, and then told Kenzie, 'I could give you an injection of pethidine into your thigh, if you like? That should help relieve the pain, but it might make you feel a bit sleepy.'

'Thanks, that would be good.'

'Okay.'

Rebecca prepared for the procedure, cleaning her hands with antiseptic solution and pulling on surgical gloves, leaving Cade to gather together the rest of the equipment and the medication she would need. She examined the pregnant woman, checking her blood pressure and observing the contractions, as well as monitoring the foetal heartbeat. She made sure that Kenzie had understood that the baby would be delivered with either its bottom or its feet first. Apparently she didn't know the sex of the baby she was expecting.

'Everything seems fine,' she said, at last, hoping to reassure her patient. For herself, she had to prepare mentally for what lay ahead. Breech births could be tricky, and most doctors would prefer to deliver them in the safety of a hospital theatre.

She turned to the paramedics. 'Would you go on giving gas and air as she needs it? And perhaps one of you could see to it that we have suction apparatus to hand?'

'Will do.' They both nodded and the other paramedic, who was also the driver—Marcus—said he would keep in touch with the hospital by radio.

'Thanks.' She glanced at Cade. 'Perhaps you could monitor her vital signs and keep an eye on the baby's condition?'

'Of course.' Cade was already preparing the woman, cleaning an area of skin on her thigh, ready for Rebecca to give the injection. 'It'll take a few minutes before you feel the effects of the pethidine,' he told Kenzie, 'but it's a good pain-reliever.'

It wasn't long before Kenzie's contractions became stronger, and soon they were coming at faster intervals. 'She's fully dilated,' Rebecca said. 'I can see the baby's bottom. I may need to do an episiotomy—a small cut,' she told Kenzie, 'to make it easier to deliver the baby. I'll anaesthetise the area first, so you won't feel it.'

She waited awhile, letting nature take its course, and then, as more of the infant's rear end came into view, presenting at a sideways angle, she carefully turned the baby so that its back was facing upwards—the safest position for delivery.

'I'm going to very gently insert a finger, so that I can bring down the baby's leg on the right side,' she told the woman. 'Are you okay?'

'I think so. I just want this to be over.'

'I can imagine… It shouldn't be too long now. You're doing really well.'

Rebecca concentrated on delivering the first leg, and then adjusted the baby's position once more to enable her to bring down the left leg more easily. It was a delicate manoeuvre, and she held her breath as she performed it, taking care not to cause any damage to either mother or baby.

'That's good,' Cade said, smiling his relief. 'Both legs are out safely,' he told the mother. 'Oh, and it's a boy!'

Kenzie gave a soft gasp of delight. 'A *boy*! That's what my husband was hoping for.'

'We'll let nature take its course for a while,' Rebecca said quietly.

Gradually more of the baby's body descended, until she could see an elbow peeping out. Two more careful manoeuvres and gentle turning motions helped bring down the infant's arms one by one. She let out a slow breath. Feeling her way, she placed her middle finger at the back of the baby's head and supported its body underneath with her forearm, placing two fingers either side of his nose. Then she slowly tilted the infant so that his head could be delivered fully.

Exposed to the air, he let out a protesting cry and Rebecca felt a lump forming in her throat. He was safe. He was perfect.

Quickly Cade suctioned the baby's nose and mouth and wrapped him in a blanket. Then he laid him in his mother's arms, smiling at her blissful expression. Kenzie was exhausted, but all the pain and difficulties of the last few hours receded in an instant as she held her newborn infant for the first time.

Rebecca watched Kenzie and her baby, a joyous picture of unity, and despite her happiness for them felt unbidden pain suddenly tug at her heart. Would she ever hold her own baby in her arms that way? How certain could the doctors be that it would never happen? Was it hopeless? They'd told her the scans weren't good—that her ovaries might be affected by scar tissue, too. It was a nightmare situation.

She'd debated the possibility of having surgery at some point in the future, but Drew hadn't been prepared to await the outcome. 'I'm sorry,' he'd said. 'I know it's not your fault but…I can't do this…'

He'd wanted perfection, and he had made her feel as if she was somehow defective. It made her wonder if all men would react in the same way…

She blinked, as though that would blot out the image before her, and made a determined effort to pull herself together. Perhaps, as Emma had said, events were still too raw in her mind. It had been several months since the break-up now, but she was still at a low ebb healthwise, and that had made things seem far worse.

Cade glanced at her. His pleasure at the birth was undimmed, but now his gaze was curious. He knew something was troubling her, but she ignored his unspoken question and brought her attention back to her patient.

'I can give you an injection to help the placenta come away,' she told Kenzie, and the new mother nodded. She was too absorbed in her baby to care very much either way, Rebecca guessed.

She gave her the injection, again in her thigh, and waited for a minute or two before clamping the cord. Delaying the clamping gave the baby a better initial blood supply from the placenta—one that was full of nutrients, especially iron.

Cade continued to monitor the baby's condition, but it looked as though the infant was fine. Once the placenta had come away, and the episiotomy cut had been stitched, Jimena stepped in to see to the mother, and Rebecca moved back to give her room.

The other paramedic, Marcus, had been talking on the radio for the last few minutes, keeping in touch with the hospital and the ambulance service, and now they all chuckled as he announced, 'Backup's arrived.'

He climbed down from the vehicle to go and greet the new ambulance crew. 'Sorry we took so long,' his colleague said. 'How are things going?'

'Mother and baby are both doing well.'

Rebecca cleaned up and then stepped down from the ambulance, conscious of Cade following close by. She gave a report on the mother's condition, and Cade did the same for the baby.

'He's a little cold,' he said, 'so he'll need to be warmed.'

'We'll make sure of it. Don't worry.'

'Thanks.'

They said their goodbyes and then walked quickly back to Cade's SUV.

'You did a great job back there,' he said as he set the car in motion. 'You were fantastic every step of the way.'

'Thanks. I'm just glad that things worked out all right.'

Darkness was all around them as they drove back along the country lanes towards the town, but it looked as though the rain was finally beginning to ease off. She settled back against the luxurious upholstery and closed her eyes briefly.

'Are you okay?' he asked. 'I thought something was bothering you, back there in the ambulance. Do you want to talk about it? I wish you would let me help you.'

'No. It's all right. I'm fine—really. It's just been a difficult day, that's all.'

It was the truth. The day had seemed endless already—full of worries, problems and complications—and they still had to go back to the hospital and wait for news of baby Annie.

'And I'm still worried about Emma.' She fished her phone out of her pocket and tried calling her sister once more. 'I keep trying to get in touch with her,' she told Cade.

He must have guessed she was prevaricating, not wanting to talk about her other worries, but he said nothing more about it, driving on and concentrating on watching the road while she dialled and waited. And waited.

'Is she still not answering?' he asked.

'No.' She frowned. 'It's not like her not to phone me. I'm sure something's wrong.'

'As I said, the phone network may be down—or

she may be busy, or sleeping. It's getting late now, you know.'

'Yes, perhaps you're right. But if I don't hear from her soon I think I'll have to go and find her...to make sure she's okay.'

She settled back in her seat once more, trying to calm herself and get some rest before they arrived back at the hospital. After a while her phone burbled and she checked the caller information.

'It's William,' she said.

'Ah.' He sent her a fleeting sideways glance, his brows drawing together. 'He probably wants to meet up with you again.'

'Yes, maybe...' She answered the call and chatted with William for a while, asking him about his work day and about his father's illness. In turn, he asked about Emma.

'I still haven't been able to get in touch with her,' she told him. 'I shan't feel happy until I know she's okay.'

'I know how you feel,' William said, with more emotion in his voice than she'd expected. 'I'm worried about her, too. But it's probably nothing—just a problem with the phone signal in the village.'

'You're probably right,' she said. It was strange William was so worried about Emma, given that they didn't really know each other that well. Emma had that effect on people, though. She was friendly and caring and everyone seemed to like her.

'I could finish work at the plantation early tomorrow afternoon,' he said. 'Take you out to cheer you up. Maybe we could go to the beach once the storm clears up.'

'Bless you—you're an angel,' she said, smiling. 'It sounds wonderful. I'd like that.'

'Me, too,' he murmured.

She cut the call a minute or so later. Cade was frowning.

'Sounds as though you and William will be getting together again?' he said, and she nodded.

'He's promised to take me to the beach,' she said.

'Oh, I see.' He said it as though that bothered him. 'You and he get on really well together, don't you?'

'Well, we're friends. We have a lot in common with one another.'

'Hmm…'

She sensed that he was battling with feelings of jealousy. The way he had kissed her during the storm had been so full of raw passion and command, and yet he clearly felt unsure about what it had meant. As did she. It had played on her mind—and her senses—ever since. And no matter how much she insisted that she and William were just friends, it was clear his worries persisted.

His frown had deepened, and to divert his train of thought she said, 'He says his father is now being given corticosteroid medication to reduce the inflammation around his heart, and they've given him a different kind of tablet to regulate his heart rhythm.'

'Let's hope that will help things improve.'

He was quiet the rest of the way to the hospital, and she wondered if he was thinking about his uncle. It *was* a worrying situation.

Things were no better in Accident and Emergency.

'Annie's showing signs of pulmonary oedema,' said James, when they met up with the consultant once more in the Emergency Unit. 'It can happen, I'm afraid—as

I'm sure you know—even several hours after being rescued from near drowning. We think a patient is doing okay, and then they suffer a downturn.'

Pulmonary oedema meant that there was fluid in the lung tissue, causing the infant to have difficulty breathing. It was what Rebecca had been dreading.

'Presumably you're giving her a diuretic to try to remove the water?' she said.

'Of course... Along with medication to stabilise her heart rhythm and regulate her blood pressure.' He laid a hand lightly on her shoulder. 'Believe me, we're doing everything we can for her.'

'I know... I'm sorry... I'm not doubting you...' She hesitated. 'Perhaps I should go and see to some of the other patients on your list? I need to keep busy.'

'All right. If you're sure.' James nodded. 'If you don't mind, I need to get on—so I'll leave it to Cade to show you the ropes.' He left them, hurrying away to see to the list of people who were waiting.

Cade frowned, studying her closely. 'Don't you think you've had enough for one day? It's very late—I could take you home. I've already rung Harriet to ask her to get a guest room ready for you. She'll have some supper put by for us, too.'

She shook her head. 'I don't want to go anywhere until I know Annie's all right.'

'Okay...' he said doubtfully. 'But if it gets too much for you there's always the couch in my office. If you need anything at all, you must let me know.'

She glanced at him. 'I will—but you don't need to worry about me, you know. I'll be fine. You're the one who needs to take time out and get your head down for a few hours—you came to the cabin to see me after being on call. To be honest, I don't know how you're managing to keep going.'

He gave a crooked smile. 'Years of practice,' he said, 'along with supreme body fitness, of course… From my regular workouts, great energy levels, vitality, suppleness…' He was struggling to keep a straight face.

'Yeah, yeah…' She laughed and waved him away. There were patients waiting to be seen.

But she couldn't help but eye him surreptitiously as he walked away. He certainly was in good shape—lithe and supple, in top form. She was glad she wasn't his patient—he'd make any woman's heart race just by being in the same room with her.

They worked for a couple of hours into the night, seeing to patients who had been injured in the storm and coming across one another briefly as they compared notes or when he signed her treatment records.

'Shall we go and look in on Annie?' he suggested. 'Her parents are with her doctors at the moment, so there'll just be nurses with her.'

She nodded. 'Have you heard anything? Has James said any more about how she's doing?'

'He says she seems to be responding to the treatment.'

Encouraged, she went with him to the observation ward, where the baby lay in a cot, surrounded by monitors that showed her temperature, respiration rate, heart-rate, blood pressure and blood oxygen level. She was sleeping, her pale cheeks showing small patches of pink colour.

'Her vital signs are coming up to something near normal,' she said, relief washing over her. 'She's going to survive—do we know if she's all right neurologically?'

Cade glanced through the baby's file. 'Apparently she recognises her parents, and she's responded to them. Things are looking good.'

'Thank heaven. That's so wonderful to know.' She gave a heartfelt sigh. 'It's been a nightmare. It feels like the whole day's been one long trauma.'

As a doctor, she was used to dealing with situations like these, but somehow over these last few months her emotional safety net had been shredded.

He must have read the self-doubt in her eyes, because he reached out to comfort her. 'Not much of a holiday for you, eh?' He laid an arm gently on her shoulder. 'Time to go home, I think. We could both do with some sleep. You'll feel a whole lot better in the morning.'

'I expect so.'

'I'm sure of it.'

He drove to the plantation, following the winding road up into the hills. The rain had slowed to a drizzle and the wind was dying down—the storm had lasted a relatively short time, by all accounts, but it had been bad enough to bring down bridges, flood roads and cause landslides that had created havoc.

'I'll phone my landlord first thing in the morning,' she said. 'I expect he'll want to organise repairs straight away.'

'It could take several days for him to fix things, you know. Tradesmen will be in demand all over the island.' He sent her a sideways glance, as though to gauge her reaction. 'It could mean you staying at the plantation house for around a week…possibly longer.'

'Oh, I see.' She frowned. 'I suppose I don't have many alternatives… So if you're all right with that…?'

'I'm more than happy for you to stay with me.'

The plantation house was lit by a lantern in the porch, and security lights sparked into life on the veranda as they came up the drive. Cade parked the car and showed her into the hallway, leaving her to look around while he went back to fetch her cases from the boot. It was a two-storey building, with a wide staircase leading from the central hallway to the upper floor.

'I'll show you to your guest room,' he said, hefting the cases as if they were lightweight. 'It's an en-suite room, so you'll have your own bathroom, and there's plenty of wardrobe space.'

He led the way to the room, setting her luggage down on the floor beside a double bed, and then showed her around.

'There are doors that open out on to the upper veranda,' he said. 'I think you'll love the view from here when you see it in the morning.'

'It's a lovely room,' she said, taking time to look around. There were voile drapes at the windows and beautiful silk covers on the bed to match the pale upholstery of the chairs and the dressing-table stool. A built-in dressing table and wardrobes took up the whole length of one wall.

'Harriet said she's left us some supper—cold cuts of meat and salad, with fruit for dessert. We could have it downstairs, in the kitchen, or I could bring a tray up here and you can help yourself whenever you're ready?'

'That's really thoughtful of you—and of Harriet. Thank you. I think I'd like a tray up here, if that's okay?'

'Of course.'

He came over to her and placed his hands lightly on her shoulders. If he was disappointed that she wasn't going to share the meal with him, he managed to hide it. There was just the faintest flicker of a shadow in his dark eyes as he looked at her. Perhaps he accepted that they were both tired after a difficult and draining day.

'You can have whatever you want. You did so well today…and I know it was hard for you. I'm not sure what went wrong for you in your job back home in England, but I sense you have a huge problem, working in obstetrics, don't you? I felt it in your reactions—but I know you don't want to talk about it…it's okay. I understand.'

He kissed her gently on the forehead, a kiss as light as thistledown, and she looked up at him in bemused wonder.

'What was that for?' she asked softly, and he gave a faint shrug.

'I just felt you needed it right now,' he said, 'and I want you to know that I'm here for you.' He straightened and reluctantly let her go. 'I'll leave you to get ready for bed and I'll bring supper up here for you. Don't worry if you're in the shower. I'll leave a tray on the table.'

'Thanks,' she murmured.

It seemed that she was in his debt yet again. He'd rescued her at the harbour on that first afternoon and he'd come to her aid today when the storm had damaged the shingles on the cabin roof. Now this.

She smiled tentatively as he turned to leave the room, but she was welling up with emotion inside. How had it happened that she had started to feel such tenderness and affection towards him? It was gratitude, surely, for everything he'd done for her…? But, no…it was more than that…much, much more.

It had been all too easy for her to grow attached to him, to want to have him close by. It was reassuring to know that he was only a heartbeat away.

She'd been so tempted to invite him to stay with her…and he would have accepted in an instant, she knew. From the way he had kissed her earlier, and the tension in his body as he'd held her just now, she could tell he was also struggling to hold back.

But that would have led to all sorts of complications. It wouldn't do for her to fall for him, would it? That could bring about all kinds of heartache. It would be unbearable to love him and have it all go wrong when he learned that she was so terribly flawed.

CHAPTER FIVE

'HI, THERE.' CADE LOOKED across the room as Rebecca came into the kitchen the next morning. His eyes glinted approval, his gaze resting on her for a fraction longer than was necessary, taking in the curving lines of the pencil-slim skirt that hugged her hips and the sleeveless top with spaghetti straps that revealed a smooth expanse of golden skin.

The toaster pinged and he jumped slightly, distracted and disorientated for a second or two. Rebecca went over to him. It was somehow gratifying to know that she had such an effect on him.

He was obviously trying to multitask, toasting English muffins and whisking up what looked like a Hollandaise sauce at the same time. As she approached him she saw there were a couple of eggs gently poaching in a pan of hot water on the hob.

'Did you have a good night?' he asked.

'I did—thank you. I fell asleep as soon as my head touched the pillow. And you were right about the view from the French doors—it's fantastic.' She'd stepped on to the balcony first thing this morning and seen the rainforest laid out in front of her, sloping down the hillside, and in the distance the bay had been a vivid blue.

'I'm glad you took the time to look.' He smiled. 'I thought I would make eggs Benedict for breakfast…is that all right with you?'

'Oh, that sounds wonderful. I'm starving. It must be the fresh air that's giving me an appetite. You wouldn't know there had been a storm here, would you? Everything just looks as though it's been washed clean.'

He nodded. 'We get these storms from time to time, and after a downpour everything springs to life—plants and trees green up and flowers open.'

'It's beautiful.'

Sunlight streamed in through the tall windows and a warm breeze drifted in through the open glass doors. Out on the veranda she saw that a table had been laid with a white damask cloth, and there was a jug filled with fresh juice, along with two glasses.

Cade slid the hot buttered muffins on to plates that were warm from the oven and topped them with slices of smoked salmon. Then he added the lightly poached eggs, drizzled smooth Hollandaise sauce over the top and sprinkled chopped chives over that.

'Mmm…it looks and smells delicious.'

'Good…that's what I was aiming for. Let's eat outside, shall we?'

He led the way to the veranda, carrying the food on a tray that also contained a coffee pot and porcelain mugs. The aroma of freshly brewed coffee drifted on the air and Rebecca followed it as though mesmerised.

'This is heavenly,' she said as they sat down to eat. 'It must be the best way to start the day.'

This part of the veranda looked out over the garden, a wonderful landscape of fruit trees—lemon, tamarind and pineapple among them—and there were palms that surrounded an immaculate lawn area. Showy purple bougainvillaea and scarlet kalanchoe brought colour to the borders, along with sweet-scented pink and yellow frangipani. The delicate fragrance drifted over to them on soft air currents. In one corner of the garden there was a lily pond bordered by masses of bright pink sedum.

'I'm glad you like it. I was keen to get the plantation underway, but the house and garden were my next priority. We're fortunate out here that everything is so lush. Plants grow very quickly, so it just takes a bit of landscaping and a gardener who can keep on top of things to make it all come together. I love sitting out here in the mornings before work. It's tranquil, and it helps to set me up for the day.'

'I can see why it would do that.' She savoured the taste of the smooth sauce and runny egg yolk on her tongue and sighed with satisfaction. 'This food is wonderful—I thought you said you couldn't cook?'

He shrugged, making a crooked smile. 'Let's say my repertoire is limited. I can manage a few egg recipes, pizza and maybe toss a pancake, so you wouldn't go hungry if you were relying on me. That's about my limit, though.'

'Perhaps you've never had much time to spend in the kitchen?'

'That's true—especially in the last couple of years, with my work on the plantation and the house.' He looked around. 'As I said, this place was pretty much run down and in need of some tender loving care when I took over. It's taken a while, but I think I finally have things on track.'

He poured coffee for her and she added cream and

sugar. She said, 'From what I've seen so far it's a big house. It must have taken some doing to get it right. The kitchen is absolutely lovely. You have very good taste.'

He smiled. 'Thanks. I've always preferred light-coloured units, with display cabinets and plenty of glass shelving. And of course the central island unit is very useful.' He swallowed some coffee and then added, 'I'll show you around the rest of the house if you like?'

'That would be great, thank you—if you have the time. Do you have to go to work at the hospital today?'

'I'm on call this morning, and at some point I'll have to go in to deal with some paperwork. After that I have a couple of days' leave due to me—I'd planned to use it to finish off overseeing the building of my new fermentation sheds...though perhaps that's something William could get involved in.'

They finished breakfast a few minutes later and set off on their tour of the house.

The living room was long and wide, with three sets of French doors opening on to the veranda. They had been flung open to allow the warm air to circulate. The room was furnished along pale, uncluttered lines, with pale oak flooring and a corner sofa with matching armchairs. The coffee table was made of pale green-coloured glass, and that same green colour was reflected in the ferns placed at intervals around the room. Outside, beyond the veranda, there was more greenery, with graceful palm trees and yuccas and climbing philodendrons.

They went upstairs and he showed her several bedrooms, each with its own bathroom. They were all exquisitely furnished with stylish fabrics and restful colour schemes. Each room had doors opening out on to the wide balcony.

'This is breathtaking,' she said, looking around in wonder. 'The whole house is beautiful.' Her mouth curved as a thought struck her. 'I've no idea how you're going to fill all these rooms, though. Maybe you plan to have a lot of visitors?'

He smiled. 'I do have visitors, from time to time, but you're right, of course. It *is* a big house—but that's one of the things that drew me to buy this particular property.'

He leaned against one of the French doors in the main bedroom, looking out from the balcony over the forest and the curve of the bay in the distance.

'I like everything about it, and I'm hoping that perhaps one day I'll have a family of my own to fill it. It's not something I dwell on, or that I'm specifically planning, but it's there in the back of my mind—something to aim for. I didn't much like being an only child, but my parents' marriage broke up so there were never going to be any brothers or sisters. I want something different from that for my own future.'

She met his gaze as steadily as she could, with an equilibrium she didn't quite feel. 'Family's important to you,' she commented. Unaccountably, her heart was sinking. She should have known it was foolish to get to know and like him…to have deeper feelings for him. She was hurting already, and a heavy ache was starting up deep inside her. 'It's something that's been missing from your life.'

He nodded, moving away from the balcony and back into the bedroom. 'I suppose so. I haven't really analysed my feelings as such, but in the back of my mind I think I bought this house with the idea that it would be a happy family home one day.'

They went out into the hallway. She said slowly, 'Of course that would depend on you meeting the right woman. You *did* say you'd had some problems with that…'

He laughed. 'Well, yes. Perhaps I've been unlucky in the women I've dated so far.' He stopped on the landing, by the balustrade, his gaze meshing with hers. 'That could change, though. Who knows what life holds in store? After all, here I am with an incredibly beautiful girl—someone who's thoughtful, sweet-natured and caring—it's the stuff that dreams are made of.'

He moved closer, reaching for her, his hand resting on her waist, drawing her to him and folding her into his arms. He kissed her—a tender, coaxing, sweetly gentle kiss that stirred her senses and made her pulses rocket out of control. His hand stroked warmly along the curve of her spine, bringing her even closer to him so that her breasts were softly crushed against his chest and their thighs tangled.

The breath caught in her throat. For a moment—for a heartbeat in time—she almost gave in to her deepest desires and leaned into him. Then she came to her senses and reluctantly, with a feeling of angst rising inside her, put a hand on his chest to ward him off. She couldn't get involved with him. No matter how much she wanted to…she couldn't…

'It might not be,' she said softly.

He was teasing her, surely, and she batted away the notion of him wanting her before it had time to take hold. When he'd kissed her and held her back at the cabin, emotions had been running high. It didn't have to mean anything…did it?

'I'm not looking for a relationship, Cade,' she said flatly. 'I've been there, done that, and it all went very badly wrong for me. I don't think I want to dip my toe in that water again for quite some time.'

'Are you quite sure about that?' His eyes darkened and his hand gently stroked the rounded contour of her hip. 'Perhaps I could persuade you to change your mind?'

'Oh, I wouldn't bank on it,' she said, with a jauntiness she didn't feel. 'You know me—I'm here for a holiday…to have fun and take life as it comes. No strings attached, so to speak.'

She stepped back, moving away from him. It was too much of a temptation, being close to him this way, feeling the warm touch of his hand on her body. It made her want what she couldn't have, and she felt a sudden desperate need to escape. She turned around and started to go back down the stairs, conscious all the while that he was following her.

'And doing that will involve William, I suppose? *I* don't figure anywhere in the equation, do I?' His expression was taut, a muscle flicking briefly in his jaw. 'You want to be with *him*.'

It felt as though she was on a course of self-destruction, but she plunged on. 'Well, he did see me first—and he did offer to take me down to the beach this afternoon. I'm quite looking forward to that.'

It was cruel—a harsh way to treat him, perhaps—but wasn't this better than hurting him even more deeply in the long run? He wouldn't want her if he knew the truth about her, and she couldn't bring herself to tell him right now. Perhaps saying it out loud to a man she cared about would make it inevitable—the desperately dreadful aftermath of her illness. She didn't want to admit the finality of it even to herself.

He stared at her in an arrested fashion, thrown by her flippant reply. She might have slapped him, judging by the way he'd reacted. It seemed he was about to say something in response but his phone beeped and he hesitated, a soft, unspoken curse hovering on his lips.

'I should take this—it might be the hospital,' he said.

She nodded and he quickly checked the text message that had come up on screen.

She glanced at him after he'd put the phone back in his pocket. 'Was it the hospital?' she asked.

'No, but it's a call-out.'

Rebecca frowned. 'I'm sorry. You must go, of course.'

He braced himself, straightening his shoulders. 'I don't want to leave you stranded here,' he said. 'If you want to go out and about anywhere, I can arrange for Benjamin to drive you.'

'No.' She shook her head. 'There's no need for that. I'll have to sort out some form of transport while I'm on the island. I can't rely on you and William all the while. I'll see if I can rent a car.'

He was thoughtful for a second or two. 'Actually, it's just occurred to me,' he said. 'I have a four-wheel drive car you could use. It's a few years old, but it's been maintained well and it will get you around reliably. My uncle uses it sometimes, when he works on the plantation, but he's not up to driving at the moment. It's yours if you want it—until he's back on his feet again.'

'Oh…really? Thank you.'

She looked at him, a smile curving her lips. She

didn't deserve his kindness. He was doing this for her despite their recent altercation, though she suspected part of his motive for making the offer was to make her less reliant on William… His cousin was more than willing to help her out, and Cade clearly wanted to nip that in the bud.

'That's settled, then,' he murmured. 'We have insurance to cover us for any driver, so there's no problem there.'

'You're being very good to me,' she said. 'And I do appreciate it, you know? It'll give me the chance to explore the island.' And maybe she could even go and look for Emma. That was her first priority.

He studied her, his brows drawing together. 'You're welcome. I should have thought of it before. The car's just sitting around in the garage at the moment…it'll be ideal for you to get around.' He seemed a touch hesitant as he added, 'It's probably best to avoid going up into the hills, though—especially right now. Road conditions will be tricky after the storm.'

He looked at her musingly for a moment or two longer, trying to gauge her thoughts, and she tried to put on an air of innocence. After all, he hadn't really been able to read her mind…had he?

'Have *you* driven up there?' she asked. 'Into the hills?'

He nodded. 'There are hairpin turns and in places there are sheer rock faces on either side of you, with vertical drops. It's not a drive for the faint-hearted.'

'Oh, I see.' She frowned, thinking about that.

She wasn't normally of a nervous disposition, but she balked at taking to roads where she wouldn't see a hedgerow or houses or at least something fairly solid on either side of her. But she hadn't heard from Emma for a few days now, and she was concerned about her. Something was wrong—she was sure of it… And, no matter that Cade had warned her against it, she would have to go in search of her sister sooner or later.

'It will be good to have a means of getting about, anyway. Thanks again.'

A frown cut into his brow but he simply said, 'We could go and take a look at the car right now, if you like?' He glanced at his watch. 'I have to go out to look at one of my workers who's been taken ill—the text message was from Harriet, to tell me about it. We could take the car for a spin over to his house if you want to get used to it.'

'Sounds like a great idea.'

She went with him to the garage—which turned out to be an old stable block at the back of the house. It had been renovated, and now accommodated a number of vehicles—including the new truck.

Cade stowed his medical bag in the boot of a smart silver-coloured vehicle and then handed her the keys. 'Okay, you're in charge. I'll give you directions on how to get there. Agwe lives in a village some six or seven miles away from here. It's a tourist area, where people go to fish in the river, and when he isn't working on the plantation he helps out with the catch. They run competitions and weigh the fish. Unfortunately his village was hit by the storm several hours before we were. There are flood waters all around.'

'Do you think we'll be able to get through to his home?'

'It should be possible. The bridge held up, and his house is on higher ground.'

'Okay.' She started the car, pleased when the engine fired into life straight away. 'What's wrong with him—do you know?'

He shook his head. 'The message was a bit vague. Flu-like symptoms, muscle pains, headache…'

'Do you treat *all* of your workers when they're ill?' She turned the car on to the road leading away from the plantation and set off towards the south of the island.

'I usually try to do what I can for them. Medical bills can be an unwanted expense—their insurance premiums might be affected by any claims they make—so if it's at all possible I'll help out. It's part of the package they get, working for me. So far things have worked out all right.'

The car handled well, she discovered, and once she was used to the gears and the instrumentation, things went smoothly. They reached Agwe's village only a few minutes later.

'Thank you so much for coming,' his wife said. She was a middle-aged woman, with springy black hair and dark hazel eyes. 'Come in…come in.' She ushered them into a small cottage. 'I'm really worried about him. I thought maybe he needed to go to the hospital—but he won't listen to me. He says he doesn't want to be a burden to anyone.'

'He's not a burden, Marisha,' Cade said. 'Has his condition worsened in the last few hours?'

She nodded. 'Yes, I think it has. He's feverish. He's not well at all.' She led the way to the bedroom. 'He was taken ill yesterday. We thought it was just a virus, and it would pass, but he seems to have gone downhill since then.'

At Marisha's invitation Rebecca went with Cade into Agwe's bedroom. The woman hovered in the doorway.

Her husband was lying in bed, beads of perspiration breaking out on his forehead. 'Hi, Agwe,' Cade said, going over to him. 'I'm sorry to hear you're not well.'

Agwe mumbled a response. 'My wife shouldn't have bothered you. I'll be fine.'

'You don't *look* fine,' Cade answered. 'I'd like to examine you to see if I can help, if that's all right?'

Agwe nodded wearily, clearly unwell, and Cade started by taking his temperature and running a stethoscope over his chest. He checked his pulse and blood pressure.

'You're running a fever, and your heartrate is very fast,' he said after a while. 'Added to that, your blood pressure is low, and you say you're having problems with your waterworks—it seems as though you've picked up an infection of some sort.'

He looked at a graze on the man's hand.

'It's just a thought, but have you been handling fish from the river recently?'

'Yeah…a few days ago. I caught my hand on a fishing hook.' Agwe frowned. 'Why?' He was becoming breathless and finding it difficult to speak. 'Is it important?'

'I'm trying to work out what we're dealing with,' Cade answered. 'There are a number of possibilities… but there have been one or two cases of Weil's disease admitted to the hospital recently, and your symptoms are similar. It's a bacterial infection that can be caught in various ways—through contact with contaminated water or soil, for instance. That graze of yours would have been an ideal entry point. I really think the best place for you is the hospital, Agwe.'

Agwe's wife said worriedly, 'So you think he has this disease?'

Cade nodded. 'It's very possible.' He turned back to Agwe. 'We need to get you to hospital so that they can do some tests and put you on intravenous antibiotics. I'm going to give you tablets to take right now, to start the treatment straight away.'

Agwe looked as though he was about to protest, but his wife stopped him with a look. 'Dr Byfield says you need to be in hospital, so that's where you're going. No argument.'

Cade smiled at the interchange and glanced at Rebecca. 'Are you up for driving there? It'll be quicker than waiting for an ambulance. I'll ring ahead to tell them to expect us.'

She nodded. 'Yes, I can do that—if you can make him comfortable in the back of the car.'

She knew Cade was worried about the possibility of kidney failure. Weil's disease could be very dangerous, and treatment should be started as soon as possible if there was to be a successful outcome.

They set off a few minutes later and Rebecca covered the distance in short time, thankful that the main roads had been cleared of debris. It hadn't taken her long to get used to the car, and she really appreciated Cade's offer to let her borrow it.

Once they reached the hospital Cade handed his patient over to the emergency team. The man's wife stayed with her husband, going to sit by his bedside.

'We'll bring in the renal consultant,' the doctor in charge of the team told Cade. 'I think you're probably right about the diagnosis—we'll start him on intravenous therapy straight away. He may need corticosteroids, too. Thanks for bringing him in.'

'I was glad to help.'

Cade left Agwe in capable hands and went over to Rebecca, who was waiting to one side.

'I have to stay and sort out my paperwork,' he told her. 'It'll take me some time, so you might want to take the car and get back to your holiday. I can make my own arrangements for getting back home. I'm sure someone here will drop me off later.'

'I don't mind waiting,' she said, but he shook his head.

'You've already done more than enough to help out. Besides, I think I ought to stay around here for a while, to see how Agwe's doing and talk to his wife. She's upset, and could probably do with knowing a bit more about what's likely to happen to him. He'll be in hospital for a few weeks, I expect.' He ran a hand down her arm in an unexpectedly tender gesture. 'This is your holiday. Go and enjoy it.'

'Are you sure you don't want me to stay?'

She frowned, uncertain about leaving him. Then it struck her that clearly he was no longer concerned about her seeing William this afternoon, and perversely that troubled her. Had she been all too successful in pushing him away from her? Wasn't it for the best? Then why did she feel so dreadful? Her stomach clenched in despair.

'I'm positive,' he said. 'Perhaps I'll see you at the house for dinner later this evening?'

She nodded, not willing to answer him outright. Now that she had a car at her disposal she only really had one thing in mind—as soon as possible she would go in search of her sister. She didn't want to involve Cade in what she was planning, because this was her problem to resolve on her own. Perhaps she was worrying unnecessarily, but she wouldn't rest until she was certain all was well.

She drove back to the plantation, stopping off to buy a few supplies, but hurrying because William would be arriving to take her to the beach in a short time. She thought about calling to put him off, but she didn't want to disappoint him. He was anxious about his father, and maybe some time at the beach would be good for him.

'Hey, it's good to see you, Becky!'

William arrived just as she'd finished packing a holdall with the things she thought she might need for a trek up into the hills. The storm might have caused problems up there—she didn't know what to expect—so she'd included a change of clothes, fresh water, food supplies… She put as much as she could cram in her backpack, together with medication she'd bought from the local pharmacy. She wanted to be prepared in case Emma was ill, or had been cut off by the storm. She couldn't imagine what had happened up there in the village, but if she'd been able Emma would have been in touch by now, she was sure.

William glanced at the holdall she'd left in a corner of the kitchen. 'Are you planning on leaving us?' he asked. 'I thought you were staying on the plantation for a few days.'

'That's the general idea,' she said, smiling, hoping to throw him off track. She hadn't expected him to notice the bag. 'That's just a few things I've scrambled together in case I decide to go exploring.' It wasn't exactly a lie, was it? Although she had filled a backpack, too… 'There's such a lot of the island I haven't seen—including your beach…'

He laughed, taking the hint. 'Come on, then. It's perfect out there just now. The tide's out, and there's a soft, warm breeze.'

'Sounds idyllic. I'll just put this holdall up in my room and then we'll be off.'

They spent a couple of hours by the sea, alternating between splashing in the calm waters and lying on the sand and soaking up the sun. William went over to one of the tilting palm trees that grew along the shoreline and shimmied up the trunk to get to the coconuts. He picked one and brought it over to her, cracking it open on a rock and handing it to her so that she could drink the juice.

'Mmm…wonderful…' she murmured. 'I'm having the greatest time.'

'Me, too.' He was quiet for a moment or two. 'I bet Emma would love it here. She said how much she likes to spend time on the beaches around here. Have you any idea how long she was planning on staying up at the village?'

She shook her head. 'None at all. She didn't say.'

'I suppose her colleagues would have let you know if anything was wrong?'

'Yes, I'd have thought so.'

Only she hadn't been able to contact any of them. It was disturbing. There *was* the possibility that a phone signal wasn't available up there, but she couldn't help wondering if her sister had been taken ill or been involved in an accident of some sort.

William dropped her off at the plantation house and

apologised for having to leave her so soon. 'Cade asked me to check on the new fermentation buildings,' he said, 'to make sure the workmen are doing everything according to the plans—and then I need to go with my mother to visit my father in hospital. He's on this new medication and we're hoping it's going to help him get better.'

'Good luck,' she told him. 'I hope things start picking up for him soon.'

After he'd gone she made a swift check to see if there was anything else she needed to take with her on her journey up into the hills. She quickly changed into jeans and a T-shirt and then downloaded a map from the Internet and printed it out. She hurried—she was anxious to get away before Cade returned from the hospital.

At last, she was ready. There were still about three hours left before sunset—surely it wouldn't take her more than an hour to make the drive up to the village? There would still be plenty of daylight to make the journey there *and* back, if need be.

She set off, driving carefully along a road that turned out to be exactly as Cade had predicted. It became progressively steeper as time went by, and there were potholes left by the recent storm, so she bumped and clattered and worried about the car's suspension. It was an all-terrain vehicle, though, so that shouldn't be a problem.

The landscape she passed through was awe-inspiring. She caught glimpses of mango and avocado trees being grown on small farms, and as she climbed higher into the hills saw slopes that were thickly forested with tall chataignier and spiky breadfruit trees. Vines grew everywhere, winding around tree trunks and climbing upwards towards the sunlight. As Cade had said, the tropical vegetation on the island was lush, thriving in the warm, humid atmosphere.

She drove on, and the road became more narrow and winding, with deep chasms falling away to one side. She slowed the car, alarmed by the increasingly craggy landscape and the towering cliffs that had been battered by the recent storm. As she went further, she saw there were landslips, where soil and rubble and other debris had accumulated in falls down the rock face. It looked precarious—as though it might tumble on to the road at any moment.

Rounding a tight bend, she held her breath as she negotiated the difficult turn—and then gasped as she saw what lay up ahead. A large portion of the cliff had been undermined by rainwater and the softer sedimentary rock had sheered away from the volcanic grey basalt beneath. It had fallen across the road in a mass of boulders, tree roots, branches and rotting leaves.

She stopped the car and sat for a moment, debating what she should do. There was no way she could risk taking the car beyond this point, but she'd come too far to go back—she would have to go the rest of the way on foot.

She parked the car in as safe a place as she could find, as far off the road as possible, just in case anyone else might be as reckless as she and try to venture up further into what was virtually a small mountain. They would need room to turn around. Perhaps this was why Emma hadn't come home. The road was blocked.

Rebecca pulled on her backpack, took her holdall from the boot of the car and set off along the road. Even up here it was hot, and without the benefit of the car's air-conditioning she was wiping beads of perspiration from her face within half an hour. She sat down to rest on a flat outcrop of rock at the side of the road and gazed around her. She caught the green flash of a parrot's wings as it flew among the branches of the mountain cabbage palms. If only she could fly…

How much further was it to the village? According to the map it was only some twenty miles from the plantation, and she must have covered a good deal of the journey by now, surely? Perhaps she'd miscalculated somewhere… The sun was already getting low in the sky and she'd still not come across the small settlement of houses she was expecting to see.

Perhaps she ought to call someone and report that the road was blocked? She checked her phone, but there was no signal. She'd not really expected it to work up here, but it was a bit daunting to find that she was totally isolated, with darkness coming on. Had she been completely foolhardy to start out on this expedition?

She stood up and started on the road uphill once more. Cade would certainly have something to say about her actions when she finally returned to the plantation house. Her thoughts lingered on him. She felt strangely empty inside, with a feeling of unaccustomed loneliness washing through her. She missed him and wanted to be with him.

A soft sigh escaped her. He would have left the hospital some time ago. Was he wondering why she wasn't around to have dinner with him? Guilt ran through her. He'd been nothing but good to her and she'd pushed him away.

Lost in thought, she trundled on—until, bizarrely, from out of nowhere she heard someone calling to her.

'Hey, Rebecca! Wait…wait up…' The words cracked across the air like a whiplash.

She froze in her tracks, hearing that familiar deep voice coming out of the wilderness. It couldn't be Cade—could it? Was she hallucinating? Had she conjured him up out of pure wishful thinking?

Slowly, as though in a trance, she turned around and looked back at the road. Giant tree ferns covered the hillside, verdant among a stand of tall Caribbean pine. Then her glance settled on a lone figure and her heart leapt in her chest.

She shook her head briefly. This wasn't real. She was imagining he was there, surely? But, no, he was standing in the road, tall and broad-shouldered, his hefty medical pack slung over his back.

'Rebecca…thank heaven I've found you.' Cade walked briskly up to her, studying her from under dark brows. Putting his medical kit down on the ground beside him, he reached for her, his hands circling her bare arms. 'Are you okay? You don't look quite right.'

'It…it must be the shock of seeing you,' she answered huskily. 'I thought I was alone out here. How did you know where to find me?'

He gave a short, harsh laugh. 'It wasn't too difficult. I had the feeling you'd come after Emma. I guessed she'd been on your mind ever since she came up here. So when I got back to the house and you weren't there I rang William. He said you weren't still with him, but he told me you'd packed a holdall and taken it up to your room, so I went to check. It wasn't there, and it was fairly easy to guess the rest.' His mouth tightened. 'You've no idea how worried I've been.'

'There was no need for you to worry,' she protested.

'And you didn't need to follow me out here. This is my problem—not yours. I didn't want to involve anyone else.'

His eyes glittered, skating over her. 'Can't you imagine how concerned I was when I realised you'd taken it into your head to come up here?' He shook his head, tugging her close to him. 'How could I let you do this on your own? You've no idea what you might come up against. I've been so worried about you. This is a dangerous road and you're not used to the car.' His voice was edgy and tinged with impatience.

She looked into his smoke-dark eyes, trying to gauge the depth of his emotions. She was feeling overwhelmed. He'd actually come after her—had cared enough to make sure that she was safe—but he seemed to be rigid with tension.

'You're angry with me?'

'Angry? No. Not angry. Frustrated…concerned… It's getting late, and there's no way we can go back down that road in the dark. There could be another landslide at any moment and we need to be on the lookout for it.' He wrapped his arms around her. 'Rebecca, I was so afraid something might have happened to you…that you might be hurt…'

'But I'm fine—'

'You're *not* fine.' His tone was clipped. 'You're a pain in the neck, going off like that without a word. Anything could have happened.' He drew her up against him, holding her tightly, his whole body pressuring hers. 'I wish I didn't feel this way about you—but I can't help myself—'

He bent his head to hers and kissed her on the mouth, crushing her lips with intense passion—as though he couldn't get enough of her, as though he would rid himself of the demons that were driving him.

Her soft curves meshed with the hardness of his chest and her legs collided with the taut, powerful muscles of his thighs. A wave of heat ran through her from head to toe. She ought to be putting up some kind of a protest, she knew, even as she kissed him in return and lifted her arms to let her fingers caress the silky hair at his nape.

She was so glad that he was here, that he'd bothered to come after her. She'd been fully prepared to do this on her own, but now that he was with her she felt as though she could move mountains. He filled her with strength. Together, they could do anything...

Her body melted into his in an involuntary movement of longing, of deep, instinctive yearning. A soft moan rumbled in her throat. She wanted to run her hands all over him—over his arms, his chest—wanted to tell him how much she needed him, how glad she was that he was here with her.

His lips left a trail of kisses over her mouth, her cheek, her throat, and his hands made sweeping forays over her curves.

'I need you,' he said, the words hot against her cheek, and she felt her body tremble in response.

A soft, shuddery sigh escaped her. What was she doing? What was she thinking? How could she go down that road again? Falling for a man who would turn his back on her as soon as he learned the truth about her?

'I can't,' she whispered. 'I should never have let this happen.'

The breath caught in his throat and he stared down at her, his gaze hot with desire. 'Don't do this to me,' he said, his voice roughened. 'You kiss me as though you want me every bit as much as I want you, and then you change your mind and call a halt. You can't behave that way. You're driving me crazy.'

'I'm sorry.' She stared up at him, tears in her eyes. 'I'm *sorry*.'

He gave a ragged sigh and appeared to be making an effort to pull himself together. Slowly he put her away from him, holding her at arm's length.

'Okay,' he said. 'Explain it to me. You want to have fun. No strings attached. I can do that. I'm willing to give it a try. What's the problem?'

'It won't work,' she said, her chest heaving. 'Not with you and me. Not like that. It just won't work.'

He stared at her, trying to fathom what was going on in her head. 'Sooner or later,' he said, 'you're going to have to talk to me and tell me what's going on with you. Right now, I don't understand what makes you tick. But I *will* find out, Rebecca. That's a promise.'

CHAPTER SIX

'WE NEED TO find the village before nightfall.' Cade's tone was clipped, decisive.

'Yes. I'm not sure exactly how far it is.'

Rebecca sent him a swift glance as she picked up her holdall. Just a few moments ago he'd been holding her in his arms but now he was remote from her, as though he was steeling himself to keep a distance between them—at least physically.

He looked at the setting sun and lifted up his medical pack—it was a very large immediate-response kit, designed to provide every available means of helping patients in the dangerous time before they could reach a hospital.

'It looks as though you came prepared for trouble,' she said.

He nodded. 'I thought it was best to be on the safe side.'

She frowned as they set off once more along the road. 'But I thought you believed I was worrying unnecessarily?'

'No, that's not true. I didn't say that. I didn't want to upset you by agreeing that your sister might be having problems. There was no point in making you any more anxious than you already were.'

'But if I'd known you *agreed* she might be in difficulty I might have been persuaded to come up here earlier.' She sucked in a breath, upset by the waste of time. He knew this country and its idiosyncrasies far better than she did.

'You could hardly have come up here while the storm was raging. We couldn't even have got rescue helicopters in the air to check things out. Besides, as I recall we had our hands full—with a baby rescue and a breech delivery.'

'I suppose so,' she acknowledged, giving it some thought. His logic was unassailable.

They trudged up the hill, rounding a bend in the road. A tarmacked path led off to the east, and they turned in that direction.

'It can't be far now,' she said, cheering up a bit. 'That's the landmark I was searching for. I knew there was a place where a side road turned towards the village.'

In the distance the land rose still higher, the slopes covered with luxuriant rainforest, broken only by the cascade of waterfalls that cut into the rock face and pooled far below into a wide lake. Just here a river tumbled down the hillside in a torrent fed by the recent rains. As Rebecca and Cade went further along the path it soon became clear that there had been a lot of flood damage up there.

'The path's been broken up by the water and the boulders that have been washed down,' Cade remarked. 'It'll be impossible to get supply trucks through here.'

Ahead of them they could see the outline of some painted wooden houses set out in a clearing.

The ground was now soft and muddy underfoot, and Rebecca stopped for a moment to pull a pair of boots from her backpack. She was wearing jeans and a T-shirt, and now she put on a light jacket. A light breeze had sprung up and she was beginning to feel apprehensive, not knowing what they might find when they reached the settlement.

'At least we should soon have some answers,' Cade said, glancing at her as they set off once more. 'It looks as though this place has been cut off by flood water—it's beginning to recede now, but from the state of the houses it must have been pretty bad while it lasted.'

He was right. It appeared most of the houses had been submerged up to a foot from the ground. There were dirty marks left on the houses' framework, from where the water had risen and then gradually started to ebb away.

'I expected to see more movement,' Rebecca commented. 'People going about the business of clearing up. Everything's so quiet…it's like a ghost town.'

'It's odd, definitely,' he agreed. 'Perhaps the families moved out of the lower-lying houses into those on higher ground—out of the path of the water. There's some kind of communal building and a few dwellings over there that should have missed the worst of the damage.'

They headed towards the communal building—a large wooden structure. The entrance door swung open when Cade pushed it, and soon they were standing inside a long, wide room.

'This must be the school,' Rebecca murmured.

Desks had been pushed to one side to make space, and chairs were stacked neatly against the wall. Instead of being used as a place of learning, the hall had been turned into a hospital, with half a dozen beds arranged in a row, facing the windows. Three children lay in bed, covered by mosquito nets, whilst adults sat quietly next to them, reading or talking to one another in low voices. They looked up as the newcomers walked in, surveying them with tired interest. Two further beds contained adults who were sleeping.

Rebecca and Cade introduced themselves to the people in the room. 'We're here to help—any way we can,' Cade said.

A door at the end of the room opened, and Rebecca drew in a sharp breath when she saw Emma walk in. She was pushing a medicine trolley, obviously trying to go about her work as usual, but Rebecca was shocked by the change in her sister. The vital, energetic and bright young woman who'd been laughing and joking at Selwyn's Bar had disappeared completely, and in her place was someone who looked ill and drawn. She was very pale and looked intensely weary, walking stiffly as though she was in pain.

Emma glanced across the room and saw the visitors. Relief seemed to wash over her. 'Oh, *Becky*,' she said in a choked voice. 'I *knew* you would come. I knew if anyone could get through it would be you.'

Rebecca went over to her sister and hugged her. 'What are you doing up and about? You don't look well,' she said. 'Why aren't the other nurses looking after you?'

Emma shook her head. 'There's no one else here— only the people you see in this room. When the floods came we had to evacuate as many people as we could to the next village.' She paused to get her breath. 'I said I would stay behind and take care of the patients. They were going to come back for me—but I think the villages must have been cut off from one another. They never came.'

She reached for a chair and sat down, suddenly losing strength.

'How long have you been feeling ill, Emma?' Cade asked.

'A few hours. It came on quickly. I'm tired, I suppose. I've been working through the night, looking after the patients.'

He frowned. 'From the state you're in, I think it's a lot more than tiredness. Do you have the same symptoms as the others?'

'No.' She tried to shake her head and cried out, wincing as pain shot through her. She held her hand to her neck and rubbed gently. 'The children have spotted tick fever. They're beginning to recover—I've been giving them antibiotics. They're due for another dose now… the adults, too.'

She started to get up to go to them but Cade gently pushed her back down.

'We'll see to all that. You need to rest. We have to find out what's wrong with you.'

'But it's time for their meal.' Emma's brow creased with anxiety. 'I've got to find something for them, but there's not much left—we're just about out of food.'

She drew in a shaky breath and shivered a little, wrapping her arms around herself for warmth.

'I've scrambled together what I could find, but the storehouse was flooded and everything was ruined. I don't know what we're going to do. The power's out, and the water pipe gave way on the first day—since then we've been managing with bottled water.'

She sank back in exhaustion.

'I've a couple of canisters of water and some food supplies in my holdall,' Rebecca told her. 'It's only protein bars and chocolate, and some nuts, but it's all high-energy stuff. It should keep everyone going for a while, at least.'

'And more help should be on its way before too long,' Cade put in.

Rebecca sent him a quizzical look. 'How can that be?'

'I have a friend who works with the air rescue service,' he explained. 'I called him from the hospital this afternoon and he said he would take the first opportunity to fly over the area and see if anyone was stranded. He said they were busy with other rescues, so he might not be able to do anything today, but he'll try tomorrow. We need to get something up on to a roof to show him there's a problem—something he'll be able to see in the daylight.'

Her eyes widened. 'So you've been thinking all along that there might be an emergency situation? You were never going to leave things to chance?'

'That's right.'

She frowned. 'You didn't tell me.'

'I wasn't sure I'd be able to reach him, or if he'd be able to help. I would have told you if you'd been at the house when I came home.'

'I'm so glad you managed to get in touch with him.' She smiled at Cade and then said quietly, 'What should we put up on the roof?'

He thought for a moment, and then asked Emma, 'Are there any paint supplies around here? All the houses are painted, so I'm assuming there might be.'

'Yes. In the store room.'

'Good. I'll paint a large SOS on the roof.' He shot Rebecca a quick glance. 'Can I have a word with you? We need to sort out how we're going to organise things.'

She nodded, then turned to Emma. 'Stay here and rest. I'll come back and check you over in a minute—see if we can make you more comfortable. We'll see to everything so you don't need to worry... I'm assuming there are treatment charts for all the patients?'

'Yes, of course.'

Natural light was still coming in through the windows, but Emma closed her eyes as though it was too bright for her.

'My head really hurts,' she said. 'I'm so glad you're here, Becky.'

Rebecca laid a hand on her shoulder. 'So am I. Get some rest. I'll be back before you know it.'

She went with Cade to stand a short distance away.

'I'm afraid your sister is very ill,' he said in a low voice. 'Whatever it is that's wrong with her, she needs treatment right away.'

She nodded. 'I know. I'm really worried about her—*and* about the other patients. We need to get things sorted quickly.'

'Okay. I'll do a medicine round and then see what food we have—if we hear a helicopter I'll go outside and wave my arms or something.'

'Thanks, Cade.'

She laid a hand on his arm in an affectionate gesture, but he stiffened at her touch and she gazed at him, disturbed by his reaction. She'd really hurt him in her rejection of him earlier.

He seemed to brace himself, and she took her hand away from him.

Taking a quick breath to steady herself, she said, 'Thanks for telling your friend about this. When I came out here I didn't know if I should be worried or not—whether I'd be able to handle things by myself. I'm so glad you decided to come after me.'

'I would never have left you to do this on your own. I'd already made up my mind to find out what was going on up here.' He frowned, studying her briefly, taking in her uncertain expression. 'Any time you have a problem I'll help you any way I can. I'll *always* help you—with anything.'

'Thank you,' she said softly.

She wished that could be true. How would he respond if she confided in him? If she told him that her illness had left her damaged, that she couldn't let herself fall in love with him? He wanted children, and that was something she couldn't promise him. She couldn't allow him to get involved with her, because in the end he would discover her deepest imperfection and then he would turn away from her—just as Drew had done.

She didn't think she could bear that. And nor could she cope with having an affair with him—a temporary fling—because already she cared too much for him. It would hurt too badly when it came to an end. Was it already too late? Had she already fallen in love with him? Why did this hurt so much?

'All right,' he said, straightening, ready to move on. 'Let's get on with this. Go to your sister—take my medical kit with you.'

'Thanks, I will.'

Rebecca hurried back to Emma. 'Where have you been sleeping?' she asked. 'I think we should get you to bed.'

'In the back room.' Emma started to get up, swaying a little and leaning on Rebecca for support. 'Oh… I feel really sick. I've been vomiting a lot. I can't seem to keep anything down.'

'I'll help you. Don't worry about it.' She waited with Emma while she was being sick in the bathroom, and then helped her into bed. 'I'll do a quick examination,' she told her.

Emma's hands and feet were cold, she discovered, but it was fairly clear she was running a fever. Things weren't looking good. Rebecca already had a horrible suspicion about what they were dealing with, but she put on a calm, reassuring front as she checked her sister over.

A few minutes later she packed away Cade's stethoscope and blood pressure machine and spoke gently, attempting to explain what she thought was wrong with her.

'Your blood pressure's low and your breathing and heartrate are quite fast,' she said. 'I'm pretty sure you have an infection—a bacterial infection—so I want to get you started on an intravenous antibiotic right away. I'm going to give you dexamethasone at the same time, to prevent any inflammation.'

Emma lay back against her pillows. 'You don't need to wrap it up in cotton wool for me, Becky,' she said, her breath coming in short bursts. 'I'm a nurse. I'm pretty sure I know what's wrong with me… It's meningitis, isn't it?'

Rebecca sighed softly and nodded. 'I think so. We won't know for certain until we get you to hospital and they do some tests, but we can't afford to take any chances. Luckily Cade has the medication we need in his kit, so we can start you on the treatment right away. All you need to do is try to get some sleep. I'll give you something for the headache.'

'Thanks, Becky.' Emma closed her eyes. 'It's so good to have you here…'

Rebecca stayed with her until she was sure she'd done everything she could, and then went in search of Cade.

She found him playing a card game—Snap—with one of the children, a boy of around five years old, who was sitting up in bed, recovering from his illness. They were laughing, because the boy was winning and Cade was pretending to be put out by it.

'We'll play again later,' he told the boy, and stood up, leaving the child's mother to collect the cards and find a storybook to entertain him.

'Okay. I'll win again,' the boy said with a wide smile.

Cade chuckled and came over to Rebecca. His mood immediately became serious. 'How is she?' he asked.

'She's sleeping right now. I've put her on an IV drip and I'm giving her oxygen, but we need to get her to hospital as soon as possible.'

'Meningitis?' he guessed, and she nodded.

'I think so.'

The danger lay in the swelling of the protective membranes around the brain. This was causing Emma's bad headache, and if it became worse she might start having seizures. Then there was the awful worry about blood poisoning. That could cause all kinds of problems. Rebecca didn't even want to think about that.

'How are the other patients?' she asked.

'They're generally not too bad. It's a farming community, so the youngsters were exposed to tick bites from the goats their parents herd. They're being given doxycycline to combat the infection. There are two five-year-old boys who are well on the way to recovery. The little girl is three years old—there's still some swelling on her leg, where she was bitten by a tick, and she's a bit fretful, having nightmares—they're part of the way the illness presents.'

'Really? I've never come across this kind of tick fever before.'

'Well, along with a high temperature and a rash, sufferers get bad headaches and muscle pain. The rash doesn't itch—which is a blessing, I suppose.' He looked over to the beds where the adults slept. 'Those two are suffering from chest infections. They're on oxygen and antibiotic therapy, as well.'

'It sounds as though everything's under control—what about the food situation? Did you manage to put a meal together?'

He pulled a face. 'After a fashion. I'll show you the facilities.' He walked with her towards a small kitchen at the back of the building and pushed open the door. 'There's no electricity, so I've had to make do with very little. I thought we'd better save the protein bars for tomorrow.'

She nodded, glancing around. The room was utilitarian, with a deep sink, a cooker and a fridge—neither of which were working—and a counter for food preparation.

'Let's hope your friend gets here with a rescue team

before too long. Heaven knows what we'll do if we have
to stay here for any length of time.' She gave a shuddery breath, thinking of Emma.

He laid an arm around her shoulders. 'I'm sure we'll
find a way to cope, whatever the situation. You had the
foresight to bring provisions—I brought a medical kit.
We make a good team, you and I, don't you think?'

'Yes, we do.' She pulled herself together. With him
by her side she could move mountains. 'Do you want
me to help you with painting the SOS? Maybe we need
to do more than one?'

'No, I'll do it in a few minutes—before it gets dark.
But first I should get you something to eat. I bet you
haven't had anything since breakfast, have you?'

'Um…no, actually…' She hadn't even thought about
eating until now. Maybe she'd been too stressed. 'I'm
not really hungry—and anyway I need to stay with
Emma.' Anxiety rose up inside her once again. 'I should
get back to her.'

'That's okay. You can do that. I'll bring some food
to you in there…see if I can tempt you with cold leftover rice and tinned peas.'

'Oh—stop…such a gourmet meal—how can I resist?' She gave a broken laugh in spite of her anxieties
and he smiled.

'That's better—we'll get through this together…
you'll see.' He looked into her eyes. They were damp
with unshed tears and he said softly, 'I think you need
a hug…would that be all right?'

She nodded wordlessly and he folded her against
him, kissing her lightly on her forehead. 'We're doing
everything we can for her—for all of them,' he said.
'You're doing fine—you're a great doctor and a good

person to have around in a crisis.' He stroked her back, his hands gliding over her in a tender gesture. 'I can't think what your ex was thinking of, letting you slip away from him. Whatever happened between you must have destroyed your faith in men.'

'It wasn't Drew's fault—not really,' she said huskily. 'Things just didn't work out for us. He's a decent man, but things went wrong. I was ill—appendicitis—and there were complications. I ended up in intensive care for a while.' She sighed. 'He didn't handle my illness very well. I think I realised then that he wasn't the right man for me, but perhaps there were signs before that…we were opposites in quite a few ways. He could be quick-tempered and impatient, whereas I tend to be a bit more laid-back. With hindsight, I think we would have gone our separate ways before too long anyway.'

'I'm sorry. It sounds as though you cared for him very much and that finishing with him has had a bad effect on you. But it would be a pity if you're going to let it put you off all relationships.'

'Maybe.' She straightened. Talking about Drew was bringing back memories of things she would far sooner forget. 'I think I should go to Emma.'

'Yes. All right.' He let her go, easing his long body away from her. 'I'll fix some food for you and then see to the SOS. Don't worry about the patients. I'll look after them.'

'Okay.'

She stayed with Emma through the night, and by morning was thankful that her condition didn't seem to have worsened too much. She was sleeping a lot, and complaining still of a bad headache, but at least the vomiting had stopped. As ill as she was, she'd even managed to let Rebecca know how concerned she was to find out how her patients were getting on.

'I'm going to look in on them now,' Rebecca told her. 'I'll be back in a few minutes.'

When she went into the main room she saw that Cade was sitting with the three-year-old, wrapping a blood pressure cuff around her teddy bear's arm. The child watched him, utterly absorbed in what he was doing.

'Well, I think Teddy might be feeling a bit better this morning,' he said. 'I'm wondering if he might even like to try a cookie?'

The infant nodded cautiously. 'I'll give it to him… can I?'

'Yes, all right…if you want to… But you might have to show him how to nibble at it. What do you think?'

'Yep. I can do that.'

'Okay, then.' He handed her a plate with several cookies. 'Maybe he can eat the whole lot?'

She screwed up her nose. 'Nah.'

'Oh. Well, perhaps you'll have to help him, then?'

She nodded, picking up a biscuit and putting it to her teddy's mouth. Then she took a small bite for herself, tasting the honey and oats and deciding she liked them. Cade smiled, and Rebecca felt a lump form in her throat. He was so good with the little girl, just as he had been with the boy the day before. He would make a wonderful father.

Satisfied that the child was eating, Cade stood up and came over to Rebecca, leaving the infant with her mother to watch over her.

'She hasn't been wanting to eat up to now,' he said, 'but I think from the looks of things she might be feeling a bit better today.'

'That's good news. You were brilliant with her, from what I could see.'

She looked around the room. The two boys were in bed, eating protein bars and doing what looked like simple crossword puzzles set out on sheets of paper.

'I thought they would keep them amused,' Cade said. 'I used to make up crosswords for William when he was little. The five-year-old can read, so he can manage simple words, and the seven-year-old is doing well with slightly harder ones. They were getting bored, but they're not strong enough to be up and about yet. Doing that and colouring pictures seemed like the best option for now.'

'You're full of surprises,' she murmured, helping herself to a few nuts and a protein bar from the selection of food he'd laid out on a table. He was a natural with the children, and they clearly liked him.

'How's Emma doing?' Cade asked.

Her mouth flattened. 'Much the same, I think. I'm worried that there's still a lot of inflammation around her brain. She's a bit confused, which would suggest things haven't improved, but at least the antibiotic seems to be keeping sepsis at bay.'

'That's something to be thankful for.' He poured some water into a glass and sipped slowly. 'We need to get everyone ready for evacuation. If the rescue helicopter arrives we should have things all packed up and set to go.'

'Yes, I've been thinking about that. I've made a start with the medication. Each adult patient should take his own treatment chart, drugs and any equipment like IV lines with him. If there's any problem—like limited numbers of passengers—then the most seriously ill should go first. My sister, the man with pneumonia, and the little girl.'

He nodded. 'With any luck the rescue team will be here some time this morning. I've marked out a landing pad for them, where I thought it would be safest. We'll have to stretcher people over there.'

There was still no phone signal, so they had no means of knowing what to expect, but a couple of hours later they heard the heartening drone of an aircraft overhead.

The helicopter landed shortly after that. Relieved, they hurried to greet the crew.

'How many people do we have?' Cade's friend asked.

'Three children,' Cade said, 'and three adults—all of them sick—and four parents. That's ten people, plus Rebecca. She needs to go with her sister to make sure she's okay on the journey. Can you carry that many?'

'Three little ones and eight adults? Yes, we should be able to manage that.' The man frowned. 'What about yourself?'

'I need to go back down the road to get my car. I'll join you at the hospital later.' He turned to Rebecca. 'I'll send someone to pick up the other car and take it back to the house.'

'Okay. Thanks.' She was anxious to get Emma on to the helicopter, but at the same time worried about Cade making the journey back alone. 'What if there have been more landslides? What will you do?'

He shrugged. 'I'll deal with that as it comes. You can load my medical kit on to the helicopter—you might need it, and it'll make the going quicker for me.' He made a crooked smile. 'If I don't turn up at the hospital in, say, a couple of hours, you can send William to find me with a search team.'

'I'll do that,' she said. 'You're making a joke of it, but I mean it. I didn't like the look of those rock falls on the way here.'

'Go,' he said firmly. 'Don't waste time… You need to get out of here.'

Together they supervised the transfer of all the patients on to the helicopter. Rebecca made sure Emma was secure for the flight, and then sat by her for their journey to the hospital. She was worried about her. Her sister was becoming very sleepy, and showing signs of delirium, and soon after that she deteriorated badly and started to have a seizure.

Alarmed, Rebecca quickly searched in Cade's pack for medication to control the fitting. Any seizures might increase the pressure on Emma's brain and cause her to become even more desperately ill. She had to do everything she could to stabilise her condition fast.

The pilot radioed ahead, so that when they landed on the helipad at the hospital medical teams were waiting to take care of the patients. Emma was whisked away to a treatment room where doctors took over the responsibility for her, doing everything they could to save her life. Rebecca had to stand by helplessly, watching and waiting.

Cade's friend James was the consultant in charge of her care, and he came to see Rebecca around an hour later. 'We've given her drugs to try to stop the swelling on her brain and prevent any more seizures,' he told her. 'It'll be some time before we know if the treatment's going to work. We've done tests, and now it's up to the lab to tell us if there's any other antibiotic we can use that will combat the infection more effectively.'

'Thanks, James. I know you're doing everything you possibly can.'

He nodded. 'Why don't you go to Cade's office and get a coffee? There's nothing you can do hanging around here. I'll tell Cade to come and find you when he arrives.'

'Okay.'

She went to Cade's office and phoned William to keep him up to date with what was happening before switching on the coffee machine. He was immediately concerned, both for Emma and for his cousin. 'Is he not back yet?'

'Not yet, no.'

The hot brew was reviving. She sat down on the couch and finished her drink, and then leaned her head back against the cushioned upholstery. Last night she'd watched over Emma and had hardly any sleep. She was so tired...

There was a knock on the door and then William walked into the room. 'Rebecca?' He came over to her. 'I had to come as soon as I heard. You must be worried sick.'

'Yes. There's been no more news. It could be several days before we know if she's going to be all right.'

He sat down beside her and wrapped his arms around her. 'I'm so sorry,' he said. 'I went to see her and she looks so pale...so still. I can't believe this has happened to her.'

'I know. It's a shock. But they're doing all they can.' She glanced at him. 'This must be a difficult time for you—I know you like her—and you must be so worried about your father, too. He's at this hospital, isn't he?'

'Yes, I've just come from seeing him. At least he's

responding to the new medication, so we're very relieved about that.'

'I'm really pleased for you.'

He nodded. 'Emma will pull through, Becky. She's young and strong—so full of life. You and Cade were there for her, and she has every chance. She *has* to get better.'

'I hope so. I hope she's strong enough to fight it…'

Tears trickled down her cheeks and William drew her close, comforting her. She laid her head wearily against his shoulder.

Cade found them like that a few minutes later. He walked into the room and ran his glance over them in a shocked, steely, hard look that told Rebecca he'd completely misconstrued the situation.

'William.' He looked at his cousin, clearly trying to keep himself under control. 'You obviously came here as soon as you heard?'

'Yes.' William nodded. 'Becky rang me and told me what was happening. I was worried sick.'

'Of course. You two are becoming very close to one another, aren't you? You were bound to be anxious.'

Rebecca frowned, gently disentangling herself from William, and sat up, her spine rigid. 'He was worried about you, too—but you've made it back all right. I'm so glad that you're safe.'

'I'm okay. Actually, I rushed over here because I didn't want you to be on your own at a time like this… but I see I needn't have worried.' His eyes darkened as he surveyed them once more, but he kept his thoughts to himself, going over to the coffee machine.

'Becky's upset about Emma being so ill,' William

said. 'I wanted to come and give her some support. I've been to see Emma…she looks very sick.'

Cade nodded. 'James tells me there's no change in her condition. We just have to wait it out.' He glanced at Rebecca. 'It's probably good news that there's been no change. It means she's stable for now.'

'Yes.' Rebecca watched him, taking in the tense lines of his body. He obviously didn't like the fact that William had been holding her—perhaps he thought that she and his cousin might get together at some point, become more serious in their relationship? He clearly didn't believe they were just friends, but this surely wasn't the time to get into a discussion about it? She was too upset about the events of the last few hours.

Emma was her priority right now—she would talk to Cade privately later. She just hoped he would listen to her.

CHAPTER SEVEN

'EMMA LOOKS A little better today, don't you think?' Rebecca glanced at Cade for confirmation and he nodded.

They'd just left the isolation room where her sister was being treated and were heading for the car park. A week had passed since Emma had been admitted to hospital, and for most of that time she had been in intensive care, sedated, and hooked up to monitors that checked her vital signs. It had been a worrying, nerve-racking time.

'She does. I think the new antibiotic must be working. James will perhaps be able to lessen the sedation soon, now that the inflammation around her brain is subsiding.'

The lab had identified the specific bacteria that were causing the problem, and for the last few days James had been able to combat the infection with a more suitable medication.

'William will be pleased,' she said. 'He's been coming with me to see her whenever he has the chance—he said he was going to see his father anyway, and felt I could do with the support.'

Cade frowned, but nodded. 'My uncle's doing well now—that's been a huge relief all round. Obviously

William's still worried about him—and about Emma, too—so this news will buoy him up a bit.'

'Yes, I wanted to tell him but I couldn't get through on the phone just now.' She frowned. 'Last time I saw him he said he was going to be extra-busy this next week, because you have him overseeing the building work at the plantation.'

'That's right. I want him to make sure the carpenters stick to the drawings.'

'Is it really so important for him to keep an eye on the tradesmen the whole time? William said they all seem very good at what they do.' She studied Cade thoughtfully for a moment or two. 'I can't help thinking you're giving him this work so that he doesn't have time to be with me.'

'Do you blame me? You know how I feel about you, Rebecca…and yet you and William are so close at times.' His jaw clenched. 'You were in his arms that day at the hospital—how do you think that made me feel? It was gut-wrenching.'

'I'm sorry you felt that way.' She touched his arm lightly, in a soothing, coaxing embrace. 'William's just a friend, that's all. He was trying to comfort me.'

'Oh, yes? Is that so?' His eyes were dark with disbelief. 'I don't think William sees it that way.' His mouth made a flat line. 'I've always looked out for him— heaven knows, I want him to be happy—but I can't see him with you without wanting to break things up.'

'There's nothing going on between William and me.'

He gave her a sceptical look. 'Perhaps he just hasn't made his feelings clear to you yet. It's obvious to me that he cares about you. I saw for myself the way you two hooked up on the boat over here, and you've been to the beach together, as well as meeting up at other times and talking on the phone.'

Annoyed, she flashed him a quick dismissive glance. 'This argument is getting us nowhere,' she said tightly. 'I told you. We're just friends. I like him…he makes me laugh—and he's been good to me.'

'I don't think young men and women can have platonic relationships,' he said.

'Really? Well, that's your problem. You'll just have to deal with it the best way you can.'

He grimaced, walking with her through the main doors of the hospital. 'All right. I'll accept that you perhaps can't see what's going on with William… But I know I'm right. He has feelings for you…and I think you are more than fond of him.'

She sucked in a harsh, annoyed breath and he shot her a quick look as they crossed the car park.

'Look, perhaps we should call a truce?' he suggested. 'You've been under a huge strain this past few weeks, with everything that's happened and now your sister being ill. It would be good for you to be able to relax a bit and get some of that Caribbean holiday you came out here to enjoy. Perhaps you'd like to take some time out to have lunch with me?'

She thought about it. 'I'd like that,' she said. 'And a truce sounds good.'

He took her to a delightful restaurant a few miles along the coast. It was built on clean lines—a white stone building with wide terraces, set into the tree-covered hillside overlooking the rugged seashore.

A waiter showed them to a table in the loggia, which was decorated with tubs of glorious flame-coloured hibiscus. Rebecca sat down and looked around, immedi-

ately absorbed by the breathtaking view of the glittering
blue sea. There were yachts in the harbour below, bob-
bing gently on the water, and in the distance she could
see white-painted houses with ochre-tiled roofs dotted
about the hillside.

'I've spoken to the landlord about the repairs to the
cabin,' she said, when the waiter had brought their first
course to the table. She dipped her fork into a golden
pastry basket and speared a tasty scallop, drizzled with
a delicious Chardonnay bisque sauce. 'He says he can't
get anyone out to fix the roof yet because all the tradesmen are in demand after the storm. It'll be a few more
days at least—I hope you don't mind me staying at the
plantation for this length of time?'

He raised dark brows. 'Of course I don't mind. You
can stay as long as you like.' He smiled. 'I like having
you around.'

She relaxed back in her seat, relieved. 'That's good. I
don't want you to feel that I'm taking things for granted.'

'I think you worry too much,' he said. 'You were
supposed to be here for a holiday, and so far you've had
precious little chance to enjoy it. If I can make life easier for you in any way I will. I could take you out and
about, if you want, show you the island?'

'That would be lovely,' she murmured. 'I just need to
be sure that Emma's well and truly on the mend. Maybe
then I could go out with you?'

'I'll keep you to that,' he said, his mouth curving.

They finished off their starters and the main course
arrived—braised lamb with risotto and roast vegetables
served with a Merlot and shallot gravy.

'The food here is wonderful,' Rebecca said. 'Have
you been to this restaurant before?'

He nodded. 'A few times. I've entertained suppliers here, and people who've helped me get the plantation on its feet or helped me with work on the house.'

She was relieved he hadn't mentioned bringing any other woman here. Just thinking about it made her stomach tighten.

They talked about the food, and then about the plantation and his workers. Agwe was on the mend, he said. 'He's been fortunate—the illness hasn't done any permanent damage to his kidneys. And Thomas's hand is healing up nicely.'

'I'm pleased for both of them. They're lucky to have an employer who looks after them and takes their welfare so seriously.'

They finished off their meal with a fruit dessert, followed by cups of richly flavoured Columbian coffee accompanied by thin dark chocolate wafers.

'I'm so full,' Rebecca said, rubbing her stomach. 'I haven't eaten such a great meal for ages. That was perfect.'

He paid the bill and they left the restaurant, walking at his suggestion through the botanical gardens that covered the hillside. They passed along a trail where avocados and apricot trees grew in abundance, alongside hanging bird-of-paradise flowers and flamboyant heliconia that attracted the attention of tiny hummingbirds searching for nectar.

It was incredibly peaceful out here, and in the tropical heat of the late afternoon they stood for a while on a small wooden bridge over a large lily pond and watched the parrots flit among the trees. Cade put his arm around her and pointed to where bright pink flamingos paraded at the side of the pool. One female was feeding its youngster—a small bird that was pure white.

'Oh, aren't they beautiful?' she exclaimed softly. 'The chicks are adorable.'

He laughed softly. 'So are you,' he said, hugging her close and dropping a kiss on her startled lips. 'It's great to see you looking happy.'

She looked up at him in wonder, still dazed by the unexpected gentleness of that kiss. Her lips tingled with excitement and her heart leapt, her pulses racing in anticipation that he might do it again. Slowly, bending his head towards her, he obliged, brushing her mouth with his, sending a trail of fire to course through every part of her body.

She wanted more—wanted to have him holding her and running his hands over her, tugging her to him. And even as the thoughts entered her head, he satisfied her inner yearning, tenderly shaping her body with his palms.

She kissed him hungrily, lifting her arms and running her fingers over the corded muscles of his shoulders. 'You've been so good to me...' she whispered. 'Taking care of me, offering me a place to stay... I've never met anyone who's been so generous, so thoughtful.'

'I think the world of you,' he said. 'In fact... I think I've fallen in love with you. I've never felt this way before, nor met anyone quite like you, and ever since I first met you I've never stopped wanting you.' His voice was husky, ragged. 'If you knew how you make me feel you would take me into your heart and trust me. I would never hurt you—you need to know that.'

It was what she wanted to hear more than anything.

She lifted a hand to his face, stroking his cheek, running her fingers lightly along his hard jawline. 'I wish I could be sure of that,' she said quietly. 'I wish I knew how to make things turn out the way I want. I can't. But I do wish things were different.'

He frowned, and she suddenly realised he might have misinterpreted her words.

'You mean you're still not sure about whether you want to keep your options open? If you're only with me because you're grateful for the way I've looked after you—'

'No, it isn't like that—' she interrupted, but she didn't have the chance to talk to him about it any more because suddenly, alerted by footsteps in the distance and chattering voices, they realised that they were no longer alone.

They moved apart as other visitors to the gardens approached, coming out from the arbour and moving towards the pond.

Wordlessly Rebecca and Cade walked to the other side of the bridge and followed a path through the lush undergrowth on the route back to the car park.

When they were alone once again he drew in a deep breath and said, 'I can't help the way I feel about you, Rebecca. I was lost the moment I first saw you.'

'But—'

He put a finger to her lips, stopping the flow of words. 'There's a barbecue on the beach in a few days' time. I thought you might like to go with me?'

'Yes, that sounds good.' She smiled at him tentatively.

There was little point in arguing with him, in pointing out where his thinking was flawed. And she *wanted* to be with him. Her efforts to keep him at bay all this time had been for nothing, because she had well and truly fallen for him. She had to admit it to herself. He was everything she wanted in a man, but she wasn't sure how it had happened that she'd come to love him.

How could it ever be right for her to be with him—knowing that she might never be able to give him the family he wanted? She wasn't being fair to him, letting this go on, and yet she couldn't bear *not* to be with him.

She had to find a way to sort things out, to come to terms with the kind of future she might have. Was it possible for her ever to be with Cade?

Over the next few days Emma gradually gained strength and was able to sit up in bed. Before too long she was even able to chat without getting too tired.

'You're looking so much better,' Rebecca told her. 'I'm so glad you're on the mend.'

'It's you I have to thank for that,' Emma said, leaning back against her pillows.

'Hmm… I think there's more to it than that,' Rebecca murmured.

She looked at the bedside table, bright with colourful flowers and cards from well-wishers. There was one, she noticed, from William—an especially beautiful embossed card, inscribed with affectionate sentiment.

She looked closely at Emma. Her sister's long chestnut hair had regained some of its sheen and her blue-grey eyes were bright. 'Could that sparkle in your eyes be due to the fact that you've had a handsome young man visiting you every day while you've been here?'

Emma blushed. 'You noticed? It's true—William's been coming to see me every chance he gets. He brings me fruit and flowers, and he's doing everything he can to cheer me up.' She glanced at the bedside locker. 'He brought me those beautiful roses, and there's a note with them that says he's thinking of me always.'

'Well, well…isn't *that* a lovely turn of events? How do you feel about him?'

Emma's cheeks reddened even further. 'I really like him, Becky. He has such a good sense of humour, and we have so much in common. I think we clicked the first time we met.' She studied Rebecca thoughtfully. 'You feel the same way about his cousin, don't you? I've seen the signs, and I'm pretty sure you're in love with Cade?'

'What makes you think that?'

'I saw the way you looked at him when he came to the cabin—*and* when we were at Selwyn's Bar. You were laughing and joking with William, but it was Cade you were watching when you thought no one was looking. And I've seen it when you've both been here to visit me.' Her mouth made a crooked shape. 'To be honest, I don't think men can see beyond their noses.'

Rebecca sighed. That was true enough. Cade wouldn't listen when she told him she and William were just good friends.

'I don't know what to do, Emma. Yes, it's true—I do love Cade. And I know he feels the same way about me. But there's no future for us, is there? How can I be with him if I can't have children? He says he wants a family, and I can't deny him that. I don't know what to do.'

'There's one thing you can do.' Emma reached for her sister's hand. 'Go for treatment…have surgery to try to open your fallopian tubes.'

Rebecca frowned. 'But the doctors back home weren't keen on that—they said it's not done very often.

They told me my best prospect would be to try in vitro fertilisation in the future—and that will depend on my ovaries being unaffected by the scar tissue...which they aren't. Besides, IVF isn't always successful. You hear of people having several courses without a good result.'

'That's a negative way of thinking. You're better than that, Becky. You were always a positive person until this happened to you. If you're worried about IVF you should go and make an appointment at a clinic—talk to someone about having specialised surgery to open up your fallopian tubes and remove any scar tissue that's causing a problem. What's the point of waiting? Not knowing if there is anything you can do about it is making you put your life on hold.'

'I suppose you're right.' Rebecca tried to think things through. 'I'll think about it. It's such a big step, though.' She closed her eyes briefly. 'I think I've been putting it off in case it doesn't work.'

'Don't just think about it. Do it. At least then you'll know definitely, won't you? And then you'll be in a position to make proper decisions about your future. At the moment you're in limbo.' Emma squeezed her hand. 'Don't waste any more time, Becky. In fact—pass me my handbag from the bedside locker, will you? I did some research when I knew you were coming over to stay for a while. There's a clinic on one of the islands that would be just right for you. I checked into them and they're really good, by all accounts. The surgeons there are really skilled.'

Rebecca did as she asked and Emma fetched a card out of her bag.

'Here. Give them a ring,' she said. 'Do it today. They told me they should be able to fit you in at short notice if you're a private patient.' She frowned. 'And for goodness' sake talk to Cade.'

Rebecca shook her head. 'I can't do it now—not while you're still in hospital. What if they can do it straight away? I would be so worried about you. I'll ring them in a few weeks…when you're up and about.'

'No, no… There's no time like the present. I want you to do it now… I'm feeling so much better. I'm not in danger any more, and with any luck by the time I'm out of here you'll be back from the clinic, so we can spend some time together at the cabin. You might only need an overnight stay in hospital. Rebecca—call them and make an appointment.' She smiled. 'William will be here to keep me company when he's not at the plantation. You don't need to worry about me.'

'I can't. Not now. I need to be here with *you*.'

'Those are just excuses.' Emma pursed her lips determinedly. 'I'll do it for you.' She started to reach for her phone.

'No, don't do that.'

Rebecca looked at the card once more. The clinic was situated on an island nearby—just a ferry ride away. She *could* do it, couldn't she? At least then she would know if things were ever going to be all right for her, wouldn't she?

'Okay,' she sighed. 'I'll do it. I'll give them a call.'

'Good. Put it on speaker phone so I can hear what they say.'

Rebecca dialled the number on the card.

'You're in luck,' the receptionist at the clinic said, when Rebecca had introduced herself and explained the situation. 'We've had a couple of cancellations—one patient has a family crisis to deal with and another has decided to try an alternative treatment—so Mr Solomon has some free time. I can book you in to see him tomorrow, if you like? That will be an initial appointment, and he'll arrange any other details with you when you see him.'

Rebecca shook her head. That was far too soon. 'I wasn't expecting to be seen so quickly,' she said. 'I'm not sure—'

'She'll do it,' Emma said, cutting in on the conversation. 'Make the appointment, please.'

'Madam?'

'Sorry, that's my sister…adding her two pennyworth.' Rebecca took a deep breath. 'Okay, then. Thank you. I'll come in tomorrow. We'll take it from there.'

She cut the call a couple of minutes later and sat quietly for a bit longer, getting over the enormity of what she was doing. She had to think of practicalities. There would be a ferry later today. If she hurried she could throw a few things into her holdall and be on her way. Once she arrived on the island she could think about booking a hotel room near to the clinic.

'I came over to the Caribbean to see you and to ask your advice,' she said, looking at Emma. 'I knew you'd know what I should do.' She gave Emma a hug. 'You're my best big sister,' she said. 'I love you to bits.' Glancing at her once again, she added, 'And now look what I've done—I've tired you out with all this talking. I'm sorry.'

'I'll be fine.' Emma smiled. 'I'm feeling so much better now…and I'm getting up and walking about a bit every day… But they say they want to keep me in for several more days to be certain everything's all right.' She sent her a meaningful look. 'Time enough for you to have the surgery,' she said. 'You can call me from the clinic.'

They talked for a minute or two longer and then Rebecca stood up to leave. 'I'll go and see if I can find Cade,' she said.

She found him in the main area of the Emergency Unit, talking with a man and woman who were standing by the main desk. He had his back to her, but she went up to him and laid a hand lightly on his arm.

'Hi, I've just been up to Emma's room and I thought I'd come down here to see you, if you're not too busy.'

'I'm never to busy to see you,' he said, turning to face her.

He was smiling, obviously in a good mood, and she suddenly recognised the couple with him.

'It's Mr and Mrs Tennyson, isn't it?' she said, her eyes widening.

'That's right. We wanted to come in and thank everyone for looking after us so well…and especially to thank Dr Byfield for saving Annie.'

They both looked well—much better than when she'd seen them last, when Jane Tennyson had been suffering with broken ribs after the car accident and her husband Paul had been concussed from his head injury.

'You seem to be recovering well,' Cade said.

'Oh, yes, we're on the mend,' Jane said happily. 'My ribs are healing, and Paul is just fine. And as for little Annie—she's doing brilliantly.'

'I'm so pleased she's recovered.' Rebecca looked around. 'Where is she? Is she not with you today?'

'Oh, she's here.' Jane smiled broadly. 'The nurses were so happy to see her they whisked her away to show her off to everyone. Here she is now.'

Greta was carrying Annie back to them. The little girl looked the picture of health, and she put her arms out to Cade to be picked up. She moved her fingers impatiently, wanting his attention.

Paul Tennyson chuckled. 'Oh, she can't get enough of you. You're her favourite person today.'

Cade smiled and took Annie into his arms, giving her a cuddle. 'You're a real cherub, aren't you?' he said. He tickled the little girl's tummy and she giggled.

Watching them, Rebecca felt her heart contract with pain. She longed to hold the infant herself, but didn't trust herself not to break down. She wouldn't want to give her back.

'She's gorgeous,' she said, trying to keep a firm lid on her emotions.

Cade was jiggling the little girl gently up and down and she was laughing, loving the sensation and wanting more.

'Again!' Annie squealed with delight. 'Again.'

'Enough, sweetheart,' Cade said after a minute or two. 'Your mum wants to hold you.' He handed her to her mother and the trio said their goodbyes and went on their way.

He turned to Rebecca. 'We'll go into my office. We're having a quiet time in Emergency just now.' As he led the way he said, 'It was great seeing them now that they're more or less back to normal, wasn't it?'

She nodded, trying to get a grip on herself. He sent her an odd look. 'What is it, Rebecca?' He opened the door to his office and ushered her inside. 'Has something happened? Is there something you want to talk to me about?'

'I... Yes...' She took a deep breath.

She'd wanted to talk to him about them maybe having a future together, but seeing him with the infant had thrown her into a quandary. What if her treatment was unsuccessful? How could she put him though that?

'I've decided to go away for a few days,' she said finally. 'I'm going over to Barbados for a short break.'

His dark brows drew together. 'When are you going? I could perhaps get some time off and go with you.'

'No… I'm going today. I've made up my mind… It was a spur-of-the-moment decision and I'm getting the ferry later this afternoon.'

'I don't understand.' He looked bewildered. 'Why would you leave when your sister's still in the hospital?'

'She's…she's feeling much better now… She thinks I don't need to worry about her…and she'll have William to keep her company.'

His frown deepened. 'Wait a minute… That's what this is about, isn't it? It's about William. Is he with Emma? I had hoped you were over him—that you might—'

'I've *never* had any romantic feelings for William,' she said, cutting Cade off unexpectedly. 'I told you, I like him as a friend. It's you I want… I love *you*…'

He drew in a sharp breath and she went on hurriedly.

'I didn't mean for it to happen, and I tried to stop it, but it just… It's impossible—I can't love you, Cade. It would be wrong for us. It wouldn't work out.'

'But *why* wouldn't it?' He was bewildered. 'We're so good together, Rebecca. And now that you've told me that you love me, too, what's to stop us?' He drew her to him, kissing her fiercely, as though he couldn't bear to let her go. 'We'd be perfect together.' He murmured the words against her mouth. 'I love you.'

The kiss was her undoing. Her lips softened under the tender onslaught and her whole body quivered as he ran his hands over her, shaping her to him. 'I know your ex let you down,' he said in a roughened voice, 'but don't let him come between us. I love you...you say you love me...what could possibly be wrong?'

An alarm bell started to ring in the Emergency Unit and a nurse's voice came over the speaker system to say that a patient was being brought in by ambulance. Cade stiffened, but didn't let her go.

Rebecca laid a shaky hand on his chest. 'Cade, the truth is you've told me you want a family and I don't think I can give you that. I told you I was ill, and there's a lot of scar tissue...adhesions. My doctors have said they don't think I'll be able to conceive. I don't want to put you through that. It wouldn't be fair to deny you something you've always dreamed of.'

He was staring down at her, a shocked look on his face. 'You can't have children? That's a *terrible* diagnosis. Why on earth didn't you tell me this before?'

Before he'd fallen in love with her?

'I don't know—I'm not sure. It was painful for me and I couldn't face up to it. The time never seemed right. I was too busy trying to stop myself from falling for you.'

'Was that because of how your ex reacted?'

She nodded. 'After I told Drew what the doctors had said he went away for a while to think things through. Then he told me he'd thought long and hard about it but he couldn't stay with me if there was the possibility of my not having children.' Her face crumpled. 'I couldn't bear to have you say that to me. I'm sorry.'

A muscle flicked in his jaw. 'We need to talk about

this,' he said. 'It's such a shock…coming out of the blue like this. I'd no idea.' He frowned. 'Look, I have to go and deal with this emergency, but we have to talk some more.' He stared at her, his eyes smoke-dark, flickering with a troubled mixture of pain and anger. 'You should have told me, Rebecca.'

'I know. I'm sorry.'

He left her, reluctantly, to go and deal with the patient who was being brought in, and Rebecca made her way out of the hospital, went back to the plantation.

Once there, she quickly packed a bag and called for a taxi. She wasn't going to use Cade's car any more. It wouldn't be right. She would have to send for the rest of her things at a later date.

Things were surely over between them. He'd been utterly shocked and dismayed by her revelation, and all the talking in the world wouldn't make things come right. He deserved better. He deserved to find happiness with a woman who could give him the family he wanted. This was her burden to bear. It didn't have to be his.

She hurried out of the house as the taxi driver pulled up outside. 'Where to, miss?' he asked.

'The ferry port,' she said.

She looked back at the house as they drove away and inside she felt as though her heart was breaking.

CHAPTER EIGHT

REBECCA OPENED HER eyes and looked around the unfamiliar room. For a moment or two she was disorientated and couldn't remember where she was, but then a nurse approached the bedside and smiled.

'Oh, you're back with us! You came round from surgery and then went to sleep for a couple of hours. How are you feeling?'

'I'm okay…I think.'

'Good. It'll take some time for the effects of the anaesthetic to wear off, but you don't need to do anything. Just rest for a while. I'll take your blood pressure.' The nurse wrapped the cuff around Rebecca's upper arm and checked the monitor. 'It's a little low,' she said after a moment or two, 'but that's to be expected after surgery.'

'Do you know anything about how the surgery went?' Still a little groggy, Rebecca struggled to sit up in bed. She was a bit sore from the procedure she'd undergone, and there was a dressing on her tummy where the surgeon had stitched up a small incision.

'Dr Solomon will be in to explain things to you in a little while,' the nurse said. 'You were so fortunate to have him as your surgeon—he's a brilliant man—very skilled at doing tubal surgery.'

'So I've been told.' Perhaps it was the after-effects of the general anaesthetic, but Rebecca was feeling overwhelmed, and above all isolated and lonely. She was on her own in this—but then she'd known that from the beginning, hadn't she?

She tried to put a brave face on things, but the nurse must have guessed how she was feeling, because she said, 'How about a cup of tea? That should help to cheer you up.'

'Thanks. That would be lovely.'

'Oh, and you have a visitor… Are you up to seeing anyone yet?'

'A visitor?' Rebecca echoed.

Who could that be? No one knew she was here except for Emma. She'd phoned her sister yesterday, to tell her that the surgery was being done on a daypatient basis—the doctor had found an operating theatre slot for the day after her first appointment. He'd said that if all was well she would be able to leave hospital about four hours after the procedure.

'Oh, yes. He said he came over on the ferry this morning. Looks like a dark thundercloud, but gorgeous with it. He's been here since you went to theatre, pacing up and down, wearing a hole in the waiting room floor. Mind you…' The nurse grinned. 'He could come and pace *my* floor any time!'

'Cade's here? Dr Byfield?'

'That's the one. That'll be two cups of tea, then, will it?'

Rebecca nodded, still trying to take it in. What was he doing here? How had he known where to find her?

The nurse left the room and a moment later Cade came through the door. He stood by the doorjamb, studying her, not saying a word, his face taut, his expression one of controlled anger.

She swallowed apprehensively. 'I wasn't expecting to see you,' she said in a quiet voice. 'Come in and sit by the bed. How did you know where to find me?'

He strode towards the bed, but ignored her offer of a seat. 'I asked Emma where you'd be. She was surprised you hadn't told me. So was I. I thought we were going to talk. Yet you took off without another word.'

'Okay. Okay, I'm sorry.' She looked at him doubtfully. 'We can talk now, if you want.'

'It's a bit late, isn't it…? A bit overdue? I can't imagine why you would leave like that, without saying anything or telling me where you were going. What were you *thinking*?'

She frowned. 'I don't know, exactly. What's the point in talking if I might not be able to have children? I may have to get used to the idea, but you don't.'

'So you walked out on me? You decided I didn't need to know what was going on—that I wouldn't want any part of it?' His jaw was clenched, his mouth a flat, harsh line. 'I told you I would help you any way I can—that I would always be there for you. Did you think they were just meaningless words?'

She gave a half-hearted shrug. 'People say all sorts of things on the spur of the moment, when nothing much is at stake. Drew promised he'd love me for ever, but that fizzled out a very short time after I became ill.'

'I'm not Drew. It's high time you stopped comparing me to him.'

'But you made it very clear to me that you want children—that you want a large family to make up for what you missed out on in the past. I couldn't be certain of giving you that—what was I supposed to think or do?'

'You should have talked it through with me. Yes, I want a family—but I've fallen in love with you, Rebecca... How can I ignore that? Do you *really* think I'm the kind of man who will reject you because you can't give me everything I want? Do you *really* think I'm that selfish?'

Her shoulders lifted. 'I don't know what to think. Are you going to sit down or not? Did you just come here to quarrel with me?' she queried grumpily. 'Because I can pick a fight with myself—I don't need you to do it for me.'

He laughed—a short, sharp sound that cracked on the air. 'No, I'm sorry.' Finally he pulled up a chair and sat down beside her. 'I came to see how you are...and to make you see that I'm nothing like your ex. I *will* be here for you, Rebecca, no matter what happens.'

She swallowed against the lump that had suddenly formed in her throat. A sheen of tears misted her eyes. 'I never expected that,' she said in a muffled voice. 'I'm so glad you're here, Cade.'

She put out a hand to him and he grasped it reassuringly, enclosing her palm in his long fingers, resting their entwined hands on the bedcovers.

'So how did the surgery go?' he asked.

'I don't know,' she admitted. 'They haven't told me yet. The surgeon will be in later to see me.'

The nurse came in with a tea tray and set it down on the bedside table. 'There you are. Help yourselves. Mr Solomon will be here soon. He's just talking to another patient.'

'Thanks.'

'You're welcome.' She glanced at the monitor. 'Your heartrate's gone up in the last few minutes.' She waggled an admonishing finger. 'Not good.' Then she glanced at Cade and sighed. 'But hardly surprising, really.' She sniffed and left the room.

Rebecca laughed, and then held on to her tummy, where the stitches were under pressure. 'She thinks you're gorgeous,' she said.

He raised a dark brow. 'Oh? And what do *you* think?'

'I think you're pretty wonderful, all told. I just don't want you to get swell-headed about it.'

'There's not much likelihood of that. I don't have time to be swayed by what people think. I'm a very practical kind of man. I like to know where I stand, make plans and see them through.'

'That can be difficult. Things don't always go to plan.'

'That's true.'

There was a knock on the door and Mr Solomon walked into the room. He was a tall man, dressed in an immaculate dark suit.

'Hello,' he said, smiling. 'It's good to see you sitting up and with a bit more colour in your cheeks. Is it all right if I come in and talk to you about the results of your surgery?'

'Yes, please. Come in. Sit down.'

Cade glanced at her. 'Would you prefer it if I leave? I can wait outside.'

She shook her head. 'No, it's all right. I'd like you to stay.'

Mr Solomon sat down. His expression became serious and Rebecca immediately sensed trouble. She watched him, her shoulders stiff, trying to prepare herself for what was to come. It didn't look good.

'You'll recall we talked about the tests we did yesterday?' he said, and she nodded. 'There were a lot of adhesions around your ovaries and both fallopian tubes, and the hysterosalpingogram showed us that the tubes weren't viable in that state.'

'Yes…' It was almost a whisper.

'As we discussed, with that much scarring it's not always easy to remedy the situation, but we went ahead and did as much as we could.'

'And the result?'

'The good news is that one of your ovaries is now completely clear…'

She sighed with relief. It meant that IVF might be an option at least.

'Also, one of your fallopian tubes was blocked at the uterine end, which was good as far as we were concerned, because it was easier to clear. So, it means that with one fallopian tube and a functional ovary your chances of conceiving a baby are much better than they were before you came to see us.' He frowned. 'There is a possibility, though, that the surgery in itself might cause more scarring. But at the moment I'd say you have a forty to fifty per cent chance of getting pregnant.'

She smiled. That was so much better than no chance at all. 'Thank you, Mr Solomon. I'm really grateful for everything you've done…and for seeing me so quickly.'

'I'm glad to have helped…and I had a cancellation so there was no problem getting you into theatre.' He checked the monitors. 'We'll check your blood pressure and temperature again, and when they're satisfactory, we'll let you go. The nurse will go through your aftercare instructions with you. Any problems at all—come back to us.'

'Thanks again, Doctor.'

He left the room and she sat with Cade, waiting for the news to sink in.

'It isn't perfect,' she said. 'But it's better than I expected.'

He squeezed her hand. 'I'm glad for you, Rebecca. You did the right thing, coming here. But you should have told me. You should have trusted me. You should always have faith in me.'

He kissed her gently on the mouth, and then leaned back in his chair as the nurse came back into the room.

'I need to check your blood pressure again,' she said, 'and then we'll see about sending you home.'

Rebecca left the hospital with Cade a few hours later. They took a taxi to the ferry port and managed to time things just right, with the boat leaving for St Marie-Rose shortly after that.

The crossing was smooth, the sea a tranquil, glassy blue. They sat by the deck rail, looking out at the coastline, sipping ice-cold mango juice and eating cool slices of melon.

'How do you feel?' Cade asked. 'Did they say anything about how long it will take you to recover from the surgery?'

'I'm feeling okay. It shouldn't take too long at all, really. I'll probably be back to normal in a couple of days.'

'That's good. We'll get you settled in back at the house and you can rest up as much as you need. I'll take you to see Emma whenever I can, or I'll arrange for Benjamin to take you there and bring you back.'

'That's good. Thank you… I can't wait to see her.' She frowned. 'I should be with her when she goes home to the cabin. She'll need someone with her for a few weeks while she's convalescing.'

'Erm…and what about *you*? You've just had an operation yourself, so you'll both need some looking after! Why don't you both stay at the plantation house? There's plenty of room, and you'll be a lot more comfortable there, I expect…and Harriet will love being able to cook for more than just me.'

'I'll ask her.' She smiled at him and laid her hand on his. 'Thank you…again.'

A week later she was starting to feel a little better. The small laparoscopy wound was healing up and she had managed to visit Emma earlier in the day. She had been greeted with the news that she was soon going to be able to come home.

'Stay at the plantation house?' Emma had been thrilled by the invitation. 'Oh, wow! That sounds fantastic…and I'll be so much nearer to William, won't I? He says he has a cottage not far from there. Oh, it gets better and better. I can't wait to get out of here.'

Cade had already started to move Emma's things from the cabin to the plantation house. He seemed to like having a house full of people. He'd told Rebecca to pick out a room for her sister and that he'd do whatever she wanted to make her comfortable there.

Now, though, Rebecca was getting ready to go out for the evening with him.

'There's that barbecue on the beach, remember?' he'd said earlier. 'It starts just before sunset and goes on till people start leaving.' He grinned. 'I think it's time for you to have some fun. If you're feeling up to it, of course?'

'Yay!'

She didn't know what to wear, but in the end picked out a colourful sarong that had a thin halter-neck strap and left her shoulders bare. It wrapped around her, nipping in at the waist and gliding over her hips in soft folds, and gave a glimpse of a long tanned thigh as she walked. She'd pinned her hair up, so that curls massed around the back of her head and fell in gentle tendrils to frame her face.

When she had finished dressing she went downstairs, ready to leave as soon as the taxi arrived at the front of the house. Cade had been looking around for his house keys, but when he saw her approach he stopped what he was doing and stared at her, transfixed.

'Oh…Rebecca… Oh…you look stunning.' His dark gaze moved over her as though he was captivated by the vision before him. 'You look so lovely…'

'I'm glad you think so.' She ran a hand over the sarong. 'I wasn't sure what people wear at these parties.'

'Whatever they wear, you'll be the most beautiful girl there. I won't dare let you out of my sight for an instant.'

She laughed and went out with him to the waiting cab. The driver whisked them away, stopping to drop them off at the shore a few minutes later.

They walked on to the sand and watched the setting sun dip slowly on the horizon, casting an arc of gold over the blue sky. Palm fronds waved gently in the light breeze and gradually the sky turned a dusky pink.

Behind them the bartender had opened up his wooden shack and was serving fruity rum punch and piña coladas. At the same time the chef had fired up the barbecue, so that soon the aroma of steak and chicken filled the air. People were soon queuing up to sample tasty titbits.

'Try these jerk chicken wraps,' Cade said, taking her over to where a buffet table had been set out. 'They're delicious.'

She tasted them, along with seafood skewers and spicy roast pork. 'Mmm…mmm…mmm…' she said. 'You're right. Everything tastes wonderful. I *love* Caribbean food. And I definitely want to try those coconut kisses for dessert.'

The musicians struck up a rhythm on their steel drums and people started to dance, swaying in time with the music. Cade led Rebecca on to a flat stretch of sand and for a while they moved together to the sound of calypso and reggae.

As the sky darkened and the moon glittered on the sea he held her close and kissed her tenderly. 'I love you,' he said. 'Will you marry me?'

'I love you, too,' she said softly, her heart leaping with joy at the unexpected proposal. 'And I want to marry you more than anything in the world.'

He pulled in a quick, shaky breath, his face lighting up in a smile. He lowered his head and kissed her passionately on the mouth. She clung to him, wrapping her arms around him.

'Have you thought this through?' she asked after a while, when they came up for air. 'I've had the surgery, but it isn't a guarantee that everything will be all right.'

'I want to be with you,' he said simply, taking her by the hand and leading her by the water's edge. 'If children come along, that will be wonderful. But if they don't…we could go for adoption or find some other way of satisfying that need.'

He looked at her.

'It's early days, but perhaps you should think about going back to working with children—even if it's only part-time? You have a lot to give, Rebecca. You've had a lot to think about these last few months—this year— but now you have a chance to be happy again. We *both* have that chance.'

'I could be happy with you,' she said. 'Being with you is what I want more than anything.'

He slid his arm around her waist and they walked along the beach, the sound of steel drums floating on the air, the fading light dancing on the water.

'We'll be good together,' he said. 'I feel it inside. It's as though I've been waiting for you to come along my whole life.'

They stood in the shelter of a coconut palm and he took her in his arms. His kisses filled her with exhilaration and made her body tingle with joyful anticipation.

There was a lifetime of love ahead of them. She knew it.

EPILOGUE

'REBECCA, THE CATERER wants to know where to put the large fruit basket.'

Cade was frowning and Rebecca smiled. For a man who was so good at dealing with emergencies and handling people, he was being strangely inept when it came to dealing with the intricacies of organising his cousin's wedding.

Of course he'd had more than usual to contend with these last few days, with the plantation house full of guests. Her family had come over to the Caribbean to stay for a few weeks, and his family was here, too.

'Tell her I thought it would look good on the end table,' she said. 'The one at the far end of the marquee.'

'Okay.' He came over to her and placed a hand lightly on her tummy. 'How's the bump doing today? Oh…he's kicking.' His mouth curved and he stayed very still for a while, waiting for his son to move around some more.

'Yes, he is.' She laid her left hand on top of his, the gold wedding band glinting brightly in the sunlight that streamed in through the windows. 'He's been doing that all morning. It must be all the excitement, and I think he's feeling cramped in there…only four more weeks to go.' She sighed, looking down at her large abdomen. 'Trust William and Emma to decide to get married when I'm as big as this—I wanted to wear something special for their big day.'

He placed a gentle kiss on her soft lips. 'You look lovely. And think of it this way—at least our boy will be at his auntie's wedding.'

She laughed. 'Okay, I'll grant you that. But let's hope we get the timing right with the next one.'

He wrapped his arms around her and kissed her tenderly. 'Of course we will. It'll be perfect, I promise you. When our children come along the timing will always be right.'

* * * * *

DISCOVERING
DR RILEY

BY
ANNIE CLAYDON

Published in Great Britain 2016
By Mills & Boon, an imprint of HarperCollins*Publishers*
1 London Bridge Street, London, SE1 9GF

© 2016 Annie Claydon

ISBN: 978-0-263-25432-7

Our policy is to use papers that are natural, renewable and recyclable products and made from wood grown in sustainable forests. The logging and manufacturing processes conform to the legal environmental regulations of the country of origin.

Printed and bound in Spain
by CPI, Barcelona

Dear Reader,

For me, writing isn't just a job—it's a lifeline. When something's bothering me I write it down. When I'm happy about something I write it down. For as long as I can remember the page has been my faithful confidante.

So I can understand how Cori Evans operates. As an art therapist she is used to helping children express themselves through the medium of art, and her painting expresses her own thoughts and feelings as well. But Tom Riley's burden of secrets is her greatest challenge yet.

I hope you enjoy this book—it's one I've long wanted to write. I always enjoy hearing from readers, and you can contact me via annieclaydon.com.

Annie x

To Lynn
With thanks for helping me count the days

Books by Annie Claydon

Mills & Boon Medical Romance

Visit the Author Profile page at
millsandboon.co.uk for more titles.

CHAPTER ONE

'Do me a favour…'

There was more than a hint of flirtatiousness about the tone of the request, but Tom Riley knew that Dr Helen Kowalski's designs on his person were far from recreational. A Sunday afternoon, a doctor at a loose end and a phone call from a busy A and E department added up to only one thing.

'You want me to come down and see someone?'

'If you're not busy on the ward. We've got a kid here who's driving everyone crazy.'

'And since he's under sixteen, you thought you might pass him on to me.' Tom smirked into the phone. 'Because awkward customers are my speciality.'

Helen snorted with laughter. 'I could say something about it taking one to know how to deal with one.'

'If you do, I'm going home. I'm not even supposed to be at work today.'

'Get down here, Tom.' A crash sounded from somewhere in the background and Helen muttered a curse. 'Please…'

'I'm already on my way.'

The source of all the trouble turned out to be eight years old, with a shock of red hair. He was sitting on the bed in one of the cubicles, swinging his legs. Tom gave him a wide berth to avoid being kicked, and smiled at the woman sitting next to him.

'I'm Dr Tom…' He winced, stepping back as he realised that he'd underestimated the reach of the boy's flailing feet.

'I'm so sorry… Adrian, please don't do that, you'll hurt someone.' It looked as if Adrian's companion had come straight from some half-completed DIY project, with her dark hair fastened at the back of her head and bound with a scarf. Paint-stained overalls had been slipped from her shoulders, with the sleeves tied around her waist, to reveal a Fair Isle sweater with a darn at one elbow.

'No harm done.' Tom dismissed the urge to rub his leg where Adrian had kicked him. 'What brings you here?'

When she looked up at him, it registered that she had violet eyes. Whatever *had* brought her here seemed suddenly unimportant.

'It's Adrian.' She turned wearily to the boy, laying her free hand on one flailing leg in an attempt to restrain him. Tom noticed that the other was held fast in Adrian's own hand. 'He's hit his head. There's a lump.'

'Okay.' Tom wondered whether Adrian was usually this badly behaved. 'Anything else? Any change in his demeanour?'

Her wry smile was directed at the boy, who promptly stopped kicking his feet. 'He always has plenty of energy.'

That was one way of putting it. 'So what happened?'

'I was up a ladder and Adrian was playing. He brushed against the ladder and we both ended up on the floor. He banged his head, so I thought it was best to bring him here and get him checked over.'

She tipped her face back towards Tom, raking him with her gaze. He could almost feel it caress his face, before she looked away.

'You weren't hurt?' Instinct told him that Adrian had probably careened straight into the ladder, rather than merely brushing against it. And the stiff way that she moved told him that Adrian wasn't the only one who should see a doctor.

'I'm fine.' She couldn't even meet his querying look. 'Adrian, don't do that, please.'

Tom focussed his attention back on the boy and saw that he had started to meticulously shred the paper cover that had been laid over the top of the bed. First things first. 'Right, young man. Let's take a look at that head of yours.'

Adrian's freckled face and red hair seemed to flame. He clutched fiercely at the woman, and she winced. Tom backed off. Experience had told him that it was always good to listen to adults, but that you learnt a great deal more by looking at a child.

Pulling a chair away from the bed a little, he sat down, leaning back and folding his arms. Now that there was no imminent danger of being wrestled from the grip of his companion, Adrian calmed, regarding him steadily.

'All right, Adrian.' Tom stretched his legs out in front of him, as if he had all the time in the world. 'How are we going to do this?'

This doctor was a dream. Cori had known that taking Adrian to A and E was going to be a challenge, but he

needed to be examined by a doctor, and on a Sunday
afternoon there wasn't a great deal of choice but to join
the queue and try to reassure him and keep him calm.
The loud farting noises that he had made in the waiting room had ensured a circle of empty chairs around
them, and the woman doctor that Adrian had seen at
first had been kind and efficient but clearly too busy to
give him the time he needed.

She hadn't caught this doctor's second name, and
perhaps he hadn't given it. He wasn't wearing a name
badge like the other staff in A and E, but more im-
portantly he'd had the time and the inclination to sit
back and let Adrian dictate the pace. He'd explained
everything that he was about to do, and nodded when
Cori had added the piece of information that she knew
Adrian needed to hear. He'd be going home with her,
as soon as they were finished here.

The man was blond and blue-eyed, but gifted with
enough hard edges to indicate that he was probably no
angel. He hadn't tried to part her and Adrian either, but
had somehow contrived to examine Adrian while he'd
still clung to her. When his fingers had accidentally
brushed her cheek, she'd forgotten the pain in her hip
and shoulder and had felt herself automatically relax.

'Right, then, Adrian.' Tom grinned. 'I'm officially
giving you a clean bill of health. That means you can
go home with your…' His gaze flipped questioningly
towards Cori.

'Sister.' She volunteered the closest description she
could manage without a lengthy explanation.

He nodded gravely, clearly taking a shot at estimat-
ing the eighteen-year difference between Adrian's age
and hers. 'Right. Your sister.'

Perhaps he'd come to the conclusion that they came from a large family, which was close enough to the truth. Cori nudged Adrian, who was now beaming at Tom.

'Thank you,' Adrian responded to her prompt, and Tom smiled again. He had a nice smile, which came packaged up with a small nod, as if he was sharing a secret. Cori reminded herself that, whatever the conspiracy was, it was probably between him and Adrian and not her.

'You're very welcome. You were right to come.' He turned his attention to Cori, and she felt her fingertips tingle. That was probably the effect of having fallen hard on her left side, although why her right hand should be affected as well was beyond her.

'How are you getting home?'

'My father's coming to pick us up. He should be here by now.'

'All right. What's his name?'

'Ralph Evans. But—'

'Stay there.' Tom's look brooked no argument. 'I'll see if I can find him.'

Adrian was clearly still determined not to be parted from his sister, and so Tom was going to have to find a way of examining her without distressing the boy. Because however much Adrian wanted to go home, and however much his sister tried to hide it, she was clearly in pain. And as much as he prided himself on his medical skills, Tom was unable to tell whether her ribs were broken by simply looking at her.

He caught Helen's eye as she hurried past. 'Have you

got a minute? I want you to have a look at the woman that the boy came in with.'

'What's the matter with her?'

'She's had a fall. If you could just check her over…'

Helen shook her head. 'If she's not urgent then she'll have to wait. The boy's father was here a minute ago.'

'You get on. I'll find him.'

Helen shot him a smile over her shoulder, and Tom looked around the busy department for some clue as to who the father might be. Maybe red hair, which matched the boy's…

A middle-aged man turned towards him, following the receptionist's pointing finger. 'Dr Riley? I'm here for Adrian Harper, I'm his guardian.'

Tom's surprise must have shown on his face. In his experience you could often explain a child's behaviour when you met the parent, but this man, with his relaxed manner and dark, salt-and-pepper hair, bore no resemblance to Adrian at all. Before he could frame the question, the man had reached into his pocket and drawn a card from his wallet to identify himself.

'Adrian's your foster son?'

Ralph nodded. 'Is he all right?'

'He has a bit of a bump on his head.' Tom remembered the pamphlets on aftercare that were stacked behind Reception and reached across, selecting the right one and handing it to Ralph. 'You should keep an eye on him for the next twenty-four hours.'

Ralph chuckled. 'We always do. Is Cori all right?'

'His sister?' Tom realised that he didn't know her name. Her smile and the extraordinary colour and warmth of her eyes had seemed enough.

'Yes. When she called she said that Adrian had cannoned into a ladder. I was rather hoping she hadn't been up it at the time.'

Cori had obviously rationed out the truth, giving little bits of it as and when she'd reckoned necessary. 'She told me he brushed against the ladder and that she'd fallen. I'd like her to see a doctor, as she's obviously in pain, but Adrian won't let go of her.'

Ralph nodded, clearly not fazed by any of this. 'Okay, thanks. I'll take Adrian home and make sure that Cori sees someone.'

'Today.' Tom peered through to the waiting room, which, if anything, looked even fuller than it had been half an hour ago. 'If she comes back here, I'll try and find someone who'll see her quickly.'

'Thanks. I know how busy you are, and I appreciate it. She'll be back as soon as I've got Adrian into the car.'

Cori walked back from the hospital car park. Adrian had been mollified by her assertion that she wasn't coming with them because she was going straight back to her own flat, but Ralph had insisted quietly that she do nothing of the sort. Now she had at least another two-hour wait in front of her before she saw one of the doctors in A and E.

The pain in her shoulder and hip was getting worse, though, and now that she was alone Cori suddenly wanted to cry. She couldn't be injured, not now. Tomorrow morning she'd be starting an eight-week attachment, here at the hospital, which might lead to getting the permanent post that she really wanted. However hard she'd fallen, she couldn't afford not to get up and get on with it.

'Hey, there.'

That sounded suspiciously like Tom's voice, laced
with a hint of the conspiratorial quality of his smile. She
looked up, and saw him standing outside the entrance
to the A and E department, a cup of coffee in his hand.
He looked like a dream come true.

'Come along.' He took a long swig of the last of his
coffee and spun the paper cup into the bin.

She wanted to just go with him, without asking
where or why. But that wasn't going to get her out of
there any quicker. 'I've got to go and register at Reception. Get my place in the queue.'

He grinned and Cori hesitated. When he smiled, he
was the most perfect man that she had ever seen. Wherever it was that he wanted her to go, it suddenly seemed
like a good idea.

'You've just jumped the queue.'

'But…' It was tempting. 'There are people waiting.
You should see them first.'

'I'm off shift, and there's nothing more for me to do
here. And you've already waited once.'

Did he have to be quite so persuasive? 'It's okay,
really. I appreciate it, but you should go home if your
shift has finished.'

His brow darkened. '*You're* not going to kick me,
are you?'

She shook her head, silently.

'Good. In that case, you'd better follow me.' He
turned on his heel, not waiting for the objection that
Cori felt duty-bound to make, and led the way back
into A and E.

Tom hadn't given her the chance to protest any further.
He'd taken one look at the rapidly forming bruises on

Cori's shoulder and hip, and filled out a form for her to take down to X-Ray. While he was waiting for her, Helen had made the most of the opportunity and passed a couple of minor cases to him, telling him that she couldn't bear the thought of seeing him bored.

When they came through, he reviewed the X-rays carefully, and then went to find Cori. She was sitting on a chair in one of the cubicles, a hospital gown pulled down over her knees, her T-shirt and sweater wrapped in a bundle and hugged against her chest.

'I wanted to say thank-you, for being so nice with Adrian. And that I'm sorry he kicked you. I hope he didn't hurt you too much.' She blurted the words out almost as soon as he drew the curtain across the entrance to the cubicle.

'It's okay. I've had worse.' A lot worse. He'd grown up with it, and Tom had learned to just take the blows and move on. To cry later, when he was alone in his bed. He pushed the memory away, wondering why it had chosen that moment to surface. Maybe it had been something to do with the gentle way that Cori had treated Adrian. Tenderness always seemed to awaken an obscure feeling of loss in him.

'So what were you painting?' He didn't want to think about it any more, and Cori seemed nervous. Small talk would hopefully rectify both those issues.

'It was a wall.' She seemed to relax a bit. 'Actually, a mural. In my spare time I work with a group of artists, which donates wall art to charities and schools.'

'Sounds great. Only Adrian had different ideas?'

She stiffened. 'He didn't mean to do it. He's not usually as naughty as when you saw him…'

He liked the way she rose to the boy's defence, her

eyes flashing defiance at him. 'That's okay. I'm not blaming him for anything.'

'No. Thank you. Adrian hasn't had things very easy in the last few years.'

'Your father told me he's fostered with your family.'

'Yes, that's right. He's had a few really bad experiences with hospitals.' She clutched at her sweater, as if she felt she'd just made a *faux pas*. 'Not this one.'

'No hospital's an easy place to be for a child. We do our best, but…'

'I know. You were great with him, and I really appreciate it. It makes a difference.' She seemed unwilling to let the point go. 'When he was little, he was taken into his local A and E department with his mother. Drugs overdose. The boyfriend forgot all about Adrian and he got left in the waiting room on his own. The staff found him curled up in a corner.'

A little boy, lost and alone. Tom felt a sudden heaviness in his chest, as if something was trying to stop him from breathing. 'Which is why he wouldn't let go of you?'

'Yes. And why I said there was nothing wrong with me.' She shrugged, and winced painfully. 'I shouldn't be telling you all this, but I guess it's okay, since you're his doctor. And I wanted you to know how much the way you treated him will have meant to him. He doesn't have the words to say it. Not yet anyway.'

For a moment, Tom really couldn't breathe, and felt himself begin to choke. Then self-control came to his rescue. 'Thanks for telling me. Adrian's lucky to have you to speak up for him.'

'I'm adopted too.' She gave him a bright smile. 'I

was lucky to have someone speak up for me when I needed it.'

And now she was paying it forward. Tom turned quickly, trying to shut out the *what if*s. The fact was that no one had spoken up for him when he'd been a child, and it was far too late for anyone to do it now. He moved the bed down so she could sit on it without him having to help her up, and motioned her towards it.

'Your X-rays are fine, so there are no breaks or fractures, but I'd like to check on the movement in your shoulder.'

She nodded, rising stiffly from the chair and sitting down on the bed. Tom raised it until they were almost face to face, trying not to allow her eyes to distract him from the job in hand.

'I'm going to rotate your shoulder. It's going hurt a little bit but try and relax.'

She smiled again, almost as if she was trying to reassure him. But he wasn't supposed to be noticing her smile, let alone allowing himself to react to it like a teenager. 'It already hurts a little bit.'

'Right. Then it's going to hurt a little bit more.'

It hurt. He was gentle, and measured, but it still hurt.

'Sorry… Nearly done.'

She let out the breath she'd been holding. Somehow she'd let go of the edge of the bed, and her fingers had clutched at the closest thing to hand, the material of his white coat. She felt herself flush, and let go, hoping he hadn't noticed.

'Everything's fine there. I just want to take another look at the bruising. If you could slip the gown off your shoulder…'

Cori did as he asked with trembling fingers. It was nothing. She'd shown her shoulders in public before without a second thought. But even though Tom had his back turned and was scribbling something on her notes, she was suddenly embarrassed. In the moment before she'd let go of his coat, she'd felt hard muscle flexing beneath her hand.

He was cool, and professional, his gloved fingers gently probing her shoulders and back. That just made things worse. If he'd cracked a joke, at least she could have come back with a smart reply to take the edge off the tension. Cori squeezed her eyes closed, dropping her head forward.

'Okay. That's good.' He didn't seem aware of the fact that her forehead was resting against his shoulder, and that they were in an awkward replica of an embrace. When he stepped away again, she wanted to pull him back.

'You can get dressed now.' His cool professionalism told Cori that the closeness was all in her head. She was just another patient in a never-ending line of them, and he'd been nice to her because he was probably nice to everyone.

'Thanks. I appreciate everything you've done.' She waited for him to lower the level of the bed so she could slip off it easily.

'All part of the service. I'll write a prescription for some painkillers, and see if I can find a leaflet for you to take away.' A hint of humour shone in his eyes. 'Apparently we have a leaflet for pretty much everything.'

He turned his back and then he was gone, leaving Cori to pull her T-shirt and sweater back on as quickly as her shaking, painful limbs would allow.

* * *

When she'd let out that choking gasp of pain, and reached for him, Tom had almost forgotten what he was supposed to be doing and given her a hug to comfort her. Then he'd reminded himself where he was, and had drawn back. He gave her more than enough time to get changed, and headed back to the cubicle, finding her dressed and ready to go.

He handed her the leaflet and she took it, scanning the page. 'This tells you what you can do to make yourself more comfortable. You should take it easy for a few days. You have some deep bruising and it'll hurt in the morning.'

She twisted her mouth downwards in an expression of dismay. 'I start a new job tomorrow. Here, actually.'

'You'd be better off staying at home.' Then the words sank in. 'Here?'

'Yes, I'm an art therapist. I'm here for eight weeks, starting tomorrow…'

Cori? Corrine Evans? Suddenly Tom's mouth went dry. *This* was the woman that he'd tried to keep out of his department?

'It's going to be quite a challenge and I can't take time off…' She looked at him earnestly.

He was the challenge she was talking about. And the determined look on her face told him exactly what she meant to do with that challenge.

'I'm sure…'

What was he sure of? That he happened to know that Dr Thomas Riley, Acting Head of Paediatrics, would be more than happy to give her the next two days off? That he'd actually be more than happy to give her the whole of the next eight weeks off?

Before he could come to a decision on how to break the news, she stood up. 'I won't take up any more of your time. Thank you. I really appreciate all you've done.' She shot him a bright smile, thanked him and then she was gone.

Corrine Evans. Even her name seemed to have gained an allure now that he had met her. He'd expected that he would be able to largely ignore the new art therapist, sideline her by giving her a few things to do that couldn't cause any trouble, and get on with his own job of running the department. In eight weeks' time she'd be gone and out of his hair.

Something deep in the pit of his stomach told him that it wasn't going to be that easy.

CHAPTER TWO

CORI WOKE FEELING as if she'd been run over by a steam-roller in the night. Perhaps she'd feel better once she'd had a shower and got moving.

There wasn't much choice in the matter. Her supervisor had told her that Dr Shah, Head of Paediatrics, had taken extended medical leave, and that the acting head had expressed concern about her being allowed to work in the unit. She wasn't going to give him any excuses to dismiss her before she'd even had a chance to show what she could do. Not turning up on the first day would be like presenting him with her head on a plate.

She'd packed everything she'd thought she might need for the day in a large canvas bag, which sat in the hall. Taking the heaviest and least essential items back out, she pulled the strap across her shoulder, decided she could manage, and called a taxi.

The two miles to the hospital was easy, but by the time she'd found her way through the maze of corridors to the paediatric unit her shoulder was on fire and she needed to sit down. The entrance doors to the unit were locked, and pressing the bell didn't elicit an immediate response.

'I thought I told you to stay home for a couple of

days.' The voice behind her was unmistakable. Dammit. What was *he* doing here? A and E was on the other side of the building.

It was just as well that Cori could only turn slowly as it gave her time to think. 'Actually, you told me to take it easy for a couple of days.'

He didn't look best pleased. 'So I did. And I can see that you're following my instructions to the letter.' He reached past her and punched a code into the pad by the door, then held it open for her. Dressed in a suit, instead of the dark blue chinos he'd been wearing yesterday, he seemed a lot less approachable, if no less handsome.

'Thanks. I'm looking for the admin office…' Hopefully Tom wasn't going to be staying around long enough to mention that she'd turned up to work against doctor's orders. That wasn't the start she'd been hoping to make.

'I'm Tom Riley.' He pulled the door closed behind them. 'Acting Head of Paediatrics.'

Suddenly Cori's shoulder stopped hurting, in response to an instinctive urge to either fight or fly. The effort of doing neither left her staring at him in dumb horror.

A flicker of remorse showed in his eyes. 'I didn't realise who you were yesterday, until you'd gone.'

At least he had some idea of the position he'd put her in. And if this wasn't quite an apology, at least it wasn't a declaration of out-and-out war.

'I didn't catch your surname.' She flushed, remembering that Adrian had kicked him before he'd had a chance to say it.

'Let me help you with the bag.' He was suddenly closer than she'd like. 'I know you've got to be hurting.'

Cori thought about telling him she could manage, but it was much too late for that. He'd already seen the bruises. She'd already betrayed far more about herself than he needed to know, and then she'd allowed herself to fantasise about those innocent-as-sin blue eyes. The detached professionalism which she'd intended to hit Dr Riley with this morning wasn't going to work.

'Thanks.' She grabbed at the strap of her bag, trying awkwardly to lift it over her head, and he came closer still to help, grimacing when he felt its weight.

'How did you get here?' It was probably just concern on his part, but Cori couldn't help but feel there was an edge of criticism to the question. She took a breath, lacing her answer with a smile.

'By taxi. If I'm going to be reckless, I'd prefer to do it the easy way.'

Taking the gamble of joking with him didn't come off well. He seemed about to smile and then reconsidered, turning abruptly to lead the way past the reception desk. Cori followed him along a snaking corridor, her eyes fixed on his back, trying not to count the number of ways that she might be in disgrace.

He threw open a door. 'We've set a room aside for you.'

'Thanks…' Cori caught her breath. The health authority scheme, linking art therapists with local hospitals, had produced a set of guidelines that stipulated a separate room, but most of the therapists in her group had been given a large cupboard at best. Tom might not approve of her presence, but he'd given her a bright and airy room, with two large tables to work at and a small seating area in one corner.

'This is…' Perfect. Wonderful. Suddenly it was quite

unbelievable. 'Are there any limitations on when I can use the room?'

'Nope. It's all yours for eight weeks.' The breath of a smile played around his lips. 'That's what the guidelines requested.'

'The guidelines asked for more than anyone expected to get.' Cori looked around. 'This is perfect, thank you.'

His nod indicated that he'd heard, but conveyed nothing else. 'I have a meeting in a minute, so I hope you don't mind if I leave you to it. I'll get Maureen, the unit administrator, to show you around and then perhaps you can use today to get settled. It would be good if you could draw up a list of proposals for the kinds of activities you want to run, as well.'

She already had a list of proposals. Okay, so she hadn't seen the space she was going to be using, but she'd made sure to include options that covered almost anything from a broom cupboard to Buckingham Palace. But Tom seemed to be intent on getting out of the room as quickly as possible and was already halfway to the door. Taking a breath and thinking first, before she said anything rash, was the thing to do now.

'Thank you. Maureen, you say…?'

Was that a smile? Maybe he was congratulating himself at not having to bother with her any more this morning. 'Yeah. She probably won't be in yet, but I'll leave a note on her desk. If you stay here, she'll find you.'

'Okay, thanks.'

This time there definitely was a smile. As swift as it was melting, it sent warmth tingling through her followed by a sudden, empty feeling of loss as it was withdrawn. She almost choked.

'Coffee machine's in the main office. Help yourself.'

He was gone. Taking with him his smile, the fresh scent that Cori had tried not to notice, and any hope that she might have had of winning him around at their first meeting.

She sat down with a bump, wincing as she did so. This morning hadn't quite gone as she'd intended, but she was still here. And she was still in with a chance of finding out exactly what Tom had against her being here, and of changing his mind.

Not so long ago, the only thing expected of Tom when a pretty young woman arrived on the unit was that he would turn on the charm and ask her to dinner. But then Dr Shah had suffered a heart attack, and it had fallen to Tom to keep the unit running while he was away on extended leave.

It was a mystery to him that Cori was even here. He'd seen the bruises and knew that she must be hurting like hell. It wasn't as if there was any hope of a job once her eight weeks in the hospital were up. Funding had been withdrawn, and the only reason this placement hadn't been cancelled was that it had been considered too late to stop it. But she seemed determined, and it was his responsibility to provide her with as many opportunities as he could.

Thankfully Maureen was already at her desk, reviewing the contents of her handbag before she started her day. At least he could send someone else to provide Cori with the welcome that he'd entirely failed to give.

'Was that the new art therapist I saw you with?' Maureen dispensed with the usual *Good morning* and *Did you have a nice weekend?*

'It was. Do you still have time to show her around?'

'Of course. What have you said to her?'

'That I'd see if I could find you…'

'So, in other words, you ducked the issue.'

'I know it looks a lot like that. Now I'm Acting Head of Department, I think I'm allowed to call it delegating.' He grinned at her and she rolled her eyes. Maureen had been in the department for twenty years and there was no one, including Tom, who hadn't been picked up and dusted down by her at one point or another in their career.

'I'll tell you now that I've no intention of playing good cop. Or bad cop, for that matter, if that's what you're asking.'

'I wouldn't dream of it.' He imagined that the woman he'd met yesterday in A and E would spot such a game a mile off, and probably outplay him. 'I just want you to keep an eye out for her. Let me know how she's doing.'

'And the better she does, the less you'll like it?' She looked at him thoughtfully. 'Does she know that?'

'It's not as simple as that…'

'No. Nothing ever is.' Maureen got to her feet, pulling her jacket straight in a no-nonsense motion. 'Just as long as I'm not the one who has to explain that to her.'

Tom Riley was almost certainly a better doctor than he was a boss. Cori considered the matter carefully as she tidied up the pens and paper from the afternoon's art session. It had been fun. Children from the ward had been joined by parents and siblings and more than one person had said that it was a great addition to the pastoral care that the unit provided. The only problem was that it hadn't been art therapy.

The next eight weeks might not be precious to Tom

but they were precious to her and time was trickling away. A day, then two, now three…

As expected, Ralph and Jean had provided comfort food, followed by advice over the washing-up.

'You know this isn't your fault, don't you?' Ralph was soaping plates vigorously.

'That's how it feels.' She could share those fears with Ralph. He knew that was how she'd felt when she'd been a kid, rejected by one family after another. It had almost been too late by the time he and Jean had finally found her.

'So you'll be getting up at six in the morning to do the housework?' A smile played around Ralph's mouth. 'You want a hand with that?'

Cori chuckled. That was exactly what he had said when he'd found her in the kitchen, seven years old and trying to reach the switch for the washing machine, reckoning that if she made herself useful Ralph and Jean might keep her for a while. She'd liked their relaxed, cluttered household from the start and being allowed to stay had seemed like the first time a dream had ever come true for her.

'I think I've got it covered. I'm not going to be washing Dr Riley's socks.'

'Glad to hear it.' Ralph stacked more plates onto the drainer, his brow puckered in thought. 'So let me get this clear. There's an initial eight-week period, and if that's a success the post becomes permanent.'

'Yes, that's right. It's such a good opportunity, working with children, close to home. It's exactly the job I want.'

'And this Dr Riley doesn't want you. Why on earth did he agree to it in the first place?'

'That's the thing, he didn't. His predecessor, Dr Shah, agreed to it, and now this Dr Riley has got his reservations. I've emailed the scheme's supervisor to ask her why, but she's now on holiday. And I'm sure Dr Riley's avoiding me.'

'Is there anyone else you can talk to?'

'Only Maureen, the unit administrator. She's been really welcoming, but it's up to Dr Riley to refer specific patients on to me if I'm to do any clinical work. If he doesn't do that, then all I can do is general art sessions.'

'And you're taking that personally, eh?'

'How else can it take it? Every time I see him he either rushes off before I can get to talk to him or he says he's busy and he'll get back to me.'

'Is he like that with everyone else?' Ralph frowned as he turned the problem over in his head.

'You saw what he was like with Adrian, he's fantastic with the kids. They all think he's the coolest doctor ever.'

'What about the other staff?'

'Everyone says he's great. That he always listens and is very fair about things. They seem to like him a lot better than Dr Shah. He was apparently pretty autocratic.'

The frightened child in her, who had blamed herself each time a fostering arrangement had fallen through, had been tugging at Cori's sleeve for the last three days. Keeping her behind after work, even though her sore ribs were screaming for a hot bath, working to make the best of the room she'd been given.

She'd succeeded. The children loved the room, and no one had been able to walk across the threshold without being tempted to touch at least something. The problem had been that Tom Riley hadn't yet found time to walk across the threshold. And that rejection outweighed every other expression of delight.

Ralph shook the suds from his hands, and wrapped his arm around her shoulders. 'There's no shame in saying this place isn't right for you, Cori. You don't have to prove yourself. They're the ones who have to be good enough for you.'

She hugged him tight. 'Thanks. Spoken like the best dad in the world.'

Ralph gave a small chuckle of pleasure. 'So what are you going to do, then? We're around at the weekend to help you with some more job applications, if you want to come over.'

It seemed like a plan. Since this job didn't seem to be going too well, it would be good to keep all her options open. But she wasn't ready to give up on Dr Riley just yet.

'Thanks. I think I'll give it another week or so, though. I've still got a couple more things up my sleeve.'

It had been a long and busy week and all Tom wanted to do was go home, fling himself onto the sofa and think about nothing. Heading up the paediatric unit wasn't as easy as Dr Shah had made it look. But slowly he was cracking it. One problem at a time. One patient. One member of staff.

The light glimmering on his windscreen hadn't stood out amongst the other reflections from the overhead strip lighting in the car park. In truth, he'd been thinking hard about something else, and it wasn't until he'd flipped the central locking that Tom switched his attention to his car.

Perched on his windscreen wiper was a fairy. Actually, it was a bundle of scrunched-up silver wire, some sparkly fabric and a bit of tinsel. But the whole was a great deal more than its parts, and the resulting fairy leaned as if inspecting the exact spot where he was standing, her head tilted slightly in a questioning pose.

'What do you want?' Tom shot the creature a glare. It was a little late to start believing in fairies now. Particularly on a cold, wet Friday evening.

The fairy ignored him. Whatever she was doing here, it was clearly none of his business, even if she was sitting on his windscreen. Tom looked around, and saw that his car was the only one that sported an otherworldly being.

It was just a bundle of wire and gauze, which had somehow landed here by accident. The significance of its pose was a trick of the light. Tom reached for the fairy and then hesitated, as the bundle of wire and glitter seemed to scowl at him reproachfully. Its outstretched hand held a wand.

His gaze followed the direction in which the gently glowing tip of the wand was pointing. The passage of car tyres over the concrete floor had scattered it a little, but the trail of glitter was still easy to see.

There was only one person who could have done this, and he'd been avoiding her all week. Slinging his briefcase into the back of his car, and giving the fairy one last baleful stare before he locked it in the glove compartment, he followed the trail of glitter that Cori had laid.

As soon as he stepped onto the frosty path outside the car park, Tom could see where he was headed. It was pretty much impossible not to notice the tiny lights, glimmering amongst the spreading branches of the tree that stood by the main entrance to the hospital. A nurse passed him walking in the other direction, holding a fairy in her hand, the little LED light at the tip of its wand glowing in the darkness.

When he got closer, he saw Cori leaning against the dark shadow of the tree trunk, her face lit up by the twinkle of lights in the branches around her. She did him the courtesy of not pretending to be surprised to see him.

'People usually find that leaving a note on my desk works.' Tom was trying hard not to be enchanted by this method of catching his attention.

'Do they?' She grinned up at him, her eyes dark in the shadows. 'You seemed so very busy.'

He supposed he deserved that. Each day that he'd transferred his meeting with Cori onto his 'to do' list for tomorrow, it had been easier to put it off. When Friday had come, the difficult problem of what exactly he should say to her had seemed quite naturally to fit into next week's timetable instead of this week's.

'Okay.' He was in the wrong and if it had been anyone else Tom would have apologised. But an apology was meaningless unless one intended to change in some way, and right now changing his mind was out of the question. 'So what's the point of all this?'

She folded her arms across her chest, looking up at him. 'You're my point.'

A sudden breathless feeling seemed to spread heat across his chest. 'How, exactly?'

Cori shrugged. 'I know you have your reservations about my effectiveness in the unit...' A little quiver in her voice told Tom that this mattered to her.

'I have no doubts whatever about your effectiveness.' Tom glanced at the fairies, cavorting around them in the tree. Some touch of magic had turned them from confections of wire and glitter into personalities, each one thrilling with life. There was a small group obviously arguing about something. Some preened themselves, and others beckoned watchers closer, looking no doubt to cast some kind of spell on them.

'Then…what?' She stared at him, nonplussed.

It seemed that she needed to hear him say this. He couldn't for the life of him think why, but if it would get her off his back, then he was more than happy to oblige. 'Look, Cori, your CV is very impressive, your work is great and the kids are enjoying it…'

'You haven't seen any of my work yet.' She looked ready for a staring match. From somewhere, the craving to respond hit him, the urge to look deep into those violet eyes, and break down all her defences.

'I do take a look around the unit once in a while. And I quite often talk to my patients, as well.' Tom resisted the temptation to add that talking to children was a damn sight easier than navigating the uneasy waters of adult office politics. 'I can see that you've been making a difference…'

'And making a difference is a good thing, isn't it?'

Tom wondered if she was deliberately playing dumb, or she really didn't know. Surely she knew that the funding had been cut. It was impossible that no one had told her.

'You have the potential to be a real asset for the unit, Cori. But now that we have no funding for a long-term appointment, and it's just this eight weeks…'

She was staring at him as if he'd just grown a pair of

wings and was about to flutter off into the branches with the fairies. Her mouth formed an 'O', and she covered it with her gloved hand. 'So… There's no permanent post…after these eight weeks are over?'

'No. I'm sorry. Once your work placement is finished, there are no plans for any permanent post until next year at the earliest. Didn't the scheme supervisor tell you that?'

She shook her head and abruptly turned away, as if there was something she wanted to hide from him. Disbelief, maybe. Tears? Anger? It was difficult to say, and, if he was honest, he would rather not have to deal with any of those emotions. He should go now, let her think about things over the weekend and they could talk again about what she wanted to do on Monday morning.

'Hey, Tom! What's going on? Can anyone join in?' A voice came from behind him and Tom turned to see a couple of off-duty nurses, one of whom was trying to draw his attention to a little girl, transfixed by the lights in the tree and trying to escape her father's grip on her hand. It seemed that they had just come from A and E, because the man also carried a younger child with a bulky dressing on her arm.

Cori had already seen them and was moving towards them. 'Would they like to come and take a look?' She spoke to the man first, and when he nodded she bent down to the little girl at his side. 'If you want, you can take a fairy home.'

The answer to that was a clear and overwhelming yes. She led the little girl under the sparkling canopy, and her father followed, the child in his arms reaching up with her uninjured hand to touch the fairies. It was touching, heart-warming, and Tom wanted to be a part of the magic that Cori was able to create, more than he could say. Which was exactly why it would be much better if he went home. Now.

CHAPTER THREE

NOT SO FAST. Cori could see Tom out of the corner of her eye, pulling his car keys out of his pocket. She'd spent all of yesterday evening making fairies, and her lunchtime today attaching the little LED lights to the tips of their wands. He'd found his way here, and if he thought he was going anywhere before they talked this out, he was mistaken.

'Dr Riley. We need some help here.'

She called over to him, indicating the child beside her. Tom turned, his eyes narrowing in an indication that he knew full well that she wasn't playing fair, and she grinned at him in reply.

He moved across the grass towards her with all the affability of a tiger caught in a trap. He lifted the child up in his arms so she could reach the fairy that she wanted, never taking his gaze from Cori's face.

'Thank you.' The little girl responded to a prompt from her father and thanked him, and Tom's face broke into the kind of smile that Cori would have decorated the whole hospital with fairies for.

'You're very welcome.' He bent down, watching as the child inspected the fairy. 'What's her name?'

'Only *I* know it.'

Tom nodded gravely. 'Right. Well don't forget to take good care of her. She needs to have breakfast every morning.'

'Porridge?'

'Yep. I'm told that fairies are very partial to porridge. Particularly during the winter.'

The child nodded. 'Can Hannah have one?'

Tom allowed himself to be drawn into choosing and obtaining a fairy for the child with the injured arm. Before he was finished, Cori had given away another four, as hospital staff and visitors stopped to look at the tree.

'Dr Riley?' A man in a suit and overcoat was marching across the grass towards them. Tom turned away from the children, and the corner of the man's mouth twitched downwards.

'Now we're in for it…' He murmured the words as he passed behind Cori, moving forward to meet the man. 'Alan. Have you come to make a wish?'

It didn't look as if the man believed in fairies. Cori noticed that a couple of the nurses who'd been lingering under the tree had melted away, leaving the sparkling branches to those who were obviously not employed at the hospital and therefore not subject to the disapproval of its administrators.

'Just came to see what's going on.' Alan was looking round with an assessing gaze.

'Make-a-wish Friday.' Tom's smile would have cracked an iceberg, but he was obviously improvising, and Cori stepped forward. If anyone was going to get into trouble for this, then it should be her.

'It's all my…' She felt fingers close around the sleeve of her coat and Tom pulled her back a couple of steps.

'These are all Cori's creations. She's attached to the

unit temporarily and she's been doing some stupendous work. We had some leftover fairies and I thought it was a shame for them to go to waste.'

'You're supervising this?'

'Absolutely. Can't have people wandering around hospital grounds making unsupervised wishes.'

Cori opened her mouth to speak and Tom turned to face her. For a moment his gaze met hers and she forgot what she was about to say.

'I suppose…' Alan looked around and gave a small shrug. 'There *is* a procedure to go through for anything like this in the hospital grounds, though.'

'Yes, I know. I apologise, but it was an off-the-cuff thing. Next time we'll go through the right channels.' Tom's gaze swung around to Alan, and for a moment it was touch-and-go as to who was going to outstare who. Then Alan backed down.

'No apologies needed, I'm sure. Good work…um…'

'Cori Evans.' Tom smiled beatifically in Cori's direction.

'Good work, Ms Evans. Thank you. You're the new art therapist?'

'*Temporary* art therapist.' The years when she'd moved from one foster home to another, before finding a home with Ralph and Jean, had taught Cori that the 'T' word was one to be both respected and feared. Knowing the difference between something that might work out and something that was strictly temporary was vital to one's own sense of self-worth.

'Did I mention that the unit could really do with someone on a permanent basis?' Tom broke in again.

'Several times.' Alan bestowed a hurried smile on

Cori, and obviously decided it was time to retreat. Tom watched him go, his face impassive.

'I'm sorry.' She'd tried to get Tom's attention, and had ended up getting into hot water. And, unlikely as it might seem, it had been Tom who'd come to her rescue.

He shrugged. 'It's okay. Alan's all right, he just gets a bit scratchy when you don't fill in the necessary forms. Next time you take anything out of the unit, let Maureen know. She'll notify the right people.'

'Yes. I'll do that.' There wasn't going to be a next time. This had been all about getting Tom's attention, finding out why he seemed so dead set against her working in the unit. And Cori had found out a great deal more than she'd wanted to know.

'Look…' He turned suddenly. In the darkness, his hair seemed every colour from blond to tawny. 'I thought that you knew that the funding for the art therapy scheme had been cut. I don't know who omitted to tell you that, but I intend to find out.'

'It's okay…'

'It's not okay.' He frowned.

'It will have been the scheme supervisor at the local health authority. She's been under a lot of stress recently, so I suppose she must have forgotten, and she's on holiday now so she hasn't responded to any of my emails.' Cori shrugged. 'Please. Leave it. I don't want to get her into trouble.'

'In that case, I'll deliver the reprimand to myself, for not making sure that you understood the situation.'

'No. Please, don't do that either. It won't change anything.' She could feel tears pricking at the sides of her eyes now, and hoped that the darkness would hide them from him. 'This is why you have your reservations about me doing clinical work in the unit, isn't it? You don't want me to start something when there's no chance of any follow-up.'

'Yeah. I just don't think it's fair to offer therapy to someone and have it stopped after only eight weeks. I'm sorry, Cori.' He seemed suddenly very close. Close enough to put his arm around her, and if he did that she would make a fool of herself and start crying.

'Don't…' She took a step backwards. 'There's no need to be sorry. You're right.' He was acting in his patients' best interests and Cori couldn't argue with that. But she couldn't just accept it either.

'Will you give me an hour? Please? Just one hour of your time.'

He shot her a melting look that seemed to say he understood all her hopes, all her fears. 'In all fairness I have to tell you that I can't change my mind. You're welcome to hold general groups and sessions on the unit, but I won't offer you anything more.'

'Maybe there's something else I can do… Please. Just an hour.' He hesitated, and Cori took her opportunity. 'What harm can it do to listen?'

He shook his head. Then he smiled, and suddenly she was looking at the Tom Riley who had such a special connection with the children under his care. The one who could make people feel that everything was all right with the world.

'Okay. But you come alone. No fairies.'

'Of course not. That would be an unfair advantage.'

He nodded. 'I don't have much time next week. But I'm dropping in to the hospital tomorrow and I'll be finished at about four. Will that suit you?'

'Four o'clock is fine.'

'Okay, I have your mobile number, I'll call you then.' He looked around at the fairies. 'What are you going to do with these?'

Cori shrugged. 'There doesn't seem to be any shortage of takers for them. I think I'll stop here for another fifteen minutes and give them away.'

'You don't want to save them for another time?'

She shook her head. 'Nah. I can always make more, and I think these all deserve a home now.'

'Having done what they were meant to do for tonight?'

He'd come uncomfortably close to the truth, but Cori wasn't about to admit it. 'You think this was all for you?'

'I'm not that self-centred. I think you want to be of benefit to the children, and to do that you need to catch my attention. And that you found a way to do that which also highlighted your own skills.'

Was that a compliment or a warning? Was he telling her he knew what she was up to and that he was more than a match for her? Before Cori could even begin to work it out, he was walking away.

Tom parked in the tree-lined avenue at the address that Cori had given him. A large Victorian mansion, converted into flats, stood back from the road. Running his finger down the row of names next to the door, he found Cori's and pressed the bell alongside it, hearing a chime sound from somewhere deep inside the house.

She answered almost immediately, wearing a padded coat that engulfed her small frame, accessorised with striped gloves, a scarf and a brightly coloured woollen beret, set at a rakish angle. Tom found himself wondering whether jeans and a leather jacket were quite right for the occasion. Somehow a suit would have made this outing feel more professional and less like a date.

'Is this thing you want to show me far?'

'We only have an hour, so we'll go by car.' Tom's gaze followed her pointing finger to a small, rather battered blue car. 'We could take mine, but the heater's broken…'

He imagined that the suspension was as old as the bodywork looked. And although it was nearly a week since he'd examined the bruises on her shoulder and hip, some of them had been deep enough to still be hurting her. 'We'll take mine. You can give me directions.'

She nodded, looking slightly relieved. 'Yes. More comfortable.'

As he opened the door for her, and she slid carefully into the passenger seat, the world suddenly felt right again. Working in the unit today had carried with it a sense of dislocation, as if something was missing, something that he had been doing his best to ignore. Now that Cori was in his car, Tom realised what that something had been.

'So what is it you want me to see?' They'd driven through a maze of back streets, until he'd lost his bearings.

'I'd rather it took you by surprise.' When he glanced across at her, her face had taken on an impish expression.

'Ah. So it would be wrong of me to try and guess.'

'Very wrong. Turn left here.'

They drew up outside a building that Tom recognised as the old town hall, which now housed a community centre and various offices. Cori led the way along a broken path that wound its way to the back of the building, and then down some metal steps into a gloomy passageway that led to the sub-basement space. Tom squinted at the metal plate on the door, recognising the name of a local charity working with families affected by domestic violence.

His heart felt as if it were stopping. How could she know? No one knew. His childhood was the one part of Tom's life that he kept strictly private.

'What's this?' His voice sounded distant, as if he'd left his body and was already halfway up the steps and out of there.

'I've been working here with some friends from art college. I want you to see what we've been able to do.' She pressed a rather ancient-looking buzzer on one side of the door.

'Your CV says you've been working at another hospital.' Suspicion clawed at him. If she was trying to gain his favour, by thinking she knew what made him tick, she was going about it in quite the wrong way.

'Yes, that's right. I was there for a year, covering for one of the therapists who was on maternity leave. I worked here at the weekends.' She turned to him, her face bright in the darkness. 'We finished up last Sunday. Or rather the others finished up. I was unavoidably detained elsewhere.'

So this was what she'd been doing when she'd fallen off the ladder. Before Tom could think about apologising for the suspicions he hadn't voiced, the door opened and warm light flooded out into the gloomy passageway.

'Cori.' The woman at the door hugged her gingerly. 'How are you doing?'

'Fine, thanks. I've been resting up.'

'Glad to hear it.' The woman turned a smile onto Tom, as if she suspected he'd probably had something to do with that. 'You're Dr Riley? Welcome. I'm Lena Graves, the centre's director.'

Lena motioned them both inside, into a small reception area. It was then that Tom realised why he was there.

CHAPTER FOUR

A FAINT SMELL of new paint still lingered in the place. Three of the walls were painted cream and the fourth was a riot of colour that stopped Tom in his tracks.

'Fabulous…' It was a glimpse into a world of pure fantasy. Lushly painted trees and flowers formed the framework for animals and birds, engaged in familiar, human pursuits. In one corner, a group of hedgehogs was holding a tea party. In another, flamingos were gossiping together.

The design was covered with clear plastic panels, running the length and height of the wall. 'These are to protect it?'

Lena chuckled. 'Not really.'

Cori picked up a marker pen from a box on the reception desk and handed it to him. 'You're supposed to draw on it. Have a go.'

He almost didn't dare. 'And it wipes off?'

'That's the idea. I've wanted to do something like this for a while, and Lena agreed to let us try it out here.'

'It's working well so far. The children love it. One little guy spent all afternoon here yesterday. He drew a picture of himself sitting in a chair next to the hedgehogs.' Lena grinned. 'The staff like doing their thing with it too. At the end of the day we just wipe it all down, ready for tomorrow's designs.'

The tip of the marker pen hovered over the smooth, clear surface. 'You're thinking too much.' He heard Cori's voice close behind him.

'Yeah. Guess I am.' Tom stepped back, putting the cap back onto the pen. 'What happens if someone... if the drawings the kids make become challenging?'

'Challenging to who? The people who draw, or the people who are looking?' She looked up at him thoughtfully. 'Does that matter?'

'It might. If it's disruptive.'

'This area's always supervised. And most of the children who come here with their parents are traumatised because of their family situations. I imagine that Lena will tell you that drawing isn't the most disruptive way of revealing that trauma.'

'Not by a very long chalk.' Lena grinned. 'Anyway, sometimes it's the ones who sit quietly in the corner, and can't bring themselves to reveal anything, who worry me the most.'

'As opposed to someone like me, who reveals everything by painting all over your walls?' Cori chuckled, nudging Lena.

'We're not getting into that. We'll be here all evening.' Lena turned to Tom. 'There's more I'd like to show you. Through here, when you're ready...'

'Yeah. Thanks.' Tom couldn't take his eyes off the huge painting. It was like Cori, disturbing and confronting and yet captivating. Something he wanted to touch, but he knew that once he did so he would be unable to conceal the feelings that had the power to destroy him if he let them have their way.

* * *

'He's the only one.' Lena shrugged, mouthing the words to Cori as Tom turned from the painting, walking briskly away from it. He was the only person, adult or child, who had stood in front of the wall art with a pen in their hand without making their own addition to the design, however tiny.

And it was Tom Riley, the man who was in charge of her future for the next seven weeks, who had turned out to be completely immune to the temptation to draw. The one man she wanted to impress, and her best shot at doing just that had left him cold.

Maybe he was just trying to be objective. To not get involved so that he could make a better decision. Cori held on to that thought, allowing Lena to usher him into the activities room.

He spent a while looking at everything. The child-sized painted chairs, each of which had an individual design snaking up the legs and across the back. The art table, which she had arranged like a sweet shop, different pens and paper displayed with an implicit invitation to touch, to pick up and to draw.

'We got the chairs from a recycling charity.' She had to say something to break the silence. 'Some of them were a bit rickety, but we fixed them up and painted them…' This morning it had seemed like a good idea to show him this. Now she was wondering whether she hadn't blown things completely.

'They're great.' Finally, he smiled. Not the conspiratorial, we-know-a-secret smile that she liked more than she cared to say, but it was something at least.

'The wall here is painted with a wipe-clean surface.'

She ran her hand across the hard, white finish. 'It's a different experience from the one outside. A clean slate.'

He nodded. 'You're encouraging the kids to paint on the walls?'

Lena came to her rescue. 'Just this wall. This is an experiment too. If we find too much graffiti all over the place then we'll paint over it and put it down to experience.'

'It's a lot of effort just to paint over.'

'If we try something and it doesn't work, that's not wasted effort. We learn and do better the next time. Lena's been great in allowing us to experiment a bit.' Cori flashed a grin towards Lena, who nodded, encouraging her to go on. 'You wanted to see something where the benefits didn't rely on having an in-house art therapist. I think this is it.'

'And how much did all of this cost? Just a ballpark figure.'

Cori caught her breath. If he was going to dismiss it out of hand, surely he wouldn't have asked that.

'Cori's group is self-funding.' Lena stepped in again. 'We couldn't have afforded this on our budget.'

He turned to her. The approval in his eyes was breath-taking. 'How much?'

'I'd…have to work it out. I can supply you with figures, but… Well, I'd prefer it if you would come to see our fundraising operation.' Nothing ventured, nothing gained.

'You have an…operation?' He raised one eyebrow.

'Well, that might be a bit of an overstatement…' No. They did. And she was proud of it. 'Yes, we do. And when you've finished looking around here, I'd like you to see it.'

* * *

As they left the building and walked back to the car, the cold evening air on his face seemed to jolt Tom back into the here and now. 'Where are we going this time?'

'The High Street. You carry on down here, take a left and then keep going until you get to the traffic lights.' She settled herself into the passenger seat of his car and buckled the seat belt, clearly not inclined to give any more information about what he was going to see.

'Right.' He started the engine, wondering what she was going to come up with next.

There were no clues from the place she indicated as a parking spot, and he became more baffled as she led him into a bright, warm tea shop, bustling with activity. Sitting down at a table, she loosened her scarf and coat, and signalled to a waitress.

'Hi, Cori. Pot of green tea?'

'Yes, thanks. Tom…?'

At some point in the course of the afternoon she'd responded to his request to stop calling him *Dr Riley*. Tom couldn't remember quite when that had been, but it felt good, as if she'd acknowledged that he might be at least partially on her side.

'Earl Grey, please.' He settled back in his chair, looking around. 'You run a tea shop?'

'No, of course we don't. Where would we get the time to do that?' She grinned, jerking her thumb at the back wall. 'That's our fundraising operation.'

The wall was covered with canvases, ranging from tabletop height almost as far as the ceiling, jostling together in a chorus of colour. 'You painted all of these?'

'I wish. There are over a dozen of us in the group, and everyone contributes a few paintings. The tea shop displays them for us and gets ten percent of sales. It brings people in here and they have something to put on their walls. It's a mutually beneficial arrangement.'

'And you use the money to fund the work that you do for charities.'

'Yes. Charities, schools, hospitals…' That impish grin appeared again. 'Actually, we haven't done any hospitals. But we would, if we got the chance.'

Tom chuckled. 'Anywhere in mind?'

'No, not specifically. We're just open to the possibility.'

'I see.' He could think more clearly now. 'So can you tell me what all this has to do with art therapy?'

She laughed. 'I was wondering when you were going to ask me that.'

'It's the obvious question. As I understand it, art therapy is all about the process of engaging people in some kind of artistic pursuit in a safe environment, and working through the issues that it raises for them. I've only seen the first half of that process today.'

'It has its benefits, though.'

'I'm not denying that.' Tom nodded a thank-you as the waitress put a cup and saucer and a small teapot down in front of him. 'I think what you've done at the centre is fantastic. It's welcoming and inclusive, and at the same time it's challenging…'

'But you're right. It's not art therapy.' She flashed him a smile. 'It *is* sustainable, though, and it's helping to create a culture where users of the centre can use art to express themselves. I'd like to have a conversation with you about doing something of the sort in your department.'

This was something that she lived for, that set her

alight, the way that medicine set Tom alight. And fire suited her. He wondered what it might be like to feel her heat flickering across his skin, warming him on a cold night.

'That's going to be a fairly lengthy conversation.'

'I hope so. And I imagine we'll have a few creative differences along the way. Are you up for it?'

Tom reminded himself that Cori would be working as a part of his team. The only fire that he should be sharing with her was the one that would temper their working relationship.

'I'm up for it.' His gaze found hers, and heat began to throb through his veins. 'There's one condition.'

'Okay.'

'I want to be sure that this is an arrangement that we can both benefit from. I imagine you've already got a few ideas about things that could be done in the unit?'

'One or two.' Her grin told him that it was more than one or two, but that she was planning on surprising him.

'In that case, I want a list of clearly defined benefits, to us and to you. I can't offer you any long-term prospects of employment, so I'd like to know how you feel the work you do will help your career after you leave us.'

Her eyebrows shot up, giving Tom the satisfaction of knowing that he was able to pull a few surprises out of the bag, as well. It seemed that working with Cori was not only going to be possible but more fun than he could have imagined.

'That's… Yes, that would be valuable for me.' She seemed to be ruminating on the thought. 'You know, you're not such a bad boss after all…'

'I'm a work in progress as a boss. I'm a much better doctor.' Tom held out his right hand. 'Do we have a deal?'

Her fingers brushed his, and then gripped tight. 'Yes. We have a deal.'

CHAPTER FIVE

WHEN TOM DREAMED that night, it wasn't of Cori, neither was it of his father. The jumbled landscape of his dreams rarely made any logical sense. He had been standing in front of the vivid wall painting but was shrunk to the size of a child, so that he was on the same level as the hedgehogs' tea party. The creatures seemed to be moving, beckoning to him, and he wanted to join in but his feet were stuck to the floor. He struggled, but whatever was binding him wouldn't let go.

He woke suddenly, an obscure feeling of relief accompanying the realisation that he was in his own bed, in his own house. In his own life, away from the unpredictability of his father's temper. He could be who he wanted to be, someone who made a difference in the world instead of a frightened child, whose greatest desire was to make himself invisible so that no one would notice him.

Tom had never known what he might have done had his mother lived. But she'd died from cancer when he was twelve, and when Tom had got a place at medical school he'd been free to walk away from his father, without looking back. That freedom hadn't amounted to much at first, but he'd worked on it. Worked his way through the night terrors and the flashbacks that had started to haunt him, and the anger and grief that had surfaced as soon as he had begun to feel safe enough to feel anything.

And now Cori was beginning to chip away at the armour he'd so carefully put in place. He'd woken up in the middle of the night, too sleepy to realise what he was doing, and reached for Cori, wanting her to be there. And he didn't do that sort of thing. The acclaimed master of the romantic weekend break, he had only one rule, and that was that he never asked a woman back to his place. Keeping himself at a distance allowed him to be the man he wanted to be.

He got out of bed, stumbling towards the bathroom. Cori's particular brand of unpredictability might be very sweet, and a world away from his father's, but it still wasn't for him. The best thing—no, the *only* thing— to do now was to ignore that enchanting way of hers and the undoubted spark between them, and concentrate on how her eight weeks in the unit might benefit his patients.

Cori was now in no doubt that Tom had made up his mind to lead by example. On Monday he had wheeled a young patient into her room, introducing his parents to Cori, and had sat down with the boy to help him with paper and crayons for ten minutes. Three slightly older girls arrived, after Tom had reported the possibility that fairies might be on the premises, and a couple of boys came to enquire whether Tom's hint of intergalactic warriors was more than just an unfounded rumour.

By Thursday, the whole unit had been in receipt of

the gossip concerning a long, and sometimes animated, meeting in the staff canteen at lunchtime the previous day. Tom had waved away anyone who had attempted to join them, and had spent more than an hour going through Cori's portfolio of photographs and suggestions.

And where Tom led, the rest of the unit followed. The staff began to automatically include the art room when telling patients' families about the facilities that the unit offered, and gradually it was becoming a hub of activity instead of a rarely visited outpost.

By Friday, the prospect of an hour on her own at lunchtime was a welcome respite. As the last of the children were taken back to the ward Tom's secretary appeared in the doorway.

'Hi, Rosie.'

'I brought you some tea.' Rosie held two mugs, which were obviously her excuse for coming to have a look around.

'Thank you, that's really nice of you.' Cori pulled out a chair. 'Will you join me?'

'Thanks.' Rosie was small, blonde and very precise, and dusted the chair before she sat down. 'How does this all work?'

'Art therapy, you mean?'

'Yes. It looks as if it's just painting sessions at the moment.'

The words hurt, but that wasn't Rosie's fault. Cori forced a smile. 'I'm only here for eight weeks. There's a limited amount I can do in the time.'

Rosie nodded. 'I'll mention it to Tom.'

Cori bit back the temptation to say that she'd already mentioned it. Rosie seemed to like her position as secretary to the head of department, and clearly felt that a measure of Tom's authority automatically devolved to her.

'Thanks. Although it's really just the way that things are.'

'You'd be surprised what Tom can do when he puts his mind to it.' Rosie tucked a stray lock of hair behind her ear. 'I haven't been working for him for long, but I've really got to know what makes him tick.'

What made Tom tick? It had been a question that had taken up more of Cori's time than it should have, and it appeared that Rosie had cracked it. Cori dismissed the thought that perhaps Rosie just *thought* she'd cracked it as unfair.

'How long have you been working for Tom?' She supposed she should show some interest.

'Not long, just a couple of months. Dr Shah's secretary used to look after Tom as well, but she's gone on maternity leave. I'm the one with the most seniority in the department after her.'

'So you got the promotion?'

'Yes. I don't think that Terri's coming back after her maternity leave. I heard her talking to Maureen…' Rosie gave a little self-satisfied nod, as if to indicate that she knew more than Cori about the internal workings of the department.

Silence seemed like the best option at this point, and Cori sipped her tea.

'So what *do* you do, exactly?'

That she had an answer for. Cori grinned, pushing a pile of paper closer to Rosie. It was beautifully printed, with blue and gold swirls, and she'd been keeping it for something special, but it seemed that the situation warranted it.

'That's gorgeous.' Rosie picked up a sheet. 'Textured…'

'Feel nice?' Cori moved the pile away from Rosie. One sheet was enough to make her point.

'Yes, it does. You've used it for folding… That's lovely.' Rosie nodded towards a paper crane that Cori had suspended from the ceiling.

'You want me to show you?'

Cori picked up a square of rough paper, and Rosie carefully followed the folds that she made. They worked together until the blue and gold bird was finished and lay in Rosie's hands.

'See, it feels good to make something.' Cori smiled at her.

'Yes, it does. And this is what you do?'

'No, it's the start of what I do. Painting, drawing, making things are all ways of relaxing, and feeling safe about expressing ourselves. It helps people talk about the things that they sometimes can't talk about otherwise.'

'So you're practising on me?' Rosie flushed a little.

'No. Just making a paper crane. I'm on my lunch break.'

'Okay. Can I take this?'

'Of course. You made it. Want to help me with some more?' Cori pushed the cheaper paper towards Rosie. One blue-and-gold crane was enough, and she couldn't afford a whole flock of them.

'Yes, I've got half an hour.' Rosie took a sheet of paper and started folding. 'Then I'll have to go. I usually give Tom's office a tidy up when he's out of the way as he doesn't like it when I do it when he's around. He's called a meeting about new projects in the department.'

'Really? The meeting's in half an hour?' Perhaps this was what Rosie had been supposed to tell her all along, and she'd just got sidetracked.

'No, it's already started. That's where everyone is.' Rosie smiled. 'Apart from us. Makes a nice change to have a free lunch hour.'

The lump that had formed suddenly in Cori's throat made words out of the question. She'd rather hoped that she might be a contributor to at least one new project in the department. And yet Tom had excluded her from this meeting. Maybe he'd decided that he was going to turn down the proposals she'd presented on Wednesday and had resumed his earlier policy of avoiding her rather than breaking the bad news.

'He should do something like this…' Rosie was still talking, seemingly unaware that she'd lost her audience. 'It would do him good. He's very tense.'

'Uh?'

'Tom. He's very tense. It's not surprising, really, he's got such a lot of responsibility now. Lots of people don't notice because he hides it. I do, though, because I suffer from tension myself.'

Cori concentrated on the paper folding. Maybe Rosie would get the hint and shut up for a minute.

Not any time soon. Rosie admired her second crane and reached for a new piece of paper. 'Of course, sometimes he needs saving from himself.'

Cori didn't reply. Much as she might have liked it to be, saving Tom from himself wasn't her own special mission. She knew that.

'I'll bet no one's really mentioned it, but you should

know.' Rosie leaned towards Cori confidingly. Something about the gesture seemed to indicate that this was what she'd really come to say, and that the tea and the interest in her work had just been polite preliminaries.

What if this was something she really did need to know and not just idle gossip? 'Yes?'

Rosie moved closer, obviously keen to unburden herself of this particular piece of information. 'You know, don't you, that he has…a reputation.'

Cori bit back the temptation to ask what Rosie meant. It was quite obvious from the look on her face that she was talking about Tom's love life. 'Really?'

That was enough to open the floodgates. 'Yes. I'm surprised no one else has mentioned it. Tom's very charming, well, I imagine you've noticed that already, and he dates loads of women. It never lasts, though.'

It wasn't her business, and it actually wasn't Rosie's either. But short of putting her fingers in her ears and singing loudly, it seemed that there was no way that Cori was going to be able to avoid hearing this.

'He always seems quite friendly with them, and they never seem to talk about it. That doctor down in A and E, Helen Kowalski, do you know her?'

Cori remembered vaguely that the first doctor who Adrian had seen had been called Kowalski, and that it had been her who'd called Tom. She decided not to encourage Rosie. 'No, I don't think I do.'

'Well, she's very pretty. Beautiful, actually, with very nice skin. She and Tom dated for a short while, a couple of years ago. She's with someone else now, I heard they were getting engaged…' Rosie's brow puckered slightly as if she was making a mental note to check on that piece of information. 'Anyway, it was all very civilised and Helen never said a word about what had happened. They still seem perfectly friendly…'

'That's…very professional.' Clearly Tom liked beautiful women who knew how to keep their mouths shut. The thought that the second characteristic probably ruled out anything much happening between Tom and Rosie was needlessly unkind but Cori couldn't help it.

'Oh, yes. He's always very professional. He's never been anything other than very professional with me.' Rosie's look invited Cori to answer the unasked question.

'Um… Yes, absolutely. Completely professional… with me.' Cori tried not to think about the smouldering look that Tom seemed to save for moments when they were alone together. *He* probably couldn't help that.

Rosie nodded, a hint of triumph in her smirk. Clearly this had been on her mental list of things to find out and the answer pleased her in some unspecified way. 'I suppose I'd better be getting on. Can I take the cranes I made? They'd look nice hung up by my desk.'

'Yes, of course. Help yourself.'

Rosie picked up all the folded paper birds, those that Cori had made as well as her own, and made for the door, leaving her empty teacup behind on the table. Cori stared at it, as if it might contain some clue as to what had just happened.

But no. Undoubtedly the lipstick mark on the rim contained Rosie's DNA, but that wasn't a great deal of use. It might feel as if the Tom Riley who had been haunting her dreams for the last two weeks had just been stolen from her, but no actual crime had been committed here.

The one redeeming thing was that she hadn't shown

her own hand. She hadn't made a fool of herself over a man who was apparently just as unreliable as he was good-looking.

Cori closed her eyes, breathing slowly and deeply. Okay. She knew three things. Tom had excluded her from a meeting that concerned her, which pretty much everyone else in the unit had been invited to. That hurt. Second, it seemed he had something of a reputation. That ought not to hurt, because it really wasn't any of her business. And, third, she'd just been warned off by his secretary.

Tom slipped his coat from the hanger, slinging it over his arm. Today had been a good day, and everything was right with the world. There was no requirement for fairies or trails of glitter this Friday. He'd seen that the light was on in the room that Cori had made her own, and that was all he needed to go to her.

'May I buy you a coffee?' She was sitting at the table, staring at a child's painting. When she looked up at him her eyes were cool, like the blue waters of the Mediterranean at night.

'No…thanks. Would you come here a minute? There's something I'd like to show you.'

Something serious, from the look on her face. Tom let the door swing closed behind him and walked over to where she was sitting.

'It might be nothing.'

'Which implies it might be something.' He threw his jacket across the back of a chair and sat down.

'You see this? I've just noticed it…' She slid the painting she'd been studying towards him.

'Yes.'

'See how it slants? And there's a gap, here.' She swept her hand across the paper to indicate what she meant.

'Yes. Does that concern you in any way?' As far as Tom could see, it was simply a child's painting.

'Well, I don't know whether this is something that's already been picked up, I haven't seen the medical notes. But I think that this child has some kind of difficulty on his left side. Maybe his eye or in co-ordinating his left hand with what he sees.

Tom glanced at the name, written in Cori's clear hand in the corner of the painting. 'That's not something I'm aware of. Peter's broken leg is the result of him skidding and falling over on some ice.' He looked again at the painting. It did look a little lopsided but, then, Peter was only seven, and to Tom's untutored eye it was pretty much what he'd expect from a child his age.

Out of the corner of his eye he saw her straighten next to him. 'Okay. I'd like to have it put onto his notes, though, just in case. For reference…'

'There's no need for that.'

'I think there is.' Cori was obviously steeling herself for a confrontation, and Tom was snared by the temptation to play devil's advocate. Watching her defend the children in her care always gave him a kick.

'There's no need because I'm going to take a look at him right now.' Tom imagined he'd get plenty more chances to fight with Cori, without manufacturing one now, and got to his feet, snatching up his coat. 'Coming?'

She should have known that Tom's unreliability wouldn't extend to the children in his care. He swept into his office, throwing his coat and briefcase onto the chair, taking off his jacket and loosening his tie, the way he always did before he went onto the ward. Opening his desk drawer, he rummaged for a moment, before pulling out a penlight, and then turned quickly, almost bumping into her on his way out.

'Sorry…' They both moved the same way at the same time to avoid each other, and he muttered an apology, frowning when Cori tried to move out of his way and ended up blocking his path again.

When he took her by the shoulders she realised that she was shaking. He moved her gently to one side and led the way out of his office. She followed, almost running to keep up with him, and slid to a stop as he slowed suddenly before entering one of the wards.

Tom's relaxed gait revealed nothing of the purpose that he'd showed just a moment ago. On the wards he was always relaxed and ready to talk to anyone.

'Hey, Peter.' The boy grinned up at him, and Tom shot one of his conspiratorial smiles back, before turning his attention to Peter's mother, who was sitting next to his bed.

'Sarah, this is Cori.' Tom had given every indication of having forgotten that she was there, and Cori jumped when she heard her name mentioned. 'She's an art therapist attached to the unit.'

'Hi.' Peter's mother turned to Cori. 'Are the folded paper dinosaurs your work?'

'Mainly Peter's. I just helped.'

'Thank you.' Sarah nodded a smile of appreciation towards Cori, before turning to Tom. His nonchalant attitude had fooled Peter into assuming that the only reason for their presence there was to discuss dinosaurs, but Sarah's instincts were a little sharper.

'I'd like to take a quick look at Peter's eyes. Just to make sure everything's okay.'

'His eyes? Why wouldn't his eyes be okay?'

'We've noticed that he doesn't seem to see as well out of his left eye.' Tom was watching Sarah, gauging her reaction. Caring for her, just as much as he cared for her son.

'Is that a problem?' Worry lines were spreading across Sarah's face, like hairline cracks on a vase.

'I'm just making sure.' Tom smiled at her reassuringly, flipping through Peter's notes. 'You said that he didn't hit his head at all.'

'Not as far as I know. It all happened so quickly.'

'Yes. The A and E team examined him pretty thoroughly, and there's no mention of any bumps.' Tom focused his grin on Peter. 'What do you say we take another quick look, eh?'

He seemed to evoke the same relaxed magic as when he had examined Adrian. A few jokes, a little kindness, and the impression that he had all the time in the world. Cori saw that, with as little fuss as possible, Tom's attention strayed from Peter's eye to his left hand.

Turning, he summoned a nurse and Cori stepped back from the bed. Tom gave some instructions and the nurse hurried away. Then he rose, drawing the curtains around Peter's bed. Brightly coloured curtains, which effectively told Cori that she wasn't wanted there any longer. She was on the outside, and anyone who mattered was on the inside.

She looked around the small ward, wondering whether it might be acceptable to go and sit with one of the other children and wait, to see what happened next, but all of them already had visitors. There was nothing else to busy herself with, and Cori was pretty sure that if she returned to the art room and stayed there to wait for Tom to come and find her, she'd be there all night. She wasn't needed any more and that was that.

This kind of thing happened all the time in hospitals. How many times had she initiated something at the last place she'd worked without getting to see the outcome? Working on her own in a small unit, rather than as part of a large team of therapists, she'd hoped that things might be different here, but that obviously wasn't the case.

What really hurt was Tom's attitude. She wasn't able to trust him but she wanted so much to do so. It just wasn't fair that he could ignore her so easily, and yet everything he did seemed to burn itself into her consciousness like a brand.

Cori marched back to her room and pulled on her coat, winding her scarf around her neck so vigorously that she almost choked herself. It was Friday evening, for goodness' sake. She was supposed to be getting ready for the weekend. Picking up her bag and resolving to do just that, she marched out of the unit.

CHAPTER SIX

WHEN SHE OPENED the door, and saw Tom standing on the doorstep, the smile slid from her face. Not a good sign. Maybe Saturday afternoon was a bad time to call, but he owed her an apology, and since Cori hadn't been around to receive it that morning Tom had decided to deliver it to her doorstep instead.

'Hi. You're in.' Of course she was in. How could she answer the door if she wasn't? Tom wondered if he sounded as tongue-tied as he felt.

'Yes. I'm in.'

Right. That was that one settled. On to the next thing. 'I just popped round on the off chance. I've been at work this morning.'

'Okay.' Her face betrayed nothing.

'I came to apologise. For leaving you hanging yesterday evening.'

She shrugged, her shoulders the only part of her body that divulged any clue to what she was thinking. 'No apology necessary. You were busy with Peter.'

'Yes. I thought you might like to know how he's getting on.'

His one last-ditch attempt at reaching her worked like a charm. Cori stepped back from the doorway.

'Yes, I would. Come in, I was about to make some coffee.'

'I don't want to disturb you if you're in the middle of something.' For the first time it occurred to Tom that she might not be on her own, that there might be someone she shared her Saturday afternoons with. Those entrancing eyes, the smile that had made him feel that she was somehow his couldn't have failed to go unnoticed by other men.

'No. I was doing some painting but I don't seem to be able to get it this afternoon.' Finally she smiled at him. 'Some days it's better just to leave it alone.'

He couldn't have left if he'd wanted to now. Tom stepped across the threshold and followed her along the hallway to her own front door, which was propped open by a large piece of stone that had been hewn in half to reveal a crystal inside. She nudged the doorstop out of the way with her foot and closed the door behind them.

It was hardly puzzling that he was beginning to find the scent of paint erotic, but it was disconcerting. Being at the mercy of his senses like this was not something that Tom liked to encourage in himself. But Cori... It was impossible not to let her presence flood over him. Like warm syrup. Or iced water. Whatever she did seemed to provoke in him an exaggerated reaction of either pleasure or pain.

She took his jacket, hanging it up in the narrow hallway, and led him through to a large, open-plan room which incorporated a small kitchen in one corner and a hotchpotch of furniture, most of which was probably second-hand. In the curve of a large bay window stood an easel, tilted towards the light so that it was impossible to see what the canvas on it showed.

Somehow, despite the fact that nothing matched, there was a feeling of harmony about the room. It was a bright, peaceful place, which calmed Tom's senses.

'So how is Peter?' She flipped open one of the kitchen cupboards and took out two mugs.

'He has a small tear in his retina. That's why he left a blank spot in his painting; he couldn't see that part of the paper.'

She whirled around suddenly to face him. 'Will his sight deteriorate?'

'Hopefully not. It's classified as an emergency and he had surgery this morning. I went in to be with him and talk him through it, and the ophthalmic surgeon is very pleased with the way things went.'

'Was it a result of his fall?'

'We don't think so. It seems to be a pre-existing condition. That's often a problem with diagnosing children, they don't always say when something's wrong, they just work around it.'

She set the mugs down with a clunk onto the kitchen counter. 'So I was right in coming to you?'

'Are you saying that you were considering *not* raising a concern about a patient because you might be mistaken?' Tom shot her a deliberately confrontational look.

'No, of course not.' The little toss of her head made him smile. 'Why, were you considering not doing anything about it because I might be mistaken?'

'Not for a moment.'

Now that was cleared up he could get to what he'd come here for. 'My apology…'

'Yes?' Suddenly she had him pinioned with her gaze. This feeling of powerlessness was something he'd avoided his whole life. Tom swallowed down a sudden and completely irrational urge to run.

'I came to apologise for offering you coffee and then leaving you standing there.'

Surprise flared in her expression momentarily, before she covered it up. 'That's okay. I didn't even notice.'

Perhaps she had and perhaps she hadn't. In any case, she seemed much better disposed towards him than she'd been five minutes ago. 'You had more important things to do.'

'Yeah, I did. That doesn't mean I can't apologise.'

'Apology accepted. I'm just glad that I could be of *some* use in the department.' There was hurt in her eyes, and this time she didn't bother to cover it up.

'What's the matter, Cori? Last week you were very insistent on telling me exactly what you thought. This week you seem to be dropping hints.'

'Things change.'

She turned away from him, frowning at a small red coffee machine that stood on the counter. Tom settled himself on the high stool that sat next to the divider between the kitchen and the living space. Whatever had changed between last week and this week, he wasn't moving until he found out what had happened.

She was looking suspiciously at the coffee machine, as if it was about to blow up. It looked new, although it was difficult to tell because everything was so clean it all looked as if it hadn't been used yet.

'It won't bite, you know.' Tom folded his arms.

'No, I know. I had it for Christmas, and I'm not quite sure…' She was pressing each one of the buttons on the machine in turn.

She was normally so practical, so capable that it was

unexpected to see her conquered by something as simple as a coffee machine. Tom couldn't help grinning. 'Have you got some capsules?'

'Yes. My brothers bought me some to go with it.' She flipped one of the cupboards open and Tom peered inside to see four unopened boxes of coffee.

'Which do you want?' He assumed she'd looked at the outside of the boxes at least.

'I'll have what you're having.'

Tom opened the box that contained the strongest brew, reckoning there was a good chance he was going to need it. Reaching across her to plug in the machine, he switched it on and dropped a capsule into the holder. Cori retreated to one of the high stools, seemingly content to let him get on with it, and Tom filled the machine's reservoir with water.

'You don't cook all that much?'

She didn't reply and Tom took that as a *no*. Anyone even vaguely interested in cooking generally didn't have a coffee machine for two months without at least reading the instructions and working out how to use it.

'Espresso? Or cappuccino?'

'Um. Espresso.'

He suspected that she'd chosen the option that sounded easiest. 'Cups?'

'There are some smaller cups in the top cupboard…' She was watching him steadily, as if waiting for him to do something. Tom finished making the coffee, setting hers in front of her.

'Would you be able to have some sessions with Peter next week?' He leaned back against the kitchen counter, taking a sip of his espresso.

'He's not having specific therapy for that eye?' Her face still showed no emotion.

'Yes, it's all arranged. But eye operations can be very difficult for kids, and he already has a relationship with you.'

'I could… I mean, I'd *like* to talk to him about it…' She seemed almost hesitant in asking.

'I did think that you might want to see things through with him.' If she didn't, he was going to drink his coffee, go home, and think hard about how he could have misjudged her so badly.

'Yes, I would. Thanks. I won't wait until Monday, I'll go and see him tomorrow if that's all right with you.' She smiled at him, and suddenly it looked as if he was going to stay.

Ridiculous. Crazy. Just because Tom had arrived on her doorstep, shown himself to be equal to the coffee machine, and dropped a few crumbs to salve her wounded pride, it didn't mean that he was to be trusted. He was still excluding her. And although Rosie's assessment of him was probably not coming from an entirely rational place, Cori believed her.

So why did she feel like flinging herself into his arms? Ripping his clothes off and dragging him through to her bedroom? No, actually taking his clothes off very slowly would be a lot better…

Cori dismissed the thought. He'd been so enthusiastic about their plans for the art room and now it seemed he'd dismissed them out of hand, without telling her why. If he could reject her so easily, she should be more careful about what she wished for where Tom was concerned.

She wouldn't allow herself to fantasise about him. Temporary families, temporary jobs, temporary lovers… None of them were worth breaking her heart over.

'So what *is* the matter?' He was regarding her steadily, giving her that *everything's okay* look that he gave the kids, only this was the grown-up, X-rated version that was melting her insides and making her tremble.

'Nothing…'

'And since you don't trust me enough to tell me, then you're obviously not going to trust me enough to confirm if I guess correctly.'

'That doesn't necessarily follow.'

'So there *is* something.'

She may as well say it. She wasn't being petty, she was a professional who reacted with her head. 'Okay. Well, I would have hoped that if you were calling a meeting about the unit's new projects, it might have been an obvious move to invite me.'

He stiffened suddenly, his eyes darkening with something that looked like anger. 'Who told you?' He held his hand up. 'No. Actually, don't tell me. I think I already know.'

'I'm not a sneak. Anyway, a department meeting is no big secret. And I have skills and expertise that can help you. I thought we'd agreed on that.' She could feel her heart pounding in her chest. This was where it all broke apart. Tom couldn't deny that he'd excluded her, and now that it was all out in the open she couldn't just meekly go along with it.

'Yes, we did. Which was exactly why you weren't at that meeting, because we could hardly talk about you if you were sitting right there.'

'You talked about me?' Cori wasn't sure whether she liked the sound of that or not. She walked over to the sink with her empty cup, to cover her confusion.

'Yes.' He moved his weight from the counter top behind him and took a step towards her. 'I said that I thought the unit had been given a unique opportunity, and that we should grab it with both hands. I said that your skills had the potential to make a measurable improvement in the services we offered our patients and their families.'

'Ah…' Perhaps it was her turn to apologise.

'I also said that I thought we should consider very carefully how much money we could raise in the next few weeks to finance some of the proposals that you made to me on Wednesday.' He seemed to be getting closer.

'You… I told you that the artists' group is self-funding.'

'Yes, you did.' He was definitely closer now. Close enough to stretch out his arms either side of her and plant his hands on the edge of the sink behind her. 'Your group works hard for its funding. I think it behoves us to work equally hard to help raise money for work that you're offering to do at the unit.'

'I…' He was far too near for anything other than honesty now. The whole truth and not just part of it. 'I've made myself look like an idiot, haven't I?'

'No. I can see how it must have looked to you. I've made some preliminary enquiries with the hospital's building maintenance group, and it seems that it's my decision as to whether we go ahead or not. But I felt that I should at least discuss it with Dr Shah.'

'And you didn't want to tell me about it until you had.'

'I've spoken to him on the phone, and he was very

enthusiastic. I'm going to see him at home tomorrow afternoon to show him your proposals. I don't think he's going to disagree with me.'

'Thank you, Tom.' Cori tried to avoid his gaze but couldn't. 'I've misjudged you.'

'Of course you did. How could you have done anything else when I've consistently neglected to discuss things with you?'

'You… It would be wrong to promise something you couldn't deliver.'

'Yeah. That's my excuse.' He was very close now, and his eyes promised something that Cori knew for certain he could deliver. In full, and then some. All she had to do was reach out.

She stood on her toes, brushing her lips against his cheek. 'Thank you. For everything you've done.'

'You're welcome. I don't suppose you'd like to do that again?'

'This?' She kissed his cheek again.

'Yeah.' He didn't move his hands from the counter top, but dipped his head to touch his lips to her forehead. All that Cori could think about was making this real. Letting go of the pretence and doing the one thing she wanted to do. She slid her hand over the soft wool of his sweater, up to the neck of his shirt. At the first touch of her fingers on his skin she heard his uneven intake of breath.

When she curled her arm around his neck, pulling him down towards her, he drew her in close, making sure that she felt his body against hers before she had a chance to feel his lips. He wanted her. The knowledge spilled into her like a bright light penetrating a very dark place. He wanted her.

His kiss told her that too. The way he took it slowly, savouring it and then going back for more. Deeper this time, just by a fraction. She could do this all day and all night, until they both reached their limits.

'I really don't want to stop…'

'But you think we should?' She knew that he was offering her a way out. If they went back now, then they could both pretend nothing had happened. No harm done.

'I think that… I think it's going to compromise both of us if we take this where I want it to go.' He wound a few strands of her hair around his finger with an expression of regret. He was good at this. He knew exactly how to let a woman down gently. Cori found herself wondering how many times he'd done this before.

The *how many times* made her hesitate just a moment too long. Suddenly his hands were on her shoulders and he had her at arm's length. 'You know, what I really want is to spend some time with you. Just to talk.'

Despite her raging want for him, this was the most thrilling thing of all. His scent might make her feel giddy, his touch might send shivers through her body, but this was something different. Hadn't Jean always told her, in those difficult teenage years, that finding someone to sleep with was easy enough, but finding someone to talk to was a lot harder?

And Dr Tom Riley, the man with the reputation, wanted to talk to her.

Perhaps Rosie had exaggerated things, but Cori somehow doubted it. 'Talking would be…something different.'

His eyes narrowed as he scanned her face. 'So you heard? I'm told I have something of a reputation.'

Tom was obviously expecting her to say that she'd heard nothing of the sort, because his eyebrows shot up when Cori nodded.

'Who...?'

'I'm definitely not going to tell you that.'

'No. That's probably for the best.' His sigh was perhaps a bit too theatrical and clearly for her benefit. 'Things were a lot easier before I took on this job.'

'I think you make a very good head of paediatrics.'

'*Acting* head...' He slicked his hand back through his hair in a gesture of frustration. 'Which makes it quite impossible for me to mention that your eyes are beautiful. Even on my day off.'

'They're not beautiful.'

'So what are they, then?'

Cori wasn't sure. A little too noticeable for her face maybe... 'Startling.'

He chuckled. 'I'll give you that. Startlingly beautiful. Although, of course, I shouldn't be saying that. Or probably even thinking it, at least not for another six weeks.'

Was that what he thought? That the only reason they made a potentially explosive and dangerous mix was that he was her boss? What about the volatile mix of a man who didn't play for keeps and a woman who did?

'You know what. You said you wanted to take another look at the paintings. Let's go down to the tea shop and we can have something to eat and talk about your plans for the unit.' Getting out of there before they both gave in to temptation seemed like the way to go.

He gave her a grin that radiated sex and sent blood rushing to her head. 'Good plan. We'll take this relationship to another level, shall we?'

He'd always been so careful. Always made sure that his partners knew that he didn't really do long term. Before long, word had got around and his reputation precluded the need for that awkward conversation. Tom Riley would be good company, a good lover, he'd end it well and never breathe a word about anything after that ending. But the one thing he didn't do was for ever.

He wasn't proud of that. For ever was something that he'd seen most of his friends embark on, and each time he'd wished he could do that himself. But surviving his father's emotional and physical violence hadn't come without a cost. Tom had shut it all out and learned to make a life for himself, and now opening himself up to anyone seemed an impossible risk.

'So which ones are yours?' He tucked those thoughts away, out of sight, where they belonged.

'Hmm. I don't think I'm going to tell you.' She flashed him a smile over her tea cup. 'You might feel the urge to be nice.'

'I don't *have* to be nice. It's my day off, remember. No rules.' Cori always made him feel as if there weren't any rules. He'd almost disregarded all his personal and professional rules and blundered into something... He didn't need to think about that either. They'd brushed against the point of no return and then drawn back. And the rules mentioned absolutely nothing about enjoying someone's company.

'I'm not telling you, all the same.'

'A test, then.' He grinned at her. 'To see if I can pick yours out as the best, without having known that they were yours.'

She flushed a little, confirming his suspicions. 'I don't expect you to do that.'

'You'd like me to, though.'

'I'm an artist. Of course I'd *like* you to. But I'd appreciate your honest opinion.'

'Okay.' He leaned back in his chair, aware that Cori was sitting bolt upright, her fingers clutching her cup tightly. 'Well, this is going to be tricky.'

He picked a seascape, which he was pretty sure wasn't Cori's but that he liked anyway. He was sure the vase of flowers, a cascade of blues and purples with a twist of individuality, had to be hers, but she shook her head, grinning.

'That's Marianne's. We were at art school together.'

'Close but no cigar, then.' His gaze ranged over the wall. The intricate pencil rendering of a London skyline wasn't hers, neither was the abstract. Cori was far too involved with people. He rather hoped that the dark rendering of a crowded, rain-soaked street at night wasn't hers either. There was something disturbing about it, although Tom couldn't quite work out what.

'What are you thinking?' She was looking at him intently, and Tom realised that he'd been staring at the painting.

'I'm…' He was suddenly at a loss for words. 'That one's…challenging.'

'Yeah? Challenging how?'

'I don't know. I'm no expert on art.'

She grinned. 'But you know what you like. Everyone knows what they like.'

'I suppose so. It's not that I don't *like* it, I just couldn't live with it.' Tom studied the picture carefully, trying to work out exactly how he felt about the painting. The figures on the street seemed so alone, hunched over and hurrying to escape the rain. 'I can't quite get to grips with it…'

He turned as Cori snorted with laughter.

'I've put my foot in my mouth, haven't I? It's yours.'

'Yep. It's mine.'

He should have known. He couldn't take his eyes off the picture, and he didn't know what to make of it. Who else could have painted it but Cori? 'Sorry. I didn't mean...'

'Don't be silly. I love that it makes you feel something.' She looked over at the painting. 'It's called *Walking Home Alone*. It's about isolation, in a crowd.'

Tom looked again. The more he looked, the more it seemed to be speaking just to him. It was almost an effort not to stand up, walk over to it and touch it.

'When you painted it... It seems very personal. Is it something you know about?'

She nodded, looking at him thoughtfully. 'I think we all do in one way or another. When I was a kid I used to feel I was the only one in the world who didn't have a family. I was quite wrong, of course.'

'And then you were adopted.'

'Yes. Then I went to Ralph and Jean. Best thing that ever happened to me.'

Tom nodded. Cori may have found her way out of the loneliness that the painting portrayed so starkly, but he'd never quite shaken the feeling. It was the loneliness of having a secret. Keeping it, until it became so much a part of you that you couldn't let go.

'That one's mine too.' She seemed to sense that he'd had enough of this guessing game and pointed to another painting, this one of children playing on a beach.

'That one I like.' It was warm, uncomplicated and portrayed the kind of childhood everyone should have.

'Yeah. I painted it to be liked.'

'Not the other one?'

She smiled. 'Not particularly. I like that you picked it out, though.'

He'd done something right, even if he wasn't quite sure what. And he'd made Cori smile, which was fast becoming the one and only object of his afternoon.

CHAPTER SEVEN

CORI WAS WORKING harder than she had ever done in her life. Together, she and Tom were exploring the things that she could do in eight weeks, rather than the things she couldn't. There was a whole unit full of children with different medical conditions and different needs, and only a few short weeks remaining to leave something lasting behind.

The whole unit had been invited to come up with fundraising ideas, and suggestions came flooding in. It became apparent that Tom had been doing some serious promotion of the gallery at the tea shop, and the artists' group couldn't supply enough canvases to keep the wall completely full. She suspected that Tom had purchased a painting too, and noticed that *Walking Home Alone* had been sold, for cash, to an unknown buyer. At this rate they were going to have enough money to provide murals for the whole hospital, but Tom had jealously chased away any other heads of department who'd had the temerity to try and divert Cori from her work in the paediatric unit.

If only this could last. She made the most of every moment, knowing that this was the job she wanted more than anything, and consoling herself with the thought that when her eight weeks were up she could always return to help out on a voluntary basis with some of the projects she was starting.

Tom's alarm had gone off an hour early and he lay in bed, wondering why. He had a horrible feeling that there was somewhere he'd promised to be.

His phone rang and he answered without looking at the caller display. It had to be the hospital at this time in the morning. 'Tom Riley.'

'What are you wearing?'

'Cori?' His hand slid over his chest. If she really wanted to know what he wore in bed, she could come over and find out…

'If it's not running gear, you'd better hurry up. I'm just about to get into my car so I'll be with you in twenty minutes.'

Right. He remembered now. There was nothing like an early-morning wake-up call to remind him why he usually ran in the evening after work.

When Cori arrived, clad in leggings and a fleece jacket, the day brightened considerably. It was only a short way to the park, and Tom began to feel the familiar surge of strength in his body as it warmed up, ready to take on a little more speed.

'How far is it around the perimeter?' She stopped at the park gates to stretch a little, and Tom followed suit, trying to keep his mind off the slim curve of her hips.

'About twice as far as we'll have to run for the challenge. I reckon we take it slowly until we get to the halfway mark, then see what we can do.'

'Okay. I'm a little nervous about this. I only run three times a week and I don't know if I can go at the pace we need.'

'We'll see what our time is first. Then we can worry about whether we can do it or not.' Tom knew that he had the speed, and if it was humanly possible to get Cori around the course, he'd do it.

The idea was simple enough. Five teams of runners would complete a relay through the streets of central London. The twist to it was that the runners weren't racing against time, or each other, but against five teams who were travelling by public transport, using their wits to find the quickest route on the day.

It was possible. Buses and trains covered the distance much faster, but over short stretches the runners had the advantage of not having to wait for traffic or the next train. The idea had already caught everyone's imagination. They'd had little trouble finding enough people to make up all the teams, and the 'Runners' and 'Riders' were already busy planning the quickest routes between the handover points.

They finished their warm-up and started to run. Cori had a sweet style. Graceful and economical, she seemed to float along, easily keeping up with Tom on the first half of their circuit.

'Ready to speed up?' He shot a grin at her as they approached the halfway mark.

'Yes. Go for it.'

She seemed to be handling their present pace pretty well, and the exhilaration of running with her egged him on to speed up, perhaps a little more than he should. But she responded, and Tom felt a rush of pleasure. This was going to be a lot more fun than he'd bargained for.

* * *

Tom began to push a little, and Cori lengthened her stride, seeing his nod when she didn't fall back. When they were close to the end of the circuit he pushed it up another gear, his strong frame making mincemeat of the now punishing pace.

She was falling behind. Cori fixed her eyes on his back and concentrated on closing the space between them. She made a little headway and saw him glance behind.

Keep going. She willed him not to slow down, digging deep for just a little extra speed. She wanted to show him that she could do it.

'Come on…' His shouted words of encouragement spurred her on, and she put her head down and sprinted. As they reached the gates of the park she drew level with him.

'Nice.' There was real approval in his tone, even though Cori was gasping for air and he seemed hardly out of breath.

'Time…' She managed to get out just the one word.

He consulted the stopwatch strapped to his wrist. 'We're pretty much on target already. If we keep training, we'll do it without any problem at all. I reckon two fast-paced runs for a couple of weeks, and then step it up to three.'

'Two…' She gave up the unequal struggle and just nodded to indicate that she was up for that.

He waited for her to recover and then fell in step with her as she began to jog through the park gates and onto the pavement at a gentle speed. She felt exhilarated beyond the expected endorphin effect. She'd kept up with Tom and earned his respect.

And running beside him made her feel good. He felt strong and dependable, and he was able to set a pace and keep to it. It was even permissible to admire his body, under the guise of assessing his muscle tone.

'I'll see you at work in…an hour?' Tom stopped by her car, looking at his watch.

'Yes. Thanks for this morning. I really enjoyed it.'

He nodded, bending to brush his lips against her cheek. It was the very briefest of encounters, but it took Cori's breath away. He turned, without waiting for any response from her, and walked away quickly.

The text was ordinary enough—when she had a moment, could Cori come to Tom's office? But when she got there she wished she hadn't waited the twenty minutes until the children in her charge were ready to go for lunch. Tom looked dreadful, pale and haggard, as if he might be bleeding to death from some concealed wound.

'What's wrong?'

'Nothing.' He avoided her gaze. 'I just wondered if you could help with a patient.'

'Of course.' Cori sat down quickly in the chair opposite his desk. Something *was* bothering Tom and she didn't want to leave until she found out what.

'I… We have a new patient in Bay Six. Seven-year-old boy, with newly diagnosed diabetes. He's going to be here for a couple of weeks while we stabilise him.'

'Okay. And I can help with that?'

Tom shook his head. 'No, we've got that covered. I want you to see if you can get him to talk.'

'About what?'

'He has a lot of bruises.' Tom's gaze dropped to the surface of the desk in front of him.

'And that's not due to the diabetes?'

'Increased susceptibility to bruising and slow healing *are* a symptom of diabetes. I want to make sure that's all it is, though, and I'd like you to work with him.'

Cori caught her breath. Tom must think that it was serious or he wouldn't have even suggested this. 'You have concerns about him?'

'I have.' He shook his head. The blankness in his eyes was beginning to frighten Cori. 'I have a feeling. That's all. I've spoken to the hospital's social worker and we've agreed that I'll try to find out more from him over the next few days.'

'And you want me to talk with him.'

'Yeah. Or paint…or whatever. Whatever you need to do to find out whether there's any need for further action on our part.'

'Okay. You've spoken to him?'

'No.'

Something prickled at the back of Cori's neck. The very same instinct that Tom was experiencing with the boy perhaps. Something was wrong and she couldn't put her finger on what it was.

'Is there a reason why you haven't spoken with him yet?'

'Cori, can you just do it?' His tone was level, but his hand was shaking. Tom gripped the arm of his chair in an obvious attempt to steady the tremors, and seemed to take a deep breath. 'I'm sorry. I didn't mean to snap. Today's turning into a bad day.'

'That's okay. I wish you would.'

'Would what?'

'Snap. I wish you'd snap.'

He smiled at her. That luminous, melting smile that

reached all of the pleasure centres of her brain. It made her blood run cold.

'Don't do that, Tom.'

'Do what?' He spread his hands in a gesture of innocence.

'Stop pretending that there's nothing going on.' The illusion of a man who was untroubled was so perfect that Cori almost began to doubt herself. But it was too perfect. Somewhere, locked behind the barrier of Tom's impenetrable good humour, there was a wounded soul, screaming to be heard.

'There *is* nothing going on.' He was regarding her steadily.

'Okay.' She got to her feet. She had to move before she started raging at him, and Cori's instinct was that her rage would only make him retreat even more. 'I'll go and see the boy this afternoon. I'll let you know what my thoughts are.'

'Thank you. I'd appreciate that.'

That look. The one that said nothing was the matter and betrayed just a trace of relief that she was going along with the lie. She couldn't bear it. Planting her hands on his desk, she leaned across until they were face to face.

'We're not done yet, Tom.'

Turning quickly, before he could come out with any more denials, she walked out of his office.

Tom wondered whether she was aware he was watching her, and came to the conclusion that she must know. But Cori didn't seem to mind, and it settled Tom's raging emotions to do so.

He'd seen children who had been abused before, far

too many of them. And although every mark inflicted on a child's skin was unacceptable, he'd seen cases that were a lot worse than this one. So why now?

Because of Cori maybe. He watched as she smiled at Jamie, sitting down by his bedside. She didn't push the paper at him but did quite the reverse, putting the brightly coloured pencils and the paper just out of his reach, as if it was a coincidence that she had them with her. When Jamie reached for them himself, she slid them a little closer, smiling in that impish way she had.

If he'd had someone like Cori when he'd been a kid... Tom had thought about that prospect more than once. Someone who might have come to his rescue when he was still young, before all the hang-ups had become an inseparable part of him, as if they were set in stone.

Suddenly, in his imagination, he was Jamie's age again, sitting in the warmth of Cori's smile. Right away he knew that wasn't really what he wanted. In the imaginary world where anyone could be any age they liked, he narrowed the age gap between them and imagined her at six years old and himself at eight. *He* would be protecting *her*, holding her hand and being her friend. And that, somehow, would heal his own pain.

'Tom!' Someone spoke insistently behind him and he jumped.

'Yeah, sorry.' He turned away from Cori and the image dissolved, taking a little bit of his heart with it.

Kate, the senior nurse on duty, handed him the notes for the child in the bed across from Jamie's. 'Do you need anything else?' Her querying look reminded Tom that a visit to this particular bay wasn't on his schedule for the day.

'No, it's fine. Thanks, Kate, I'm just checking up on

something.' He focused his eyes on the notes in front of him and then handed them back. 'Fine. That's fine. Thanks very much.' Tom strode out of the ward, leaving Jamie in Cori's care.

He was almost disappointed to find that his car was just as he'd left it. No fairies on the windscreen, no folded dinosaurs under the wipers. Tom wondered whether she would have left something, just a sprinkle of glitter maybe, if Cori had known how he felt right now.

His hand shook as he reached into his pocket and his keys slipped through his fingers and fell to the concrete. He wanted to forget about all that had happened today and just talk with Cori. Just be with her and feel her warmth.

He let the phone ring three times and then hung up. Cori wasn't answering. It was suddenly calming to know that he was alone. If he was alone then he couldn't hurt or be hurt.

He took a deep breath, picked up his keys from the ground and disengaged the locks on the car doors. Automatically, he went through the motions. Opening the back door to throw his briefcase and coat onto the seat. Getting behind the steering wheel. He was in control now. It had been stupid to think that he needed anyone else.

His phone rang, and he jumped. When he looked at the caller display he almost didn't answer. Then he heard Cori's voice on the other end of the line, almost as if someone else had answered for him.

'Tom… Are you there?'

'Yeah, sorry. I must have pocket-dialled you.'

'Okay.'

From the tone of her voice she didn't buy that for a moment.

'Look, I've just walked in through my front door. Would you like to come over?'

'What for?' He knew exactly what for. This was an invitation to explain himself.

'Nothing in particular. Just pop in if you feel like it. I've learned how to make hot chocolate. Once I got to grips with the coffee, I felt I wanted to branch out a bit. It's pretty good.'

'That would be great. But can I take a rain check? I've got something to do tonight. Another time.'

'Of course.'

There was a pause, as if something else needed to be said but neither of them was going to make the first move.

'Look after yourself, Tom.'

'Yeah. See you.'

He always *had* looked after himself, there had never been anyone else that he could depend on. He'd grown up and become strong enough to defend himself. No one could touch him now, not even Cori.

CHAPTER EIGHT

CORI WAS TWIRLING her brush thoughtfully in a dab of scarlet paint, wondering whether a red slash of colour on the canvas was what she really wanted to do, when the doorbell rang. Dinner was served.

She hurried through the hallway and threw open the main door. Tom was standing on the doorstep, under a large umbrella.

'Oh.' The brush slipped from her fingers and clattered onto the floor. 'You're not my pizza.'

'No, I'm not.' He bent to pick up the brush and handed it to her. 'Is that a problem?'

'No. I just wasn't expecting you.'

'I came to…' Tom clearly had no more of an idea than she did about what he was doing there. But when she looked up into his face, she thought she saw pain.

'Whatever it is, you can't do it on the doorstep. Come in.'

He gave a small nod, folding down the umbrella and giving it a shake, before propping it in the porch. Each one of his movements was sparing and controlled, and it seemed like he was trying to keep it all together.

He sat down wearily on the sofa, as if he'd come a

long way to get here. Cori sat down silently next to him. Whatever happened next, it had to come from him.

'I should apologise. I…' He shrugged, seemingly lost for words.

'You have nothing to apologise for. You seem to have something on your mind, and I'd really like to help, if I can.'

Her doorbell rang. Damn, this wasn't the time.

'Your bell…'

'I know. It's my pizza. Forget it.'

'Aren't you hungry?' A twitch at the corner of Tom's mouth said that he knew that he'd quite literally been saved by the bell. That he'd got himself in too deep and he was looking for a way to retreat gracefully.

She wasn't going to help him with that. 'Yes. But I want to hear what you've got to say more than I want to eat.' The bell rang again, this time more insistently.

'This can wait. And he'll only keep ringing…'

Cori frowned. Tom was right, you couldn't just leave a pizza delivery guy standing on the doorstep. He'd press the doorbell for every flat in the building. 'Okay. Stay there.'

She ran to the door, flung it open, snatched her pizza and pressed the money for it into the young man's hand. Slamming the door in his face, before he could thank her for the generous tip, she threw the pizza box onto the kitchen counter and sat back down on the sofa, next to Tom. The whole operation took about forty-five seconds.

'Don't you want to put that in the oven?' Tom's demons were making a last-ditch attempt to preserve their hold on him.

'I'd prefer to talk about whatever it was that brought you here in the first place.'

'You promised me hot chocolate.' That smile. The one that seemed so open and inviting and yet hid so much.

'Later. It's too early for that.'

'That's not what you said on the phone.' His tone was suddenly flirtatious. That was Tom's answer to everything that came a little too close for comfort.

'I thought it went without saying that you'd like a progress report on Jamie first…' Cori gave him the sweetest smile she could, in the face of his blistering, thousand-watt gaze.

He flopped back onto the sofa cushions, grinning. 'All right. Yes, of course I'd like a progress report.'

Cori swallowed hard. If she'd thought that talking about work was going to make things any easier then she'd been wrong. The sizzle between them retreated a little, but not far enough to allow her to think with any clarity.

'We spent a couple of hours together—he seemed to enjoy it and we talked quite a bit. He said nothing about the bruises and I didn't ask.'

'What about his drawings? I saw that you gave him crayons…' Tom was thoughtful now, staring at the ceiling.

'He's been ill, he's in a strange place, and there are obviously some things on his mind. I'm waiting for him to tell me.'

'Do you have any guesses?' Tom turned his head, and his gaze hit her like a bolt of lightning. These were the moments when he was so irresistible. It was the way she'd first seen him, a concerned and committed doctor, who had no reason to hide his passion. As a man, a lover, Tom Riley seemed always to be hiding from something.

'My guess is that this is a process I can't rush. He'll tell me when he's ready.' Cori supposed that Tom would do that too. Only the years had given him a better defence strategy than Jamie was likely to have.

Tom nodded thoughtfully. 'You have a way with the children. They trust you.'

'Thank you…' There was something about Tom's praise that made her crave more, and he seemed to know it.

'You're kind and creative. You know how to weave a spell…' He leaned in a little closer, his gaze mesmerising her. 'A little pushy at times, but I'm getting to like that too. And you have gorgeous eyes.'

Her breath caught, almost choking her. 'Tom, I…'

Maybe her confusion was showing on her face. He seemed to sense it. 'Am I embarrassing you?'

'Well, yes. A little.'

'I just like to pay you compliments. I think you deserve them. But I could stop now, if it makes you uncomfortable.'

She couldn't help smiling. 'Yes. I think you should.'

He nodded. 'Would it be all right if I mentioned that you fold a very mean dinosaur?'

'What are you doing here, Tom?'

'I wanted some company.'

'Why me?'

'Only you would do.' He smiled. That we-know-a-secret smile that rocked her world. 'Can I cook for you?'

'Cook for me?'

'Yeah. I'm a really good cook. Didn't I tell you that?'

'You might have mentioned it. I'm not sure that I entirely believed you, I thought you might be bragging. And there's a perfectly good pizza there that we could heat up.'

He rolled his eyes. 'That pizza's going to be as hard as a brick by now. I can pop to the deli around the corner and get us something better to eat. Don't you want to find out if I'm as good as I say I am?'

'Ohhh!' He was good. Very good.

'You like that?'

'Oh, yes.' Cori felt as if she was melting. 'Again.'

'Wait…wait.' He chuckled quietly. 'Anticipation's the key.'

'You're going to kill me.' Tom's first course had been delicious, melt-in-the-mouth pasta with a seafood sauce. She'd challenged him to surprise her with the second course, and he'd risen to that challenge.

'No, I'm not.' He let the spoon brush her lips, leaving a smear of molten chocolate, then withdrew it. 'Keep your eyes closed.'

She heard the spoon scrape in the bowl and then felt it touch her tongue, cold this time. 'Mmm. Sorbet. Vanilla sorbet. With something else.'

'Lime.'

'Uh. Nice.'

He let the cold spoon linger against her lips, just a few moments longer than he really needed to. This felt just like sex. It had taken the same kind of trust, closing her eyes and letting him feed her. And she was rapidly getting very turned on.

'Try this.'

She felt the spoon at her lips again, warm this time.

She could smell the chocolate. Cori had never stopped to smell chocolate before, but this… He let her have the whole spoonful.

'More?'

'Not yet.' She wanted to savour each note of the bittersweet taste in her mouth.

'Now you're getting the idea. Did you know you have hundreds of thousands of taste receptors in your mouth? Different tastes trigger responses at different times, which means that good food is always worth taking your time over.'

She could think about the science later. Right now, all she knew was that each one of those receptors was on high alert and begging for more. If any other guy had tried this, he would have found himself kicked out and unable to walk without pain for a week. But Tom wasn't any other guy, and she'd let him do it. In return he seemed to be doing his best to drive her totally mad with pleasure.

'Here.' He picked up her hand, running her finger around the cool bowl of a drinking glass. There was a sweet fruity smell as he raised the glass to her lips. 'Take a sip.'

'Mmm. That's really nice. Dessert wine… Hey, what are you doing? Are you drinking it too?'

'Just a mouthful. I'm enjoying it with you.' Cori felt the glass against her lips again and took a little of the wine, wondering whether he'd allowed her to drink from the place where his lips had touched the rim. The thought made her head reel.

'I concede. You were right and I was wrong. Food's a sensual experience.' She wondered whether the admission was going to call a halt to this. She hoped not.

'Now I've won you round to my point of view…'

A sweet, unmistakable smell made her smile. 'Mmm. Strawberries…'

Tom woke up with a start. The sensation that Cori was in his arms was still so real that for a moment he thought she was. He rolled over, burying his face in his hands. What on earth had happened last night?

It had all started when Cori had thrown down a challenge. She'd said that creating a desert to die for in half an hour was impossible, and he'd shown her differently. Then she'd shared her own passion with him as they'd sat together in front of a blank canvas. Slowly his own face had emerged, half smiling back at him. As she'd worked, he'd felt her body relax against his, drawing him into her own world of happiness.

He couldn't remember when he'd had a better evening, or ever having been so loath to say goodnight. But sex with Cori…

His body reacted to the thought, and Tom rolled out of bed, hoping that the chill air might go some way towards dampening his ardour. Being her boss might be a good enough excuse for the next month or so, but sleeping with Cori would be breaking the rules on a far deeper level than that and at some point he was going to have to face up to the real reason. They weren't two friends, sharing something special, on the explicit understanding that it wasn't permanent. If she took him into her bed she'd make him her lover and Tom doubted if he'd walk away from Cori in one piece.

He switched the shower on, shivering at the touch of the cool water. Maybe he should paint her a picture, one that would tell her everything she needed to know about him.

No. Not that. Maybe a letter. Perhaps he should just write down all the things he couldn't say, and then she'd see that he wasn't the man for her. The idea grew in his head, blossoming as the water grew warmer. It was one way to salvage their friendship before he did anything stupid.

CHAPTER NINE

THE NEXT FEW days should have been perfect. Tom was supportive at work, and his creative approach to bureaucracy meant that there were no obstacles to the plans for making the art room into an environment that children would love long after Cori was gone. On Friday evening, a staff meeting in the pub to exchange ideas for fundraising had been well attended and had gone on until closing time.

She told herself that this was all she wanted. Even if Rosie's assessment of Tom wasn't necessarily to be trusted, he hadn't denied it. He was a great boss, a good friend and that should be enough. Cori wasn't in the market for a fling, particularly one that she suspected might just break her heart.

When her phone rang on Saturday morning, she turned over in bed, keeping her eyes firmly closed. Whatever time it was, it was too early.

The phone stopped and started again. Whoever it was wasn't taking no for an answer. She grabbed the handset from the nightstand and held it to her ear.

'What?'

'Still in bed?' Tom's voice came down the line.

'Yes.'

'Then I suppose I shouldn't really ask what you're wearing.'

'You can if you want. I'm not ashamed of being caught wearing pyjamas. Why are you calling?' If he told her that he'd woken her up for an early morning chat, she was going to find and throttle him.

'You asked me to. Call me in the morning, you said, or I'll never make it into work.'

'Okay, you called me. Thanks, Tom.' She cut the line and sank back into the pillows.

The phone rang again.

'Tom!'

'Yeah. You didn't sound really committed about the getting-out-of-bed thing.'

'I'm not.'

'It's just that you said that you wanted to pop in to see Jamie and a couple of the other kids today, and that you had things to do this afternoon, so you needed to get an early start.'

'Uh.' Cori was beginning to remember. She *had* got a busy day today, and she had asked Tom to call her. 'Sorry, I…'

'No matter.'

The doorbell rang. Cori dragged herself out of bed, and somehow managed to get her arms into her dressing gown, while still holding the phone. 'Where are you now?'

'On my way to the hospital.'

'Okay. I'll see who it is at the door, and I'll be on my way in about ten minutes.'

'No, you won't…'

'Why?'

'I've just left breakfast on your front doorstep. Don't hurry it.'

Cori scrambled to the front door and found that Tom had already gone. There was, however, a cardboard box, which on inspection proved to contain hot coffee, warm croissants and a chilled fresh fruit salad.

An hour after he had left breakfast on her doorstep, and then raced back to his car and driven off, Cori walked into the paediatric unit. Tom was sitting in the reception area, looking through the plans for the mural that was to be painted there and trying not to let it appear that he was waiting for her.

She was obviously going somewhere this afternoon, and she looked fabulous in slim-fitting jeans and ankle boots that made her legs look impossibly long. A red knitted jacket, with a matching, multi-coloured scarf slung across her shoulders, accentuated her dark hair and the porcelain of her skin.

'Thank you for breakfast.' A slightly brighter shade of lipstick than usual made her lips look impossibly kissable. The fact that she bent down to deliver the words directly into his ear was rather more than Tom had bargained for.

'You're welcome. I would have come and cooked something, but I decided that would probably constitute housebreaking.'

'Maybe. I wouldn't have reported you, particularly if you were making me breakfast.'

'In that case, I might give it a try.' Tom got to his feet, gathering up his pile of notes. 'Are you ready to see Jamie?'

'Yes, I'll spend some time with him, and then there are a couple of other things I need to do.' She reached into her large leather handbag and pulled out a rag doll. 'Do you think Molly will like this?'

'I think she'll love it.' The doll had red hair like Molly's and freckles. It also had a small lump under its pretty green summer dress, and when Tom investigated a little further he found that it was a replica of Molly's insulin pump.

'I'll leave it on her bed while she's having her lunch.'

Tom had noticed that one of Cori's favourite things was leaving little presents for the children to find. If she could, she'd hide nearby to see their excitement, but if not she'd simply walk away, grinning. He was beginning to see the appeal. If he hadn't seen Cori get such pleasure out of it, he would never have thought to leave breakfast on her doorstep and just drive away.

They walked together to Bay Six, but Jamie wasn't in his bed. A quick check of the toilets and then the art room became a slightly more comprehensive search of anywhere that Jamie might be.

Kate was the senior nurse on duty today, and was the first to be told. 'When did anyone last see him?' Cori could hear the concern in Tom's voice.

'About half an hour ago.'

'That's something. I've been in the reception area for the last three quarters of an hour and it's unlikely he could have slipped past me and out of the unit.'

'All the same, can't be too careful…' Kate's voice was thick with worry. Something like this was potentially one of the unit's worst nightmares, and no one wanted it to happen on their watch.

'Yeah, you're right. I'll call Hospital Security, and get

them to review the CCTV tapes opposite the entrance door and check outside for any open doors or windows.' Tom thought hard, remembering the procedure to be followed in the event of a missing child. 'Kate, we'll need six members of staff, to split up into pairs and search the three sections of the unit. We'll do an initial search, and then contact the child protection nurse and the patient services co-ordinator. I'll stay here and I want everyone to report back to me after ten minutes.'

'Got it.' Kate hurried away.

'What can I do?' Cori was at his elbow still, frowning, and Tom remembered that he had resolved not to make the mistake of excluding her again.

'Come with me.'

Tom had taken up his position at the nurses' station so that he could co-ordinate all the people searching for Jamie. He sat down, motioning for Cori to sit with him. 'Okay, so we've covered the systematic approach. What can we add to that?'

Cori thought hard. 'Well, we've already checked the places we'd expect to find him.' She reached into her handbag, pulling out her tablet computer, relieved that she'd brought it with her that morning. 'I've got all of his paintings scanned in. Let's take a look.'

She switched the tablet on, and flipped through the pictures that she'd scanned after each session with Jamie. Stopping at one, she heard Tom's sharp intake of breath behind her.

'I asked Jamie to tell me about this picture, and he said that the figure was him. These heavy lines, almost obscuring him, can be indicative of a desire to hide.'

She looked up at Tom, who was staring at the screen. 'You recognise this?'

'I...I don't know. Maybe.' He shook his head. 'This isn't about me, Cori.'

'It's about both of us, using our instinct and imagination to work out where he might go. If you have something to bring to this, then you should do it.'

He didn't reply. She flipped through the pictures slowly, and was almost at the end before he stopped her again. 'Look, he's afraid of something and he thinks you'll protect him.'

'What makes you say that?' Cori had already seen Jamie's fears, a monster with large teeth in the corner of the picture, but she hadn't picked up on her own presence there.

'See there. That sunflower with the smiley face and the beautiful eyes.'

'Oh. You think that's me?' The face had red lips and bright purple eyes.

'Can't you see the resemblance?'

'No, not really...' Cori studied the picture carefully. 'These all give some indication of his general state of mind, but there's nothing that tells us where he might be.'

'Okay, so look at it another way. What's his general state of mind?' Tom's brow was furrowed in thought.

'He generally seems quite a happy little boy, but there is something bothering him. Something that frightens him.'

'So he might be hiding?'

'Maybe. Where would *you* hide if you wanted to keep out of everyone's way?'

Tom shrugged. 'I'm a bit bigger than Jamie. The only place I can find to hide around here is my office.'

'Hmm. Has anyone actually checked your office?'

'I don't know. Jamie doesn't even know where it is, does he?'

'Of course he does. His bed is by the entrance to the bay, and there's a glazed panel that lets him see all the way up the corridor. He watches you going in and out all the time.' Cori wondered if she'd just betrayed the fact that *she* had been watching Tom too from Jamie's bedside.

They stared at each other for a moment. It suddenly seemed the obvious place that Jamie would go.

'Only one way to find out.' Tom was on his feet, striding past Bay Six, where Jamie's empty bed was, towards his office door. When he twisted the door handle, it didn't give.

'Did you lock it, Tom?'

'No, but I left my keys on my desk.' He raised his knuckle to the door to rap on it and then thought better of it. 'I don't really want to frighten him if he is in there.'

He tried to peer through the glazed panel to one side of the door, but the blind between the two panes of glass was closed. Cori saw that the skylight, above the door, was unobscured, and tapped his arm.

'If you can give me a leg up, I'll look through there.'

She took off her boots, expecting him to lace his fingers together and boost her up the two feet she needed to peer through the skylight. Instead, he lifted her bodily upwards, and she clung to his shoulders for balance.

'You're a lot stronger than I thought...' She gripped hold of the edge of the skylight to pull herself up a little higher.

'Yeah. You're a lot heavier than I thought…'

'Thanks!'

'What? I thought fairies didn't weigh any more than a mustard seed. What can you see?'

'Hang on…' Cori peered through the glass and then she saw him. Jamie was sitting in Tom's high-backed chair, staring solemnly at her. Cori grinned, waving at him. 'Hi, Jamie…'

'He's there?'

'Yep.' Cori gave the boy an encouraging smile. 'Sweetie, can you unlock the door?'

Jamie shook his head.

'What's he doing?' Tom's hand had strayed to her bottom, but since she felt much steadier that way, Cori decided not to protest. Needs must.

'He's just sitting there, grinning at me. And it doesn't look as if he's going to open the door.'

'How does he look? Is he drowsy?'

'I'm no doctor, but he looks absolutely fine to me.'

'Ask him to unlock the door again. I don't want to frighten him by having to break down the door… Kate…' The nurse appeared at the other end of the corridor and he called to her. 'He's in here. Will you let everyone know they can stop looking for him now?'

Cori made a few funny faces at Jamie and he made a few back. Then she asked him again to open the door and he shook his head. 'He isn't going to do it. Let me down for a minute.'

She felt herself sliding down his body, and tried not to think about it. He set her down onto her feet, the trace of a smile on his lips.

'Perhaps I can pick the lock.'

Tom's eyes widened. 'You know how to pick a lock?'

'You learn a lot of very handy things in a children's home.' Cori picked up her handbag, searching for something that might do the job, and felt her fingers scrape against an old nail file.

Kneeling down, she peered into the lock. 'The key's in there, but I think…' A sharp, well-placed jab with the nail file meant the key fell out of the lock on the other side. 'Just as well he doesn't know the old trick of turning the key a quarter turn.'

She heard Tom's chair creak, and light footsteps running to the other side of the door. Jamie's eye appeared, looking through the keyhole at her. 'Hi, Jamie. Go and sit down, sweetie.'

Cori straightened up. 'He obviously reckons this is some kind of game, I can hear him laughing. We'll have to get him away from the door. I'm not jabbing a nail file into the lock if he's on the other side of it. And you can't break the door down either.'

Tom's brow furrowed in thought. 'We'll just have to reason with him. Wait there.' He strode to the end of the corridor where a small group had gathered to see what was happening. Sending one off in one direction, and following another the opposite way, he reappeared a few moments later, carrying a small stepladder.

He planted it on the floor outside the door and climbed the three steps to the top. 'Hey, Jamie…' Cori heard the boy scamper away from the door, so that he could see Tom. 'I've given the nurses the slip and come to rescue you.'

It was an approach. And from the muffled sounds of Jamie's greeting through the door, it was working. 'Jamie… Jamie, you need to take cover while we get the door open. There might be a bit of an explosion, so hide under the desk.'

'Oh, please…' Cori heard Kate behind her, muttering under her breath. 'They never grow up, do they?'

Cori chuckled, and turned to see her holding a crowbar. 'Here.' She handed it up to Tom.

'Ah, you've got it, thanks.' He turned to look through the skylight again. 'That's right, Jamie. Right underneath. That's it, mate. Now stay there until I tell you to come out.'

'I could try the lock, now that he's away from the door…' Cori volunteered. 'Might take a little while.'

'Let's play it safe and get him out of there now.' Tom stepped down from the ladder and fitted the crowbar between the door and the jamb. 'Keep an eye on him, make sure he stays put, will you?'

Cori took his place on the ladder, peering through the skylight. 'Okay. He's under your desk, and he's got his hands over his ears.'

'Yeah…' Tom twisted the crowbar in a short, sharp movement. There was a crack and the door drifted open a couple of inches. He handed the crowbar back to Kate, and then made a show of stumbling into the room, almost collapsing onto the floor.

Kate let out a sigh, shaking her head. 'And I have to work around all this…' She was grinning, though, obviously as pleased with the creative approach to problem-solving as Cori was.

Jamie appeared from under the desk and started to run around, hallooing. Tom herded him behind the desk and lifted him up into his chair. 'Okay, mate. Let's have a look at you, and make sure you're all right. That was pretty exciting, wasn't it?'

'You banged down the door…' Jamie was clearly impressed with Tom's efforts.

'Yes, that's right.' Tom picked up his keys from the floor and pocketed them, bending down in front of Jamie. 'Sit still for a minute.'

He quickly examined Jamie, nodding towards Kate. 'Okay, he's all right. Perhaps we could get him a drink. Would you like something to drink, Jamie?'

Jamie nodded. 'I want to stay here.'

'Well, I've got some things to do, so maybe you'll look after things here while I'm gone. Perhaps Cori will sit with you, eh?' Tom's gaze found hers and Cori nodded, smiling at Jamie.

'We'll make dinosaurs, shall we? I've got some paper in my room, I'll just go and get it.'

'Yes-s-s!'

Jamie had finally said it. After days of letting him know that it was okay to say whatever he wanted to her, he'd explained the bruises. Kate was sitting quietly by the door, and exchanged a quick glance and a nod with Cori.

After half an hour Jamie seemed relaxed enough to go back to the ward, and Kate took him away.

'He'll have someone with him?'

The nurse nodded. 'Yes. I'll make sure someone's keeping an eye on him.' She gave Jamie the special smile that all the nurses seemed to reserve for their young patients. 'We'll go and get some lunch, shall we, Jamie? Adventurers all need a good lunch…'

Tom was in the reception area, deep in conversation with one of the junior doctors, and Cori hung back, waiting for him to finish. When he saw her, he shot her a smile. She mouthed that she'd be in the canteen and he nodded, returning to his conversation.

As she walked to the door, a man pushed past her, almost knocking her off her feet. He was tall and burly, with anger seeping from every pore. Cori turned to see if there was anyone to deal with him, and saw him marching towards Tom.

'You...I want a word.'

Everyone in the reception area jumped as his voice rang out.

'Mr Morton—' Tom didn't get a chance to say whatever it was he was about to say to Jamie's father as a woman who had been running in his wake put herself between the two men.

'Jack, don't.' Tears were running down her face and her voice cracked into a pleading tone. 'Please... She told us not to say anything...'

'It's okay.' Everyone else seemed to have shrunk away from the man, but Tom squared up to him. 'Perhaps you'd like to come to my office and we can talk about what's on your mind.'

His reasonable tone seemed to enrage the man even more. He moved his wife out of the way and held his fist in Tom's face.

Tom didn't even flinch. It was as if he was entirely indifferent to whether the man hit him or not, but Mrs Morton started to cry in earnest now. 'No, Jack, you're making things worse...' She turned to Tom. 'He's not like that, he's just angry...'

'Be quiet, Marion, and sit down. This is between him and me.'

That was one thing that the two men seemed to agree on at least. Tom guided Mrs Morton to one side, and

Kate led her firmly away. Then he turned back to face Mr Morton.

'Mr Morton, you need to calm down right now.'

'No. *You* need to buck your ideas up a bit. I've had enough of you people. You're supposed to be looking after my son and this morning I find out that you lost him.'

'Jamie was found in my office, no more than fifteen minutes after he went missing. We called you to let you know.'

'Don't think that I don't know what you're up to. I heard about your little plan to take him away from us and you're not going to do it.'

'Mr Morton, there's no plan, we're simply responding to Jamie's needs and to questions that have arisen.' Tom's voice was still calm, still measured, even though he must be asking the same silent questions Cori was. Who had told Jamie's father about their suspicions? Nothing had been made official yet.

'And how would you know what's best for *my* son?' The man was still shouting at the top of his voice. 'Don't think that I don't know where you're coming from. Your father beat you and you think that all fathers are the same. Wake up, mate, because they're not.'

There was a sudden, shocked silence. Cori could almost see the life draining from Tom, leaving just an expressionless husk behind.

'I think we should take this conversation somewhere else.' Tom went to move Jack Morton towards the door.

'What, I'm too near the truth for comfort?'

'No, you're too near a ward full of sick children to be raising your voice like this. We'll take it elsewhere.'

'We'll take it nowhere…' The door of the unit clicked

shut and Cori looked around to see two of the hospital's security guards walking towards them. Mr Morton turned and took a swing at Tom.

Tom saw it coming and stepped back, but he couldn't avoid the fist entirely. There was a dull smack and blood started to trickle down Tom's chin.

Then everyone seemed to be moving. One of the security guards took Jack Morton's arm, pulling him away from Tom, and someone produced a paper towel, which he held to his lip. Tom seemed to be trying to calm everyone down.

The guards were hustling Jack Morton out of the unit, no doubt intending to defuse the situation. Tom was about to follow when Cori caught his arm.

'I have to talk to you. Now.'

'Can't it wait?' There was nothing in his eyes. No pain or anger. Just nothing. Was Jack Morton right? Was this the thing that Tom hid so carefully from everyone?

'No, it can't wait. It's about Jamie and it's really important. You need to speak to me before you speak to anyone else.'

'Okay. Later.' Tom signalled to the security guards, and exchanged a few words with them, suggesting that a cup of tea in one of the quiet rooms might give everyone a chance to calm down. The two of them ambled off on either side of Jack Morton, who was visibly regaining his composure.

'Tom…?'

He exchanged a nod with Kate, who was shepherding a sobbing Mrs Morton after her husband. Then he turned abruptly, without a word to anyone, and without even looking in Cori's direction he strode out of the unit.

CHAPTER TEN

HE COULD HEAR her voice behind him, but Tom didn't stop. He didn't know where he was going, he just needed to put some space between himself and everything that had happened this morning.

'Tom! Slow down.'

He increased his pace, walking out of the main doors of the hospital and into the freezing wind. Cori was one of the few people who knew about his concerns for Jamie, and the only one who knew that he had a personal reason for not talking to Jamie himself. She had to have worked it out, and the thought that, while she'd said nothing to him, she must have said something to someone else made Tom want to curl up and disappear.

'Tom...'

He'd thought that he could make good. Thought he could leave his childhood behind him when he'd left home and come to London. He'd made a life for himself, untainted by his father's violence, and now it had come back to smack him in the gut in the very worst way possible. Cori had betrayed him.

'Tom! Face me!' Her tone had turned from supplication to challenge. Tom whirled around, before he quite knew what he was doing.

'What? You think I can't?'

She was jogging to catch up with him, her cheeks pink and her eyes hot with emotion. 'No. I think you can't face how angry you are at being on the end of someone's fist.'

She was wrong. He'd learned to swallow that anger, to push it away. 'No, Cori. What I can't face is someone going behind my back. It's unprofessional.'

Unprofessional, and it hurt like hell. He'd allowed Cori in and she'd got to the very heart of him. Now he was paying the price.

'You think…' Her cheeks flushed deeper now. 'You think it was *me*?'

'I think you spoke to *someone*. Maybe you didn't realise the consequences…'

He'd thought that he was just giving her a way to confess without losing too much face, but fire flared in her eyes and Cori glared up at him.

'Don't patronise me, Tom. I'm perfectly well aware of the consequences of breaking a confidence.' She shot him a meaningful look. 'Even one that's not explicitly a confidence.'

She was right. He'd hinted at the truth but had never told her not to say anything. Maybe on some level he'd wanted her to know. Tom never would have thought she'd use that knowledge for this, though.

'Who else could it be, then? You were the only one who knew…' He broke off and turned away from her. He couldn't do this. Couldn't see the look in her eyes when she finally ran out of excuses and admitted that it had been her.

He took two steps, and then he felt her grab his arm. He could have shaken her off easily, but if he knew Cori at all he knew she'd hang on for all she was worth. It took an effort to calm himself and face her, but somehow he did it.

Her face was determined. 'I won't deny that I put two and two together, and thought that you had some personal experience of violence as a child. And I could probably manage to prove that I didn't talk to the Mortons. But I'm not going to do that, because I'm asking you to just believe me. I didn't speak to anyone, about you or about Jamie.'

'You want me to just take your word for it.' Suddenly that didn't seem so much to ask. And suddenly Tom knew it was what he wanted to do, more than anything.

'Yes, I do. I'm trusting you that you're not going to reject what I say out of hand.'

Then he saw it. The child who had been rejected time and time again had turned into a woman who was brave enough to reach out and demand his acceptance. And she didn't do it lightly. She did it because she knew that she deserved it.

He took a deep breath. 'I'm sorry, Cori. I… I do believe you.' The words weren't as difficult to say as he'd thought.

'Thank you.' The fire in her eyes died suddenly, and one tear rolled down her cheek. *His* tear. Suddenly he knew that it was for him alone, and Tom bent, brushing it away with a kiss, which stung as the salt found the cut on his lip.

'I bet that smarts.' She smiled up at him.

'Yeah. Sorry… Look, you've got a little blood on your cheek.'

She rubbed at her face, never taking her gaze from him. 'That's okay. You've got a little salt in your wound.'

'Yeah. Quite a lot, actually.'

'And it hurts?' She clearly wasn't talking about the cut any more.

'Hurts like hell.' He didn't want to tell her it was okay, or that it was all behind him now and none of it mattered any more. He'd been telling himself that for too long.

She nodded. 'I'm sorry that happened to you.'

He gave a small stiff nod, not wanting to think that this was anything more than just the right thing to say, not daring to imagine that she understood how he was feeling. 'Go inside. You'll catch a cold.'

She'd come out without a coat, and she was shivering now, but she shook her head. 'Come back with me.'

The last thing he wanted was to go back to the unit. Everyone would be talking about what Jack Morton had said, and wondering whether it was true. However much they might understand, however sympathetic they might be, he'd spent the last eighteen years distancing himself from it and he just didn't want to go back there.

'No.'

'Then I'm going with you.'

'Cori, you have no idea where I'm going.'

'Yeah, I do. You're going back to that place where you're humiliated and hurt and you can't escape. Trust me, I know exactly where that is. And you're not going there on your own.'

'Cori…' He turned away from her, and the freezing wind seemed to slap him in the face, making his jaw throb and his cut lip sting. He might not have any idea what he was going to do next, but suddenly it didn't feel as if walking away from Cori would solve anything.

He took off his jacket and tried to wrap it around her

shoulders, but she shrugged him away. She had tears in her eyes.

'I'm going to the canteen. Are you coming?' He didn't wait for her answer, and wouldn't let her escape this time when he bundled her into his jacket. He put his arm around her, and hurried her across the courtyard.

At least he'd stopped running. She let him hustle her inside, and through the doors into the warmth of the canteen.

'Tea?' He felt in his pocket and pulled out a handful of coins. 'I left my wallet in my desk drawer, but I think I've got enough for a buttered bun between us…'

She felt in her jeans pocket and found a pound coin. 'Get two.'

'Okay. Find a table.'

He brought the tray across and unloaded the cups and plates onto the table. Careful and precise, it was as if he had to think about everything he did at the moment.

'What was it you wanted to tell me? About Jamie.'

Maybe he was just trying to change the subject, get onto easier ground. But the situation with Jamie's parents demanded that he hear this sooner rather than later. 'We were making dinosaurs and he was getting one of the models to fight with the other. He said he was going to bash Kevin like that.

Tom raised an eyebrow. 'Kevin?'

'Apparently Kevin is his babysitter's boyfriend. From what I can gather, the babysitter has her boyfriend round when she's alone in the house with Jamie. He gets left to his own devices to get himself washed and into bed. They lock themselves in the living room and if Jamie wants something and bangs on the door, the boyfriend isn't too pleased about it.'

'So it's not the father?'

'I never got that impression, from the way that Jamie talks about his dad.'

'How does he talk about him?' Tom looked puzzled.

'Well, for a start, he talks about him. He told me how he's been building a shed in the garden, and that he lets Jamie help him.' Cori imagined that Tom hadn't mentioned doing anything with his own father in the course of conversation for the last eighteen years.

Tom nodded, the twitch of a pulse showing at his temple. 'I'm glad it's not his father. But why didn't he tell someone?'

'He was afraid.'

Sadness and pain showed on Tom's face. 'I'd better go. I have to sort this all out…'

'It's okay. They don't need you. Kate was with me and she heard everything.' But Tom was obviously not going to allow Kate to deal with this if he was on the premises, and was already reaching for his coat. 'Why don't you call Kate? It may well be better if you stayed out of the way for a little while.'

Tom didn't look convinced, but he made the call. Whatever Kate had to say seemed to put his mind at rest.

'She's called the duty social worker and they've talked to Mr and Mrs Morton, and reassured them as best they can. They're with Jamie now. It appears I'm surplus to requirements for the moment.'

'Good. Then we can stay here and talk. About what happened to you, if you want?'

'I don't usually talk about it.'

His gaze dropped from her face to the floor. This was always the worst of it. Kids who felt ashamed of the fact that they were victims. Adults who kept on carrying the shame, unable to set it down. In Tom, it was somehow unbearable. She reached out to him, brushing her fingers against his jaw.

'Don't, please. It's…'

'I know.' His voice was harsh. 'It's nothing to be ashamed of, I've been told that. I'm nothing like my father. I've heard that one too.'

'Who told you?' She was hoping against all hope that this wasn't the first time that Tom had talked about this. That someone had been there for him.

'For the first year or so, after I left home and went to medical school, it was as if I was suddenly free. And then…'

'It all came back and bit you?'

He nodded. 'I couldn't sleep, and when I did sleep I had night terrors. I felt such rage, and it scared me. So I went to a counsellor and talked it through. She suggested ways to control the anger and got me back on track.'

Maybe it would have been better if his counsellor had suggested ways for Tom to get the anger out of his system, not just control it, but Cori knew that now wasn't the time to mention that. 'Is that why you decided to go into paediatrics?'

He grinned suddenly. 'That's what my counsellor said. Apparently I'm saving my internal child.'

'Maybe. People's motives aren't always as clear-cut as that. I imagine there was some element of conscious choice about it.'

Tom nodded. 'I know it's what I'm best at, and where

I can do the most good. That's more than enough for me. If it's a consequence of what happened when I was a kid, then it seems a little ironic.'

'Maybe you're just sticking two fingers up at your father? Turning what he did into something good?'

'I like that idea much better.' He leaned back in his seat, looking at her steadily. 'You know I've wanted to—'

He stopped talking suddenly, his thoughts obviously racing.

'You've wanted to what, Tom?'

'You were talking about making sense of things by painting.'

'Yes. That's one of my ways of dealing with the world.'

'I was trying to make sense of things. I'd decided to write a letter… I started on it late one evening when I was in the office, but it just didn't seem to say what I wanted it to. I thought I'd leave it and come back to it, and locked the pages in my drawer.'

Immediately the thought came to Cori. Rosie. But she shouldn't say anything, not yet. There had been enough rash accusations flying around already today. 'Are they…still there?'

'I don't know.' He took a sip of his tea, winced as the hot liquid touched his lip, and set the cup down into the saucer with a rattle. Tom seemed in no hurry to go and have a look.

'I'll go. Give me your keys and—' He shook his head abruptly.

'Thanks, but you don't need to. This is my problem.'

'No, it's the unit's problem. Someone is talking to a

patient's parents, giving them information that's both confidential and traumatic.'

'I know, and I need to sort that out. But I don't want to drag you into this.'

When was he going to learn? He might be able to do it all by himself, but he didn't need to. 'Okay. There's something you need to know, Tom.'

His gaze didn't waver. 'I imagine there are lots of things I need to know.'

'Well, this one's important. Letting your friends help you isn't a sign of weakness.'

The bustle of the canteen no longer registered and all she could see was the anguish in his eyes. For long moments she held his gaze, hoping against hope that she could get through to him somehow.

'This one's for the door…only I guess you're not going to need that.' He'd pulled his keys from his pocket and was holding them up. 'This one's for the desk. Top drawer on the left. Right at the bottom there's an A4 envelope. It should be sealed.'

She took the keys. 'Thank you. I'll bring the envelope straight to you, if it's there.'

'Don't you want to know what's inside?'

'Of course I do. But I'm not going to invade your privacy to find out.'

He shook his head, a wry smile on his face. 'You're missing the point, Cori. The letter was addressed to you.'

Waiting for her wasn't as bad as he'd thought. Letting someone do something for him… It was a warm feeling, as if suddenly there was a place for him in the world. Tom tried to ignore the thought that maybe the important difference between this and all the other times that he'd turned away from anyone who'd got too close was that this time it was Cori.

He found that he had enough change to get another cup of tea, and this time he got a straw to drink it with. It must look a bit odd, but it meant that he could drink without getting the metallic taste of his own blood. Picking up a discarded paper from a neighbouring table, he turned to the crossword and tried to concentrate on the answers to the clues, instead of thinking about what Cori might be doing.

By the time she got back, he'd only got two of the easy ones. Sitting down opposite him, she drew a familiar manila envelope from her bag.

'I imagine this isn't how you left it.' She handed the envelope to him and Tom examined the flap. It had been carefully peeled open, and then stuck down again. He might not have even noticed if he hadn't taken the time to look.

'No, it isn't.' He laid the envelope down on the table. He could feel that there was more to come.

'Kate and the duty social worker have talked to the Mortons. We know who did this.' She waited for his nod before she gave him the name. 'Rosie.'

'Yeah. I… That doesn't come as much of a surprise.' Everyone knew how much of a gossip Rosie was. He'd just never thought she'd take things this far.

'No. Not to me either. Apparently Mrs Morton came in to see Jamie yesterday evening, and she decided to go and have some tea afterwards. Rosie approached her in the canteen.'

'Rosie approached her?' Tom had been hoping against hope that this was somehow a mistake, something that someone had let slip. But it looked as if Rosie had gone out of her way to talk to Mrs Morton, and if she had, Tom couldn't protect her from a hospital disciplinary board.

'Yes. She told her about the concerns for Jamie, said that she thought we'd got it all wrong and why.'

'Why didn't Mrs Morton come back to the ward and ask what was going on?'

'Because Rosie made her promise not to. And, anyway, she wanted to talk with her husband first, and he works nights. So the first opportunity she got to discuss it was this morning.'

'So Rosie not only told her something enormously worrying about her own child, she also asked her to keep it a secret. That poor woman.' Tom shook his head. He supposed he wasn't really one to talk about keeping secrets. 'I imagine there's a fair amount of upset on the unit at the moment…'

'I didn't notice any.' She bit her lip. What the unit needed now was strong leadership, and Cori knew that as well as Tom did. He picked up the envelope, put it into his jacket pocket and stood up.

'Are you coming?'

She frowned at him, as if he'd just thrown her a mortal insult. 'What do you mean? Of course I'm coming.'

The unit had been sizzling with questions and uncertainties, and it seemed that Tom had the answer to all of them. He walked back into the unit and took charge straight away.

His first task was to talk to Mr and Mrs Morton, apologising to them both on behalf of the unit and shaking Mr Morton's hand. After some time spent alone with them, he emerged and made for his office, glancing at the staff assault report form that the social worker had left on his desk before screwing it up and throwing it in the bin.

Cori waited. Tom spoke to Kate for a while, and his body language was reassuring when concern shone from Kate's face. He joked with other members of staff and smiled at them, as far as his split lip would allow. Then he left Cori in the reception area and disappeared back into his office to speak with the hospital social worker. Just when it seemed that everyone was settling back into a normal Saturday lunchtime routine, Rosie walked through the doors of the unit.

This was *not* the neat, precise Rosie that Cori had got to know. Her coat was open and her scarf was dangling messily from her neck, while her face was streaked with tears and her hair scraped back into a messy ponytail. Cori moved in her direction to head her off, vaguely aware that Kate was doing the same, but Tom got there first.

Rosie gulped something about someone calling her, and that she needed to talk to him, and Tom hesitated for a moment. She gasped an agonised 'Please' and then he nodded, shepherding her towards his office, managing to give the impression of shielding her without actually touching her. Kate caught Cori's eye.

'He can't do that.' Kate knew as well as Cori did that in these circumstances it was a risk for Tom to go anywhere with Rosie on his own. She had no doubt that Tom would treat her kindly and with scrupulous professionalism, but with no witnesses, whatever was said or done it was Rosie's word against Tom's. And Rosie had already proved herself unreliable.

'I'm going after him.' Tom had waved both Kate and Cori away, but he was just going to have to live with her disagreeing with his judgement on this one.

Kate twisted her mouth. 'Good luck...'

She was walking so fast that she almost bumped into Tom, who was coming out of his office. She ignored him completely, craning around his bulk to see Rosie, sitting quietly now, being comforted by the hospital social worker.

Come to save me? He mouthed the words at her. His smile, lopsided because of the cut on his lip, made it clear that he liked the idea.

'No. I came to see whether I could get some tea for you.'

'That's a nice thought. Thank you.' He pulled the door closed behind him.

'Three cups and an ice pack?' They were alone in the corridor, and Cori risked brushing her fingers momentarily against his swelling jaw.

'Actually, just two cups, I don't think I can manage another one. The ice pack would be great, thank you.' His gaze caught hers, and heat sizzled between them. They'd come through this together. Tom, the man who needed no one and wanted no one, had accepted her help.

She turned quickly, before the touch turned into a kiss. 'Okay. I'll be back in a minute.'

They'd been closeted in Tom's office for almost an hour. Then Rosie had left with the social worker, and Tom had been ordered into one of the treatment rooms by Kate.

After that came the most tricky part of the morning.

'You're very rough. I hope you're not like this with the kids.' Tom shot Kate a rueful glare.

'She's not rough. If you'd just put that mirror down and stop trying to do it yourself, it would all go a lot quicker.' Cori grimaced at him.

Kate was shaking her head grimly. 'Doctors are always the worst.'

'Second only to nurses…' Tom's words were beginning to get a little slurred as the local anaesthetic took effect.

'I broke my finger. I don't think you fully appreciated just how much that hurt.'

'I seem to remember that you made it very clear at the time.'

Kate frowned at him. 'Are you going to stay still, or do you want me to call for restraints?'

'You keep your personal life out of this…'

The easy procedure of putting a couple of stitches in the cut on Tom's lip was performed with the maximum amount of fuss. Finally, Kate pronounced him likely to heal without a scar and Tom called a 'Thank you' to her retreating back.

'Are you ready to call it a day?' It suddenly seemed inconceivable to Cori that either of them should go anywhere without the other.

'More than ready.' He got to his feet and walked to the door, but instead of pulling it open he closed it. 'I've told Rosie to stay at home on Monday. I imagine that the HR department will be wanting to see her at some point, about speaking to Mrs Morton the way she did, but there's no need for her to be here.'

'That's thoughtful of you. You're not going to put

in a complaint about her going through your personal stuff, are you?'

'No. She's in enough trouble already. I'm not going to make things any worse for her.'

'That's more than she deserves. It's difficult to imagine that she didn't know how much this might hurt you.'

'Maybe she did, and maybe she didn't. Maybe she thought that Mrs Morton would do as she asked, and keep what she said a secret.' Tom shrugged. 'In the end perhaps the secret itself is the most corrosive thing of all.'

He leaned back against the door, seeming suddenly tired. 'Come here.'

He'd always been so professional up until now, making sure he never touched her, never lingered in her gaze too long when they were at work. But this somehow felt right. As if now the different pieces of Tom's life, which he'd worked so hard to keep separate, were finally beginning to come together.

His arms were ready for her, and she felt a thrill of excitement when he folded them loosely around her shoulders. 'How do you feel now?'

'I want to kiss you. Although this isn't really the time *or* the place.'

'I won't tell if you don't…' Cori stretched up onto her toes, feeling his body react as hers moved against it, and kissed his cheek.

He hugged her tight. 'I'm… On second thoughts, I think I need a bit more time…'

'That's okay.' She moved away from him and he pulled her back.

'What I mean is that I can't kiss you right now because I have no feeling in my lips.'

'Ah. Well, you'll just have to let me do it for you, then.' Lightly, she kissed the very corner of his mouth, on the other side from the stitches. 'Can you feel that?'

'Yeah. Nice.'

'This?' She brushed her lips against his cheek, gently tracing the tip of her tongue around the curve of his ear, and heard Tom's sharp intake of breath.

He was luxuriating in her touch. Holding her close, as if that could chase away everything else that had happened today.

'Why don't you come with me to Ralph and Jean's this afternoon?'

He gave her a slightly sceptical look, which wasn't an outright no. 'You want to take me to meet your parents?'

'No, it's not like that. Ralph and Jean have open house on Saturday afternoons. Everyone drops in, they bring friends and friends of friends. It's like…'

'One big happy family?'

'You should try it.' The idea of finding comfort with your family had probably never occurred to Tom. Perhaps now was the time to show him what that was like.

They'd stopped off at Tom's house so he could change out of his blood-spattered shirt, and then at the supermarket to get a bottle of wine and some cheesecake, which Cori assured him would be exactly the right thing. He'd added a bunch of flowers for Jean to their basket, a bright arrangement of yellow and white blooms.

'I don't think I've ever met a girlfriend's mother before.' The large house was set back from the road and four cars blocked the driveway at the front so Cori swerved across the road to park.

'Well, there's no reason to start now. I'm not your girlfriend.'

That was actually wearing a little bit thin. They might not have had sex, but Tom didn't recall waking up in the middle of the night after an erotic dream about any of his other friends. Neither did he recall looking forward to every moment he saw them, or finding that whole evenings had slipped away in their company and that he still wanted to talk a little more.

'No. Well, that's a relief. How many brothers did you say you had?'

'Four.' She turned to him, grinning. 'Don't tell me you're afraid of my brothers.'

'Terrified. That's why you brought me here, wasn't it?' Tom got out of her car, wondering if anyone would notice if he walked around to open the driver's door for her, and in a burst of courage he did it anyway.

'You look gorgeous.' He allowed his fingers to brush against the soft fabric of her jacket, and she smiled up at him, slipping her arm through his.

The lion's den wasn't as challenging as he'd thought it might be. Ralph shook his hand and expressed concern over the bruise that was rapidly forming on his face, and Jean fussed over him, taking his arm and leading him through to the kitchen, where a buffet lunch was laid out.

Adrian careened up to him, wanting to know whether he'd treated any really gory cases recently, and was shushed away by a woman who introduced herself as Cori's sister. Then Adam, the brother who was a member of Cori's artists' group, found him and plied him with questions about the unit, his enthusiasm just as great as Cori's. All the while he could feel her gaze, and whenever he was alone for a moment she was at his side.

'You like my family?' They were in the spacious conservatory, watching while everyone else traipsed outside into the large back garden to inspect the summer house that Ralph was building.

'They're like...' Tom had no point of reference for this. 'They're like a happy ending on TV. When everyone gathers round the table for lunch together and the camera pans out, leaving them to it.'

She chuckled. 'We have our ups and downs. Quite a lot of them, actually.'

'A happy ending doesn't mean there won't be any ups and downs. Just that you'll deal with them.' Tom surprised himself with the insight. He'd always been more comfortable with the kind of happy ending that involved a fulfilling career and resolute control over his personal life.

'Is that what you really think?' Cori clearly didn't quite believe what she'd heard.

'Just trying the idea for size. And, yes, I really like your family. Thank you for bringing me along with you.'

She smiled, flinging herself down into an armchair. 'They're the best thing that ever happened to me.'

'How old were you when you came here?'

'Seven. I'd been in and out of children's homes and foster-care before that. My father left my mother when I was a baby and she started drinking. She'd get herself straight and I'd go back to her, then she'd start drinking again and everything would go pear-shaped.'

'Do you have any contact with her now?' Tom

walked away from the conservatory window, sitting down opposite her.

'No. When I was four years old she went on holiday with her new boyfriend and left me with a neighbour. When she didn't come back after two weeks, the neighbour called Social Services.'

'She never came back?'

'No. I found out later that Social Services had found her but she'd refused to return. When I was twenty-one I wanted to find out what had happened to her, and Ralph helped me. She'd moved around a fair bit, got married for a while and gone to live in Spain under another name. She died there. Liver failure.'

'I'm sorry.'

'It's okay. Actually, leaving me behind was the best thing she ever did for me. I couldn't believe it when I first came here. I used to get up ridiculously early in the morning and go downstairs and try to do the housework so that they'd keep me.' She grinned at him. 'I think Jean was afraid that if she taught me to cook, I'd be whipping up a Sunday roast at five in the morning.'

'So they taught you to paint instead. Sounds reasonable.'

'Actually, Adam taught me to paint. He's the same age as me but he was adopted at birth. So he got the job of making me feel at home when I arrived.'

'You're all adopted?' Tom was becoming fascinated by Cori's family. How it had been pieced together and yet seemed so solid.

'Yes, Ralph and Jean wanted kids but couldn't have any. Ralph had his own company, and had made a load of money through internet start-ups, and they decided they wanted to make a change. It was either this or go and drink cocktails on a beach somewhere. Ralph says that there are times when he wishes he'd chosen the cocktails.'

She turned as the door to the conservatory opened. 'There you are.' Jean smiled, flipping on the light, and Tom realised that it had begun to get dark while they were talking.

'I've been telling him the story of Ralph and Jean, and their incorrigible gang of kids.' Cori grinned up at her mother, and Jean laughed.

'I wouldn't say you were quite a gang. Are there any dirty plates in here?'

'Nope.' Cori got to her feet. 'You look tired, Mum. Sit down, and I'll do the washing-up.'

'That's all right. Grace and Adam are in there.'

'I'll go and help them, then. Sit down, will you?'

Jean nodded wearily. 'Yes, I think I will. Just for a minute.'

Tom went to stand and follow Cori into the kitchen, and Jean waved him back into his seat. 'You should be taking it easy too. That face looks painful.'

'It's not as bad as it looks. I want to thank you for your hospitality this afternoon. I imagine Cori told you that this morning's been difficult...'

'No. But I've seen enough split lips in my time to know that someone punched you.'

'Yeah. It was a misunderstanding. I'll have to work on doing things a little better next time.'

'Don't shoulder too much of the blame. A misunderstanding's never any excuse for violence.' Jean made the observation quietly.

In the last few moments Tom had just confided more, and received more back, than he'd ever shared with his own family. He felt suddenly thankful that Cori had found Ralph and Jean.

'I appreciate you saying that.'

Jean smiled, leaning back in the comfortable armchair. 'It's been a pleasure having you here. Cori's very excited about the project at the hospital. She says she's learning a lot.'

'Well, we've had our ups and downs.'

Jean looked at him thoughtfully. 'A learning experience for both of you, then.'

'It certainly is. Cori gives as good as she gets.'

'Always.' Jean smiled. Her eyelids were fluttering as if she was fighting off sleep. 'I'm…shlore…um… shlertain…'

'Jean?' Tom was suddenly alert. When Jean didn't respond to him, he rapped out her name. 'Jean!'

Her right arm fell from the arm of the chair. When Tom knelt down in front of her, he saw that her right eyelid was beginning to droop.

'Cori… Cori…' he called into the kitchen, as he pulled his phone from his pocket and dialled.

CHAPTER ELEVEN

'HE'S VERY GOOD-LOOKING.' Grace and Adam had been teasing Cori about Tom ever since she'd walked into the kitchen, and she was just about to let them do the washing-up by themselves.

'And he seems like a nice bloke.' Adam added to the ever growing list of Tom's accomplishments.

'Got a good job.' Grace chimed in with another one. 'What's his car like? It's got to be better than yours.'

'Why do cars matter? And, anyway, what's wrong with my car?'

'Not big enough, for a start. You need a van, like mine, to transport all your stuff.' Adam nodded sagely.

'Why do *I* need a van when you've got one?' Cori looked around as she heard Tom calling her from the conservatory.

Grace cupped her hand behind her ear, winking at Adam. 'Do I hear thy lover calling…?'

There was a note of urgency in his voice, which both Grace and Adam seemed to have missed. Cori dropped the plate she was soaping back into the sink, and hurried out to find Tom.

He was kneeling in front of Jean, his phone held be-

tween his shoulder and his ear. As she entered the conservatory she heard him say the word *stroke*.

'Mum...?' Tom beckoned her over and Cori saw that
Jean's face was drooping downwards on one side.

'Your mother's having a stroke.' Tom spoke firmly,
his voice low. 'I'm calling an ambulance now.'

'What do I do?'

'Hold her hand. Talk to her.' Someone spoke at the
other end of the phone, and he turned his attention to
them.

All she had to do was listen to Tom. *Don't think...
don't question.* He knew what to do and he'd get Jean
through this. Cori took her mother's hand between hers.
'It's okay, Mum. We're all here and Tom's calling an
ambulance. It's going to be okay.'

She felt a tremor in her mother's grip that might have
been some kind of reply and might not. Tom finished
his call and slipped his phone back into his pocket.

'I'll stay here, and I want you to go and get your father.' His voice was quiet and measured, showing no
sign of the stress of the situation. 'We're going to keep
things quiet and comfortable for your mum. Do you
understand?'

'Yes. Thanks.' Cori turned back to her mother.
'Mum, I'm going to get Dad. I'll be back with him in
one minute, and in the meantime Tom's going to stay
here with you.'

She didn't want to think about whether her mother
understood, or what the convulsive jerk of her fingers
meant. Laying her mother's hand back carefully into
her lap, Cori ran through the kitchen, past Grace and
Adam and into the garden. 'Dad... Dad...come quickly,'

she called to Ralph, who turned, walking towards her over the grass.

'What's the matter?'

'It's Mum. She's had a stroke. Tom's with her.' She gripped Ralph's hand tightly. 'He's called an ambulance and we're waiting. Tom says we have to stay calm, and that we have to talk to her, reassure her…'

Ralph's face blanched, but he nodded. Wordlessly he hurried into the house, walking straight past Adam and Grace, who were on their way out to see what was happening.

'Cori…?' Adam followed her inside, catching her arm.

She repeated the news. Each time she said it, it seemed a little less unreal. Grace started to cry and Adam nodded. 'I'll tell the others and we'll round Adrian up and keep him quiet. Go with Dad.' He wound his arm firmly around Grace's shoulders. 'All right, Gracie. We'll do this together.'

Cori stopped outside the door of the conservatory, and took a breath to calm herself. When she entered, Tom stood. 'Cori, I need you to help me. I'm going to move Jean onto the couch. Laying her down will help the blood flow to the brain.'

'Let me…' Her father was hanging on to her mother's hand.

'No, Dad. Let Tom do it, he knows how to lift her.'

'Yeah. Sorry.' Ralph pressed the palms of his hands to his temples, moving away from Jean.

'It's okay.' Tom was calm and reassuring. 'Just let us make her comfortable, and then you can be with her.'

He lifted Jean carefully, while Cori supported her head, laying her down gently on the sofa. Jean moaned, trying to speak, and Tom caught her flailing hand. 'You're doing really well, Jean. Just lie quietly and we'll get you to the hospital.'

Cori pulled up a chair for Ralph and he sat beside Jean, holding her hand and talking quietly to her. Tom straightened, his gaze fixed on the pale, suddenly frail figure lying on the sofa.

'How is she, Tom? Please tell me…' Cori whispered, dreading the answer.

'We've got to her quickly, and that's going to make a real difference to how well your mother recovers. When she gets to the hospital they'll do a scan, and if it's an ischemic stroke…'

'What…?' Cori could feel tears welling in her eyes.

'If it's a blood clot, they can give her drugs for that.' She felt his hand on her arm. 'Hang in there. I can take care of what's needed medically, but it's up to you to keep things calm and quiet, and let her know that you love her.'

'Okay. Will you talk to Dad? Tell him what's going to happen next?'

He nodded, and Cori took her father's place, while Tom drew him to one side to talk to him. Somehow she found some words, and as she talked, she became more and more sure that her mother could hear her.

Her eyes filled with tears. When she'd heard Tom say *stroke*, all she'd been able to think about was an emergency, with blaring sirens and flashing lights. But he'd created a calm and peaceful atmosphere, one where Ralph had been able to hold Jean's hand and tell her how much she was loved. It was a precious gift.

She felt Tom's hand on her shoulder, and she bent

and kissed her mother's fingers, then moved away so that Ralph could sit back down next to Jean.

When the ambulance crew arrived they seemed surprised by the lack of panic in the house. Then the paramedic saw Tom, and nodded to him. Tom spoke to her quickly and then the paramedic walked over to Jean, bending down so that she was in her line of vision.

'Hello, Jean, we've come to take you to hospital…'

Cori heaved a sigh of relief. The first and most dangerous part was over.

Tom and Ralph had gone with Jean in the ambulance, and Cori had followed with her brother Iain in his car, leaving the others at home with Adrian. There had been a scan, a huddle of doctors, comings and goings, and a transfer up to the stroke unit. Through the whole process Tom had been with Ralph, guiding him and keeping him strong. Finally, they were told they must leave for the evening, and Cori kissed her mother, leaving Ralph by her bedside to say goodbye.

Iain grasped Tom's hand in his usual vigorous handshake. 'Thank you for everything, Tom.'

'My pleasure.' Tom looked as drained as Cori felt, but he still had a smile left for Iain, even if it wasn't the most effusive she'd ever seen.

'I'll wait for Ralph and take him home. Do you guys want a lift anywhere?'

'That's okay. I'll walk Cori home.' Tom spoke for both of them. He seemed to know that the thing she wanted most was just to walk for a while in the cool air and clear her head.

'Right you are. Come for lunch, eh? Soon.' Iain's

gaze included both Tom and Cori in the invitation and Cori's nod accepted for both of them.

They walked together out of the hospital, not a word passing between them, and not even the brush of his fingers against hers. But as soon as they were on the pavement Tom curled his arm around her shoulders in an expression of easy warmth.

'Your mum's in really good hands.'

'Yes, I know. Thank you.' Cori felt her lip begin to quiver. 'I told her that she was going to be okay...'

'You did the right thing.'

Cori heaved a sigh. 'I'm not going to ask whether I lied or not. I'm just going to believe that I didn't.'

He pulled her a little closer. 'That's a really good way of looking at it. However much we'd like to, no doctor can tell anyone with absolute certainty that they'll recover from something like this, but I'm as sure as I can be that Jean will. It'll take some time, and she'll need some help...'

Cori laughed. 'You've seen my family. She was there for us when we needed her, and we'll always be there for her.'

'And Adrian?' Tom had been obviously concerned for Adrian before they'd left for the hospital, making time to speak to him alone and reassure him.

'We'll all look after him until Ralph and Jean are back in action. Maybe it'll be a good thing for him in the long run, seeing her come back home and being involved a bit with her rehab.'

Tom nodded. 'He'll see that not everyone who goes to the hospital dies there.'

'Yeah.' There, a little thrill of pleasure to end a day that had held precious little to recommend it. Tom had been taking notice, the way he always did, and he'd remembered Adrian's fear of hospitals.

They reached her doorstep, and stopped. The last thing Cori wanted was to part from him now, after everything that had happened today, but she wasn't sure how to ask him inside.

'Are you tired?' He seemed to know the right question to ask.

'I should be. I'm not, though.'

'I feel the same.' He looked speculatively at his car, still parked outside in the road. 'You want to go for a drive?'

Perfect. The adrenaline in Cori's system was begging her to either fight or fly, but there was nowhere to go, and a feeling of obscure dread had been pooling in her stomach for the last hour. 'I'd love to.'

'Me too.'

They went inside to collect a flask of hot chocolate, which Cori insisted on making, even though Tom seemed to know a better recipe. She took her warm coat from the cupboard and found a dark green scarf that she hardly ever wore but which quite suited Tom when he wound it around his neck, tucking the ends into his leather jacket. And then they got into the car and just drove.

They passed through brightly lit main streets, filled with Saturday evening crowds, and quiet back streets. The road began to climb as they skirted around Hampstead Heath, houses and shops giving way to trees and parkland. Then Tom steered off the road and cut the engine.

'What a view!' Cori had driven past this spot before, where a gap in the treeline suddenly allowed a view right across London. In front of her the lights of the city were spread out like a twinkling carpet.

Tom got out of the car, opening her door and helping her out. Cori's limbs felt stiff after the hours of tension, and she almost stumbled into his arms. Almost but not quite. The last few inches were all of her own volition.

He settled against the side of the car, his arms clasped loosely around her, and she leaned against him, allowing his bulk to support her. 'I can see the London Eye…' She pointed to the right of the sparkling horizon. 'And the Shard.'

'Docklands and… What's that building? Over there?'

'I'm not sure. I don't recognise it; it must be something new. They keep building new landmarks.'

She felt his chest rise and fall against her shoulder. 'How are you doing?'

'I'm good. Thanks, Tom. If I'd gone home, I would have just cried on the sofa all night.'

'You can cry here if you like.' He bent down, his lips grazing her ear. 'It's a therapeutic exercise, and I wouldn't want to stop you.'

'No, I think I'm good.' She laid her head against his chest, watching the lights, feeling the tension ebb out of her. 'Up here, I feel that everything's going to be all right.'

'It is. I know you're scared for your mum, but she's going to be okay.'

Something wistful in his tone made her want to ask, and the intimacy of this moment made it all right to do so. 'What about your mother? Is she…?'

'My mother died when I was twelve. Cancer.' His

embrace seemed to tighten a little, as if he suddenly needed to hold on to her.

'I'm sorry. I shouldn't have asked.'

'If I hadn't wanted to answer, I would have said so.' He puffed out a breath. 'I have a lot of experience in not telling people things.'

'That's not very reassuring. I'd far rather you were a bit more…transparent.'

Tom chuckled quietly. 'You're not up for the discovery process, then?'

She turned in his arms, reaching up to clasp her fingers behind his neck. 'It might be a little frustrating at times, but on balance I'd say it's worth it.'

He folded her in what was unmistakeably an embrace. Not two friends clinging together for comfort, or huddling close in the cool air for warmth. 'There's so much I want to say…to explain to you. I tried to write it all down, but that didn't go so well. And now isn't the right time…'

'There's no such thing as the right time. And no such thing as a place to start.' She snuggled into his warmth. 'But if you ever find that you're in that wrong place and time…'

He took a deep breath, as if he was getting ready to hurl himself from a precipice. 'My mum always used to tell me not to get in his way, not to annoy him or make any noise. When he was in one of his moods, we'd both be walking on eggshells for days. When she died, I thought that maybe if I'd protected her a little better…'

'There's nothing you could have done, Tom.' She stretched up and kissed his cheek. 'You know that. You were a child, and it was up to the adults in your life to protect you. You are not responsible for your father's actions.'

He nodded. 'I know. Feels good to hear you say it, though.'

'Want me to say it again?'

'As many times as you like.' He kissed the top of her head. 'Are you getting cold?'

He'd had enough. She could feel it had been an enormous effort for him to say even that much. 'I wouldn't mind some of that hot chocolate. Can we stay here, though? Just for a little while longer?'

'As long as you like.' He let her go, brushing her hair back from her face with his fingers. 'You know, up here it almost feels that anything's possible.'

If only. Cori watched as he opened the car door, leaning inside to get the flask. If everything really were possible, then Tom would be able to see past everything that had happened to him. And if he did, he'd see that she was waiting for him.

CHAPTER TWELVE

CORI WOKE IN his arms. Not quite the way she might have hoped, but yesterday had been so extraordinary that pretty much anything went. Whatever got you through.

And last night, that had meant going back to Tom's house. He'd promised her a bed in the spare room for the night, and she'd taken him up on the offer because she hadn't wanted to be alone. And being with anyone other than Tom would have been alone. But in the quiet darkness her thoughts had begun to race, and even though she'd tried to go to sleep, she hadn't been able to. Tom must have heard her crying, because he'd been there, wrapping her in a quilt and carrying her through to his own bed.

They'd talked and he'd comforted her. And then they'd drifted off to sleep together. Now he was fast asleep, the morning light filtering through the curtains and bathing him in a warm glow. He looked like some kind of warrior angel, square jawed, his fair hair spiked around his head like a messy halo. One that had taken a little wear and tear lately, by the look of his lip and the corner of his mouth, which was now swollen and discoloured.

His eyelids flickered open, almost as if her gaze had

actually warmed his skin. However battered and bruised he was, however slow and tired, he was still beautiful when he woke.

'Hey there…'

As he began to come to his hand drifted to his lip and Cori caught it, pulling it away. 'Don't touch.'

'No.' He wound his fingers around hers. 'How are you doing?'

'I'm fine.'

'Really?' Tom rolled on his back, holding her hand above his face. 'You're not just saying that?'

'No. Thanks for last night… What are you doing?' He was examining her hand carefully, spreading her fingers, running his thumbs over her palm.

'Just looking. You have very nice hands. Soft.'

'You don't have some kind of hand fetish, do you?'

'I don't think so.' Tom thought for a moment. 'What would you do if I told you I did?'

'I'm not sure. Show you the other one, maybe?'

He chuckled, twisting around and propping his chin on his hand, turning the full force of his melting blue eyes on her. 'What happens now, Cori?'

Good question. In fact it was the only question worth asking at the moment. She'd just woken up in his bed, with Tom lying beside her. True she was wrapped up in a T-shirt, sweatpants and about three layers of bedding, but those eyes of his were as naked as sin, and about fourteen times more tempting.

'I…I suppose the excuse about you being my boss is wearing a bit thin, isn't it?'

'Yeah. It's only for another three weeks and, anyway, I'm still waiting for you to actually do anything that I tell you to.'

'It could still cause difficulties. In the unit, I mean.'

'I'm very good at keeping secrets. You know that.' He flashed her a conspiratorial look.

'I…' She faltered. She could spend all morning in bed with Tom and no one would ever know. 'I'm not…'

He nodded. 'You're not looking for a fling. In particular, you're not looking for a fling with the hospital's most notorious philanderer.'

'That's not what I was about to say.'

'No, you'd probably put it more diplomatically. But the fact remains that I didn't leave home with a blueprint tucked in my pocket, telling me how a happy family might operate. And family means a great deal to you, I saw that yesterday.'

'Does that matter so much?'

'Yeah, I think it does.' He picked up her hand, pressing her fingers to his lips. 'I might not hold any records for the length of my relationships, but one thing I've never done is lie. The only time I've been happy in my life is when I've been alone, with only myself to answer to. I won't pretend that I'm in it for keeps when I'm not. Least of all with you, Cori.'

The temptation to tell him that temporary didn't matter, and that she'd take anything that he offered, was almost overwhelming. But that would sound a lot like begging for his attention. The thought made Cori feel suddenly cold, and she sat up quickly, taking a swathe of bedding with her.

'Don't kid yourself, Tom. You're not breaking my heart.'

He looked a little nonplussed. Maybe Tom didn't realise that his honesty had touched a nerve. That saying it out loud had suddenly made his inability to commit very real and impossible to ignore.

'That's good to know.' He spoke quietly, his gaze on her face.

She was an inch away from taking it all back and flinging herself into his arms, but the consequences of that were unthinkable. Other women might be able to handle temporary, and do it with a smile, but Cori couldn't. When it came to the crunch, the small child, in pain and longing for a family to call her own wasn't so very far from the surface.

'I'm sorry, Tom.' She reached for him and then thought better of it. 'I just think that… We were both upset last night and I'm so grateful that you were there for me. Let's just leave it at that.'

'Friends, you mean.' He rolled away from her, sitting on the far edge of the bed, his back towards her. *Friends* suddenly seemed an awkward and rather cold word, an excuse for not being able to be anything more.

'Yes. Friends would be good.'

He'd got out of bed, and left Cori to her own devices, while he went downstairs to make breakfast. Pausing by the mirror in the downstairs bathroom, he gave a little groan of disgust. No wonder she'd turned him down, when he was looking like this.

The look of reproach in his own eyes stopped him short. He might have got very used to covering up awkward facts with other people, but since when had he been unable to face the truth in the privacy of his own bathroom? The cut on his lip would heal, and she still wouldn't want him. That was set in stone, immutable.

She was right. They shouldn't kid themselves. He

was the guy who didn't do for ever and he'd rashly thought that it might be okay to not do for ever with a woman who'd been hurt too much already. He should be ashamed.

'Friends, eh?' He quizzed his battered alter ego, staring at it hard in the mirror, wondering if it might come up with some much-needed advice. Tom couldn't imagine how just being friends with Cori would work out.

It was going to have to. There was nothing else. However much else he had dared to dream about, he had to put those thoughts aside, and deal with reality. Count himself lucky that he hadn't blown it entirely with her, and somehow remove the feeling, burned into his brain, that he never wanted to wake up again without her there.

It had been three weeks since Jean's stroke, and Adrian was sitting by her hospital bed, peeling the lid from a yoghurt carton. He carefully set the carton down in front of her and handed her a spoon. Cori watched as her mother slowly began to feed herself.

Tom had come to the house and explained everything to Adrian, telling him exactly what his mother needed and how he could help her. His confidence had been well founded. When Jean had recovered enough for Adrian to be allowed to visit her, they'd all seen another side to him. The boy who everyone reckoned had ants in his pants, and couldn't sit still for a minute, was gentle and patient with Jean, and the two were forming a very special bond.

'I think I've just about seen everything now,' Ralph observed, his voice quiet so as not to interrupt Jean's concentration.

Cori smiled up at her father. He was beginning to

look less haggard, and she knew that he was sleeping better than he had. Eating better too if Iain and his wife had had anything to do with it.

'Don't eat too fast. You've got lots of time,' Adrian admonished Jean solemnly, waiting patiently while she slowly enunciated her reply.

'Do you want a break, Dad? I'll stay here.'

Ralph shook his head. 'No, thanks, love. I went down to the canteen when Grace brought Adrian in after school. I'll take him home in half an hour.'

'Okay. I'll be here for a while, so I'll come up again later.'

'Working late again?' Ralph gave her a knowing look, which Cori ignored.

'Yes. When Tom finishes, which should be about half an hour from now, we're going to spend the evening building a tree.'

'Really?' Ralph raised one eyebrow, inviting her to continue. '*Building* a tree?'

'Yep. There's a playroom next to the art room, and we're building a model of a tree in there. It's a wishing tree. You know, people write things down and hang them on the tree…'

The idea of a wishing tree had come from Cori. She'd mentioned it to Tom, thinking that maybe a large branch or a picture of a tree on the wall would do the job perfectly, and then the whole thing had spiralled out of control.

'There's a wooden trunk and branches…' Cori indicated the curved shape with her hand. 'Maureen, one of the women who works here, her husband's a carpenter and he cut them from my sketches. They're going to be fixed to the wall, and the leaves will all be of different coloured fabrics.'

'I'll have to take a look at this when you've finished. Is this what you've been raising the money for?'

'No, it hasn't cost anything. I got three bags of fabric offcuts from my friend who works in a fashion house, and Tom got the wood from somewhere. It's nice wood too; I varnished a bit to try it out and it was a beautiful colour.'

'Sounds as if you two make a good team.' Ralph's eyes twinkled with humour and Cori frowned. That was exactly what she didn't want to hear. She and Tom *could* have made a great team, but that was just another missed opportunity now.

'Is that a problem?'

'No. But my placement is nearly up.'

'There isn't any rule which says you can't meet up with him after that, is there?'

No. But it wasn't going to happen. They'd made sure of that by pushing the boundaries too far. Ever since that morning, when they'd woken up together in Tom's bed, they'd been drifting apart. Their shared goals at work still drove them, but it was a journey full of awkward silences and feelings that would never be expressed.

Tom's appearance, at the other end of the ward, diverted Ralph from any more difficult questions.

'We were just talking about you.' Ralph shook Tom's hand warmly.

'Yeah?'

Cori felt herself flush, in response to the flicker of self-consciousness that had shown on Tom's face. 'I was just telling Ralph about the wishing tree.'

Ralph nodded. 'It's a nice idea. You seem to have achieved a great deal...'

Cori silenced Ralph with a glare before he could utter the forbidden word. *Together* wasn't something that she allowed herself to think about where Tom was concerned any more.

'I bumped into Jean's doctor on the way in.' Tom seemed just as eager to change the subject as she was. 'He said she's doing really well, and that she'll be going home soon.'

'Yes, we've been talking to Social Services and getting everything ready for her. We've got a way to go still, but we'll get there.' Ralph brightened a little at the thought.

'Absolutely.' Tom had always been positive, even in those first uncertain days after Jean's stroke. Cori wondered how they would have managed without him, and dismissed the thought. She'd find out soon enough how well she would manage without him.

Ralph shook Tom's hand again, as if he couldn't reiterate that message of thanks enough, and Tom turned, walking to Jean's bedside. He produced a comic from his back pocket for Adrian, and took Jean's hand, facing her to catch her attention.

'How do you feel?'

Jean nodded. 'Good. Good.' Her speech was still slurred, and she tended to communicate in monosyllables still, but she was getting better every day.

'That's great. You're doing very well.' He backed the statement up with a smile, and Jean managed a lopsided effort in return.

Adrian's enthusiasm for the comic, and Jean's obvious wish for a hug, were managed faultlessly. Tom supervised the removal of Adrian's shoes, and lifted him carefully onto the bed next to Jean, spreading the comic out in front of them, and Adrian started to leaf through it slowly. After submitting to yet another of Ralph's handshakes, Tom shot a glance at Cori and she nodded. Their next stop was the wishing tree.

It had taken three evenings to finish the tree. Tom never tired of watching Cori work her magic. She had an uncanny knack of making something out of nothing. A few pieces of wood and some material were all she needed and she'd made something fabulous out of it. The curves of the branches seemed to beckon to him to touch them, and the carefully arranged colours of the leaves rippled through the tree like sunlight.

'Well…?' She stretched her arms, suppressed a yawn and stood back to take a look. Tom could have kissed her there and then. If he'd thought for one moment that the accompanying wish would come true, he would have thrown caution to the wind and done it.

'It's wonderful. I love it.'

She nodded, surveying the tree thoughtfully. 'I think…' She selected another fabric leaf from the pile on the table and fixed it carefully, covering a square inch of blank wall. Then she moved another leaf a couple of inches to the left. Tom knew that she'd be stopping in front of the tree and making small alterations for a while before she would be completely satisfied.

'That's better.' She seemed content enough for the time being.

'Ready to make a wish?'

'Me?' Cori turned to him, shaking her head. 'No, not me. I don't want to go first.'

He should have known better than to even ask. During the last three weeks, their own wishes had been a no-go area.

'Maybe tomorrow.' Tomorrow was the last day of Cori's attachment to the unit. Maureen had been surreptitiously organising a small surprise party for her, and that would be an ideal time for everyone to share their wishes on the tree.

'Yes. That sounds like a good idea.' She was staring fixedly at the tree, as if looking at him was forbidden. Suddenly Tom wanted to share his wish with her now, not in front of a room full of people.

'Actually, I do have something.' Before he had time to change his mind Tom reached for one of the coloured tags that Cori had made.

'Do you?' She gave him a startled, wide-eyed look.

'Yeah.' He picked up a pen and wrote. 'Do you want to see?'

Cori eyed him suspiciously, but when he handed her the tag she took it and read what he'd written.

'Oh… Oh, that's really nice.

I wish that every child could grow up free from the fear of violence.

She tipped her shining face up towards him and Tom felt a little dizzy. They'd spent a lot of time together in the last three weeks, but determined activity had prevented them from daring to talk about anything that didn't pertain to their work. He suddenly realised how much he'd missed that.

'Are you sure you want to write your name?' She twisted her mouth in a wry smile. 'I think there might be one or two people on the unit who haven't heard the story of what Rosie told Mr Morton yet.'

'If there is anyone, send them to me and I'll fill them in on the details. It's been a secret for too long now, Cori. If I'm to be an advocate for children who are going through the same thing I went through, I need to be honest about what happened to me.'

'An advocate…' There was a telltale glint of a tear in her eye as she turned away from him. The thought that Cori still might be moved to tears for him made his heart lurch in a wild expression of forbidden joy.

Suddenly she was full of energy, bustling around, tidying up the mess they'd made while they worked. Hiding her tears from him. Tom tucked the wish into the pocket of his shirt. He'd hang it on the tree tomorrow, with all the others.

'I have one too.' She was still again, looking at him thoughtfully.

'What is it?'

'That I can keep up with you when we run on Sunday. And that we raise lots of money for the unit.'

'Whose idea was this?'

'I don't remember. Yours?' Tom turned his melting smile onto her.

'What was I thinking?'

He shrugged. 'I think it was rather a good idea.'

'I'm not so sure. I shouldn't have eaten all that cake on Friday. It was lovely of everyone to throw a party, but I'm regretting it now.' Her stomach felt as if it had a lead weight in it.

'The cake's not going to make any difference to you. You're just searching for something to be nervous about.'

'I don't want to mess up…'

Tom shook his head, obviously realising that he wasn't getting through. 'Just trust me, eh? I'll get you there.'

Despite her nerves, this felt like a turning point. They'd always enjoyed running together, and today the impending race seemed to have wrought a change in Tom. He seemed happier, less tense.

She felt his hand close momentarily around hers, giving it a squeeze. Smiling up at him, she took a deep breath. That was better.

The pairs of runners were working their way steadily through the streets of London, towards them. Through the City, which would be deserted on a Sunday morning, across London Bridge and then following the south side of the river until they reached the Jubilee Foot-bridge. Cori and Tom were second to last in the relay, running along the Embankment towards the Palace of Westminster.

The run was already a success. It had been talked about and re-posted from one social media account to another. People had smiled when they'd seen the post-ers that Cori had designed, and the local paper was re-porting on the run.

Donations had flooded in, and if the runners could complete the course first they stood to raise even more money. There would be enough for the project in the art room as well as much-needed equipment for the play room and the wards. What had started out as a fun run, had turned into a serious event.

'No pressure…' Cori didn't want to think about what they could do with that money. They weren't there yet.

'Nah. No pressure. Just keep up with me, and we'll make it.'

She rolled her eyes. Just keeping up was a lot more difficult than he made it sound. Numbly she followed everything that Tom did, warming up for the run, loosening her muscles, trying to keep her head clear of everything other than the oft-repeated mantra. They were going to make it. They were going to make it.

'Any minute now…' Tom seemed relaxed and ready to go. He stripped off his tracksuit bottoms and started to jog on the spot.

She could see the two runners coming towards them. There was no sign of the team travelling on the Underground yet. Helen Kowalski was running with her new fiancé and Cori stepped forward, ready to receive the baton.

She felt it slap into her hand, and her fingers closed automatically around it. She heard Helen shouting encouragement behind her, with what must have been the last of the oxygen in her lungs. Tom was off and running beside her, pacing her at exactly the speed he knew that she could match…

The pavement was wide, and this early on a Sunday morning it wasn't crowded. She felt good, strong, and she moved forward to run next to Tom. He flashed her a grin, checking the timer on his wrist.

'On schedule.' He didn't waste any words, but it was good to know. They'd started before the Underground team, but there was no way of knowing how much of a lead they had over them, or how long their opponents' journey would take. That element of uncertainty, which had helped to attract sponsors, was killing her now.

She fell into Tom's easy rhythm and forgot about everything else. Just the beat of their footsteps, the tempo of her breathing. One step at a time, each one bringing them nearer to their shared goal.

They ran together along the Embankment, Tom steering her around the people walking ahead of them. 'You're doing great. Just keep going.' He was well within his own capabilities and had breath to spare to encourage her.

Two-thirds of the way there she began to weaken. This was the crunch point, where she pushed through the tiredness and simply concentrated on keeping up with him. Her thoughts seemed to shimmer then crystallise on one thing. The smile he would give her when they made the finishing line together. It wasn't far away now and she concentrated on that.

'Cori…!' It was his urgent cry that told her she was falling. She heard rather than felt the sound of her knees hitting the pavement, and screamed in frustration.

'No…' She tried to get up but she'd lost control of her limbs. Ahead of her, only a hundred yards away, Gemma was waiting to take the baton, which seemed to be rolling away from her in slow motion.

'I'm okay. I'm okay.' She gasped the words, and made a grab for the baton. Somehow she managed to get hold of it and she pulled herself up onto her hands and knees. She was going to make it, even if she had to crawl.

Tom had stopped and was lifting her to her feet. She took a couple of tentative steps and then one leg gave way and he swung her up into his arms. 'All right. Just hang on…'

He started to run. Cori dug her fingers into his sweat-shirt, hanging on for dear life, trying to help him by supporting her own weight a little. She could hear his heart pounding, feel his breath, coming quick and hard.

'Yes-s-s…!' She heard a cheer from the group waiting by the station entrance, and felt Gemma snatch the baton from her hand. Tom stopped running, letting her feet slip to the ground but still holding her tightly against his chest. When he had caught his breath a little, he walked her the few steps to a couple of fold-up chairs that had been quickly vacated for them by the timekeepers.

He waved away the offers of help that came from the people around them. He wasn't the only doctor here—practically everyone had some kind of medical qualification—but he was the only doctor that Cori wanted and he seemed determined that he would be the only doctor she would have.

'Are you all right?' He was still breathing hard, but all his attention was on her.

'I'm okay.' She looked down at her knees and saw that blood was beginning to run down one leg.

'Sure? Let me look…'

'In a minute, Tom. I'm all right, just a skinned knee.' She felt her elbow begin to throb and peered at it. 'And elbow.'

'Did I hurt you when I picked you up…?'

'No, but you're annoying me now. Stop fussing and sit down will you?'

He opened his mouth, clearly intent on fussing a bit more, and then thought better of it. 'Fair enough. If I find out you're hiding anything, you're really in trouble.' Cori shot him a glare and he took the hint and sat down next to her.

Someone wrapped a blanket around her. A medical kit appeared out of nowhere, and Tom took charge of it.

'Blimey. You lot come prepared.' She surveyed the contents of the large box.

He shrugged. 'I suppose doctors and nurses know all the things that might happen.'

'What's that?'

'Nothing to concern you. You're obviously not in cardiac arrest...' He turned to see two figures hurrying out of the station and shot Cori that bright, melting smile that had carried her through the pain barrier. 'There they are...'

The team that had been travelling by public transport handed over their baton in a rather more civilised fashion than Cori had managed. All the same, she'd done it first, and that was what mattered. Commiserations were offered when they saw her knees, and someone fetched her a warm drink.

Kate arrived on a bicycle, bringing their things, and Cori slipped gratefully into her coat, while Tom put on his sweatpants. Kate tutted at the state of Cori's knees, and made a show of rolling her eyes when she saw that Tom was intent on dressing the wound.

'Good luck with that one. I'd have a nurse do it personally; we're much better at that kind of thing...' She laughed as Tom ostentatiously nudged her out of the way. She collected the next runners' things and got back onto her bike to take them on to the finishing post.

Cori waved her off as she set out along the cycle lane. Another cyclist, dressed in tight-fitting shorts and carrying a messenger bag, swerved across her path, making her wobble slightly, and she called a few indignant words after him as he pedalled away.

'Look, he nearly hit Kate…' Cori's indignation was shattered by a sudden, high-pitched scream, and she looked up to see a little girl of about five years old lying on the pavement and the cyclist riding away, without even looking back.

The child's mother was only two feet away, with a younger child in a pushchair, and she rushed to comfort her daughter, who flung herself into her arms, crying. Tom and a couple of the others were hurrying over to see if they could help, and Cori followed them, hobbling stiffly on her injured leg.

The woman seemed nonplussed at first, and then unable to believe her luck. Cori supposed it wasn't every day that you had two doctors and an ambulance driver on hand to help when your child took a nasty tumble. It seemed that, as Head of Paediatrics, Tom had pulled rank and was attending to the patient.

He helped the woman up, and delivered her child back into her arms. Someone wheeled the buggy behind them, and they all trailed across to the two fold-up chairs. Tom guided the woman into one, and Cori sat down in the other.

'What are you all doing here?' the little girl's mother asked.

Tom was working his charm and the little girl was responding shyly. Her mother obviously felt confident enough to let Tom get on with it.

'Oh, it's a charity run. For the hospital where we work. We're raising money to kit out an art room in the paediatric unit.'

'Good for you.' The woman smiled. 'I'm Lucy.'

'Cori.'

'I don't think that you're a *real* doctor…' The little girl's voice broke into the conversation, and Lucy flushed.

'Of course he is, Amy.'

Tom was laughing. 'She has a point.' He reached into the medical kit and pulled out a stethoscope, hanging it around his neck. 'There. Is that a bit better?'

Amy nodded, and Cori shrugged in Lucy's direction. Bringing a stethoscope to a fun run might be construed as over-packing, but she supposed it had come in useful.

'The man knocked me down.'

'I saw that, sweetheart. You took a bit of a tumble there. Can I look at your knee, please?'

Amy nodded, pulling at the large hole in her woollen tights. Her gaze wandered to Cori's leg and she craned around to look at it. 'Did you get knocked down?'

Cori laughed. 'No, I fell over. I was trying to run really fast and I tripped over my feet.'

'Ouch!' Lucy sympathised with her. 'You made the finishing line, though.'

'Yep. She made it.' Tom was smiling as he carefully swabbed Amy's knee.

'With a little help. Tom ended up carrying me for the last few yards.'

'Whatever works.' Lucy glanced at Tom, and then shot Cori a mischievous look. 'And it's all for a good cause.'

'Yes. One of the very best.' Cori let her gaze slip towards Tom. She never tired of watching him with his young patients. He had such a knack of getting children to trust him, making them smile. But, then, children had a habit of recognising a good heart when they found it.

'You've been very brave, Amy. Just one more thing to do, we're going to stick a plaster onto your knee.' Tom held up a large plaster and Amy nodded.

'Then Carly...?' Amy was having difficulty getting her tongue around Cori's name.

'Yep. Are you going to help? Since you know what to do now?'

'Yes-s-s!'

Amy supervised, while Tom swabbed and dressed Cori's knee, nodding her head in approval as he carefully taped a wad of gauze over the graze. 'You didn't say that Carly was brave,' Amy reproved him gently.

'That's right. Thanks for reminding me.' Tom turned his gaze on Cori, tenderness spilling from his eyes.

'You're very brave, Cori.'

He managed to say it all in just those few words. All the effort they'd put in, all the frustration and the pain. All the preparation and work it had taken to find sponsors. It had all been worth it for those simple words of praise from Tom.

CHAPTER THIRTEEN

SHE HADN'T SEEN Tom since the car that had taken them both home from the run had dropped her off outside her flat. Jean was out of hospital now, and Cori was staying with Ralph and Jean for the week to help them out.

Tom had never been far from her thoughts, though. In the evenings, when Jean and Ralph went to bed, Jean to rest and Ralph to read at her side, Cori painted. The canvas on which she had sketched his portrait, when she'd still believed that something between them had been possible, slowly took shape.

It seemed that he thought of her too. There were texts from him every day. Sometimes a question about the art-room project or about how Jean was doing, and sometimes just, How are you?

And on Friday evening came the text Cori seemed to have been holding her breath for the whole week.

See you tomorrow.

The tomorrow that Tom referred to was an early start. Even though Cori had told Tom that he didn't need to be there, and that the artists' group could begin work by themselves, he was waiting for her when she got to the hospital, all sleepy blue eyes and tousled hair. He helped unload the crates from the van, and when the other volunteers arrived he made tea for everyone, went to the canteen for egg-and-bacon sandwiches, and then made sure that he spoke to everyone, thanking them for being there.

The room had been cleared, and it was strictly off limits to patients and their families for today on account of the paint fumes. In amongst the bustle of activity they found themselves suddenly alone.

'Have you heard about Rosie yet?'

'Yes. They gave her an official warning and she's written a letter of apology to Mr and Mrs Morton. A secretarial post has come up in another department, away from the main hospital site, and she's decided to transfer over there.'

'It's probably for the best. After all the bad feeling in the department about what she did.' Cori couldn't bring herself to completely forgive Rosie for what she'd done to Tom, even though Tom himself had worked hard to smooth things over with the Mortons and had probably saved Rosie's job.

'We all need a second chance from time to time.' He stepped to one side to allow Adam to finish spreading a plastic sheet across the carpet. 'I'd better get out of your way.'

'Oh, no, you don't. There are some overalls in the crate over there.'

He raised a questioning eyebrow. 'You need a pair?'

'No. You might if you're going to help, though.'

He shook his head. 'I'm no artist.'

'Well, that's good, because I'm not looking for an

artist.' Cori had already decided that she wasn't taking no for an answer.

'I suppose I should… Can't I just make the tea?'

'No. What's wrong with doing a little painting?' Cori found the drawing she'd made of the final design for a quiet area in the corner of the room, and looked for the appropriate bundle of stencils, which she'd packed last night, pulling them out of the box. Tom was eyeing them suspiciously.

'I need you to paint. We can't finish without you…' That wasn't exactly true. The project had been organised at short notice, and the seven artists who'd been able to make it here today would have to work hard, but they could do it. In truth, someone willing to make the tea and keep everyone fed would be a great deal more of an asset to the team than someone who needed to be taught how to use a stencil.

She took his arm, and felt the muscle swell under her fingers as if he was about to pull away. 'Tom, whoever took this away from you, it's time to take it back.'

'You don't *really* need me…' He was looking around at the bustle of activity in the room. 'It looks as if it would be better if I stayed out of the way.'

'That wouldn't be the point, Tom. What we're doing here is all about inclusivity, getting everyone involved, whoever they are. I won't leave you behind.'

He heaved a sigh. 'I suppose maintaining that I'm not in your patient group isn't going to work, then.'

'Not for a moment. None of this is about sorting people out into groups, it's about embracing what we all have in common.'

'Okay.' He held up his hands in a gesture of mock surrender. 'What do you want me to do?'

'This corner's yours. Here's the design and the stencils, and the paint and mixing trays are over there. Do
you know how to use a stencil?'

'Nope.'

'Find some overalls, then, and I'll show you.'

All his life Tom had known that hanging on to his res-
olutions was the thing that made him strong. Whether
they were big ones, like studying hard and getting out
of his home, or the little ones, like never picking up a
paintbrush again. And yet somehow Cori made him at
least want to try to let go a little.

She showed him how the stencils worked together,
building up layers of colour until the whole design was
finished. How to fix the stencils to the wall, and how to
sponge and brush on the paint. Apparently airbrushing
was the next thing in her Pandora's box of treats, and
she intended to show him how to do that after lunch.

He was left alone with a pile of stencils, paint,
brushes, a blank wall, and a heart that was threatening
to thump its way out of his chest. Why? It was just an
old paintbox. Why did it matter so much?

'Come and see this.' Cori's voice broke into his rev-
erie, and he realised that in half an hour he'd done nothing. She'd told him to look first and then paint, so he
guessed he had an excuse.

'I thought you wanted me to paint.' He grinned at
her, hoping the smile would soften the starkly empty
wall that stood in front of him.

'You can take a break.' She ignored the fact that *taking a break* implied that he'd already done something,
and beckoned for him to follow her.

As she walked along the corridor, heading for the

ward reception area, she slipped her overalls from her shoulders, tying the sleeves around her waist. It was the way he'd first seen her. An old sweater, paint-spattered overalls, her hair tied up in a messy arrangement on the top of her head. This time she had marks around her eyes, the impressions from the goggles she'd been wearing to spray paint, and in an odd way that only added to the allure. Tom followed her with the same dogged joy with which he'd followed the trail of glitter from the car park.

There was a little huddle of people crowded around the nurses' station. As they approached, Maureen turned towards him.

'What are you doing here today?' Tom saw that there was a younger version of Maureen, obviously her daughter, standing next to her.

'What, and miss all the fun? We brought cake.'

'Home-made…' Cori was practically dancing on the spot with glee. 'Look, there's enough for everyone.'

'Maureen, you're a star. And you've brought… Amelia?' He searched for the name and found it.

'Milly…' Clearly the dark-haired teenager was of an age when her given name had become a burden and amendments were necessary.

'Sorry. Milly. It's great you came, thank you.'

'Milly was rather hoping she could paint…' Maureen leaned over towards him and Tom deflected the question with a look towards Cori.

'Yes, of course. I'm so glad you came. We have overalls and face masks to spare.' Cori beckoned towards Milly, who brightened immediately and followed her along the corridor without so much as a backward glance at her mother.

'She's growing up.' Tom remembered the shy child that Maureen had brought to work with her when he'd just been starting out in the unit. 'Bring your daughter to work day' had been a revelation to him when he'd first started work here. Seeing parents and kids who actually had conversations with each other.

'Yes, she is.' Maureen smiled after her daughter. 'She can be a bit stroppy at times, but she chose to come here today instead of going out with her friends.'

'She seems a great kid. I'll bet you're proud of her.' A lump began to form in Tom's throat. What was this? He dealt with parents and their children every day. Why did today suddenly seem so different?

'Yeah, I'm proud. In between the times I feel as if I could murder her...' Maureen turned as Cori and Milly reappeared at Tom's elbow.

'We've got an idea...' Milly's eyes were shining.

Cori turned to Tom. 'We thought we could open the blinds in the glazed wall, between our room and the next one, so that anyone who wanted to come and watch could do so, without getting any of the fumes from the paint.'

'Sounds good to me.'

'And *then* we thought...' Milly chimed in.

'Yes. Then we thought that we could make it a bit like a peep show. You know, at the seaside.' She frowned. 'I'll sketch it out so you can see what I mean.'

'Just do it. As long as it's safe, it doesn't damage anything, and you don't get in the way of the work of the unit, go for it.' They'd talked and planned for long enough. Today was a day for doing.

'Okay.' Cori exchanged a private nod of excitement

with Milly. 'Let's go, then. There are some bits and pieces in the van that I need some help with…'

He'd intercepted Cori and Milly manoeuvring a large piece of art board through the entrance doors, and had managed to guide them through to the art room without flattening anyone. He'd helped Maureen carry the boxes of cake through to the kitchen, and had then spent some time with Kate, checking on one of the patients who was giving her cause for concern. And the blank wall was still there, waiting for him.

When he got back to the art room, he found that Cori and Milly had almost finished their project. The art board had been laid out on the floor, cut to shape and painted. The quick, expansive brush strokes took away nothing from the design—it was a seaside Punch and Judy stall, with a red and white striped canvas, a couple of seagulls perched on the top and a cloudless blue sky behind it.

Cori took a moment to stand back and look at their work, and gave a little nod. 'That's great, Milly. Really nice. It'll be dry in half an hour and we can put it up outside.'

'What's next?' Milly was beaming.

'Why don't you go and see Adam? He'll show you how to help him with the spray paint. Only put your mask on.' She watched as Milly bounced over to Adam and then she turned to Tom. 'How are you getting on?'

'Still in the thinking stage.'

She nodded. 'Right. Well, that's good. Any clue about when you'll be ready to move on? Bearing in mind that we need to finish sometime before midnight.'

He grinned. 'We have that long?'

'Well, I'd prefer it was a bit sooner. But however long it takes.' She looked up at him, and suddenly he knew. Somewhere in the vibrant warmth of her eyes he found his safe place.

'You want to know something crazy?'

'Yeah, go on. Crazy always turns me on.' She was moving with him slowly away from the others into a quiet corner of the room.

'When I was eight years old my grandparents bought me a painting box. I loved that box, and I kept it under my bed, where no one could get at it. One day I spilled some paint on the carpet. I managed to clean it up mostly but…' Tom shrugged. The words had suddenly become too much for him.

'Your father took them away?'

'He smashed the box and threw it away with the paints. I told myself that I didn't like painting anyway, and that I didn't care. He couldn't touch me.'

'That's not crazy, is it?'

'The crazy part is that I haven't picked up a paint-brush since.'

'So…you want to share my paintbox?' She shot an impish look in his direction.

'I would…' Suddenly everything seemed so simple. So easy. 'Actually, I would love that.'

'Right. Let's get started, then.'

CHAPTER FOURTEEN

His WALL HAD become *their* wall. As Tom worked, stencilling the designs, he began to realise that Cori had more in mind than a simple mural of intertwining leaves and flowers. The lush vegetation that he was painting was just a backdrop for animals and birds, painted separately, ready to be mounted onto the wall to give a three-dimensional effect.

'Very neat. What are they painted on?' He watched as she laid the creatures out on the floor.

'Plastic. It's durable and light. I'll fix them on with these spacer pegs behind them so they'll stand away from the wall and give a bit of texture.' She looked up at him. 'That's the theory anyway. It's a bit of an experiment, and I'll be wanting you to report back to me on how it performs in practice.'

'You're going somewhere?' He was concentrating on dabbing paint onto every part of the wall exposed by the stencil, and the question just slipped out before he'd had a chance to think about it.

She gave him a puzzled look. 'I don't work here any more, remember?' She gestured him back to work.

He carefully peeled the stencil off the wall, admired

his handiwork and consulted Cori's sketch to see what he had to do next.

'You don't *have* to stick to the plan.' She was looking over his shoulder. 'Actually, a few more leaves here...'

She waved her hand vaguely in the direction of the design on the wall, and Tom laughed. 'I've only just got to grips with how to do this. Now you want me to start making it up as I go along?'

'All right. Since you're not quite ready to break free and follow the tide, perhaps you'll let me add a few freehand bits.'

'Good idea.' Cori would always be happiest with one toe slightly outside the boundaries. Working freehand and dealing with life as it came along. And Tom was happy to watch that for the time being.

Even though the room wasn't quite finished, it looked stunning. The kids who had gathered outside to enjoy the peep show had banged on the window in delight, and the artists working on the designs had made faces back at them. They drank tea and ate cake as they worked, continuing through lunchtime and finishing early. At four o' clock it was decided they could do no more until today's paint was fully dry, and Tom extended an invitation to everyone to meet at the local pub.

'You shouldn't have done that.' Cori was curled up in her seat like a cat, warm and with a full stomach. 'We usually have a whip-around to pay for food and drink.'

'It's the least I could do. Did you see the kids' faces?'

'Yeah. Makes it worthwhile.' She stretched languidly and settled back in her seat, smiling lazily at him. In that moment the whole of the evening and the possibilities of the night to come seemed to open up before Tom.

He could wait, though. While the artists tipped their glasses to empty them and put them down on the table, reaching for coats and scarves. While Milly, who had been allowed to come with them on the express condition that she only drank orange juice, waved goodbye and was watched to her mother's car outside. While the landlord collected the plates and glasses, leaving an empty table in front of them.

'Guess we'd better go. Unless you want another drink?'

'No. Thanks, but I think I'd like to lie flat on my sofa for about an hour.'

'Sounds good. You could lie flat on *my* sofa if you wanted. I have chocolate.'

She leaned towards him, the colour of her eyes seeming suddenly brighter. 'Are you trying to tempt me?'

He'd spent too long without her. And now it felt as if his world was shining with a brilliance that only Cori could create. He could no longer deny that he wanted to be with her tonight.

Tom smiled at her. That thousand-volt, X-rated smile, which she couldn't resist. 'I could leave the chocolate on your doorstep if that's a better idea.'

It probably was. But she didn't want today to end. Not here. Not now.

'You can't leave chocolate on doorsteps. It could rain and then it would get wet. Or the foxes might find it.'

'And that would be a sin.'

It was too late to weigh that one small sin against all the others that saving the chocolate might lay them open to. Especially as tonight they didn't seem so very sinful after all.

'So, what kind of chocolate do you have?'

'Truffles. Dusted with cocoa powder.'

She could almost feel them on her tongue. 'You keep a stock of them, do you?'

'No. I saw them the other day and thought of you.'

Satisfaction blossomed in her heart. 'So you've been planning this for a while?'

'There's no plan. That's the whole point, isn't it? There's nothing we have to do, and nothing we can't do.'

Her heart thumped in her chest. Cori could practically feel her cheeks flushing, her pupils dilating. All the little things that would tell him that *nothing we can't do* sounded just fine with her.

'Chocolate…may be a bad idea. Is there such a thing as a serotonin overdose?'

He grinned. 'Not unless you're taking medication that affects your serotonin levels. Got a headache?'

'No.'

'Feeling confused?'

'Not in the slightest.'

'I think you can stand a little more, then.' He leaned forward, and Cori shivered as his breath brushed her ear. 'Maybe a lot more.'

Warmth shimmied down her spine. 'And what about you? Can you stand a lot more?'

'I don't know. This isn't something I've done before.'

If that was his way of telling her that she was different from all the rest… Cori looked into his eyes, and suddenly it seemed that it might be.

'Then you'll be wanting me to lead the way?'

'Always, Cori. You get to call the shots.'

It took a man as strong as Tom to say that. To put what he wanted out there, and let her either accept or reject him. And she accepted him, just as he was. Wordlessly she stood, winding her scarf around her neck and pulling on her old leather jacket.

She clearly didn't quite believe him. Tom didn't totally believe it himself, but the feeling persisted. Cori really was different. He really hadn't been here before.

The car radio came on when he turned the key in the ignition and she turned the volume down a little but left the music on. They made the twenty-minute drive to his house almost in silence, and she followed him quietly to his front door. He slid the key into the lock and let her in, closing the door behind them.

He could see her silhouette and hear her breathing in the dark hallway. Smell the paint on her clothes and the light, musky scent of her skin.

'Cori, I...' He reached for her and felt her finger across his lips.

'It's okay, Tom. We don't need to talk about this.'

He curled his fingers around hers. There was every need to talk about it, however cold it seemed to say the words right now. They couldn't simply assume that they understood each other. 'Cori, I don't have any promises to give you. Tonight is the only thing I have.'

The last time they'd had this conversation she'd rejected him, and Tom wouldn't blame her if she did so now. But somehow he knew that she wouldn't.

'I know.' Her voice was quiet in the darkness. 'Tonight's enough.'

'You're sure?'

'You'll give me everything. Just for tonight?'

That he could promise. 'Yes, sweetheart.'

'It's enough, then.'

He wanted to tell her how special she was, but words could no longer compete with the dialogue of feeling that spun between them. Slowly, he backed her against the wall, hearing her sharp intake of breath as his body closed on hers. When he kissed her, she whimpered quietly.

Each one of his senses was raging, wanting her so badly that it hurt. He heard his own breathing quicken, along with hers, and buried his face in her neck. She wrapped her arms around his neck and he lifted her slightly, just enough that they were face to face, and felt her legs wind around his hips.

'I want to take you here. Right here, right now.' He whispered the words into her ear, and felt her body move against his. If she did that again, that was exactly what he was going to have to do.

'Yes… I want that too…'

'But then I wouldn't have the pleasure of soaping you clean. Wondering all the while what it feels like to be inside you.'

'Can we…?'

'We can do whatever we like…'

'To me? Will you do whatever you like to me?'

Her words broke him. Something inside snapped and then re-formed, wanting only to give Cori whatever she wished for. 'Whenever you want me to, honey.'

He'd kissed her in the darkness of the hallway until she could no longer disguise the fact that her whole body was crying out for him. Every time he touched her, heat seemed to bloom across her skin. Each time his body moved against hers, she felt her breathing quicken, her heart beat a little faster, in a spiral of longing that only he could satisfy. And Tom clearly had no intention of doing that just yet.

Finally he took her upstairs, stopping on the landing to kiss her again, before leading her into the bedroom. The heavy, cast-iron bedstead dominated the room, almost beckoning her towards it. A soft glow emanated from two table lamps, and Tom was showing no inclination to switch them off.

Cori had been banking on darkness and it taking him only seconds to undress her. It looked as if she was going to be wrong on both counts. 'I thought that I might...' She pulled at a loose thread on her old sweater. 'I thought I might do this alone.'

He looked genuinely crestfallen. 'If you want.'

'I didn't exactly have this in mind when I dressed this morning.' She leaned towards him, nipping his ear. 'I've got my passion-killers on and—'

'Passion-killers, eh? You think they're going to work?'

He didn't wait for an answer but pushed her back onto the bed, leaning over her, kissing her mouth. As he did so, Cori could feel him unbuttoning her cardigan. 'I want to undo every button. I want to work out a way of getting you out of those overalls and see every inch of you as I do it.'

He made it sound like a good thing that she was wearing her oldest clothes. 'Yeah. I'm good with that.'

He rolled over, propping himself up on the pillows and pulling her astride his hips. Sliding her cardigan from her shoulders, he set to work on her shirt. When he had that unbuttoned he slid his hand under the T-shirt underneath and found the hooks at the back of her bra. One hand on the back of her waist steadied her and the other found her breast, teasing until she cried out.

'Now, please…'

'No, not yet. There's so much more…' He rolled her over onto her back and the sharp insistence of the moment subsided into a warm haze of wanting. She wriggled luxuriantly under him, and he chuckled.

'I'll get you back, Tom Riley.' She pulled at the front of his shirt and felt his weight on top of her, pinning her down. When she moved against him, he groaned.

'Cori…'

'Yeah.' Her hand slid between them, finding the zipper of his jeans. Two could play at this game.

They played at this game for as long as they could bear it. When they'd got each other out of their clothes he took her into the black, white and chrome bathroom, and they soaped each other clean. Then he wrapped her in a towel and carried her back to the bedroom, laying her down on the bed.

He was gorgeous, his smooth, tawny skin rippling over a strong, muscular frame. His eyes were the deepest shade of blue and his hair golden, standing up in spikes from where she'd dragged her fingers through it.

He took care of everything—pillows at her back, condoms ready for when they needed them. And now they were both trembling, unable to wait any longer.

She felt his hips nudging her legs apart. His fingers wound around hers. For one moment he was still, gazing into her eyes, and then she felt him slide slowly inside.

'Beautiful… Cori, you are so beautiful…' He wound one arm around her back, the other cradling her face in a gesture of shattering tenderness. They made love, staring into each other's eyes, dragging out each moment until she felt the orgasm begin to roll inside her. When he felt it too he thrust hard, sending her over the edge into a bright cascade of feeling.

He could barely hang on before the orgasm overwhelmed him. Taking him and dashing him against the furthest frontiers of what he thought his body was capable of. He knew that he called out her name, and that he was holding her close, but beyond that Tom was just a helpless mess of sensation, broken for the first time, and in love before he even saw it coming.

When he woke in the night he found her there, ready to hold him and take him back inside her. She made him trust himself, believe that he could be the man he wanted. The man she wanted.

They slept and made love pretty much in equal measure until late in the morning. Got up slowly, showering and eating breakfast sprawled on the bed. Easing themselves into the day.

'You're going to work this afternoon?'

'Yes. I thought I'd take you home to change your clothes then we could go to the hospital together.' It wasn't Tom's usual modus operandi to spend the day with someone after sleeping with them the night before. People had things to do, and a modern relationship didn't require that two people cling together like limpets. But the idea of employing anything as premeditated as a modus operandi with Cori was downright ridiculous.

She grinned at him. 'I'll be needing new underwear.'

Tom tried to nod gravely, but could feel the corners of his mouth twitching. 'Another pair of passion-killers?'

Her brow wrinkled in thought. 'Well, you can only really get away with passion-killers if no one knows you're wearing them.'

'Something else, then?'

Cori's cheeks flushed pink. After what they'd done last night it seemed slightly incongruous that a discussion about what underwear she was going to wear should make her blush, but she somehow managed to carry it off. 'I...don't know.'

'So I guess that watching you work and imagining your perfect behind is going to take some improvisation?'

She leaned forward, running her finger along his jaw. And then, suddenly his whole world came crashing down.

'I love you, Thomas Riley.'

Rewind. Do something. Pretend your body was just taken over by aliens, and it wasn't you who said it. Panic seized Cori.

For a moment she thought that maybe it was going to be all right. That he'd laugh and tell her that he loved her too. But Tom would have to be taken over by aliens before he said such a thing.

'Cori, I...' He shook his head. 'We made an agreement.'

And he'd held to his part of the bargain. She should stick to hers, do them both a favour, and let him off the hook.

She squeezed her eyes shut, feeling tears well up against her lids. However embarrassing it was, she couldn't pretend that she hadn't meant what she'd said.

Not after what they'd shared last night. Not even to save whatever was left of their relationship.

Moments ticked away before she heard his voice, calm and quiet. 'Cori, I've never asked a woman back to my place before.'

She opened her eyes. 'Say that again. While I'm looking at you.'

He met her gaze without blinking. 'I haven't asked a woman back to my place before. It's a thing I have.'

'What sort of thing?'

'My own space has always been very important to me. It *is* very important to me.'

'What are you saying, Tom?'

'I'm saying that you're special to me, and that you always will be. But I don't do love. I never have done.'

Something cold crawled across her heart, and then pride came to her rescue. 'Let's not pretend, eh? This was never anything other than a one-night stand.'

He said nothing. Cori could see she'd hurt him, but knew he wouldn't hit back at her. She should go now, before she opened her big mouth again and made things even worse. She stood up, and somehow her legs managed to support her weight. 'I think it's time you took me home.'

When he dropped her back at her flat Cori made it clear to him that she intended to work alone today. She showered again and changed her clothes, and then walked to the hospital. It took the whole of the afternoon to finish the murals in the art room and she worked steadily, no tears, no scene. When she was done she packed up her paints and walked out of the hospital, without saying a word to anyone. She was done. Finished. In every sense of the word.

* * *

She'd said he loved him. It wasn't so much the words that had horrified him, but the look in her eyes when she'd said them. Cori had really meant it. And in that moment he'd realised that everything he'd felt the night before was real. He loved her too.

She'd put her heart in his hands, and he was so afraid of dropping it. Letting her down, finding that he really couldn't change and give her all the things that she deserved.

So he'd told her the truth. He didn't do love. He didn't know how to plan a future together, or dream of having a family. And it wasn't fair to Cori for him to do all this for the first time, make every mistake in the book, and break her heart in the process.

His father had always made everything about what *he*'d wanted. *His* moods, *his* temper had ruled their household. Tom had promised himself that he would never be like that, and this was the ultimate test. He had to put aside what he wanted. He wanted Cori but he had to forget that and concentrate on what he was able to give.

And that was a heart that equated strength with being alone. One that had been taught to shy away from the vulnerability of being in love. His father may have poisoned Tom's own dreams, but he would never allow him to touch Cori's.

Tom opened the wardrobe in his bedroom, sliding out the precious canvas and unwrapping it. Cori's painting, the one that he had bought from the tea shop. At the time his motive for buying it had been to give the fundraising a helping hand, but now it meant a great deal more to him. The loneliness, so movingly portrayed, was something that she had learned to leave behind. But it was irrevocably his now.

CHAPTER FIFTEEN

WHEN THE LETTER from the hospital arrived, Cori had stared at it for a long time before opening it. Inside was a reference from Tom.

She stared at the paper, wondering if Tom really was responsible for this. It was his signature at the bottom, but maybe Maureen had written it and just pushed it in from of him to sign.

Trembling, she read the reference, word for word.

To whom it may concern...

It started off impersonally enough. Who she was, how long she'd worked at the hospital and in what capacity. Then...*then...*

Cori is not bound by convention in her approach to problem-solving...

Cori's breath caught, tangling in the memory that he'd said that once before to her.

Her solutions are both elegant and appropriate.

A tear rolled down Cori's cheek. It was as if Tom were standing in front of her, saying all these things.

The artwork that she has left with us at the hospital is enjoyed by everyone and is increasingly becoming the focus of a new culture within the unit—one that encourages expression in a safe environment.

What is less tangible, but no less obvious, is the touch of magic that all her artwork contains.

It had to be Tom. He'd written that. Cori turned the page to the end of the letter and stared at his signature. He'd signed it. Put his name to it and sent it out so that she could show anyone she liked what he thought.

She went back to the beginning of the letter, reading it carefully, every word. Tom had covered all the bases, and he had nothing but praise for her. Then the final paragraph.

Cori was a great asset to the unit while she was here, and I am convinced that she will go on to do more good work. I am only sorry that budget constraints mean that she will be doing that work elsewhere.

She put the letter down on the counter top, breathless with emotion, tears streaming down her face. There was no way out, she couldn't pretend now that Tom didn't respect her. There was no doubt that he'd written this, and no doubt that he was sincere, even if this was the last evidence of their parting.

She should text him, say thank-you. Perhaps add that

there were no hard feelings, but after the generosity of the reference he'd written, that seemed grudging. Telling him that it meant the world to her was out, as well. It did, but it wasn't going to change things between them. He couldn't love her. And so she couldn't bear to be around him.

Cori decided to think it over. She put the reference away carefully in the drawer containing her passport, the statements of the savings account that Ralph and Jean had set up for her, and the two battered baby photographs that she had of herself. All the things that meant something to her and which had shaped her life.

A long shower didn't make things any clearer, and neither did breakfast or an hour sitting in front of her easel without being able to even lift her paintbrush. She took a walk, got some shopping and carried it home. She still didn't know what to say to him.

The truth. If you don't know what to say, just say the truth. She picked up her phone.

Thank you. I regret nothing and wish you only happiness.

Cori stared at the words. It was exactly what she wanted to say to Tom, but it was incomplete.

Goodbye.

The word was stark enough, but it was the truth. Cori pressed 'send' before she could change her mind.

Almost immediately her phone signalled that he'd answered. Cori dismissed the idea that it was unlike Tom to be so attentive to his phone and that he must have been watching for a message.

I wish you all the things I couldn't give. Most of all magic.

Then the tears came. Not the half-hearted, sliding-down-your-face tears but great, gasping, runny-nosed sobs. It was really over. How could Tom ever know that the last word he would ever say to her would hurt so much? Because losing him had taken every last shred of magic from her life.

Even a life without magic had to go on. Cori threw herself into applying for jobs, attending one interview after another. And her weekends were taken up with the artists' group, whose paintings were in such demand that they had a waiting list.

'Wait, Milly, I'll take you home.' The group had finished another assignment and were packing up to go home.

'That's okay. It's only a fifteen-minute walk.'

It was dark, and Cori had promised Maureen that Milly wouldn't come home on her own. The teenager had seemed to grow up very suddenly since she'd started working with the group at weekends, but she was still only fifteen and Cori was still responsible for her.

'I thought you might give me a hand carrying these boxes into my flat. Then I'll drop you home.'

'Okay.' Milly was surveying the finished wall painting and the subterfuge was accepted. 'What do you think?'

'I think you did really well. The stencilling you did in the corner there is lovely.'

Millie glowed with pleasure. 'I painted the little silver swirly bits on later.'

'I saw. They make all the difference.' Milly was beginning to show real promise, and her painting was improving as the artists in the group showed her tricks and techniques. It was more than that, though. Milly's art had a touch of exuberance about it. That indefinable magic that Cori had seen draining out of her own work recently, leaving it pale and lifeless.

'So you're pleased with the wall, then?'

'I…' The director of the centre had expressed her delight, and everyone else seemed satisfied. But there was something missing, and Cori wasn't sure what it was. 'I don't know. I'm going to think it over and come back next week.'

'Finishing touches?' Cori nodded in reply. 'Can I come?'

'If you like. As long as—'

'My homework's done and my mum's happy,' Milly interrupted. 'I know.'

'Yeah. Sorry about that. But you have to take care of the practical side of things first.' It seemed to Cori that the practical side of things was all there was these days. The magic had packed its bags and gone on holiday, and her joy in her art was gone. She surveyed the painting thoughtfully. Maybe that was what the matter with it was.

Milly saw it first. Perhaps because she still lived in a world where fairies existed. 'What's this?'

There was a feeble glow coming from outside the big bay window in Cori's living room. When she walked closer to the glass, she could see that it was coming from the end of a wand, and that the fairy who held that wand had a familiar look about her.

Cori didn't need to touch the twists of wire and gauze

outside, she knew exactly what this was. The fairy that she'd left on the bonnet of Tom's car had a tiny golden heart twisted inside its chest, which she'd put there to wish it luck in catching Tom's eye. And now she was suspended outside her own window.

'Cori...?' Milly was staring at her. 'You look really weird. You're not going to faint, are you?'

'No.' Cori grabbed at her easel to steady herself.

'Are you sure? I could call Mum...'

'No...no, I'm fine, really.' A trail of glitter led from the window to the small table on the paving stones outside. It snaked up the legs of the table and swirled around a circular box covered in gold paper and with a brown-and-gold bow on top.

'That's so pretty...' Milly had her face pressed to the glass. 'Did Dr Riley leave that for you?'

'What? How do you know that?'

'I don't. I don't know why I said that.' The guilty look on Milly's face said that she knew exactly why she'd said it. 'Mum'll kill me...'

Tom felt so close at this moment that Cori could swear she could almost touch him. She had to know. 'Look, I won't breathe a word, not to anyone, I promise. Did your mum say anything about Dr Riley?'

Milly hesitated.

'Please, Milly. Is he all right?'

'Mum said that he seemed really sad when you left. She says that it's a shame it didn't work out between you and him, and that she reckons he's working too hard. You won't tell anyone I told you, will you? Mum said we shouldn't interfere.'

'No, of course not. I won't tell a soul, I promise.' Maureen was probably right. It was better to leave things as they were. She would get over it eventually, and Tom would too.

She opened the French doors and looked out, half hoping to see Tom out there somewhere. It would get this over with quickly; she could remind him that there was no future for them and send him on his way. But the golden box and its fairy guardian were alone, so Cori collected them both up and brought them inside, putting them down next to each other on the coffee table.

'What are you going to do?' Milly sat down next to her on the sofa. Apparently they were in this together, and there was no question of Milly being dispatched home to allow Cori some time to think.

'I'm going to open the box.'

'Yeah. Good thought.' Milly nodded earnestly, as if they were making a decision on the right answer in a game show. 'See what's inside.'

Cori took the box on her knees and untied the ribbon. It occurred to her a little too late that it might contain something that Milly probably shouldn't see, but she dismissed the idea. Tom had more style than that.

'Oo-ooh!' The lid came off the box, and both of them sighed together.

'It's beautiful.' Milly whispered the words. Inside the box chocolate truffles were piled on golden tissue paper. 'What's that?'

'I think…' Cori twisted the box so that the tiny flecks on the chocolates caught the light. 'Yes—it's little pieces of gold leaf.'

'Really!' Milly's hand flew to her mouth. 'Real gold? Can you eat it?'

'Yes, it doesn't do you any harm.' Cori laughed. She could almost feel Milly's wonder cutting into the dead feeling that had surrounded her heart in the last weeks. 'Shall we try one?'

Despite Milly's impatience, Cori found a little cut-glass dish at the back of her kitchen cupboard and put two of the chocolates in it. Then she lit a candle and dimmed the overhead lights so that the gold decoration on the chocolate sparkled. This was just the way that Tom would have done it.

'Mmm. These are so good.' Milly licked her fingers to get the last taste of chocolate. 'Are you going to call him?'

Cori supposed that this was the reaction that she was supposed to have. But the chocolate was just lovely chocolate, not the delightful rush to the head that it seemed to be for Milly. And she wasn't going to call Tom.

'Maybe.' She couldn't quite bring herself to disillusion Milly. 'After I've taken you home.'

Milly had made a dash for her coat and made it absolutely clear that Cori was not invited in for a cup of tea on this occasion. Clearly she presumed that calling Tom would be at the top of Cori's list when she got back home and didn't want to keep her from doing that.

But chocolates and fairies didn't mean anything. They were evidence of Tom's charm, not that he'd changed. People didn't change, just like that, overnight, however much they wanted something. Cori had spent enough time waiting for her mother to change, to come back to her, to know that was a foolish dream.

She stared at the golden box sitting in front of her on the coffee table. It seemed to be mocking her now, daring her to think about everything that she'd lost. If she'd had any sense she would have given the chocolates to Milly so they weren't there to torture her, but somehow Cori hadn't been able to.

She shook her head at her own stupidity and reached to put the top back onto the box. Then she saw it. Nestled amongst the tissue paper, a ribbon with a tag on it threaded through the fob of a key.

'Tom… What have you done now?' The whispered words got no answer and Cori drew the key out of the box and read the words written on the tag.

Yours. Always.

It was an impossible dream. Tom's door key in her hand. The most precious thing he had was his own space, and now she had the key to it. Cori stared at the tag. What was hers? The key? Tom? It didn't say, and this was far too important for her to jump to conclusions.

It wouldn't work between them, they'd already tried once and failed. Cori repeated all the arguments to herself again and again, even as she was pulling on her coat and getting into her car.

A light shone from the downstairs front room of Tom's house. He must still be up. Perhaps he was waiting for her to call him or knock on the door. Well, she was going to call his bluff and use the key. When she did that, he'd realise what a crazy gesture all of this was and leave her alone.

She slid the key into the lock and it turned easily. There was no chain on the door and the deadlock was disengaged. Stepping inside, Cori felt her stomach lurch.

The noise from the heels of her boots was deadened on the thick carpet. When she pushed open the door to the lounge she saw Tom fast asleep on the sofa, a book upturned on the floor next to him where it had obviously tumbled from his hand.

She could wake him or… No, she wouldn't wake him. Just seeing him here asleep was chipping away at her resolve at an alarming rate. Quietly Cori picked the book up from the floor and put it on the coffee table, resting the precious key on top of it. Somehow she managed to turn and walk away.

'Don't…'

She froze.

'Not another step, Cori.'

'Or what?' She didn't turn to face him. 'What will you do, Tom?'

Cori was trembling. She knew that he wouldn't do anything to stop her from leaving, and when she did so she was going to be alone again. This had been *such* a bad idea.

She heard him move and he appeared in front of her, all tousled fair hair and bedroom eyes. Leaning back against the door, he pushed it shut, folding his arms. 'I'm not going to let you go.'

'You can't keep me here.'

For a moment they were at an impasse, each trying to stare the other down. Cori was the first to break. 'Tom, this is crazy.'

'You came.'

'I just wanted to call your bluff. To see you back down.'

He shook his head, the trace of a smile playing at

one side of his lips. Did he really have to make it this hard? 'Not going to happen.'

'Okay.' She marched over to the coffee table, picked up the key and dangled it in front of his nose. 'Do you know what this means? *Really* know?'

'I know.'

Yeah, right. There was no trace of nerves behind the smile that was moving across his face. Not even the slightest hint that he had any idea just how much something like this would turn both their lives upside down.

'I don't think you do, Tom. It means that you don't have your own space any more. It means I can come and go as I please. No more control, no more keeping everything under wraps.'

His chest heaved as he took a deep breath and suddenly Cori saw all the doubt, all the fear. 'Yeah. It scares the hell out of me, but nothing scares me as much as losing you again.'

She turned away from him so he couldn't see her tears. 'Why do you have to make this so difficult?'

'Cori…' He almost choked out her name. He was close, very close, she could feel him behind her. 'If you tell me to let you go, I will.'

'Wha—?' She whirled around, and suddenly she was in his arms.

'If you tell me to leave you alone then I will. But you can't tell me to stop loving you. And you'll never stop me from wanting you in my life. All over my personal space, challenging me every day, making me angry…'

'Really?'

'Yes, and loving it better. I want you to know that I mean this. I know how afraid you are that I'll let you down but I'm asking you to put that aside and give us another chance.'

She could hear his heart beating fast against hers. Feel his arms trembling around her. 'Let me go, Tom.'

Almost immediately he stepped back. Then he turned away, a cry of harsh anguish escaping his lips as he stalked over to the fireplace, slamming his fisted hand down on the mantelpiece. She could see his back heaving just from the effort that it seemed to take to keep breathing.

'You have to believe me, Cori.'

'Why? You don't do love, Tom. You said it yourself.'

He turned, his face softening when his gaze met hers. 'Don't you see? You have to believe me. I gave you up. I wanted you so much, but I let you go so that I couldn't break your heart. And then I realised. If I can love you enough to give you up, then I can love you enough to make you happy.'

'That's...' It was either complete and utter madness or the most wonderful thing she'd ever heard.

'Yeah, crazy. I know. But that's how it is.'

'You left me because you loved me?'

'I left you because your happiness is more important to me than anything.'

'You idiot!'

'If you mean that I'm an idiot for letting you go...' He shrugged. 'Guilty as charged.'

Suddenly she knew. From the tips of her fingers right down to her toes she knew.

'You want me to take the key? Then make me.' Cori reached out her hand, tracing her fingers across his jaw. As soon as she touched him, happiness washed over her like a great wave.

One lone tear fell from the corner of his eye. Just one, but it was the beginning of everything, her whole future. When Tom reached for her, her legs gave way suddenly and Cori wrapped her arms around his neck.

'Sweetheart…' He lifted her up, swift and sudden, laying her on the sofa and pinning her down with his weight.

He unzipped her jacket and undid the buttons of the sweater underneath. Then her shirt, and Cori felt his hand slide across her skin. She wriggled underneath him. 'Upstairs…'

'Oh, no. You just made the rules, Cori. And you are going to beg me for that key before I take you upstairs.'

Cori lay naked on his bed in the morning sunshine. Last night had changed everything. It had shaken him to the core that she could give herself to him with such passion, and when she'd finally taken the key he had wept. Unashamedly, for the first time in his life.

Tom traced her spine with his finger, wondering if she thought any less of him for it now that the heat of last night had dissipated. She gave a little purr of lazy pleasure and rolled onto her front and Tom kissed the small of her back, working slowly upwards.

'That's nice.' She shivered when he got to her shoulder blades and he used one of his thumbs to work out a knot in her spine. 'Will you be there to wake me up tomorrow?'

'Are you in any doubt of that?' He found a growing area of tension between her shoulder blades, which told him that maybe she was, and dipped to brush a kiss there. 'I wouldn't have left that box for you if I didn't intend to be there for all your tomorrows.'

'What would you have done if I hadn't found the key? If I'd dumped the chocolates in the bin?'

'You would have put chocolate truffles into the bin? I don't believe it.' He chuckled, the laugh an expression of pure happiness, nothing more and nothing less. There was no need any more to use a smile to defend himself from the world.

'Would you have tried again? Sent something else?'

'Every day. Until you listened to me.' He kissed her shoulder, nuzzling against her ear. 'You, my love, would have been the target of a concerted and determined charm offensive. Only without the charm, since it appears you're immune to that.'

'Hmm.' She propped herself up on her elbows, gazing into his face. 'I'm almost sorry I missed it.'

'Well, I'm not letting up. I have a very pressing need to keep you exactly where you are.'

'I can't wait.' She leaned over and brushed a kiss to his lips. 'What's the matter?'

He couldn't hide even the smallest thing from her, the most fleeting of qualms. And he didn't want to. 'I wonder if you think less of me. I'm not the guy who has it all under control any more. Maybe I never was that strong.'

'Only the strongest man I know could translate what you went through when you were a child into the kind of care you give the kids on the unit. Only the bravest could bring himself to weep the way you did last night.'

Tom pulled her close. 'You know, I think I might just be home.'

'Yeah. Me too.'

CHAPTER SIXTEEN

THE TWO MEN standing in front of the painting didn't see the couple in the corner of the gallery. If they had, they might not have recognised the artist of the work they were currently considering, but they probably would have recognised the subject.

'It's…so lovingly done.' The older man looked thoughtfully at the picture. 'And yet there's a kind of sadness there. Do we know the artist?'

The younger man flipped through his catalogue. 'Ah, here. Corinne Evans.'

'I haven't heard of her. But this is very good. It has… life. Spirit.'

'Do you think it's a contender?'

'Definitely. I'll be watching Ms Evans.'

The men moved on to the next painting, this time shaking their heads. 'They prefer yours,' Tom whispered to Cori.

'Did you hear what he said? Luther Galloway said that I was a contender.' She clutched at his sleeve.

'And apparently you're someone to watch.' Tom planted a kiss below her ear, making her shiver. 'But, then, I knew that all along.'

'I'm so glad you entered it. I wouldn't have had the

guts.' The painting usually hung in the hallway of their home, but Tom had removed it and brought it here, entering it for the Galloway Prize on Cori's behalf.

He put his arm around her. 'There are a lot of really good paintings here. But I know which one *I* like the best.'

Cori snuggled into him. 'You're biased.'

'Of course I am. I'm allowed to be biased in favour of my soon-to-be wife.'

The engagement ring still felt a little odd on her finger, and she had to look at it every now and then just to remind herself why she felt like laughing out loud all the time. A diamond, mounted on a platinum band and flanked by two amethysts, which he'd claimed were the colour of her eyes, it reminded her that this was all true and not just a dream.

'We should celebrate. Now that I'm no longer just the acting head of paediatrics, courtesy of Dr Shah's early retirement, and you're a contender for the Galloway Prize *and* have a great new job.' He leaned over to whisper in her ear. 'I was thinking that warrants a bottle of champagne and a large bowl of strawberries. In bed...'

'I love the way you think. But I should give the champagne a miss.'

'Why?'

'I didn't get a chance to tell you, when you rushed me out of the house this morning...'

'Sorry about that. I wanted this to be a surprise and I was hoping you wouldn't notice that the painting was gone from the hallway again. The excuse about reframing it wasn't going to work a second time...'

He stopped short, as understanding dawned in his eyes. 'You're...giving the champagne a miss?'

'For a while. But I'll be eating for two, so I'm relying on you to do some serious cooking. You might even have to give me some lessons.'

He ignored the small group of people that had just walked into the room and took her in his arms, kissing her. 'What do you say we bring our wedding date forward a bit? I want to be married to you when our baby is born.'

'That sounds wonderful. I love you so much.'

'I love you too.'

They sat together for a long time, watching the comings and goings in the gallery, happy just to be together. Cori gazed up at her painting of Tom.

'You know, I've suddenly realised something.'

'Yes? What's that?'

'I'm going to have to paint you again. I don't recognise that man.'

He looked at the painting, studying it thoughtfully. 'You mean the sadness.'

'Yes. You look so…haunted. And my sadness is there too.'

'That's not us any more, Cori.'

'No.'

He took her hand, leading her away from the painting and out into the sunshine.

* * * * *

MILLS & BOON®

MEDICAL ROMANCE™

THE ULTIMATE IN ROMANTIC MEDICAL DRAMA

A sneak peek at next month's titles...

In stores from 25th February 2016:

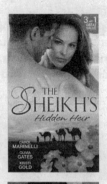

6_MB518

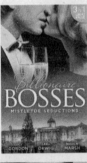

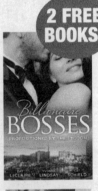
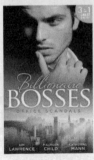
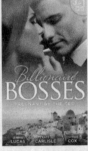
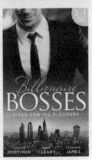

MILLS & BOON®

Why not subscribe?

Never miss a title and save money too!

Here's what's available to you if you join the exclusive **Mills & Boon® Book Club** today:

✦ *Titles up to a month ahead of the shops*
✦ *Amazing discounts*
✦ *Free P&P*
✦ *Earn Bonus Book points that can be redeemed against other titles and gifts*
✦ *Choose from monthly or pre-paid plans*

Still want more?

Well, if you join today, we'll even give you
50% OFF your first parcel!

So visit **www.millsandboon.co.uk/subs**
to be a part of this exclusive Book Club!